WASHOE COUNTY LIBRARY

P9-EKT-957

3 1235 03699 9261

the namesake

steven parlato

MeritPress

F+W Media, Inc.

Copyright © 2012 by Steven Parlato
All rights reserved.
This book, or parts thereof, may not be reproduced in any
form without permission from the publisher; exceptions are
made for brief excerpts used in published reviews.

Published by
Merit Press, an imprint of F+W Media, Inc.
10151 Carver Road, Suite 200
Blue Ash, Ohio 45242
www.meritpressbooks.com

ISBN 10: 1-4405-5457-9
ISBN 13: 978-1-4405-5457-5
eISBN 10: 1-4405-5458-7
eISBN 13: 978-1-4405-5458-2

Printed in the United States of America.

10 9 8 7 6 5 4 3 2 1

This is a work of fiction. Names, characters, corporations, institutions, organizations, events, or locales in this novel are either the product of the author's imagination or, if real, used fictitiously. The resemblance of any character to actual persons (living or dead) is entirely coincidental.

Many of the designations used by manufacturers and sellers to distinguish their product are claimed as trademarks. Where those designations appear in this book and F+W Media was aware of a trademark claim, the designations have been printed with initial capital letters.

This book is available at quantity discounts for bulk purchases.
For information, please call 1-800-289-0963.

For Janet, with love and awe at the depths of your belief.

"What was silent in the father speaks in the son."
   ~Friedrich Nietzsche

"And though in all lands, love is now mingled with grief, it still grows, perhaps the greater."
   ~J.R.R. Tolkien, *The Lord of the Rings*

Mister Pettafordi's office is examining room bright.

It makes me queasy, like I'm here for X-rays—which, in a way, I am. My art teacher slash guidance counselor slash "Think of me as your friend" wants to help. That's how I landed in the vinyl visitor chair on the wrong side of his desk. I should be in silent study, passing notes to Alexis. Instead, I'm here, embarrassed for Michelangelo's *David*. He's beside the file cabinet, a red umbrella hanging from his crooked elbow, looking a little vulnerable, naked under the lights.

I need to write this stupid essay. Mr. P's fixated on getting me a full scholarship; he says I'm his "best student ever." But then, that's what my teachers always say.

Mister P: "Evan, you need to pursue your art."

Me: "Uh-huh."

Mister P: "Evan, you've got what it takes."

Me: "Hmm."

Mister P: "Evan, follow your dream!"

Thing is, I think it's his dream more than mine now.

But I'm trying to get a jump on this heap of applications. Pettafordi said I need to "dazzle them" with my essay. I asked what I should write about.

He said, "Evan, write what you know."

As helpful as *that* was, I've chosen the opposite. See, I'm not sure I want to study art, or even go to college anymore. So I'll write what I don't know. I could do twenty pages on spark plugs or the reproductive cycle of the Andean potato weevil. Except, those I could research. No. I'll tackle the true unknown.

I never knew my father.

I don't mean that in a trash TV kind of way. Like, *Up Next, DNA Tests: Real Dads Revealed!* It's not like that. Mom wasn't a sperm bank patron. I wasn't raised by wolverines. I've lived most of my fourteen years in a room two doors down from the man, falling asleep to his snores. I could map you his morning stubble, a whorl on his chin like Madagascar.

Nope. Nothing dramatic about the Galloways. We were typical. Mom made Campbell's soup casseroles. Dad fell asleep in the leather chair on movie night. We were about as normal as it gets. At least, that's what everyone thought.

Before last April.

Now when I think about stuff, it's all about how it used to be. We used to have Monopoly marathons. Build model planes. Gorge ourselves at China Buffet. We used to . . . whatever.

A great philosopher once said, "Used-to-bes don't count anymore." Okay, it was this singer, Neil Diamond. My friend Alexis is a huge fan. But I disagree with Old Neil because, really, used-to-bes are the only things that do count anymore. Especially when today sucks so bad.

It's funny how perfectly life splits into before and after. Before, it was just life, crappy or un'. After, everything's different.

But I was going to tell you about my father.

My Father by Evan Galloway
My father is tall.
My father is fun.
My father reads stories and
Plays with me.
My father is the best, FATHER NUMBER ONE!

I wrote that in first grade. You could say my opinion of him has *evolved*. For one thing, I realized he was never all that tall. I admit the poem loses something *sans* macaroni frame, but I think it shows real literary promise. I mean, after reading that, I'm sure you can see how I ended up in Honors English, right?

Yeah, I'm smart. All through school I've been in the brain group: TAG, the Talented And Gifted Program. It's actually sort of cool, loads of field trips, elaborate, "self-guided learning opportunities." Sure, the regular kids call us "Tag Fags," but that's never really bothered me. Not much. It's jealousy, plain and simple. And come on—tag fag?—such an obvious rhyme. Leave it to a remedial reader.

Now I'm at Saint Sebastian's Catholic High School, third year, following Dad's footsteps. Yeah, he went here. But I one-upped the old man; I'll graduate at sixteen. They jumped me a couple grades. So I'm the second Evan Galloway to attend SSCHS. My family calls me "Junior," but technically, I'm not. Dad and I don't have the same middle name. Or, didn't. I do that sometimes, refer to him like he's still here. Like he didn't kill himself last spring. Like Gran didn't find him hanging from a beam in her attic Easter morning, while Mom and I were at Mass.

Sebastian's is an okay place.

Sort of an odd mix of regular high school stuff and 2,000-plus years of Catholic tradition.

Example: we have crappy cafeteria food like anyplace, but on Fridays during Lent, at least we're spared the mystery meat. There's the rare locker-room fight, but we go to Mass at the drop of a hat. Sure, the boy's bathroom has that unmistakable pot-smoke smell, but holy water's available in all classrooms.

The school hasn't changed much since Dad's time. Regular teachers outnumber priests and nuns now, although some of the oldsters remain: Sister Dolores, Brother Alphonse, and of course, Father Brendan. It's a little scary thinking Dad had Father Brendan O'Donnell for Honors psych junior year, same as me.

It's scary enough to think of a guy named Father Brendan leading his young charges through the dark, twisted mysteries of the human psyche. It's a given we'll NEVER fully explore the secrets of sexually motivated behavior.

Father Brendan's legendary. He's been at Saint Sebastian's "since God was a little kid," as Gramp would say. Every freshman has him for Christian Morality and You. He also teaches psychology to gifted juniors. In photos in the trophy case, you witness his progression from old to ancient. His glasses get larger, thicker. His forehead and waistline grow at an alarming rate. Unlike most old people, he expands with age. The guy oozes authority; even the tough kids just do not screw with him. He's like an artifact or an icon or something: enigmatic. Holy. It's like someday he might crack open and reveal a mystery.

Psychology is Tuesday/Thursday, Mods 9 and 10. Father Brendan's always there when we arrive, behind his desk, eyes closed. His is the only wooden desk at Sebastian's. All the other instructors have standard-issue, metal teachers' desks, but Father B insisted on oak. Like the man, the desk is massive. Their combined weight's been estimated at 2.4 metric tons.

Freshman year, it was eerie to see him in that trance. I'd look really close to make sure he was alive. That's how I first became acutely aware of Father Brendan's head: the translucent quality of the skin, the intricate web of veins. The age-spot Rorschach at his temple. The wild sense that if I looked deep enough, I might glimpse the brain working inside. It was like candling eggs in fourth-grade science. I was transported studying that skull, envisioning a world within. Sometimes it shocked me when Father B would open his eyes, adjust his glasses, and speak. I felt like a coroner whose client sits up midautopsy to order a BLT.

Father begins each class with a plea to Saint Sebastian to guide us. The intimacy of his prayer suggests he knew Sebastian personally. Given Father's age, I suppose that's within the realm. And Sebastian was as big a character as Father Brendan, a multimartyr. He was tied to a tree, shot with arrows, and left for dead. But his faith sustained him: He survived. Then, he was cudgeled to death. That time it stuck.

It's awesome having Sebastian as our school's namesake; you're in good hands with a guy who had to be killed twice. Then there's our team name. Our town's other Catholic schools are stuck with pretty lame mascots: "Hearts," "Doves"—not too intimidating. We are "The Archers."

That might seem inappropriate, considering Sebastian was shot full of arrows, but it turns out he's the patron of archers, so I guess it fits. Plus, it makes for great headlines in the sports section: "Archers Aim at Championship" or "Archers Shoot Toward Semis." Not that it matters to me; I'm definitely no jock.

No sports, thanks; I'm a brain. I know there is such a thing as a scholar-athlete, but I don't qualify. I've only recently broken 100 pounds, so football's out. And even though I'm tall, I suck at basketball. I just don't have the Galloway jock gene. I'm hopeless, an artist. That was an issue with

Dad. Not that he really pressured me to go out for a team or anything, at least, not after my stellar T-ball career. But his disappointment in my athletic ineptitude was always sort of palpable. Love of the game was one more thing we never shared.

We had the same name (almost) and practically the same face. We nearly even shared the same birthday. His was January 20th, oddly enough, the feast day of your friend and mine, Saint Sebastian. Mine is the 22nd, but we were separated by way more than two calendar days and a middle name. It's not like he beat me or drank or anything, not at all. He was a decent guy and an okay Dad. Well, except for the suicide thing.

But that's a pretty big flaw, all in all.

There was this kid who killed himself freshman year.

His name was Steve Austin, like the wrestler, or the guy on that old show *The Six Million Dollar Man*. He was in track, hurdles, I think. We weren't exactly friends or anything. Okay, he was a total prick. Now I realize he must've been really screwed up, molested or something. But when I try to sympathize, all I can picture is his rubbery pink smirk.

We had Art 160 together, and he was constantly busting me. Typical stuff: my supplies would go missing, he'd commandeer my work station—regulation bully tactics. He made crits a freakin' nightmare. Once, he told everyone my abstract gouache composition was really a rendering of Father Brendan's penis. Even though we were a TAG group, that sort of remark couldn't NOT get a huge laugh. Another time, he screwed with the kiln and "accidentally" blew up my ceramics midterm. Prick.

One Monday, we slouched into art class; Mr. Pettafordi was this strange shade of gray. He said, "There has been a tragic incident. Stephen is dead. Papier-mâché is postponed."

Ushered into the auditorium for prayer and silent reflection, lots of kids were crying, some teachers, too. Mr. Novack, the track coach, sat, a deflated Macy's balloon surrounded by a grim circle of teammates—a collective of hows and whys.

"Was it a car accident?" Tyler Wattrous spluttered.

"No, son. Nothing like that."

"A fire?" Kenny Nealson asked, wild-eyed.

"No, Ken. There was no fire."

"Was Steve mowed down runnin', Mister N?" The ever-tactful Randy Spiotti.

"Dammit, guys! Just stop, okay! Father will explain."

Father Brendan took the stage amid a silence so deep, the intermittent sniffle or cough seemed like a shouted swear.

"My dear family of Sebastian, may Our Blessed Mother envelop us in her protective mantle. We are, each of us, deeply flawed. We—" He seemed to lose his thread, chins pinkening. Straightening his glasses, he continued. "Without our Lord's guidance, our willful arrogance, our fear and guilt, can lead us to wrong choices, even to ruin." Again, he stuttered midthought. Staring out at us, he dabbed his brow. "May God look past the sin of Stephen's suicide, welcoming him into everlasting peace, free from the despair which led to this dreadful deed. In Jesus' name, Amen." And he motored off the stage, leaving us in silence.

Later, we found out Steve had blown his head off in the Austin's great room. At first, I was numb. I wanted to feel bad; the guy was dead. I pictured his mom calling Nurse Haggerty to report his absence. "Stevie won't be in today. He has a terrible headache." Bizarre. The bully's not supposed to kill himself. He's supposed to drive the geek to suicide. Steve had really screwed up. At my locker, I began laughing uncontrollably.

Alexis dragged me into an empty classroom. "What is with you, Evan? DO YOU GET THAT HE'S DEAD?"

"No, why don't you draw me a picture? You're good at that."

"Don't be an ass. I know you're upset. We all are."

"You're right, Lex. I'm sorry. See you at lunch."

It was easier just to agree than to explain I wasn't upset. I really wasn't anything. All I could think about was not having to dread seeing him in art class anymore. That and I wondered how they'd clean his brains off the widescreen. I started to laugh again. I know that makes me a bad person, but I honestly couldn't help it. Maybe it was shock.

The school swung into compassion mode: prayer circles, counselors up the wazoo, the whole nine yards. Being a Catholic school, Sebastian's is skilled at grief. Faster than you could say the Glory Be, Mass was scheduled for the following Monday in the auditorium. The entire Sebastian's community would attend. It would not be pretty.

What I remember most is the offertory, when they brought up the bread and wine. In this case, there was a third gift: Steve's scuffed Nike was to join the body and blood of Jesus on the altar. The shoe, his left, was borne down the center aisle relay-style by six puffy-faced track mates. It was ludicrous, ill-conceived, and totally cringe-inducing, yet somehow, an oddly touching tribute to their fallen comrade.

Then: a musical montage/slide show featuring pictures of Stevie, the Outrageously Chubby Toddler. Gap-toothed Stephen struggling to eat corn on the cob. Shots of Steve with the team, endless pictures—Stephen running, Stephen jumping—always smiling. The whole thing was engineered for maximum lachrymal effect. Someone was willing me to mourn a guy I barely knew and didn't like. They wanted me to care and I refused. Anger, not grief, welled up in me.

Un-freaking-believable! I was crying in spite of myself! Alexis drew me close, pressed her forehead to mine. My brain slammed shut. No one would extract another crumb of emotion for this punk who'd wasted himself. Screw him! But I let Lex comfort me. On some level, I guess I needed it.

At Gran's kitchen table, I catch the scent of freesia soap and old cooking oil.

Gran takes my hand in hers, says, "I have something for you, Junior."

She's going to give me $20 for ice cream; some things don't change.

"Evan."

"That's okay, Gran. I've got money."

"No, no. This was your father's."

She presses a small piece of stainless steel into my palm. I look at her hand, knobby with age, and study the smudged jewels of her family ring, a band of five. She's sapphire, ruby for Gramp, Auntie Ro is amethyst, and peridot, that's Aunt Regina. There's a stone missing on one end. She catches me looking.

"I lost that garnet last February. Your father was supposed to have it fixed."

I squeeze her hand, gently because of the arthritis.

"I guess there's no sense now." And she's crying.

"Darn it," I say, mostly to myself. I've remembered something stupid. Dad wore a garnet ring, his birthstone. When I was little, I called it a "darn it." He used to tease me, kind of a family joke. Now I'm crying, too.

"Damn! I promised myself I wouldn't do this!"

"It's okay, Gran."

"No! It's not. IT'S NOT OKAY! TEARS CAN'T RAISE THE DEAD!" She clears her throat, stands, speaks into the fridge. "If your grandfather comes in and finds us crying—we've got to be strong for him."

"That's the Gallo-Way," I say, wondering for the zillionth time whether everyone's family has such lame jokes.

"I miss him, Gran." It's the first time I've said that out loud.

"We all miss him, Evan. That's the reason I wanted you to have something. Something of his."

"A key? Gee, thanks."

"Not just the key, Smarty-pants." She dabs the corner of her mouth, surprised at the smile there. "Come with me."

I follow Gran down the narrow hall to the guest room. It was Dad's bedroom as a boy, and again, before he died. He moved back in during the trial separation that became way permanent. I avoid eyes staring from old school portraits lining the wall. A glance: Auntie Ro, front-toothless, lavender hair band—Grade 3. Next, Aunt Reg, crooked glasses on crooked nose, same wide open smile as always. Finally, a picture of Dad, about age nine. He's got a scab on his forehead. Very large ears. And a telltale redness around his eyes. Why was he crying?

"Evan." Gran's voice is like an alarm clock through a thick dream.

"Yeah, Gran?"

"I know. It's almost like looking in a mirror, isn't it? Thank goodness, you have your mother's ears, but you're definitely your father's son."

Terrific, I think.

"Well, let's take a look-see."

Following Gran into the room where Dad grew up, I'm hit with a mix of feelings. *This is so wrong.* Dolls. There are dolls everywhere, staring from shelves, peering from the floor, pale-faced dolls with big hats, bigger pouts. And floral wallpaper, rugs, pillows, curtains, quilt, and lampshades. It's like someone vomited Laura Ashley. I cannot believe my father's final weeks were spent lying on a daybed surrounded by frills. That alone is tragic. Why'd she bring me in here? To show me the décor that pushed him over the edge?

Then I notice it: the one object so totally out of place, it has to be his.

"Evan, help me, would you? Your grandfather nearly ruptured himself dragging this up from the cellar."

"Sure, Gran. Is this my legacy?"

"Ooh, you're clever. This is what I want to give you, yes. I don't know from legacy."

As I drag the footlocker past the wicker rocker, I snag the hooked rug, toppling a dolly.

"Careful, Evan! Don't be a bull! You're just like your father!"

I wince. "Sorry, Gran. What's inside?"

She runs a hand across the scratched lid, her thick nails tapping the burnt-orange surface, and briefly fingers the brass lock. "Find out."

"You mean you haven't opened it?"

"That's your job, Junior. It's just old things, his school trunk, from Sebastian's. I thought it'd be fun for you to have. Who knows, maybe he hid a fortune in here."

"Well, if he did, I'll split it with you."

"No, honey, whatever he left in there is yours now."

"Thanks for the early birthday present, Gran . . . He loved you, you know."

"It's nearly four, it'll be pitch dark soon. God, I hate January! Let's wake your Gramp and have some cake. Then we'd better get you home. They're saying snow."

I wave as they pull slowly from the curb, then slide the footlocker over snow-dusted grass. "It's just old things." But what? Secrets, answers? In my room, I shove the trunk to the back of my closet, afraid to know. Flopping on the bed, I open my fist. In it, I hold the key.

Yesterday was January 19th.

That makes today the 20th. Okay duh, what I mean is, today would've been my father's birthday. It's funny. I woke up sweating at 3:18, panicked, thinking *HOLY CRAP! I forgot to get Dad's present!* It took several minutes blinking at predawn blackness for reality to come tap-tap-tapping on my windowpane.

Once it did, I thought, *Whoa, this year, it'd be especially tough to find him the perfect gift.* I mean, what do you get for the dead guy who has everything? I guess I could pick up a little something for the cemetery, to jazz things up a bit. Maybe a "World's Greatest Dad" magnet to put next to his name. I wonder if a magnet would stick?

See, my dad's in a drawer. Maybe it's just me, but I find that way worse than a hole in the ground. It just totally lacks the permanence of six feet of earth. You can see the mausoleum from the road where I wait for the bus every morning. It rises, like a ziggurat on the hillside, looking all mysterious and exotic, like some reject from EPCOT.

I never knew what to expect from a mausoleum; had no reason to think about it, 'til last year. I figured it'd be like a *mu*seum or something inside: cool, dark, whisper-quiet. Formal, with stained glass. But, it's not like that at all. First off, it's roofless, so there really isn't an inside. The structure's open to the sky, with outer walls surrounding an area like a patio—minus the barbeque. You descend into it, along this winding sidewalk.

When they wheeled him down, I swear, all I could think of was the Winter Olympics: one-man bobsled, his coffin picking up speed, ricocheting off walls, shooting sparks. I had to bite my cheek to keep from yelling, "Go, Dad, go!"

Once you hit bottom, the center of the maze, you're surrounded by these sky-high walls. You face west toward normalcy. There's a sliver of a view of the valley: houses, trees, the DB Mart on the corner of Edgewood and Aurora Avenues.

Then you study the walls covered with names and dates.

At first, it seems like they're just plaques. Until you notice the handles. Fact is, it's more like a giant filing cabinet than anything else. The funeral guy slides one open, and you realize it's your dad's new home. Too bizarre, as if you could drop by anytime, pop the latch, and there he'd be. It's creepy, like keeping your father in a giant crisper drawer.

I had a hunch I'd be feeling morbid. Today clearly won't be a typical, birthday type of day. To begin with, we're heading to Mass first thing. Aunt Ro, in her infinite wisdom, thought a birthday remembrance would be just the thing to "help us soldier on through our grief." She actually said that! I can hardly wait. I mean nothing against the Father, the Son, or the Holy Ghost. I'm just not exactly overjoyed at hauling out all these feelings on a cold Monday morning.

His birthday would've been tough enough without having to face the relatives, the friends, the blue-haired flock of daily Mass attendees. I'd anticipated a regular school day with its mundane distractions, even planned to hit chapel during study hall. Maybe I would've gotten a Peggy Lawton brownie at lunch in his honor. Now, instead of waiting for the bus, uniformed, backpacked, I'm here in the kitchen, wearing my funeral suit, contemplating a mound of pancakes and rough seas ahead.

"Evan, sweetie, finish your breakfast. It's quarter to seven! They'll be here soon."

I don't know how she can sound so perky, given the hour and the circumstance, but that's my mother. She could stand on ceremony, even if her feet were repossessed.

"Okay, I'm done." I down a last gulp of milk. "Sure you want to do this, Mom?"

"Do what, honey?"

"Ma! This whole Mass thing. What'd you think I meant, the dishes?"

"Tone, Junior. This is not an easy day for me either."

"I wish you wouldn't call me Junior anymore, Mom. I never really was one, anyway."

"Finish up. They'll be here in ten minutes; your grandmother is always early."

We're going to Mass with Gramp and Gran. Should be a ride to remember. Gran hasn't spoken to Mom much since the suicide. I suppose the fact that each blames the other isn't exactly a chat motivator. Although Mom hasn't spoken much to me either, not about Dad. She seems to be spinning this mom-cocoon.

It's like she thinks, by serving on enough committees, baking enough muffins, reading enough books to the blind, and perpetually vacuuming, she can make people forget her husband chose death over her. Or maybe *she's* trying to forget, who knows?

As we wait for the silver Pontiac to materialize from the mist, I chip at the slush pile with the toe of my wingtip. Minutes pass. Ears tingling from the frigid air, I shift foot-to-foot, clapping gloved hands, exhaling clouds.

Mom bears the cold in silence, maybe because it matches what she's become inside.

"God, it's, like, arctic out here!" I chatter. "Aren't you freezing?"

"I'm okay. Go in the garage, if you can't stand it."

"I can take it, if you can. Besides, I want to stay with you."

She smiles.

"Mom?"

"Yes, Ev?"

"Why?" I try to put my arm around her shoulder.

She shrugs me off, pretend-searches in her purse. "Why what, dear?"

I hesitate, unable to spit out the words. Why does she need to hear them, when she knows damn well what I'm asking?

"Dad. Why do you think he . . . ?"

"Here come your grandparents. No more of this." She smoothes my eyebrow with her thumb—a maternal affection shortcut—and steps to the curb.

The Bonneville appears, a boxy, metallic ghost. Gramp glides to a stop, spraying a fine slush over our feet. As he lowers the window, an AM talk caller brays about welfare mothers. Gran switches off the radio, cradling a cardboard cup, mega-size. Java and memories sustain them now.

"Hop in, Sport. You look like you're freezin' your nuts off."

"Fred!" Gran always pretends to be shocked by him.

"Katherine, top o' the morning."

"Good morning, Fred. Maureen."

Gran nods, smiles vaguely. "Hello, Katherine. How are you, Junior, okay? Find any treasure?" She winks.

"Not yet, Gran. We'll see."

Mom looks at me quizzically, then back to Gran. Sinking into the backseat, I close my eyes as Gramp navigates the icy hills to Saint Anne's.

I was an altar boy in middle school.

Served up through freshman year, in fact. I loved it: the solemnity of the Mass, the miracle of communion. I even considered being a priest for a while. It seemed cool to have that level of communication with God. Working for Him and helping people seemed magical.

But I doubted my capacity for such devotion: no sex, no family, no house, no stuff. Seemed like a tough road. I decided to talk to Father Greg about my possible calling. He was new to our parish, and I guess to the priesthood; in his late twenties, he wore Dockers.

I lingered in the vestibule after Mass, one Sunday in October.

"Father Greg?"

He was hanging vestments, shutting lights, closing shop. "Evan, what's the scoop?"

"I wondered about you. I mean, about *being like you*, a priest," I said, uncharacteristically inarticulate.

"Wow, Ev! That's something! How long you been thinking about this?"

"Oh, a while, I guess. Do you like it?"

"Well, I'm not in it for the money, that's for sure."

"How'd you know it was definitely what you were meant to do?"

"Easy. It's like love, Evan. You just, ultimately, know when the right one comes along."

"Oh."

"Doesn't help much, does it?" He grinned.

"Well, it's a pretty parentish thing to say."

"Hey, they don't call me Father for nothing!" he said, doing a decent Groucho Marx.

"It's just, I don't know if I'm perfect enough to do what you do."

"If you judge yourself against God's perfection, you can never hope to measure up, Evan. But God made you, so you have the potential to be pretty great. Look, we just have to live up to His plan for us—not always an easy task."

"I guess I'm having some trouble unraveling His plan for me."

"Aren't we all, Evan? Aren't we all? Talk to Him, trust Him. You'll find your way."

Not long after that conversation, Father Greg left Saint Anne's. I ran into him about four months later at Big Y. He wasn't wearing his collar. I called across the produce section, "Hey, Father Greg!"

"Evan Galloway, my favorite altar boy! What's the scoop?"

"Father, I was just—"

"It's not Father anymore, Evan, just plain old Greg."

"Oh, I'm sorry." *That had to be a dumb thing to say.*

"Don't be; I'm not. Turns out, I was trying to live up to the wrong plan," he said, a half-smile crossing his lips. "Well, I should go, Evan. Good to see you." He placed a container of grape tomatoes in his cart, touched my shoulder, and wheeled off, beyond Baked Goods.

I started to walk away, sensing the world had slipped on its axis, just enough to feel it. What'd it mean, exactly? What about all the Masses he'd said, the Last Rites, the weddings? Were they somehow voided because he was now "just plain old Greg"? The sins I'd confessed in the darkness, did they still hang over my soul? But that was stupid, right? I just didn't know. And that advice: "Talk to Him, trust Him. You'll find your way." Yeah, right, it had worked great for him.

That summer I quit serving Mass. I told our pastor sophomore year was bound to be really busy. Besides, I was outgrowing the altar robes. Most of the other servers were, like, nine or ten years old. It just wasn't for me anymore. But I still went to Mass. And I confessed all the old sins, the ones I could remember, anyhow. Just in case.

It's amazing how many people turn out for your birthday, after you're dead.

I mean, my family's always celebrated in an unassuming way: Cake, presents, the obligatory, off-key serenade; that's the extent. And it's always been just family: Gran, Gramp, maybe the Aunties, Mom, Dad, and me.

Today is totally out of control. The church lot's packed; it has this traffic jam, clearance sale, parish carnival energy. Are they seriously expecting the guest of honor to show? Not likely; the crisper was locked tight this morning. I know because we swung by before Mass to say "Howdy." I didn't take him that magnet. We did leave balloons, Gran's idea.

The church teems; it's like everyone he ever met is here. I haven't seen some of these people since the funeral; it's mourner's déjà vu. Same faces, same somber outfits, even the condolences are reruns. They each want to touch me, shake my hand, gauge my grief. Luckily, the intensity level's scaled back, weeping and wailing distilled to their melancholy essence, like they're finally resigned to the truth of his absence.

Father Lessard asked me to read. It's strange because, ordinarily, I wouldn't have wanted any part of that. That's another thing I liked about being an altar boy: no lines. But Dad was a lector at Saint Anne's: Vigil Mass, 4:00 p.m., Saturdays. Everyone says they loved how he "brought meaning to the words." So I figure this could be like a present, my tribute to him. And it's weird, I'm not nervous at all.

Sitting up on the altar, I scan the assembly, remembering stuff, little details, about Dad and the people here. Dancing the Alley Cat at some wedding with Great-Aunt Lucille. Discussing Impressionist art with Mr. Ayotte, the mailman. Mock-arguing with Mrs. Pinto about the merits of mulch. Seeing him in their faces, it's like he really is here, after all. I feel close to him, maybe closer than before he was gone, swaddled in memory.

Suddenly, it's time to read. At the podium, I sense Mom's eyes on me; she nods slightly, hand on her heart. I adjust the microphone—like I've seen my father do a million times—and look down at the missalette. For a moment, I'm sure it's printed in a foreign language; words backstroke across the page. I blink hard and look out. The crowd's frozen, a painted backdrop. Clearing my throat, I stare at the book and begin.

After Mass, we meet at Alberti's for brunch.

It was my dad's favorite, a little, family-run, Italian place. I'm surprised, yet again, by the rituals of grieving. Apparently, cannoli plays an essential role in the healing process; the mood's visibly brighter after the dessert cart makes the rounds. I'm sipping a second cup of espresso, savoring it and the fact that things have gone so smoothly, when it begins.

"—because you never put him first! That's why!" Gran's voice rises and breaks.

Forks stop midway to mouths; heads turn.

"How dare you accuse me? You can delude yourself as much as you please, Maureen, but don't you try to pin it on me!" Mom shrills.

"Girls, girls, behave." Gramp attempts a chuckling intervention.

But there's no stopping. It's full-steam toward an emotional train wreck.

"All I know is my son is dead! You drove him out, and now he's gone!"

"*I* drove him out? As if I had any control over his decisions! He lived to please you people; Evan and I were afterthoughts! Your apron strings choked the life out of him, left *my* son fatherless!"

"MOM! STOP!"

She recoils, like I've hit her. Then she's leaving, stunned silence in her wake.

Gran chokes out a sob, sits down hard. Gramp holds her. All eyes are on me, naked, powerless. What do they want? An apology, an explanation? In a quavering tenor, I sing.

**"Happy Birthday, Dear Da-ad.
Happy Birthday to You."**

Not surprisingly, no one joins in.

When my aunts find me in Alberti's walk-in, I explain I just needed to cool off. They like that. Auntie Ro says, "It's emotionally very healthy that you can find some humor in the situation." Aunt Reg just hugs me.

They tell me Mom took a taxi home; she asked them to drop me. Gramp's taken Gran to a matinee; no lie. I guess they haven't had enough drama for one day. Or, more likely, they couldn't face going home. It must be hard for them, being in the house where he did it. You can't avoid the attic forever.

I tell the aunts, "Thanks, but no thanks."

I want to be alone for a while. Checking my watch, I realize all that turmoil was packed into an impressively brief interval. It's only 10:55. The better part of the day lies ahead—hopefully. Once I persuade R & R I'm okay, they pile into Regina's Fiat, beep, and drive off. I thank Mr. Alberti for the spread.

"Evan, you father, he was a good guy." His milky-brown eyes swim with tears.

"Yeah?"

"Yeah." He takes my shoulders, and for a second, I think he's going to kiss me. "You family will get through this, but it'll be messy. That's what family is. You mother, you grandmother, they trying to figure out who they are without him, you understand? They come around, you see."

I hope the old man's right. As I walk toward the cemetery, the January wind pinches my cheeks, like Gran did when I was small.

Balloons thump rhythmically against the nameplate of Dad's upstairs neighbor.

They do nothing to brighten the surroundings. The cemetery's defiantly bleak, the sky so overcast it's impossible to tell where stone walls end and clouds begin.

I half-expected something dramatic, I'm not sure what, to happen when I got here. It didn't. I stand for a long time, staring at the words on the drawer front.

Evan Frederick Galloway
Loving son, husband, father

I'm struck by finality in two-inch-high characters.

I think, *Why doesn't it say "Hung Himself"? Wouldn't that be more honest?* Why should he be allowed to take his place with the Natural Causers: cancer victims, accident fatalities, who fought valiantly to hold onto life, however broken? They used to bury suicides outside hallowed ground. They were considered an abomination. I don't know who changed the rules.

Maybe that's harsh; I'm not sure anymore. I just can't find a lot of pity for a guy who decided his misery was more important than his wife and kid. He didn't leave a note—no explanation, nothing! His last words to me were, "Got to help your gran get some Easter stuff from the attic. See you tomorrow, after church. Sleep tight, Junior."

Bullshit. He knew what he was planning for Easter morning. "See you tomorrow." Liar. I remember thinking he sounded happier than he had in a long time. I'd hoped Easter would be a new start—maybe he'd come back home to stay. So pathetic, it's almost funny. Thanks, Dad. For the Easter gift. I'd have preferred a chocolate egg.

I guess I wasn't worth sticking around for. If I was, he'd never have moved out last February. Okay, I'm not stupid enough to think the separation was my fault. I mean, I'm no dumb-ass little kid. I know he didn't kill himself because he was disappointed in me not turning out to be a chip off his friggin' block. But he also didn't stick around to see what I'd become, who I'd end up being. I can't forgive him for that. I won't.

And it's not just about me. What about Mom? Or Gran, finding him like that? We're still not sure how she got his body down from the beam. Aunt Ro said, when they found them in the attic, it looked like the Pieta. I think of poor Gran, cradling him like Jesus at the foot of the cross—the attic floor littered with plastic Easter grass—and it makes me want to go crazy. This was no sacrificial lamb. He didn't die for a higher purpose, to fulfill prophecy, save souls. He was a selfish, gutless loser.

"I HATE YOU!" I pound the metal plaque, raised lettering biting into my fist. "I hate what my life's turned into because of you! I hate that it'll never be the same as before! Screw you, Evan Frederick Galloway! ROT IN HELL!!" My voice reverbs in the empty cemetery, spooking a blue jay into noisy flight.

I wheel around, shocked at my own anger, shaking. Sliding to the ground, back thudding against metal drawer handles, I'm breathing hard, face slick with tears and snot. I retch, the sour taste of espresso coating my tongue.

After several minutes, I clear my throat, spit into the crust of snow. Looking toward his name, I see balloons bobble. "Freaking balloons!" I pull them toward me by twisted ribbons. Purple Mylar, unbelievable; my father hated purple. Gran had to know that, but purple's her favorite. I laugh in spite of myself, then tears return. It's like every memory's double-edged, tainted. Shaking my head, I climb the concrete path toward sky.

There's no way I'm going home to face Mom.

I head to the library instead, always a refuge for me. When I was nine, I ran away from home—straight to the nonfiction stacks. Miss Gillenhall, the Jurassic librarian, ratted me out when she spotted my Official Spiderman bedroll under one of the reading tables. I won't attempt a sleepover this time; I only want to lose myself for a while. Besides, Old Gilly retired last year, so there's no danger of anyone calling my mother.

I push through double doors into the familiar: that too-dry, airless, winter feeling, the unnatural quiet. Comforting. I stare at the huge clock above the reference desk. When I was little, it seemed big as the moon: 1:20. Feet shooshing across faded carpet—a static-shock in the making—I hook a left toward Genealogy and Local History; you can count on it being empty back there. I sit in a frayed armchair by the radiator and shiver; my feet are size eleven Popsicles. Funeral wingtips aren't exactly the footwear of choice for a midwinter hike.

I suppose I could get some research done for my soc paper. From my seat, I scan shelves. Random titles catch my eye: *American Pots of Gold: Irish of New England*; *Mill Town Murder*, by Alice Clapper; *Local Heroes*,

Myths & Mores. Does anybody read this crap? I text Alexis, ask her to meet me here after school.

Flipping through a pictorial town history, I study photos of the Old City Hall fire, the flood of '55. One chapter, on town architecture, has a section on the library. There's a photo of the then mayor Swanson presiding over the groundbreaking. In another, some tycoon presents a giant check to the library board. On the extreme right, an impossibly young (and hot, in an Andrews Sister way) Miss June Gillenhall. It's wild to see her pre-old, to know she's got a first name.

Turning the page, I'm smacked by this surge of unreality. There's a black-and-white shot of a kid my age, in this very chair. I'm sure it's him: Dad. Then I read the caption: *A young patron—July, 1962.* Impossible. My father would've been in diapers when it was taken.

Still, I search the image for some clue to the guy's identity. Sagging in his exact position, one leg over the chair arm, I try shifting into his head. What was he doing in the library: schoolwork, or reading for fun? Did he know his picture was being taken? Was he the bastard son—or teen lover—of Miss Gillenhall? And where is he now? I craft a scenario to answer each question. Somehow, it's easier contemplating his situation than dealing with my own. Closing my eyes, I slip into this guy's life, this happy kid who undoubtedly still had a father.

A hand touches my shoulder; a soft voice calls, "Evan, wake up."

"June?" Young Miss Gillenhall leans over, her lips brushing my cheek. I pucker, sigh.

"Eeeuuww! Evan, wake up!" A sharp poke to my ribs; it's Alexis.

"What—hey!" I shake my head. "Back off!"

"Sorry to disturb your siesta, Beautiful Dreamer, but you seemed close to a moan. Figured I'd save us some embarrassment. You, the humiliation of a wet dream in the library. And me, the utter skeeve of not only witnessing it but having to admit I know you."

"You really are charming. Does it come naturally?" I yawn.

"It's a gift. So, who's June?"

"You don't even want to know."

"Okay, Romeo, I'll take your word."

Beyond the moon-clock, the real thing glows in the January sky. It's 6:20. I've been asleep for at least four hours! I'm stiff. And starving.

"Want food?"

"Your treat?"

"Sure, I'll pay. But honestly, Lex, it's a treat just being with you."

We do that fake puking thing like always, and she punches my shoulder. I think, and not for the first time, *I've really got to kiss this girl one day*. Instead, I shove her; then we tango through double doors into the ridiculously chilly night.

Beneath the golden arches, Lex takes my hand. "Hey, you had that Mass and Munch thing today, didn't you? How'd it go?"

I stroke the fluff of her pink mitten. "Well, I'll tell you . . . not half bad." And we walk, arm in arm, into the emporium of American shit food.

Lex revs her Happy Meal toy, biting McNuggets into animal shapes. I snarf my Extra Value Meal and relate, in excruciating detail, the events of the day. We actually laugh. It's odd how grief, shared with a friend over fries and shakes, seems less overwhelming.

It's Father/Son Day.

For as long as I can remember, Dad and I had this tradition. Because our birthdays were only two days apart, we'd split the difference and spend the in-between day together, just us. Time with my father was a novelty; he was always either at work or otherwise involved. But January 21st was different: our one day.

When I was little, this meant the night before was filled with sweet anticipation. I'd lie awake obsessing about the day to come. Would it be museum or movie? Hockey game or tobogganing? On F/S Day, Dad was King Spontaneous.

When I was six we took a train into New York City, spent the day exploring Chinatown. I remember freaking over heads-still-on dead chickens hanging in store windows. Dad said, "Don't be a baby; they're the same as the ones at the IGA." But IGA chickens almost never stare back.

One time, I woke with Dad by my bed, holding a picnic basket and volleyball. He said, "Let's grab some summer in the dead of winter! We're hitting the beach!"

In the car, he played this tape he'd made: '80s Beach Tunes, featuring "Walk Like an Egyptian" and other annoyingly peppy retro hits. Made for a long ride, but it was kind of fun hearing Dad attempt harmony.

Spreading our blanket on frozen sand, we anchored the edges with driftwood, ate potato salad, and shared cocoa from this huge metal thermos. January gusts extinguished our hibachi, so we had "just the fixin's" sandwiches: pickles, cheese, and ketchup on hamburger buns, skimming frozen patties across the surf like stones.

Fierce waves churned up incredible offerings, a carpet of splintered shells: mussel, clam, scallop, and oyster glistened with foam like the remains of an Alberti's white-sauce special. I gathered the best pearlescent shards in a plastic container while Dad kicked the volleyball repeatedly into the wind. In a seaweed tangle, I discovered a perfect, tiny sea star. I still have it, the memento of a flawless day, on a shelf in my room.

Along with cool adventures, Father/Son Day had an interesting feature. "The Question Session" was like an annual, limited-time offer. Dad and I could each ask a question—nothing off-limits—and we were sworn to total honesty. The Session generally commenced as we finished lunch.

Though I'm not totally sure how it began, I vaguely recall asking if Bloop still loved me, even though I'd flushed him. I was about five, so I'm fuzzy on his response. But it was classic Dad, turning a child's rumination on a dead goldfish into some screwy, yearly tradition. Never comfortable answering my questions on a daily basis, he apparently resolved to limit meaningful interaction to a once-yearly event. Sharing thoughts and feelings became strictly a January 21st phenomenon, like reflection was a seasonal thing. I mean, there was never a July when he said, "Come back in six months. We'll talk then." Not quite. His aversion tactics were subtler; typically, he'd joke his way out of anything significant until the magic day. So Father/Son Day was about a lot more than the activities.

As a kid, I was less aware of what was happening. I mainly grooved on the festivities. And the Session was cool, liberating to have this passkey to adult wisdom. Sure, most of my early questions were typical "Where do babies come from?" stuff. Or, "Why do gerbils have to die?" That was big. He answered succinctly, yet fully, making the most of his yearly chance to shine.

His question for me was usually a variation on a single theme: "Are you happy, Evan?"

My response varied, based on my age and the day's activity. If the events were sports-related, my enthusiasm level was inevitably low.

Age five, Disney on Ice: "That was good, Daddy! Can I have a puppy?" "No puppies."

Age seven, Celtics game: "Sure, Dad. But can we rent movies when we get home?"

Age eight, Roger Williams Zoo: "Wait 'til I tell Lex I held a tree boa! See how good I am with animals? Maybe now we can get a dog."

"I've told you, Evan. We are *never* getting a dog!"

As I got older, I began to resent the whole forced-interaction concept. And I gave up on a dog, because he'd made it pretty clear he hated them.

Age twelve, Boston Aquarium: "Happy? You and Mom fight constantly. It's like you don't even care I'm right down the hall. Newsflash: I can hear! And I've been to this dumb aquarium ten times."

My questions for him grew more combative as I tired of the arrangement. I'd ask stuff like, "Are you sorry you married Mom?" and "Did you ever wish you had different parents?"

His answers were deliberate and carefully worded: "I love your mother." (A nonanswer.) And, "It's natural to have issues with one's parents." (A vague generalization.)

On our last F/S Day, I let him have it. I figured turnabout was fair play, so I asked, "Are you happy, Dad?"

As always, he was succinct and thorough. He said, "No."

Last January, we celebrated his birthday at Gran's. Mom had the flu and didn't come. On the way home, he started to talk about his plans for the next day. I stopped him.

"I can't do it this year. School's crazy; I have exams. And Mom's sick. Besides, don't you think I'm getting a little old for F/S Day? I'll be fourteen, not four."

He didn't answer. But next morning when I got up, his car was gone.

That February, he moved in with Gran and Gramp, "for a while." We never mentioned Father/Son Day again, made no attempt to reschedule. I guess the idea had run its course.

It's ironic. Now that he's gone, I really regret missing that last installment of the Question Session. I also have to wonder about his plans for our outing. Maybe we'd have scouted lynching locales, who knows? Now that he really can't answer, I have some excellent questions for him. Basically, they all begin and end with "Why?"

It's time to open the trunk.

Dad's footlocker's been in the back of my closet since last week. I've thought about opening it, pretty much nonstop, since then. And I've kept it hidden from Mom. The only person I told about it is Alexis. She offered to come over and open it with me, but I think I need to do this alone.

I'm not sure why I've waited so long to look inside; maybe I'm afraid to surrender expectation. Because what if the contents don't measure up? I mean, I doubt there'll be a winning Lotto ticket or something outrageous, like a severed head or a jar of eyeballs.

If this were a TV show, there'd be a video. Sitting on Gran's daybed, with an audience of dollies, my father would address the camera. In a teary voice, he'd say he loves me, expressing—in tight close-up—deep sorrow for what he's about to do. With a sort of desperate nobility, he'd explain "it's the only way." His choice would make tragic sense, somehow. Then he'd walk out of frame and the screen would go all static-y. Very dramatic, very cinema verité.

Unfortunately, we're not on TV. Crap, who am I kidding? It's probably just full of old notebooks. Gran said it was stuff from his Sebastian days. Please, don't let it be crammed with clippings of his field glories: "Galloway Leads Archers to 3rd Straight Win" or "Galloway Goes All the Way." I mean, it's great Dad was a sports legend. But where'd it get him?

What if it's filled with pornos? That'd be interesting. And informative since I've never owned one. Freshman year, Randy Spiotti brought a *Penthouse* to Christian Morality. Father B was not amused. When he got caught, Randy claimed the magazine was mine, like Father would buy that. Randy scored two months' detention. Plus, he had to do a twenty-page paper on the evils of porn—with annotated bibliography. Lex nearly wet herself; we both hate Randy.

Jeez, what could be in there? Drugs? No, condoms! Drug-filled condoms? Cigarettes? Whiskey? Wild, wild women? Okay, it's probably just notebooks.

I'm losing it. With this vivid an imagination a person could go nuts speculating. Not to mention, Mom's bound to spot the trunk lurking in my closet. That's another reason it's time. Plus, it's still Father/Son Day. Okay, F/S Night, 11:54 p.m. to be exact. Since Dad isn't here for me to question, I'll take what I can get.

I flip on my lava lamp, a Christmas gift from Aunt Reg. Padding silently toward the closet, I remember lying in the dark, terrified of monsters behind that door. Opening it, I lift and swing with exaggerated slowness, to minimize hinge-squeak. I've been clutching the key for an hour; its outline's imprinted on my moist palm.

Sliding the locker out, heart racing, I squint to insert the key. For a queasy moment, it refuses to fit the brass lock face. Gran's given me the wrong one. This probably opens some forgotten padlock in Gramp's workroom. Piss! I panic. Forcing the key in, I rattle it violently, like a teenaged Marley's Ghost. The lock plate drops down with an unbelievably loud clank.

"Evan?" Mom calls groggily from the room down the hall.

"Yeah, Mom. Just catching up on some reading. Sorry to wake you. Night!" I chirp too fast, too cheery. She'll be in here pronto, maternal radar full tilt.

"Okay, hon. Jus' not too late. Love you." She trails into la-la land.

"Thank you, Jesus," I whisper, glad for her new nightly tradition: a glass of wine and a Tylenol PM.

I drag my treasure chest to the center of the room and sit, Indian-style, on the braided rug. Carefully unhooking latches, I lift the lid. A pale scent of basement and memory teases my nostrils. Hunkered over the open trunk—eyes shut—I prolong the final rush of anticipation. This is going to be big; I can feel it. I look inside.

Guess it was just one of God's little HA HAs.

Sitting in Honors Bio, I struggle to concentrate on the material: the conjugation of bilirubin in the healthy liver. I'm not sure how to account for my lack of focus. It's a fascinating topic. My teacher, Miss Delateski, looks smart in a fuchsia pantsuit; her jokes about dating "Little Billy Rubin" are a scream. I suppose it could be the near-total lack of sleep compromising my retention. Maybe it's because Randy Spiotti keeps punching my arm, whenever Miss D turns her back. Or perhaps, it's exhilaration that today is my birthday. Hoopla.

No. I'm pretty sure I'm just still shocked by my new nugget of self-awareness. Last night's lone trunk-related discovery was this: I lack intuition. I was so sure that stupid footlocker would be stuffed full of insights into the old man. I thought I might find a suicide note, or that asinine video. I shouldn't have gotten my hopes up. You'd think I'd have learned by now.

What went through my mind as I lifted the lid? *This is going to be big; I can feel it.* Sure. I was ready for discovery. And when I looked inside, here's what I found: a big, fat, steaming pile of Dad's lousy, stinking crap! Well, not literally. That would have been really nasty.

No, his "legacy" amounted to a bad 1970s time capsule. Peering eagerly into the trunk, I was greeted by the divine detectives of the Townsend Agency: Charlie's Freaking Angels! Indications are he was a huge fan. He seemed to favor the smart one, Sabrina Duncan, reed-thin Kate Jackson. I guess, pre-Mom, he went for the anorexic type. Personally, I'd pick Kelly Garrett, played by Jaclyn Smith, assuming I could trek back to an era when she wasn't nearing the century mark.

He also had that Farrah poster, the one with the slew of extraordinarily white teeth and the chipper nipple. You'd probably be hard-pressed to find a boy of the '70s who didn't at least wish he had that poster on his bedroom wall. I'm a bit shocked Gran allowed it "under her roof." I'm sure Gramp was okay with it. Hell, he probably had a copy, too.

But anyway, other than an unwanted insight into my father's high school masturbatory fantasies, the trunk experience was basically a bust. No pun intended. Although, I may keep the poster. Lex would find it totally appalling.

"—explain the difference between direct and indirect bilirubin? Evan, are you with us?"

I look up to find Miss Delateski and the entire class staring at me. I flush and stammer, "Sorry, Miss D. Just thinking how much I like that color on you."

There's a generalized groan, and Spiotti cough-speaks, "Loser!" into his fist.

"Could you repeat the question?" I ask sheepishly. It's going to be a long day.

After class, Lex meets me in the cafeteria for lunch. She insists on buying my turkey roll-up. "It's a loving birthday gesture, Ev."

At our usual table, we eat in silence. Chewing the tasteless meat, I offer a fake smile. My mind keeps wandering to the trunk. As I ball up my napkin, Lex speaks.

"Okay, close your eyes, Birthday Boy."

I squeeze them shut. "You're not planning to kiss me?"

"In your dreams, bud."

"Oh yeah, the recurring nightmare. Haven't had that one in a while."

"Watch it or *I'll* be your worst nightmare. Ready? Now open your eyes, Smart-ass."

I do, and find a homemade cupcake with a paper candle and a funky, green foil envelope, obviously an Alexis Original.

"Wow, cool. Should I open it?"

"Gee, there's a novel idea." She grins.

Gently, I peel off the ladybug seal. Lex smiles, tenting long fingers beneath her chin. The card's handmade, an intricate cut-paper peapod; I pull the curled-ribbon tendril. Inside's a pop-up, 3-D photo illustration of us, backstage at our fourth grade pageant, nose-to-nose. We're dressed in matching pea costumes. Across the bottom of the card, she's written in metallic gold ink:

Two peas, forever and always!
Happy 15th!
All My Love, Alexis
XOXOXO

"Happy Birthday!"

"I'm not sure what to say."

"Well, you could start with thanks. I practically sliced off my pinkie making that. I was never exactly Mistress of the X-ACTO Blade."

"Thank you. I, uh, I love you, too." I squint back tears.

"Hey, don't go all girly on me. That's what friends are for."

"I know."

We look at each other for a moment, before Lex breaks the gaze.

"Soooo, anyway—and this honestly isn't an attempt to ease the weird sexual tension—what's in the trunk?"

"The trunk? What makes you think I even opened it?"

"Because we've been best friends since second grade. I think I know you by now, Evster. Yesterday was Father/Son Day, right? So you opened the trunk to feel close to him or whatever. I mean, that's got to be why you're so premenstrual. The card was good and all, but seriously."

She always could pull the rug out from under me; it's irritating. "Well, you're wrong. I haven't opened it yet."

She smirks. "You're Gallo-way off base, if you think I'm buying that."

"I didn't open the damn trunk, okay? Drop it!"

Voice brittle, she says, "Don't lie, Evan, not to me. We have too much history."

I know what she's talking about, and I don't want to go there, not now, not on my freaking birthday. "Lex, don't."

"Don't what? Talk about it? Why not? I'm over it, okay? But it's important. It's part of what ties us together, part of what makes us—US." It's her turn to fight tears.

I smack the lunch tray with my fist. "Alexis, what does your stepfather have to do with me and the footlocker? They're totally separate things!"

"We can't have secrets from each other and be best friends. Not when it's something important. Didn't we learn that a long time ago?"

I nod and take her hand. "I'm sorry. I shouldn't have lied. Not to you."

Lex twists my pinkie as she says, "Well don't do it again, because I *will* kill you."

"All right, yes, I opened the trunk. But, just for the record, why couldn't I be emotional over the card? It's a great card."

"Not your style. And, just for the record, you never answered my question."

"God, you're obnoxious. Which question?"

"Could you not be a jerk, just this once?" She turns my hand palm-up and asks, loudly, "WHAT"S INSIDE THE F-O-O-T-L-O-C-K-E-R?" spelling the last word into my palm, Annie Sullivan to Helen Keller-style.

I spell and yell back, "P-O-R-N."

"Eeeuuuuuuw, no way!"

We dissolve in hysterics, slumped on the table, and risk detention staying in the lunchroom for two extra Mods. I tell Lex all about last night, and the disappointing trunk loot. We laugh about Farrah and the gang, and share my birthday cupcake.

Father Brendan was a caterpillar on a mushroom, blowing bubbles through a giant key.

Image lingering, I struggle up from the dream. It's 4:04, the morning after my birthday bash.

It was a fairly tame bash, not all the usual suspects in attendance. Dad couldn't be there, obviously. Gran and Gramp mercifully sat this one out. It's only been a couple days since the showdown at Alberti's; I'm not sure when the ice'll thaw between the two Mrs. Galloways. So it was just us five: Mom and me, the Aunts and—making her Galloway birthday debut—Alexis.

It was my mother's idea to invite Lex. I think she figured a nonrelative might help defuse the situation. I guess Alexis was there as some kind of behavioral chaperone, to keep us all in line. It's funny; I don't generally think of her as a particularly calming influence. Disarmingly blunt? Check. Wildly irreverent? Yessir! Honest to a fault? That's Lex. But I'm not sure

I'd automatically cast her as Peacemaker. So I can't say whether it was her presence, or the grace of God, but the evening was blessedly uneventful.

Mom made a lasagna; Aunt Reg brought the cake, this colossal chocolate concoction. We'll be eating it for weeks. Lex sings in concert choir at school, so with her soprano to guide them, they made a pretty passable Happy Birthday Quartet. And after I blew out my candles, they all had the sense not to ask what I'd wished for. That may have been the best gift of all.

Lex's mom picked her up around 9:00, just after the snow began. As we walked toward the Blazer, Alexis caught my sleeve, pulled me close, and kissed my cheek.

"I'm sure he'd have wanted to be here, Ev."

"Yeah, well, he's not."

"It's going to be okay, you know." She hugged me.

"We'll see."

"Evan . . . "

"Your mom's waiting, Lex. And the snow's really coming down. I'll see you tomorrow."

"Happy birthday."

"Thanks. For everything."

Watching them drive into the white, I pictured us in our pea costumes and smiled. As I opened the front door, the Triumvirate descended.

"Junior, she is a keeper!" Auntie Ro squashed my face in manicured hands.

"Rosemary! Leave the kid alone, he's blushing!" Aunt Regina to the rescue.

"No, I'm just cold. Really."

"She is a cutie, though, Ev. You two will be adorable at prom. Have you asked her yet?"

"We're just friends, Aunt Reg. Besides, I thought you were on my side!"

"Don't mind them, Evan." Mom laughed. "They were the same way with your father and me. But I agree; you do make a very nice couple."

It went on for a while, the trio insisting we were more than friends. I fervently denied Lex is my girlfriend, unsure whether I was trying to convince them or myself. Just as I began to feel like a prisoner at a sleepover camp for middle-aged cheerleaders, my aunts decided to leave before the roads iced. We bid them safe travel, closing the door against needling cold. Then Mom and I stood in the foyer facing each other, exhausted, the normal act too much.

"I'm going to leave the dishes 'til morning. Don't stay up too late."

"Mom?"

"What is it, Ev?"

"Do you miss him?"

She nodded—just barely—and whispered, "Get some rest, honey."

As she walked down the hall to her room, it struck me she looked smaller somehow. Later, surrendering to sleep, I heard her crying. I told myself it was just the wind.

Suddenly, I'm in Wonderland.

There's no White Rabbit. I didn't fall down a hole. It's just like, BAM: a new realm! Remnants of my bedroom fuse with the scenery. The moon's my blue, braided rug. On the branch of a sugar maple lounges a fantastical creature.

The cat beams an extraordinarily white smile; blond fur flows, a wild, frosted shag. Unmistakable: there on her taut, red body, a single, frisky nipple. She addresses me.

"Junior, we've been waiting. Come inside. We've mysteries to share."

"Inside? Where?"

She purrs a single word, "Leeegaaacy" and is gone. The forest dissolves.

"Mister Alberti?"

Standing atop an enormous scallop shell, he unfurls a blue tablecloth; it drops to become an ocean. My tiny vessel's battered up over cresting waves. Fingers reach for me, incredibly long in the braided-ruglight.

Lex's voice: "Evan! Don't go any further—you can't come back!"

"I have to! I need to know why!"

"I am The Why. Would you know me?" It's Steve Austin, the kid who killed himself. Floating, he rolls belly-up, face a bloated gray, mouth stretched into a wet, pink leer. His lips part. My father's within, struggling to free himself from silver shark teeth.

"DAD! WAIT!"

I throw myself from the boat to save him. A shock: I sprawl in soft grass before a colossal mushroom. On it sits a massive black-and-white caterpillar. In its teeny, grasping hand a key glitters. The worm blows huge, luminescent bubbles through the key's hole. Each "plips" out a single word. In Father Brendan's brogue.

(plip) "Evan"

"Yes, Father. Please tell me . . . "

(plip) "Your"

" . . . what am I supposed . . . "

(plip) "answers"

" . . . to do?"

(plip) "lie"

"My answers lie? You mean like 'tell a lie'?"

(plip) "within"

"Okay. My answers lie within. Jeez, this is excruciating! If this is a dream, it's obnoxious. Can we speed things up a bit, maybe drop the freakin' plips?"

(plip) "your"

"I guess not."

(plip) "chest."

"Oh, please! Within my chest? You mean, like, look inside my heart? I'm sorry Father, but that is so cliché!"

"Saints preserve us! I'm talkin' 'bout the trunk. Take another look in the TRUNK! For the love of Mike! You're supposed to be a genius, Boy!"

He doesn't plip. That's what wakes me. I snap from the dream, startled, in the center of my room. I used to sleepwalk as a kid, but haven't in years. I've also never moved bulky objects in my sleep, but I guess there's a first time for everything. I'm slumped across the footlocker. I guess that fatherpillar meant business, at least to my sleep-self.

At first, I'm dubious. A prophetic dream? What am I, Nostradamus? But then, I get to thinking, the Bible's full of them. Old Testament Joseph and the Pharaoh, New Testament Joseph and the Flight into Egypt. Okay,

I'm not a biblical figure. Shoot, I'm not even named Joseph. But, who am I to argue with a caterpriest? Besides, what've I got to lose taking another look? At the very least, I'll get a chance to admire Jaclyn one more time. It's not like I have anything better to do pre-dawn.

Standing, I flip on the lava lamp and look out at a world encased in a chrysalis. We must be getting an inch of snow an hour. No school tomorrow, guaranteed. I'll need the break; I have a feeling I won't be going back to sleep. I scoop the trunk key from the shelf, next to my starfish.

As I squat to slide the key into the lock, I whisper, "Once more into the breach." I can't remember what that's from, exactly. Has to be Shakespeare; everything is. I turn the key, remembering to catch the noisy lock plate. Thumbs poised on latches, I stop.

"I don't think I can do this alone." I've started talking to myself a lot lately. It's a bit troubling. I consider calling Lex, then say, "Yeah, that'd go over great at 4:20 in the morning."

Instead, I ask myself what she'd say. Probably something like, "If a giant talking worm told you to look in the trunk, what the hell you waiting for?"

I whisper a prayer to Saint Sebastian:

Dear Sebastian, Patron of Archers,
Make my aim for answers true.
Lead me to discovery.
I ask this in Jesus' name.

Opening the lid, I lift a stack of *People* magazines and *National Enquirers*—all Angels-related. There's a large manila envelope with black marker writing: Charlie's Angels Trading Cards. I roll my eyes, put the envelope aside, atop the stack of magazines. Rummaging further, an archaeologist on an important dig, I sift through teen memorabilia, hoping to find a remnant, some emotional scrap of the kid who was my father. Nothing. It's still just stuff, meaningless. I can't attach significance to any of it. Dad's failed me again. And now, so has Saint Sebastian. It's typical. All our heroes let us down. Why should heaven be different?

Gathering a pile of clippings, I shred them. It feels good, opposite of my usual powerlessness. Ripping a *People* cover, I wad it, crushing Angel faces. "Take that, Farrah." Next up: trading cards. Tearing open the packet with manic glee, I upend it, anticipating a shower of collector cards.

"I'll burn them tomorrow!"

Absorbed in visions of memento-destruction, for just an instant, I see the cards cascade. Reality taking hold, I stare at the braided rug. It's not littered with bubble-gum relics. Just two objects lie between my bare feet. I crouch, lifting them toward the blue lava light, straining for a mental connection between expected and actual. Squinting, I read my father's tiny printing on the cassette tape label: Suicide Songs, 1976. I shiver, place the tape on the seat of my desk chair, close the trunk lid, and sit on it. Turning the other object in my hand, I stroke the rough canvas cover. Opening the book, I read the inscription.

"My God. It's his journal," I breathe into the blue-lit room, awed by discovery.

It occurs to me I owe Saint Sebastian an apology.

"What's that tune you're humming?"

Mom's voice penetrates my fog as I stare into the microwave, tracking the slow revolutions of my Cheesy Pouch on the glass carousel. Filling oozes, lava-like, from the silver crisping-wrapper.

"Huh? . . . nothing . . . why?"

I'm beat. After another sleepless night, the last thing I needed was sidewalk duty. But the storm dumped a foot-plus, and as default man of the house, it was my job to shovel a path to civilization.

"It just sounded a lot like a song by Karen Carpenter, from my distant youth."

"Karen who?" I feign ignorance. The song's "Goodbye to Love"; in it, Karen vows she's through with romance, warbling, "There are no tomorrows" where her heart's concerned. Peppy stuff. Apparently, it was Dad's favorite. It's on his suicide tape three times.

"The Carpenters. They were a brother/sister group. Couldn't imagine you knew it. Takes me back, though. What a depressing tune."

I know all about the Carpenters: how they created a new sound, Karen's struggles with anorexia, her untimely end. See, Lex's devotion to prehistoric pop stars isn't exclusive to Neil Diamond. He's merely her all-time fave. She also has a pretty extensive collection of other "artists of the eight-track."

Plus, we sang another Carpenters' gem "Sing, Sing a Song" consisting of a syncopated sequence of "La-las" in the parish minstrel when I was in fourth grade.

"Evan, are you in there?"

"Sorry, Mom. I'm pretty tired."

"Is it any wonder?" A familiar edge creeps in. "When did you finally go to bed, anyway?"

"Not sure." I turn away, taking a plate from the drying rack near the sink.

She tsks me across the oak chef's island. "You've been staying up way too late. In that room with the door shut, doing God-knows-what. It's not healthy, honey."

"Suddenly insomnia's a friggin' crime?" I yank open the microwave and grab the pouch, burning my fingers on molten goo. "SHIT!" I fumble it onto the strawberry scatter rug. Snatching a length of paper towel, I squat.

Mom commences her rant. "Nice language! Listen, I'm serious. It's going to stop, this staying up 'til all hours. The brooding in your room. You'll end up sick, for God's sake. Or worse—like him. Well, I won't lose you too!"

"Mom, I'm fine."

I try to will her away by concentrating on the rug. Rubbing at the cheese-food-product, I grind it into the plush fibers.

"No, you are most certainly not fine! You're up to something, keeping secrets! Do you think I'm blind to what's going on? Tell me the truth, Evan. Are you taking drugs?"

I spring to my feet, waling my head on the microwave door. The force makes my teeth clack.

I snap. "Look! I can't sleep. Big freaking deal! Did you ever think, maybe, I have a lot on my mind? And, no I'm not on drugs! I didn't inherit your talent for self-medicating." A vein pulses at her temple. I move in for the kill. "Yeah, I know all about your Tylenol toddies! But thanks for the intervention, Mommy. I guess you do care!"

Ignoring her gasp, I slam the microwave; the force knocks a Delft plate from the shelf above the sink. Striking the counter edge, it explodes. We stare at it, then at each other.

Silence.

"I'm sorry, Mom. I'll fix it."

"You can't." Her voice absolutely flat, barely a sigh, she leaves the kitchen.

I stoop to survey the damage: a total loss. As I pick up the pieces, I realize it's her swan plate, an anniversary present from Dad.

January 20, 1976 (Happy birthday to me!)
Dear Journal,

Too bizarre. After the scene with Mom, I headed to the library. I'm in the stacks with his journal, reading Dad's long-ago scribblings. It feels like trespassing, a familiar feeling being an incestuous Peeping Tom, like when I was nine and caught my mother with her top down.

She was sunbathing in the backyard when I came out to get my bike. Alexis and I were planning to ride to Gardner Lake to meet her stepdad for waterskiing. I always felt a little unwelcome around Lex's stepfather, like he resented sharing her. But she'd insisted I come, said it wouldn't be any fun if it was just the two of them.

Anyway, as I crossed the yard, the phone rang. Mom sat up to grab it, and her bikini top stuck to the beach chair. Guess she was going for a strapless tan; she'd unhooked.

She didn't realize I was there. Frozen midstep, jaw slack, not wanting to look, I was paralyzed by the sight of my mother's boobies. I mean, I'd never really seen live breasts up close. A classic no-win situation: Move or speak, she'd know I'd seen. Stay put, be caught.

As Mom talked, they began to sway. It reminded me of this TV hypnotist swinging a pocket watch. He put this guy under, made him do crazy stuff: act like a ballerina, gallop, and moo. It was funny at first, but I wondered how the guy would feel when he saw the show. He couldn't help it. He was mesmerized—like I was now.

I stood for what seemed like hours, unable to look away. Finally, bits of Mom's conversation seeped through my boob-stupor, and I realized she was talking to Lex. That made it even worse. I felt really ashamed. I had to take action.

As I made a break for the porch, Mom turned to call me to the phone. Our eyes locked, and she made this squeak of sound, like when Gramp sat on my hamster. Then, grabbing for her towel, she dropped the phone and fell off her chair.

Some other kid's mom might've laughed, or let the moment pass, pretended it didn't happen—even used the occasion to discuss the importance of breast health. Not mine; she went ape-shit. She started screaming, "You should know better," like I was a perv in a trench coat. Then she stomped into the porch, slamming the door.

I picked up the phone; Lex was still on the line. I knew she'd heard. When I asked if she still wanted to go to the lake, she said she thought we'd better not; then she hung up. Mom reappeared, a windbreaker over her bathing suit. She said I was grounded 'til further notice, and Dad would speak with me when he got home.

He never did, but it was definitely a turning point. Mom acted vaguely uncomfortable around me after that, like she'd impaired my morals. She stopped sitting on my bed to say goodnight, and she insisted I wear a robe at breakfast, when I'd always been a T-shirt and underwear kind of kid.

It was also around that time she stopped trying to hold my hand crossing the street. That was odd; it'd always seemed like a total instinct, like autopilot. As we stepped off a curb, her fingers would just automatically flex toward mine. Being nearly ten, I'd usually stuff my fist in my pocket. Her hand would flutter for a few seconds, searching. It really annoyed me. But then she stopped, and sometimes I still sort of miss it.

Wow, poor me. I don't know where all that came from. Besides, I didn't come here to think about Mom; I'm Dad-excavating. It's just, I'm afraid I'm about to see more of my father than I want to. Maybe more than I have a right to. Oh well, what's life without a little emotional bungee-jumping? Geronimo.

Dear Journal,

No idea what to write. Miss Solomon's making us keep a journal (swore she won't read it) to "nurture our process" and "explore our thoughts in an evocative way." (Yeah, right.) I feel pretty dense when she yaps about "creative intent" and "examining our psychical subtext." HUH?

Otherwise she's cool (actually scorching in those ballerina tops). She twirled around my desk today, singing Happy Birthday in French. Father B would not approve. She's definitely short-term.

Well, Dad was wrong about that. Miss Solomon's still here. But now she's *Mrs.* Solomon-Baxter-Coombs. She's abandoned leotards in favor of sensible suits. I guess gravity and years of experience finally got the better of her. She's still a great teacher, though.

I had Mrs. S-B-C for Myth and Meaning last year. Of all my teachers, she handled Dad's suicide best. For one thing, she talked to me when I came back, invited me to come to her office if I needed to vent. She also encouraged me to incorporate the loss into my final project, creating my own myth. She said that was the chief function of myth-making: It was "man's effort to grapple with and tame the unendurable."

I took her advice, creating the story of an island kingdom whose monarch ended his life, hurling himself off a cliff into the hungry sea, to save his people from a deadly typhoon. When he hit the water, his body dissolving into silver foam, the storm instantly subsided.

Each dawn, the king's children gathered on the shore to mourn. On the seventh day, foam swirled into the glistening form of a sea lion. It drew them into the surf, bestowing a gift on each. To the youngest, it gave a nest of seaweed, for hope. The middle child received a heart-shaped cockle, for love. And the king's eldest was given a driftwood cross, for strength.

When the sea lion swam off, singing their father's lullaby, the children, amazed, returned home with their inheritance. Realizing he hadn't left them, they accepted their birthright, ruling wisely. Each year on the anniversary of the monarch's death, the sea lion returned, and the kingdom honored its ruler's great sacrifice. And never again did the sea threaten the tiny island.

I did this huge watercolor of the children on the sand, built a topographical map of the kingdom, and sculpted a crest showing the three gifts. For my presentation, I dressed in this robe I wore as the apostle Thomas in the school's Passion play. I wore a coronet of seashells.

Mrs. Solomon-Baxter-Coombs went gaga. I guess any teacher would've been impressed, but it seemed truly cathartic for her. When I finished reading my myth, she got up from her desk, applauded, then started bawling. She said, "You have succeeded in transforming pain into parable." After hugging me, she excused herself and bolted.

The class gaped. I just stood there, wondering what the heck had happened. She must've thought I believed my father had made a noble sacrifice. But he wasn't heroic, like the king in my myth. And instead of an enchanted pinniped, he'd morphed into a human piñata.

By the time Mrs. S-B-C returned, the period was almost over. As I started to go, she caught my sleeve. Once the class filed out, she repeated her invitation to stop by. I thanked her. She made this tiny, hiccupping nod when I asked her to keep my illustration. Bet she still has it.

I did go to her office about a week later to talk. Taped to her door was a note saying, *I shall return, toot-sweet!* I took it as a sign; never went back.

January 22, 1976
   Hey Journal!
   I'm stoked! It's love! Or GRADE-A LUST! Deena's amazing! We've been lab partners for months and nothing. Today our fingers brushed over a dissection tray and—ZAP! Who knew slicing sheep eyes was such a turn-on?
   Practice was hell and I've got tons of homework. Later, E.

January 25, 1976
   Howdy J.

You know that saying "When it rains it pours"? Well, I got a chick monsoon. Tammy called. Her father's job fell through, they're back from Boston, and she wants to get together. Deena's cool, but Tammy's primo! Hmmmm . . . why not date both? Just kidding, journal. Sort of.

Hornily, E.

February 1, 1976

Yo!

This bunny-juggling's intense! Came THIS CLOSE to calling Tammy "Deena" yesterday. Then at the movies with Deena, I ran smack into Tammy's brother! He's such a chump, he prob'ly didn't know the diff. Better split! I owe Tammy a call.

Evan, AKA "Love Machine"

Feb. 2, 1976

LIFE SUCKS.

1. Tammy's brother's smarter than I thought.
2. Tammy and Deena are cousins, and
3. I am SHIT ON TOAST.

E.

Feb. 4, '76

Journal—FRIG IT! Tammy's mother blabbed to Mom at Pathmark, so I'm really in the shit. Mrs. Granato told her everything. Mom said my behavior's "indefensible." Rosemary called me a "typical male pig" which made Reg laugh till she choked on her pot roast. (Dad actually looked proud.) Anyway, I'm off women. Maybe I'll become a priest. E.

February 10, 1976

Praise God!

Can you believe it? Right after the D/T fiasco I find THE ONE. Melody's IT! She's:

1. **stacked,**
2. **a cheerleader, and**
3. **stacked—definite girlfriend material.**

   Her locker door sticks. I helped her open it, and the rest is hist—

AAARRRRGGGGHHHH! I can't take much more of this. It's like a freakin' comic book: *The Adventures of Vapid Boy*. I mean, I feel like I'm pouring over Dad's stinkin' bicentennial soap opera. The insights! The shocking revelations! My father was a shallow, sex-obsessed freak!

So obnoxious. Maybe I should donate this piece of crap to the library. Wonder if there's an Obnoxious and Deluded section? Oh hell, I'll keep reading. Got nothing better to do. I'll just finish February; it's a short month. How bad could it be?

February 18, 1976
   Dear Journal—
   Tried talking to Tony again. In study hall. Don't know what his problem is. He's acting real strange. I mean, best friends are supposed to talk and shit! Called him after supper. Mrs. Pettafordi said he never came home. She asked me to call if—

HOLY MOTHER OF PEARL! MRS. PETTAFORDI? My father was best buds with Anthony J. Pettafordi, Art Teacher and Academic Advisor to the Intellectually Muddled Masses? How did I not know this? This is major info. All those times I talked about class, or said I had a meeting with my guidance counselor, and Dad never thought to reveal they were pals?

And Mister P never mentioned growing up with my father. It's got to mean something. For starters, it explains The P Man's lingering at my Dad's wake. Seemed a little excessive, staying through afternoon and evening calling hours. I recall wondering if the school paid overtime. And the way he blubbered graveside, he was more emotional than the relatives. I figured it had to do with artistic temperament. Now I find out they were best friends—unbelievable.

But in a way it's not. Ever since I started at Sebastian's, Mister Pettafordi's made himself a force in my life. Even before Dad died, he took an interest in me. His fixation on getting me a scholarship makes sense. He must think he has a responsibility to my father.

I wonder why their friendship was so secret. Looks like I have another mystery to solve. Or maybe it's part of the one big question. Who knows? I guess the only way to find out is to keep reading. At least it's getting interesting.

"So, what do you think it means, Ev?"

Alexis has the loudest whisper ever. We're in silent study, and Miss Delateski does not look amused. She glares over a stack of lab reports, makes a zipper motion across her lips.

I try to look calm as my stomach churns. Lex's feet twitch so fast it appears she's dealing with a fire ant infestation. I wonder if anyone's ever died from having to stay silent for five more minutes. The suspense is definitely getting to us; I swear the clock just ticked backwards.

I called yesterday from the library, told Lex about the journal, asked her to meet me. She couldn't come, so I read a couple entries over the phone. I know that seems tacky, but it feels right to share Dad with my best friend. So it's the first face time we've had since my discovery, and now we're hostages to high school structure. Forced mutes. Two minutes 'til period's over. I doodle in the margin of my soc book; Lex gnaws her gel pen, sighs.

Finally, the bell rings; changing of the guard. Miss D gathers her stuff. The new monitor waddles in. We luck out: Sister Dolores, old and enormous. Swathed in traditional black and white, she looks like a penguin that's turned the tables, swallowed a leopard seal. Lex always says Sister's bosom's large enough to support the original cross. Obviously, that's sacrilegious, but I can't help laughing.

Old Dolores strains into the creaking desk chair, closes her eyes. Uncorking a Wonder Ear, she deposits it on the blotter. For her, it truly will be a silent study. We're home free.

Lex clears her throat extra-loud and repeats her question full volume. "SO, WHAT DO YOU THINK IT MEANS, EV?"

Sister doesn't budge, but the three cheerleaders in the front row turn and bad-eye us.

"Ooh, Evan! I've disturbed the Ambers. Mea culpa, ladies! That means 'sorry.' Really though, keep up the good work. You inspire me. Rah rah, now!"

They perform a perfectly synchronized hand gesture that'd never fly at a Catholic pep rally. Lex feigns horror. Sneering, the three collect their matching designer backpacks and, risking detention, cut out of study hall early.

"Thought they'd never leave. So, now that we're alone . . . "

Sister Dolores sleep-grunts loud enough to startle us both.

"Well, almost alone," Lex smirks.

"Yeah, about my dad's journal. I don't know what to think."

Lex's eyes take on that laser focus she gets when really concentrating. "It's wild, Evan. I mean, Pettafordi and your dad all buddy-buddy—so what happened to bust it up?"

"No idea."

"Well, what's his journal say?"

"I haven't read anymore since yesterday. I just got freaked out, you know?"

"I guess, kind of like being in the confessional with my mom. She used to do that when I was little, bring me in with her. I had to listen to her sins. Truly creepy. So, do you have it?"

"The journal? Obviously. I can't leave it home. Mom would root it out. She grilled me about drug use yesterday. If she found his journal, she'd pull a Krakatoa."

Slipping the journal from my binder, I half-expect an alarm to blare. I picture Sister Dolores in a warden's uniform. Screaming: "LOCKDOWN! GALLOWAY'S GOT EMOTIONAL CONTRABAND!"

I hand Dad's chronicle to Alexis. She holds it with such care, reverence almost. It's a relief knowing she's here to share the weight.

"Are you scared, Evan?"

"Yeah. So I want us to read it together. Let's start where I left off, February 20th."

February 20, 1976
  Hey Journal—
  This Tony thing's really bumming me out. He ignored me in art again today. And when Father Fran called my watercolor "luminous," Tony looked like he'd puke.

"I didn't know your father was an artist . . . Evan?"
"Me neither. He was never interested in my painting, that's for sure."
"Well, that's his loss. You're really talented, you know."
"Uh-huh."
"Ev?"
"Hmm?"
"Turn the page."

February 21, 1976
  Journal,
  Today was bad. Definitely not how I planned to spend Saturday. Tony said some stuff.
  I cornered him yesterday. He promised to meet today at Shoppers' Plaza. We dropped a pile on art supplies at Koenig's, had patty melts and Cokes at Burger Shack.
  Tony was real quiet. When I finally asked what's bothering him, he said he's trying to figure stuff out—like our friendship.
  Then he said sometimes he hates me. I have it so easy. I'm great at sports, the perfect student, good-looking. He just went on and on, getting redder.
  He's tired of hearing about Melody, too. Said I don't give a shit about him anymore, that she's taken me away from him. I told him that's nuts, he's still my best friend. Then he started crying. I felt like decking him, so I went to the john.
  When I got back, Tony was on a bench outside. He apologized, said he's just a stupid, jealous dork.

I said, "Quit being such a spaz. You're good at lots of stuff."

He said, "Name one thing."

So I told him, "You're an awesome artist."

He started crying and said, "Father Fran likes you best."

I said that's not true. It's just I've known Father since I was a kid, but Tony started SCREAMING, "IT'S NOT FAIR! WHY ARE YOU TRYING TO STEAL HIM FROM ME?"

Before I knew it, I was shaking him, yelling TAKE IT BACK, YOU TAKE IT BACK!

Then, this lady came out of Card Shoppe to ask if everything was okay. I jolted at the question, like I'd been asleep. Tony pulled away and said, "I better go. See you on the bus Monday."

When I got home, Dad said he was sick of playing secretary. I got 7 phone calls: 1 from Melody, and 5 from "that Pettafordi kid."

I said, "That's only six." And then he blew my mind.

He said, "Right, Father Fran called. Said it was important."

I didn't return any of the calls. Now it's 3 A.M. and I feel like the living dead.

I'm sweating, and I think my intestines just unspooled around my ankles.

"Alexis, I can't read anymore."

"You've got to! There are answers in here, I know it."

"I'm not sure I can deal with them, whatever they are."

"I'll help you, Evan."

"Look, maybe there are answers, but I don't need to know them. Besides, all we've learned is that Mr. Pettafordi had an inferiority complex. What does that have to do with my father killing himself like thirty years later?"

"I think you owe it to him to find out."

"I'm done."

"Fine, let me take it home. I'll do the reading and give you a full report."

"You're joking, right?"

"Well, then we only have one choice. We go straight to the source and ask the horse."

"You mean Pettafordi?"

"Of course, of course."

"You're insane."

"I know. But it's sort of liberating."

"What are we supposed to do, ask him why he freaked and stopped being friends with my dad? Won't that seem odd, considering their friendship's like a big, dark secret?"

"No way, Evieboy. We'll be discreet. Besides, you're still in mourning. Personal crises are like a free pass for odd behavior."

"You should know."

"Yeah." Lex rocks forward, studying her feet, and begins drawing tiny purple circles, like bruises, on the back of her hand.

I reach over, ease the gel pen from her fingers.

"I'm sorry, Lex. I'm an idiot. I didn't mean that."

"It's okay. You are an idiot. But it's true. I'm the expert on personal crises and odd behavior. Another gift from Dear Old Stepdad."

"I didn't mean to upset you."

"You haven't. Really. It was a long time ago, and I'm past it. Now forget it, okay?"

"But Lex, I—"

"But nothing, comrade. Back to the plan at hand: The Subtle Interrogation of Anthony J. Pettafordi. Nice ring, don't you think? I may write a *Lifetime* movie about it one day."

"Great."

"So here's the deal. We tell him in art we want to discuss college choices. We've got Mods 13 and 14 free. We meet in his office, ask a few questions, and before he realizes what's happening, we've shined a searchlight into the past. What do you say?"

"Uh . . . gee . . . let's see . . . no."

"Come on! Life is short, be a sport!"

"You know I hate it when you rhyme."

"Evan, Evan. Big, fat seven. Kick your butt straight up to heaven."

"You are so queer."

"But that's why you love me."

"Fine, I'll do it on one condition: I do the talking. You're just there as a witness, got it?"

"Whatever."

"Promise?"

"Jeez, okay!"

"Good. Repeat after me: I, Alexis Philomena Bottaro, do solemnly swear to keep my big trap shut. And to do everything in my power to keep from embarrassing my friend, Evan Gifford Galloway, who is all good and deserving of all my love."

"I think it's so cool your initials spell egg."

"Say it, Philomena."

"Shut up!"

"Say it."

"All right, all right! I, Alexis Philomena Bottaro, do solemnly swear to keep my big trap shut—"

The bell rings. As we slip past Sister Dolores, she sleepmumbles something that sounds like "rutapeppa transgoration." Lex hovers for a moment, hoping for more. As the next monitor comes in to rouse Sister, we head out.

In the hall, Lex says, "Cafeteria?"

I shake my head. "Can't. I've got a preliminary stop before we talk to Pettafordi."

"I'll come, too."

"No. This is sort of a fact-finding mission; I'll be deep undercover. It's best I go solo."

Her head does a quizzical puppy tilt. "Sure you can handle it?"

"Not really, but I'll try. See you in psych."

"Roger that." She gives me a quick salute, clicks her heels, and starts toward the cafeteria. Then, rushing back, she pulls a laminated Helen Reddy bookmark from her binder and hands it to me, grinning. "For luck."

As Lex retreats down the corridor, I briefly consider fleeing the building. Instead, attempting to channel the "I Am Woman, Hear Me Roar" singer's bravado, I head toward Awkward Student/Teacher Conversation #1.

✠

"Well, Evan. This is a surprise. What brings you here?"

I peer across the cluttered desk like a deer in the headlights. A really hungry deer. It's lunchtime. The office smells vaguely of tuna.

My stomach butts in. "MMMRRAAWWRRGGGLLLLRRRRR."

"So, what's up?"

"Um, just thought I'd drop in and say hi."

"Really?"

"Yup."

We sit in silence as the bumblebee second hand makes two flights around the Winnie-the-Pooh wall clock.

Finally, "Ahem. Okay then. Good to see you. If that's all, I have papers to grade. My freshmen are grappling with haiku."

"Oh. Sure."

Scooping my books from the floor, I turn to leave. It was a bad idea coming here. I'm a lousy sleuth. I should be in the caf right now. The meatball grinders aren't half bad.

"Evan?"

I turn back. Behind the desk hangs my illustration, the weeping children of the sea lion king.

Mrs. Solomon-Baxter-Coombs says, "Care to try again?"

"Ma'am?"

"Why are you *really* here, Evan?"

I take a deep breath.

"Well Shirl', I'm on a quest. Lex and I have a date with Mr. Pettafordi, and things are bound to get strange. So I figured I'd screw my courage to the sticking-place, and come here first. Guess you'd call this a reconnaissance mission. I'm hoping you'll provide some ammo for my visit with the P Man. So, what can you tell me about Evan the First?"

That's just my subtext. What I really say, addressing the coffee stain between my sneakers, is, "I, um, guess I want to talk."

"Well, I'm glad you've come to me. What is it?"

"MMMRRAAAAAAAAAWWWWWWWWRRGGGLLLLRR
RRR."

"So you said."

"Sorry, Mrs. Solomon-Baxter-Coombs."

"Let's make a deal. Call me Shirley, our secret. And how about sharing my sandwich? Maybe then I'll get to hear more from you and less from your surly abdomen."

"Yes, thanks."

She opens her desk drawer and hoists out the Moby Dick of tuna sandwiches. Ripping the monstrosity in two, she plops a drippy mound in front of me. She chomps into her hunk, swipes her chin with her hand, and says, "What's on your mind?"

"I'm not sure where to start." I pop a celery cube into my mouth.

"Well, if you were crafting a story, I'd advise you to begin with a hook—a device to plunge your reader into the action. Make sense?"

"I guess. You mean something like . . . I've been reading my father's old journal, and he mentioned you, so I hoped you might have some idea why he hung himself. Is that what you mean by a hook? Shirley?" Keeping my eyes on her, I scoop a glob of tuna into my mouth.

She pauses midbite. "Holy moley! Now that's a hook!"

Chewing, I track the bumblebee. It makes two-and-a-half spins around Pooh's dopey face before Mrs. S-B-C finally says, "I'm sorry, Evan. You've thrown me for a bit of a loop."

"No doubt."

"What is it you want to know?"

"I'm not sure. What was my dad like? Did he seem happy? Who were his friends? Did he ever confide in you? Mostly, I want to know why."

"Oh, Evan. I can't offer you why. You must realize his motive is unknowable."

"I won't accept that."

"I'm afraid you may have to."

This isn't working. I stand and push my tuna pile toward her. "Sorry to waste your time. I know you've got lots to do. Thanks for lunch."

"Evan, wait."

At the door I feel her hand on my shoulder.

"Come back, sit down. I'll tell you what I can."

"I don't expect more than that."

She sighs. "Your father was a character, Evan. Don't take this the wrong way, but he could be a royal pain in the ass."

"Tell me something I don't know."

"Still, he was one of my best—and favorite—students. That seems to run in your family. Golly, I can't believe it was all those years ago."

"He said in his journal he really liked you, too. But I guess you knew that."

"Well, I never read his journal, but we had a decent relationship, once he got over the notion that 'writing is for homos.' He announced that on day one. Came in with a typical jock attitude, like it was a big waste of time. But I got him to really tap into his creativity. The well was deep. His writing ended up being very rich, very emotive."

"I wish I could read it."

"You can. The school library has every issue of *The Quill & Barb*."

"My dad wrote for Sebastian's literary journal?"

"Believe me, it took major arm-twisting, but I convinced him to submit. I told him his grade depended on it. You'll find his poetry and some wonderful illustrations; however, he insisted on anonymity."

"Anonymity?"

"He said he 'couldn't risk the team finding out.' "

She shakes her head. Finger-tapping her tape dispenser, she seems to be searching.

"What is it?"

"Pen names. I was remembering some pseudonyms he suggested. Now, which did he settle on? Van something? Ivan? Wait, I. Von. That's it! His work is credited to I. Von Tanay."

"You're joking."

"Wish I were."

"Dad always was the master of stupid wordplay."

"Yes, and very into limerick for a while there. He and his friend Tony were quite the pair, sort of a literary Abbott and Costello."

"Tony Pettafordi?"

A tiny vein begins to pulse, twitching the pouch below her left eye. "Why, yes . . . I didn't realize you knew about their friendship."

"Well, I only recently found out about Mister P. In Dad's journal. Seems like they went through something."

"Oh. I see." She manages a smile, but the skin below her eye beats like the throat of a spring peeper. "You haven't spoken to Mr. Pettafordi about this?"

"Not yet."

"Well, that's probably for the best. It was a long time ago."

"Actually, I plan to see him this afternoon. That's why I came. I thought you could tell me about their friendship, and what split them up. And why no one ever mentioned it to me."

There's an atmospheric change in the room. I half-expect to see my own breath. Mrs. S-B-C's voice takes on an icy trill.

"I'm afraid that's not my place. And you might reconsider speaking with Mr. Pettafordi. As I said, it was long ago; they were kids. I think you'd only succeed in resurrecting painful memories. Surely, that's not your goal."

Now it's my turn to fake a smile. "Shirley, it's not."

"Well, then what do you hope to accomplish, Evan?"

"To learn the truth. I want to know his suicide wasn't about me. Or if it was, I need to know that too." I grab my stuff and head for the door.

Behind me, Mrs. S-B-C shouts, "Evan! There are worse things than not knowing!"

Feb. 22, 1976 (Sunday night)
Journal—
What the hell's going on? Had a real strange conversation with Father Fran after Mass. He said he called yesterday to discuss "my relationship with Anthony." He acted like Tony and I are a couple!

Plus, he knew way too much about Tony flipping out. Obviously, they talked. I think Tony's jealous because Father and I've been friends for so long. Man! That's it for now. —E.

Dad's poetry may have been "rich and emotive," but this journal's shaping up to be a page-turner. Despite her warning—"There are worse things than not knowing!"—my meeting with Shirl was pretty encouraging. It's clear I'm onto something. I can't wait to see Lex in class.

It's about ten minutes 'til psych, so I've ducked into the boys' room to read. It's as good as the library for quiet study—aside from the smell. Time for one more entry.

February 24, 1976, 2:14 A.M.
Holy shit! Just had the most insane dream.
No chance I'm getting back to sleep. Oh, man.
It started out amazing. Me and Melody hot and heavy in the gym. She undressed as I spread my jacket on the floor. Kneeling, she giggled, unzipping my fly. I close my eyes, waiting.
But the laugh gets deeper, scary. She's talking, but it's not her voice. It's Tony's—praying, "Oh my God, I am heartily sorry . . . " Then I woke up—THANK GOD! That was psycho!

I'll say. I'm shaking. A memory leaks in: the cellar, a huge daddy longlegs drops from the rafters, skitters down my neck. I flinch, nearly drop the journal. Suddenly I don't want to read anymore. But I can't stop. I turn the page.

Feb. 25, 1976
Happened again—THE DREAM. Just snapped awake (1:43) drenched with sweat. It was even worse. Instead of Melody, Tony's mouth on me. I try pushing him off. But he's too strong. I clamp my eyes, feel myself shrink, freeze.

GOD! The whole sick dream's playing in my head like some warped movie. I can almost feel Tony's body on mine, pushing me down.

The worst part is it's familiar, almost like we—That's crazy! SHIT! Dad just banged on the wall, yelling, "Lights out!" If he knew what I was writing—

"Oh God. Oh please Dad, no."

I'm glad I'm in a stall, because suddenly what little tuna I ate makes a return trip. Dropping to my knees just in time, I spray chow into the bowl. I can't resist examining the murky whirl; I'm a vomit rubbernecker. Tuna bits spin amidst the remains of this morning's cereal bar. That's the last time I mix blueberry and albacore.

Contemplating my former stomach contents helps distract me. But then those words—"Tony's body on mine"—come back, and I heave again. Nothing comes up this time. I flush, resting my forehead on the cool porcelain seat—screw germs!—'til I'm steady enough to stand.

Exiting the stall, I go straight to the wastebasket and jam the journal in. Shirl was right; some things are better left buried. I unreel a mile of paper towel, wad it, shove it on top.

Just then, Randy Spiotti and crew strut in, cigarettes ready. I find it odd that the track team subsists mainly on beer and carcinogens, but decide not to share that observational nugget.

Pretending to analyze the faded floor tiles, I take a tentative step toward the exit. Despite my valiant stab at invisibility, Randy homes in on me like a geek-seeking missile.

"Hey, Girl-O-Way! What're you doing hangin' by the urinals? Looking for a front row seat at the Pecker Parade?"

"Good one, Spiotti!" Tyler Wattrous back slaps Randy; the others erupt in baboon hoots.

"Yeah, good one," I say, raising my fist for the knuckle-bump that will not come. Quickly abandoning any idea of winning them over, I decide to run for it.

Did I mention they're the track team? Before my neurotransmitters can fire, they hoist me airborne.

With a gleeful snarl, Randy says, "Flush him."

Though we've just been fairly intimate, I'm not quite ready to become one with the bowl. Pride gone, I screech like a little girl.

As they carry me into the stall, the bathroom door slams open. A whistle screams.

"SPIOTTI!" Coach Novack swears a blue streak and, like an airplane tray-table, I'm returned to an upright position.

"You okay, Galloway?" He cuffs my shoulder with a massive paw.

"I guess so, sir. Thanks."

"Well, no harm done. No need to report. You know these guys, always horsing around."

Their thug-to-choirboy transformation complete, the guys are all smiles.

"Sorry, Evan. We were just kiddin'." Randy offers his hand. I shake; he squeezes. Just hard enough to hurt.

I get to Father B's class ten minutes late and hand him a pass from Novack. As I slide into my seat next to Alexis, she shoots me a "what happened?" look.

Inside the cover of my notebook, I write: S-H-I-T.

She whispers, "I can see that."

Father Brendan says, "Miss Bottaro, if you and Mister Galloway would excuse the rest of us, we'd like to get down to business."

"Sorry, Father."

"Very well then, today we continue with Chapter 14. Is anyone confused over what you've read thus far?"

Stifling a nervous laugh, I think, *If you only knew, Father. If you only knew.*

"We can't go through with this."

Father B's class was a pressure cooker. Now we're headed to art. I'm not looking forward to the creative process. How can I face Pettafordi after what I read?

"Oh, Evan. Don't go all limp noodle. You know what they say, 'Cold feet sink ships.' "

"Loose lips."

"Huh?"

"Loose lips. Loose lips sink ships."

"Right. I knew it sounded funny. What is it they say about cold feet? Cold feet, warm heart? No, that's not right either." The cliché soliloquy carries her halfway down the staircase.

"Alexis!"

Noticing me in a heap on the top step, she takes the stairs three at a time and sits next to me, despite the crush of students trying to pass.

"What is it? Are you okay?"

"I can't talk about it, Lex. I'm just . . . we're not meeting Pettafordi. I don't want to know anymore. It doesn't matter."

"What happened? What'd you find out?"

"Move it, Shit Stains!" A group of senior girls mounts the stairs. They've no intention of walking around us.

I bolt up the hall, Alexis following. Shaking her off, I bury my face against a row of lockers. Lex knows not to say anything, just embraces me. We stand like that 'til I catch my breath. The hall's full of gawkers, but I don't care.

Finally she says, "All right, before we get nailed for public display, we better decide where we're headed."

"Let 'em expel me, I don't give a rat's ass."

"Charming sentiment. But I'm not buying the rebel act. Doesn't suit you. Let me figure this out—Wait! I know the perfect place: cramped, private, nearly soundproof. Follow me."

She leads me past the cafeteria and auditorium to the music rooms. Slipping into an empty rehearsal cube, we lock the door and sit side by side on a piano bench in the dark.

Alexis taps my forehead with her index finger. "Spill."

"I told you, I'm through. My father killed himself. Does it matter why?"

"Why always matters, Evan. You deserve the truth."

"No! The more I discover, the worse I feel. I'm better off not knowing."

"I used to believe that too, until it almost killed me. You deny the truth long enough, you start to doubt what the truth really is. That's dangerous—I know."

I can't listen to this. I start to get up. Pissed, Lex pulls me back.

"It's better not to know? Evan, don't you get it? I won't let you play the denial game. I was the champ. I convinced the world everything was fine with my stepfather. What's worse, I made myself believe it. All I knew was, without the game, the ache was real. But thank God, I could never convince you. You made me realize I couldn't pretend my problems away. You're the reason I finally told."

"I know all that. But this is different. What I don't know hasn't hurt me so far."

"Are you sure? Because crying in the hallway seems pretty messed up to me."

"Screw you!" I jump up and knock over a row of music stands going for the door.

"Oh that's brilliant. Another solid choice: run away! That'll solve everything!"

God, I want to hit her. Instead, I launch a pile of sheet music at the wall.

"Okay, you have all the answers, Lex? The truth is so valuable? Fine! You explain how it's helpful to know . . . to know . . . that my father and Mister Pettafordi were—"

I'm not sure whether I've run out of breath or nerve, but I can't seem to finish the sentence. I pace the cubicle, jaws clenched.

Eventually, Lex breaks the silence. "Your father and Mister P were what?"

"I think Pettafordi's gay."

Her bark of laughter makes me jump. "A POSSIBLY GAY ART TEACHER? Earth-shattering! Next you'll tell me Coach Novack was rejected by MENSA. Or that Father Brendan's—GASP—Irish! No, seriously, what tipped you off? His passion for all things batik? The way he hums show tunes while showing slides? Because really, Evan, those are just—"

I almost laugh.

"Will you please shut up? This is serious! I read about him and my dad in the journal, and it sounds like, maybe, they were more than friends."

"And?"

"And? It's . . . I don't know, gross! He's my art teacher. My self-appointed mentor, you know? It's just . . . wrong. And, and. And wrong."

"So you said."

"I'll tell you one thing. I'm through staying after to help him fire up the freaking kiln!"

"Bold move, Captain. But tell me, do you really think you've got a snowball's chance of avoiding him? Realistically? You're planning to major in art. He's your guidance counselor. Are you just going to, like, switch over to shop?"

"I don't know . . . but . . . I guess you're right. I can't just pretend none of this has happened." I sit next to her. "And Lex . . . I'm sorry I told you to screw."

"No worries. You'll pay. Anyway, I know you were just overcompensating, to assert your masculinity. It's only natural, now that you've discovered your dad may have been a Swiss Miss."

This time I do hit her, a joke shove. She expects it, but mock-falls anyway, sending music stands dominoing. They clatter to the floor; we howl laughter.

Still sprawled in a heap, Lex says, "Look Ev, I really do understand you being upset, but it's not that big a deal. I mean, it's not uncommon. I read this article that said something like 63 percent of adolescent males have had at least one same-sex experience, usually with a friend."

"That's foul."

"I realize you're squarely in the other 37 percent. It's just, I think you should try not to freak over this."

"Well, I think *you* ought to reevaluate your reading material. Where'd you see this article anyway?"

"I don't remember. *Cosmo Girl, Scientific American,* something like that. But that's not the point. All I'm saying is a little youthful experimentation's not the end of the world."

"Not to you maybe, but this is my father. And my art teacher. Yish. What am I supposed say to him? How can I even face the guy?"

"Well, you certainly can't do it alone. I say on with the plan! You, me, Mister P. His office. This afternoon."

"There's no way you're turning this into some . . . "

"What?"

I'm at a loss for a clever pop cultural reference; must be nerves. "I don't know. Just . . . you're not invited."

"Okay, if you want to risk being alone with him. After all, you are a chip off the old block. Might bring back memories, spark ideas about a little like-father-like-son action."

"You are truly demented."

"Oh, come on, Evan!"

"No chance."

She joins me on the bench. "So appealing to your inner homophobe is plainly futile. How about this? Without me you've got no witness, with me, a partner in crime."

She has a point.

"Besides, I really want to be there for you."

"How selfless. Look, I know you well enough to realize you'll never take no for an answer, so I'll give you an extremely qualified yes. You know the condition."

"Yeah."

"Say it, Lex."

"I know, I know: the friggin' vow. Cripes, are we pirates? Okay. I'll bolt me lips tighter than Davey Jones's locker. I'll take yer secret to me wat'ry grave, if it be yer will. Haargh! Satisfied?"

"You would look utterly cool with an eye patch."

"Great. Be serious, Ev. If we're doing this, you need to show me exactly what you read. Where's the journal? Your locker?"

"Uh . . . nope."

"Well, where then? You didn't leave it in study hall?"

"Not quite . . . I threw it out."

"Again, very funny, but we don't have time for this. We need to decide what to tell Pettafordi. I mean, we should be in class right now. So where's the journal?"

"Would you believe at the bottom of the barrel? I shoved it in the trash in the third floor boys' room . . . Matey."

"Oh God, you ass. What were you thinking?"

"I wasn't. I just wanted to get rid of it."

"Well, I hope you brought your hazmat suit, Cap'n Bonehead. It looks like you're going diggin' for treasure.

"Oh man, do you know how nasty that is? We're talking the *boys' bathroom* here."

"At least you won't have the Sani-Pad Factor to deal with."

"Okay, now you've crossed a line."

Lex snorts, buries her head against my chest. The cube temperature ratchets up about 15 degrees. Neither of us moves. Then, very slowly, I lift her face. We freeze eye to eye, like levitating ninjas from some action movie.

Even in the gloom, I can see Lex is beet red. I lean in to kiss the face I've known forever.

Lex springs up, pops on the lights, hand trembling. Clearing her throat, she says, "It's time we vacate. These rooms aren't THAT soundproof, and with the music stands crashing and everything, I'm amazed we haven't drawn a crowd."

"I guess you're right." Picking up our mess, we avoid eye contact. "Hey, Lex. I, uh . . . didn't mean to—"

"Skip it, Ev. Strange stuff happens in these cubes. Some say they're haunted by an angry, musical pirate. Maybe he saw the spring production of *Penzance*. That'd explain his mood."

We laugh. But we both know it's fake, polite, like laughing at a teacher's joke. I feel major liberation stepping out of that box, as if I've escaped a broken elevator.

We nearly collide with Miss Yee, Lex's choir teacher, in the hall. She looks suspicious; probably thinks we were making out in the cubicles. We flash an innocent-by-virtue-of-intellect look. Lex makes up an excuse about looking for her lost backpack. Miss Yee lets us slide on by.

Hoping to avoid anyone official, we race through the halls. The days of hall monitors are long gone, but there's always the chance a wandering nun might materialize, a specter with a detention pad.

Our trip to the third floor's almost too easy. I take a deep breath—to brace for the smell, as much as to calm my nerves—and step into the bathroom. That's when I see it: Moriarty's rolling trash tub. Hesitating, I consider an about-face, but a stall door swings open and, true to my spectacularly bad luck, I'm facing Sebastian's Guru of Garbage, Alphonse Moriarty III.

There's no way I can hightail it; too suspicious. I smile. "Hey, Mister Moriarty."

He gestures with his dripping toilet brush. "Gallagher, right?"

"Gallo*way*, sir. Evan Galloway. How's it going?"

"Oh, life's a precious gift, Sir Evan Galloway. I'm having a grand time cleanin' caked puke off a toilet. Just another fascinating day. Good of you to ask."

Lacking a chainsaw to cut through the hostility, I just nod, settling on a diversionary urinal visit. Spinning the swing top of the metal basket, as I pass, I glance inside. Empty. Shit! He's already dumped it into the bin.

I lean into the porcelain alcove pretend-peeing, mind racing. How am I supposed to search his dumpster with him here? Then, sensing movement behind me, I catch a whiff of Spruce-Glo. As his nicotined hand approaches, the skin on the back on my neck migrates skullward.

"I got something you might like." His voice is low and too close.

I've squeezed my eyes shut. Opening them, slowly looking toward him, I pray to every saint I can think of that he's not exposing himself.

Can I get an Amen? The saints come through. Atop the urinal next to mine, he's placed my father's journal.

"Spotted it when I dumped the trash in my bin. You'd be surprised, the stuff I find."

I just stare from him to the journal and back.

"I went to school with your old man. I was sorry to hear. I mean, we were never friends or nothin'. Still, it's too bad. Seems like he had a lot to live for."

Stunned by the oddness of the moment, all I can manage is, "Yup."

"Look, I'll be straight with you. I read a few pages, but it seemed like it was gettin' personal. So I figured I'd save it for when I got home. But I'm glad you come lookin'. You should have it. Anyway, take it slow."

Moriarty heads away. Holstering his toilet brush to the rolly-tub, he wheels toward the exit. I almost collapse with relief.

At the door he stops and says, "Gallagher! You ought to be more careful with that diary. It's like his legacy, you know?"

And then, he's gone. I hear him in the hall, talking to Lex, something about "a nice girl like you in a place like this."

She says, overloud, "Oh, Alphonse, you slay me!"

I grab the journal off the urinal. It's no worse for the dumpster dive. Clutching my prize, I realize I really do have to pee. A whole lot. After, at the sink, I catch sight of myself in the mirror. I wink and say, "Buck up, Gallagher. We've got work to do."

Lex and I head toward Pettafordi's, practically floating through the halls. Just finding the journal whole seems like a good omen.

We tell Mister P the SparkNotes version of the truth: "I got sick on some bad tuna, and Lex stuck with me 'til I felt better." It flies. We're pets—though I'm starting to rethink that role. We arrange to meet him later to catch up on what we missed.

I needed a journal break, since it's gone all sexually ambiguous.

So I came to the Learning Resource Center to look for Dad's poems while Lex finishes choir practice. Then we're meeting Pettafordi—unless I can talk her out of it.

Mrs. Koothrappally looks up from her monitor and smiles. Some kids laugh at her—make fun of her traditional Indian clothing, complain about the faint curry scent lingering in the stacks. They even joke about her bindi—they call her "Dot."

Head joggling slightly, she says, "I hope you found what you were looking for, Evan."

"Me too. Thanks."

I feel a bit guilty lying. I told her I'm using *The Quill & Barb* as a source for my soc report on "changing trends in teenage expression." She was only too happy to help. I expected Mrs. Koothrappally to give me a link on the school database; instead, she pointed me to a section with actual past issues. I was amazed to see an entire shelf of Sebastian's student literary magazine, stretching back nearly forty years. That's a lot of bad poetry. Dad's stuff should be in the 1976 issue.

The cover features a pen-and-ink illustration, hand gripping quill. Cliché image/decent drawing. Inside it says *Cover illustration by I. Von Tanay.*

"Oh brother." It's Dad, all right.

Thumbing to the table of contents, I see the works are divided by topic—First section: Growing Pains; Second: Tears and Laughter; Third: A Remembrance; and Fourth: Life's Lessons.

Scanning the list, I wish I could travel back to 1976 with a boatload of Zoloft, because these sound like some majorly dejected high schoolers. Sample titles: "Lying Smiles," "Elegy for Mittens," "Heart/Burnt"—Yikes! Where are the limericks?

Great, Dad's got three poems listed. First up, page 12: "Mother." Should be good.

> **Mother, by I. Von Tanay**
> **A Venus flytrap,**
> **she slowly constricts; spiked love**
> **devouring her young.**

Wow, one for the Mom's Day card! Lucky it was printed under a fake name. I picture Gran at her Ladies' Guild meeting. "Wanda, listen, my Evan wrote the most beautiful haiku!"

Next up: "Tears and Laughter." Let's see, he's on page 23.

> **One Starry Night**
> **Your brushes wept**
> **a thousand swirling**
> **colors—building**
> **cypress,**
> **steeple, cosmic whirlpools.**
> **Captive stars, trapped**
> **flat, shine**
> **yellow-to**
> **pear-green-to-turquoise**

in turbulent skies.
Are you among them now,
warm in brilliance,
His voice
calling, "Open your eyes, Vincent.
You have come
home,"?

Love the Van Gogh connection. It's sort of surprising Dad never lopped an ear off—I mean, he could've made due with *one* of those suckers. I glance at the clock; Lex should be getting out of choir about now. Flipping to section four, I spot his final piece, a sonnet.

Chasing Joy
I run the field, chasing sweet elation,
Racing the winds of doubt, escaping fears.
A helmeted centaur, swift in motion,
I conquer my enemies, riding cheers

Of adulation like a victor prince.
Triumphant, I am laurelled and adored.
None has flown so high, nor shone so bright since,
last speeding turf, my cleats and spirit soared.

Lifted o'er their heads and my own sorrow,
I ride roars of jubilating voices.
Shining like a trophy, each tomorrow
Shows my future rich with hope and choices.

But later in my solitary room,
Once more I'm trampled by my inner gloom.

Well, it certainly beats my macaroni poem, but—Yish!—what a downer. Dad in a nutshell. I mean, you're the star athlete, get over the "inner gloom," pal.

Okay, obviously "getting over it" was something he wasn't able to do. Still, it feels like I came up empty; I thought his poetry would be a little more revealing. But it's not a total waste. Any window into his head's a good thing, right?

I feed dimes to the copier; it spits out a pile of Dad's poems.

"I take it your search was fruitful?" Mrs. K's chin dip accentuates her question.

Just then, Lex sidles up, grinning. "Reporting for duty, Captain Hook."

I thank Mrs. Koothrappally for her help, and we head to Pettafordi's office, Lex improvising a sea shanty, apparently to calm my nerves. It's not working. I'm tempted to ditch her, but the truth is, I really don't want to do this alone.

The herbal tea arced from his nose in an impressive trajectory.

We all just sat there speechless. For Lex and me it was a combo-silence: aweticipation. His nasal display was so unexpected—sort of impressive, really. He scored high for distance. And when you witness something like that, sudden, startling, you almost can't help but yearn for more.

For Mister Pettafordi, the silence was simpler. The guy was mortified. I mean, one minute he's describing sunrise at the Acropolis, "the heady challenge in capturing life's fierce vermilion pulse on canvas." The next, Celestial Seasonings is coursing through his sinus cavity and—SPLASH!—he's decorating his desk blotter. Talk about life's fierce pulse!

Of course, in between Mt. Olympus and the schnoz-flume was Lex's question. I'd chalk it up to cause and effect.

Hours later at the mall, I replay the moment in my mind. I'm at Full O' Beans, Level 3, by the movies, at one of those leg-danglingly tall, Formica-top tables. Someone's carved "Life blowz!" into the turquoise laminate, along with a crude rendering of a male sex organ. While the guy obviously never took human anatomy (or spelling), I have to agree with the sentiment.

It's whirling snow outside, like in one of those Christmas globes. I stare out the huge window overlooking the lot and the highway beyond. People pick through mounting white to meringued cars. One old lady slips off the curb. Sprawling, she lies there, like she's gearing up for the perfect snow angel, 'til mall security hoists her up, brushes her off, sends her on her way.

My stomach scowls; I won't eat tonight. I've sucked down three Mochakoola Smoothies. Sadly, the resultant brain-freeze, full bladder, and caffeine hum still can't quite erase the image of Raspberry Ripper spurting from Pettafordi's snout.

It was a prime example of Lex's complete disregard for discretion. I suppose I expected it. Maybe that's even why I let her tag along. The question needed asking, and I doubt I could've done it. As he regaled us with his rendering of Grecian sunup, Lex fidgeted. When Mister P paused to sip, she lobbed the big one.

"Mister Pettafordi, were you and Evan's dad lovers?"

It's funny. In movies these things happen slow-mo, but not this time. The question, the tea-spray, the choking: rapid-fire. Ultimately successful struggling for air, Mister P next fought for composure. Dabbing the desktop, he seemed to ponder Lex's question. Finally, he tried a shameless diversion. "So. I was going to fill you in on today's assignment."

It could've worked. We might've scored a magic ticket back, hopped on the Let's-Pretend-This-Never-Happened Express. Alexis, true to form, was not about to board that train.

"The reason I ask—and believe me, I'm not about to judge you for a little teen same-sexploration—is that Evan has a right to know."

He just stared. But Lex is nothing if not persistent. She shifted in her seat, the vinyl making a meek farting noise. Ordinarily, we might've laughed. Nobody was laughing now.

"So . . . is it, Mister Pettafordi? True, I mean."

This time his reaction was more subtle, or drier anyway. His plum hue the only outward sign of unease, Mister Pettafordi's eyes narrowed. He studied Lex with a mix of hurt and disgust. Then with a calm, Clint Eastwood sneer, he said, "You'd better go now."

Up 'til this point I'd been fairly quiet, satisfied to surf the crest of Lex's manic drive. But now, I found my voice.

"Sir, I really do need answers."

The planes in his face seemed to shift as his eyes—they'd never looked so black—tore through me. He was suddenly all sharp angles, stabbing brows, but his tone remained reasonable as he said, "Well, then, you'll have to ask your father. Oh, but that's not going to work, is it?"

It was like getting the wind knocked out of me in fifth grade. I tried to speak, couldn't.

"You can't treat him like that, you creep!"

"Miss Bottaro, I suggest you go."

Alexis stood. For a second, I thought she'd do the sane thing and abandon ship. Instead, she sang. Yes, sang, a tuneful plea to "stop hurting each other."

Looking back, Lex might agree invoking the Carpenters was perhaps not the wisest choice, but at the time, I guess it seemed appropriate. Regrettably, her performance did nothing to improve Pettafordi's mood. This twitch lifted the corner of his lip and one plump tear hustled toward the tea stain on his desk. Then, what can best be described as a bellow shook the office.

"GET OUT, YOU CRAZY LITTLE BITCH!"

It was maybe not his finest hour as an educator. But who could blame him? Lex does have a way of pushing buttons.

"Well, okay then. I should probably get going." She stood and, turning toward me, mouthed, "He's all yours."

We watched her leave, so cool and conversational, as if we'd been debating the merits of matte versus gloss fixative. I totally envied her. I, on the other hand, seriously thought I might've soiled myself.

"Listen, Mister Pettafordi. I'm sorry. I—"

"No, Evan. You listen. I owe you and your friend an apology. My language was inexcusable. It's just . . . this is all very painful."

"Forget it, sir. You don't have to say anymore."

"But I do, Evan. Mrs. Solomon-Baxter-Coombs warned me you'd been asking questions, but I never quite expected this. And although Miss Bottaro's brazenness was . . . shall we say, disconcerting, she was correct on one count. You do have a right to know."

I was tempted to clap hands to ears and run screaming from the room. Could I stand to have the sordid details spilled? I mean, Mister Pettafordi can really paint a picture.

My mind ricocheted. I saw them draped in togas, Mister P feeding my dad olives beneath the Athenian sun. Then they were at the Burger Shack, sitting on the same side of the booth, Pettafordi wearing Dad's letter jacket. Finally, I pictured them rolling naked in the wave pool at Sesame Place. I have no idea where that one came from.

"Evan, are you listening?"

"Uh . . . yeah . . . sure."

"As I was saying, your father and I were best friends, nothing more, though you and Lex are not the first to assume otherwise. His teammates gave him a tough time about me, I'm afraid."

"But you were just friends."

"Yes. For a while, he was the closest friend I had. Hell, he was my only friend. Evan, your father was probably the most important person in my life. I did love him, but I was never *in love with him.*"

Luckily I have more self-control than Lex, because at that moment I felt like bursting into song myself. Anyone for a verse of "The Halleluiah Chorus"? Then it struck me.

"Mister P, if you guys were so close, what went wrong?"

"We just grew apart, Evan. Not so unusual."

But his lip twitch said otherwise.

"I don't believe that, Mister P. If you'd just drifted, or whatever, your friendship wouldn't be such a secret."

"I don't follow your meaning."

"My father never mentioned being friends with you. Not once. And you never brought it up either. Why?"

He stood and walked to the window, gazing through the venetians.

"There was no need for you to know."

"Well there is now. Please, Mister Pettafordi, tell me the truth."

He turned toward me, his face like a reluctant skydiver's.

"You want the truth? Well, the truth is, I've never really been sure what happened. We were pretty inseparable, your dad and I. Being his friend was like winning the lottery."

"Meaning?"

"He made people feel special, but the fact is he was the special one. He had it all: perfect grades, perfect girl, trophies. And it all seemed effortless."

He stopped, lifted the mug, reconsidered. I think the Ripper had lost its allure.

"You'd almost say he had too many gifts, Evan. Yet there was something else, like a dank corner he'd never let me into. I'm not sure even he knew what was in that corner, but it seemed to drag on him."

"In what way?"

"We talked for hours. And he'd always end up saying the same things: He never really felt worthy, and the good people saw in him was all a lie. I think I'm the only one he told."

"What was it? What made him feel that way?"

"I wish I knew."

"You must have some idea."

"Well, I had theories, but he never gave me the chance to find out. I think I finally got too close, and he just pulled away."

"Was this when you had art class together?"

The second the words left my mouth, I knew I'd blown it. I could almost see them thud onto the desk. I wanted to scoop them up and cram them back into my big, dumb face.

But it was too late. Mister P looked like he'd guzzled a gallon of wasabi punch. The lip twitch was joined by an assortment of tics: nostril flare, finger drumming, and the ever-popular, free-flowing flop sweat. I'd hit a nerve.

Aiming for casual, he asked, "How'd you know about that, Evan?"

A lot rode on my response. Praying he wouldn't notice my own stress indicator, rapid foot jiggle, I lied, "Uh . . . I . . . it must've been something Mrs. S-B-C mentioned."

Good answer. He nodded, satisfied. With a slow brow mop, he said, "Oh. Okay. It's just strange, you bringing that up. Father Fran's class was one of the last things we ever spoke about. I'm afraid I said some rather unkind words."

He stared into the middle distance, the way a spooked dog will fix on a vacant spot, almost unaware of me.

Like a therapist coaxing his patient, I said, "Why don't you tell me?"

"It's foolish, but he was good at so many things. I guess I wanted art to be all mine."

"So what happened?"

"I'll be damned if he wasn't a better artist as well. This is pointless. It was so long ago."

"But it destroyed your friendship. It must've been important."

"It certainly seemed important then. Now it just seems petty. I was used to being the most talented one in Father Fran's class. I lived for his attention. Then your father usurped my status as teacher's pet. And I was jealous."

"Yes?"

"First, I gave him the silent treatment, avoided him, that sort of thing. He kept asking what was wrong. I wanted him to suffer, I guess. He finally forced me to talk . . . and . . . I said some things . . . I shouldn't have. I just went too far. It's funny because you always think a real friendship can weather any storm, but human relationships can be as flimsy as paper boats in a tsunami."

I waited for him to continue, but he just sat there as if someone pressed Pause.

"So that's it? One fight and your friendship was over? What did you say to him?"

"Nothing earth-shattering, just the sort of thing you say when you want to hurt someone. I'm afraid, Evan, I've always been rather too good at that."

Leaning back in his chair, he shut his eyes. As minutes crawled by, I considered gambling on narcolepsy, hightailing it. With luck, he'd think he dreamt this whole thing. Then his lids rose; he'd been gathering strength for the rest.

"I told him it was pathetic, how he needed everyone to love him best. He already had a girlfriend. Did he need to steal Father Fran, too?"

"What did you mean, 'steal Father Fran'?"

"I don't know." The lip twitch was back. "I just lashed out, tried to knock him down a peg. But I was too successful at hurting him. His reaction was fairly strong."

Fairly strong, my left nut! My father'd nearly strangled him!

"I was ashamed. I practically ran to church to confess. Father Fran actually sounded angry. He said I should apologize immediately, that my jealousy was ungodly and I should think about my intentions toward your father."

"Sounds like a take-no-prisoners confessional style."

"Yes. Father Fran said one other thing I've never forgotten: 'He has a special grace you mustn't impede.' He said that was why he and Evan were especially close—he was your father's spiritual advisor."

"Did you talk about any of this with my dad?"

"I tried. I called his house so often that afternoon I thought your grandfather would throttle me. Your father never returned my calls. The following week, when I approached him, he wouldn't listen. And he seemed . . . grayed down, emotionally monochromatic. When I tried to apologize, he said, 'No sweat.' But everything was different."

"Different how?"

"He began avoiding me for starters. Clearly he didn't want to deal with me. I followed him to his locker Thursday and asked if he wanted to come over that weekend. He said he couldn't, he was going on encounter. That was really odd. He'd always scoffed at going. But I thought it might be my chance to resolve things. I decided to make him a *palanca*."

"That's like a 'Good luck on retreat' kind of thing, isn't it?"

"Oh no. It goes deeper than that. A palanca's a pledge, a promise to pray or even fast for the encounter candidate. I spent that entire night working on the letter. It was exceptional. I laid my feelings bare, explained how remorseful I was. I told your father how much he meant to me. That I knew we'd work things out."

"Did he accept your apology?"

He scraped with his fingernail, scribing the damp blotter, breath rasping like paper. "I don't know what happened on encounter, but it changed him. After, he was like a pod person from that movie."

"*Invasion of the Body Snatchers?*"

He nodded. "Your father seemed diminished, bled dry. He shut everyone out, broke up with Melody, refused to speak to me. He even . . ."

taking a brush from the vase on his desk, avoiding my eyes, he continued, ". . . became disruptive in art. Eventually, he dropped the class."

"Disruptive how?"

"I'd rather not say. It was so long ago."

"Did he ever mention your palanca letter?"

"Never. Finally, I decided to ambush him. I showed up at his house. Your grandmother was very kind. She must've fed me a dozen brownies while I waited for him to come out of his room. When he wouldn't, she even gave me a ride home.

"As she maneuvered the station wagon, she said, 'He'll come around. He's going through a tough time, is all. Barely leaves that bedroom. Thank God, he still has Father Fran because he's stopped talking to us.' She said they were 'trying to give him his space.'

"I started up the walk, but she yelled, 'Tony, I almost forgot! He asked me to give you this, said you'd understand.' She passed me an envelope. As I leaned in the window to take it, she kissed my hand and said, 'Be good, Anthony.' And then she drove away."

"What was it?" It couldn't have been as interesting as the gift Gran gave me.

"I ran straight to my room and tore it open. Inside was a picture of Evan and me in a canoe on Gardner Lake, the copy of *The Catcher in the Rye* I'd lent him, and my palanca letter, still sealed. He'd taped a note to the envelope."

"Do you remember what it said?"

"Gee, I think so." His lip lifted in a grim effort to smile.

Eerie. Suddenly I saw the sad kid he used to be. Staring at his hands, he recited my father's words from memory.

"'Tony, you're a good friend. But I figured out some stuff on encounter. Not that *I'm lovable* shit. Bad stuff—about myself. It's better if we stop being friends. I'm not the person you think. Not really. Don't blame yourself. And please, don't make it any harder by calling me.'"

"What did you do?"

"What could I do? I respected his wishes. Kept my distance. Hoped for the best. For a while, I believed what your grandmother said, that he'd 'come around.' By the time I accepted he wasn't going to, it didn't seem to matter."

I knew I should say something. Instead, I just sat there, mouth open, in what Dad would call fly-catcher mode.

"Well, Evan ... I hope I've answered your questions satisfactorily. Now if you'll excuse me, I've got to see to the kiln."

I hesitated for just a moment, seeing an opportunity.

"I could stick around, Mister P—if you need a hand."

He refused, politely. Still, I couldn't help feeling a pang, remembering what he'd said about tsunamis. I was afraid I'd blown our friendship out of the water.

Lex met me by the flagpole after homeroom.

"So, that went seamlessly, wouldn't you say?"

I couldn't help being pissed, even though I knew it wasn't fair. She'd done it all for me.

"Look, I don't think I can talk to you right now, Alexis."

"Don't tell me you're mad." And she did this kick-line thing, singing, "Can't regret what I did for Ev."

"That's what I mean. Can't you ever be serious, just act normal?"

"Normal's in the eye of the beholder. Besides, you got some answers, right? Somebody had to put it out there, or we'd still be hearing about the friggin' Greek Isles."

"Okay. I couldn't have done it without you. That's the thing—I wish I could be spontaneous, too."

"Believe me, it takes loads of prep to be this impetuous." Then she flashed that smile.

"Lex, I'm wiped. I'll call you later, okay?"

"Hey, are we all right, Ev?"

"We'll always be all right." I gave her a quick hug, tried not to think about paper boats.

So now I'm at the mall, draining the dregs of Mochakoola #3, dreading the walk home. I swear if these cross-town excursions continue, I seriously need a dogsled.

Before facing the cold, I put the finishing touch on my paperwork. The Pettafordi experience crystallized my next step, sent me straight to Mrs.

Teague, School Secretary, Keeper of Forms. Along with an application for encounter, she gave me that "bless your heart, you demi-orphan" look. Then she went beyond the look, saying, "I hope encounter will be a healing experience for you, Evan."

Her sudden dose of compassion seemed to surprise us both. I snatched the paper and sprinted from her office, nearly crashing into Father Brendan.

"Mister Galloway, this is a school. Please restrict your speed."

"Yes, sir, I'll be more careful."

"See that you are." He smiled, glancing at the paperwork in my hand. "Is that an encounter application, Evan?"

"Yes, I've decided to go in March."

"Excellent. Encounter is quite powerful, a prayerful weekend focused on your relationship with the Lord, but I didn't think you had any interest in attending."

"Well, I found out my dad went, so I thought it might be good for me. You know, follow his footsteps, maybe understand him a bit better."

I saw a brief flicker of something in his face. Removing his glasses, he inspected them, pointedly not looking at me. "Consider your motives, Evan." Inhaling deeply, he seemed on the verge of something important, then said, "Have you discussed this with anyone else?"

"I'll mention it to my mother tonight."

"Yes, your mother." He put his glasses on again and said, "Excuse me, I must be going."

Will following Dad's footsteps really help? Maybe it's nuts, this whole detective act. I mean, Dad's encounter was over thirty years ago. It's not like I can relive his experience. What am I expecting to learn, anyway?

Lex'd say, "The truth, Evster, nothing but." And this does feel right, like I twirled the spinner on God's board game and got Follow Dad's Footsteps on Encounter. Who am I to argue?

Besides, they say a place can hold an impression of a past event, like an emotional echo. True, they generally say this only in bad horror movies. Then again, my life has become one scary-ass flick. And maybe they're right (whoever they are); maybe I'll find traces of Dad lingering at the Holy Family Merciful Wisdom Center. Hopefully, in a phantom-free way.

Slurping my last, I sign the form. Actually, Mrs. Teague's attempted comfort came in handy. Section E of the application says: *Briefly explain what you hope to gain through encounter.*

My answer: *I hope encounter will be a healing experience.*

On the escalator to the main floor, I catch myself humming "Hurting Each Other." I wonder what Lex will think about encounter. Before stepping into churning snow, I take a last look at the completed form, fold it, and slip it into my backpack. All I need is parental permission.

Easier said than done.

I wasn't fool enough to expect it'd go smoothly. Even before Dad's rope trick, my relationship with Mom was what you might call *strained.* We love each other. It's just that interacting with her is akin to emotional maneuvers: Hide the flag, look out for landmines.

So when I got home, I'd hoped to slip in under her radar. And I was so close. But then my cloaking device failed. Miserably. She intercepted me at my bedroom door, salad tongs in hand.

"Where've you been?"

I knew not to divulge. If she caught wind of The Pettafordi Incident, she'd detonate. So I employed a classic evasion.

One part apology: "Sorry, Mom. I should've called."

One part explanation: "Lex and I stopped by the library."

Mix well and finish with a subtle challenge: "You always say I spend too much time holed up in my room."

I went for the doorknob. Tongs to the sternum made it clear our chat wasn't over.

Head tilted, eyes narrowed like a stalking cat, she said, "The library? How odd."

Her whole manner said I was toast. Ordinarily I'd have buckled, spilled my guts, but I thought I might have a chance if I stayed calm. Ignoring the frantic inner voice screaming, "Run away," I attempted Lex's supernatural cool.

I oozed innocence. "What? You expect us to make High Honors without studying?"

Mom grabbed hold of my shirt collar with the tongs. Impressive dexterity. "No. What's odd is that Alexis called for you this afternoon. Twice."

Gulp.

"So," a tong twist punctuated her question, "want to take another stab at it?"

"Uh . . . okay."

"And Evan, a friendly suggestion: the truth."

It's scary how, in such moments, the human mind kicks into hyperdrive, like there's an extra lobe, independent of the conscious brain. Miss Delateski never mentioned it, but it must be there, and apparently its purpose is rapid deception. Before I could even react, my auxiliary lobe, my "fabrication station," took over, constructing the ideal response. Brief, touching, believable, it was the perfect lie, because it was built around a grain of truth. I could hardly believe I was saying it.

"I was at the mall. By myself." Awkward pause/shoe scuff. "This is embarrassing . . . I couldn't tell Lex, because . . . I went to buy her a Valentine's gift. I like her, Mom . . . as a girlfriend. But I haven't told her yet."

I was immediately awash in emotion—chiefly guilt. Not for the lie, but the truth at its heart. It was like cheating on Lex, using her as escape hatch. But the story, or my flushed face, did the trick. Setting the tongs on the hall table, Mom pulled me into a stiff hug.

"Oh, Ev. That's sweet. But be careful. I'd hate for you to get hurt."

"Okay, Mom. Look, it's no big deal. I didn't even buy anything. I'm not sure. Maybe it's better we just stay friends."

"Friends is good."

"Yeah. Um, homework."

"I'm about to put dinner on the table."

"I'm really not hungry. I had something at the mall."

"Evan, mall food's not sufficient. I stuffed a chicken. Wash up."

There's no arguing when she's in Betty Crocker mode—or ever, really—and I figured if I played the obedient son card, the encounter thing might go easier. I washed up.

Now we're at the table. She's measuring out a dose of ranch as I put the salad tongs to their intended use. Maybe I'm emboldened by so easily ducking interrogation. Perhaps the success of Operation Pettafordi's got me feeling cocky. Whatever the reason, I go for broke.

"I'm thinking of going on encounter. There's one scheduled for the third week in March."

She pauses midchew, waits for me to continue.

"I've already finished the paperwork. I just need your signature."

"You're not going."

"Come on, Mom."

"This is not open for discussion, Junior."

"I thought we agreed you wouldn't call me that anymore."

Her volume ticks up a notch. "Sorry, it's not open for discussion, EVAN. Better?"

I hate when she's sarcastic.

"Why can't I go? It's a chance to work through things."

"You can work through things at home. I don't intend to have you traipsing off on encounter, airing this family's laundry."

"Mom, it's not like that."

"You think I don't know what goes on? A weekend of complaining about parents. Just because they include prayer and communion doesn't justify the self-absorbed nonsense. You don't need it. And Father Brendan agrees."

"What?"

"Mrs. Teague called earlier. She said Father's concerned you might not be ready for encounter. That it might be too much right now."

I can't believe this! Father B's sabotaging me? What if he spoke to Pettafordi? My cheeks reddening, I try to swallow my temper.

"Mom, it might help me to talk about . . . things."

She tsks like I've said a dirty word. "Help? I'll help you. You need to talk? I'm listening."

"Yeah right, like it's so easy to open up to you. Every time I even mention Dad, you shoot me down. It's like you want me to just forget him."

"Good God, of course I don't want you to forget him. But I need you to *get over* him—for both our sakes. I'm scared, Evan. I couldn't survive if I lost you, too. It's all I think about."

"You're not going to lose me, Mom. I'm talking about one lousy weekend away."

"Great, I'll sleep easier knowing you only want to get away from me for a few days. You know, your father started out spending *a few days* at your gran's house 'to figure things out.' "

"This is different. Can't you see I'm not him?" I bang my fist on the table. My glass tips, splashing soda.

"That's it! I am so sick of your attitude. The world does not revolve around you, Evan!" She slaps her cutlery onto her plate. "I am not signing any form. You are not going on encounter. End of story. Now eat your supper."

Pushing off from the table, she dumps her plate in the sink. With a sickening grind, the garbage disposal goes to work on her chicken. Dish, knife, fork clatter into the basin, and she stomps down the hall to her bedroom.

"Mom—"

Her door slams shut. I'm left sitting with the unfortunate fowl. I prod it with my fork. "That went well, don't you think?" The bird declines comment.

I clear the table, gnawing a breadstick despite total lack of hunger. Dumping salad into a zip-bag, I stow it in the crisper drawer and think of Dad. I shovel potatoes into a plastic bucket, plop green beans on top, burp the lid.

As I swaddle the chicken carcass in a foil shroud, it occurs to me: I can just as easily pack away my curiosity, that stupid need. Saran wrap the Dad-quest and move on. I was smart to throw the journal away. Mom's right. I should just get over him. Let life be normal.

In front of the open fridge, I offer a silent goodbye to my father. I'm through. This'll seem like a good decision in the morning; now all I feel is hollow. The weight I've carried in my gut for the past ten months is gone.

I'll have to call Lex. She won't be happy, but I'll explain. I'm giving him up for the right reasons. And if she can't understand, tough. Game over.

Sitting on the floor, the chicken on my lap like the world's greasiest housecat, I pull a jar of sweet baby gherkins off the refrigerator shelf. I wolf six before the tears start. Pinching my forearm for focus, I wipe my eyes, slide the jar back, and grab a package of American cheese food product. Removing five, perfect, yellow squares from their plastic jackets, I wad them up. Snuffling, I shove the ball in my mouth.

A squeezable jam bottle swims into focus. I tip my head back, feel the marmalade flow across my tongue. Mingled with salt tang at the back of my throat, it tastes oddly like vacation taffy. My stomach lurches; I ignore it. I won't let this sudden emptiness overwhelm me. Ripping into the shrouded bird, I begin to feed.

"Ev?"

Midturn, I catch my reflection in the oven door, like something from a zombie flick: face puffy and lopsided, eyes sunken red, nose a gloogy mess. I drop the mangled poultry.

Mom gawks as if she's stumbled on a rabid wolf in her kitchen, then she goes for levity. "I guess you were hungry after all."

I try to laugh, but it comes out a gurgle. I sob, close to choking on the mouthful of food.

"I'm sorry I blew up, Evan. I didn't mean to upset you."

She can't look at me. Whether it's my raw emotion or disgusting appearance, I'm not sure. I get up, spit a clump of chicken in the sink, flip on the disposal. Running water, I rinse grease and spittle from my chin.

As I dry my face on a dishtowel, she speaks, gently, like I'm on a ledge. "You're right . . . I haven't been there for you . . . and I'm sorry."

"It's okay, Mom." I'm surprised by my own voice, a little boy's.

"No, it's not. People always say they survived tragedy by being strong for the kids. That they'd have given up if not for their children. But that's not me, Evan. I can't be strong for you."

She kneels on the strawberry rug to clean up my debris. I join her. As she reaches for a piece of foil, I touch her hand, and she looks into my face for the first time.

God, she's aged since Easter. She's stopped coloring her gray hair, and there are purple sacks I don't recognize below her eyes. Her face is a map of worry.

"It's all I can do to get myself out of bed. I don't think I have what it takes to help you. But I want to try, Evan. What do you need from me?"

"I don't know, Mom. I just . . . I really miss him."

"I do too, honey. I do too."

We cry for him together for the first time, slumped on the kitchen floor. I'm not sure who's doing the comforting; we sit, rocking one another. And I almost feel Dad there, too.

I know it sounds cheesy, but picturing him watching over us sort of helps. I risk the moment by bringing up encounter again.

"Mom, I'd appreciate if you'd reconsider. Encounter, I mean."

She hardens, draws away. "Evan, I said—"

"Please?"

My mother inhales, folds her hands as if praying. Words seem to leak from her like air. "A weekend of wallowing . . . might do more harm than good. I agree with Father Brendan. I'm afraid it's a bad idea."

I hold her gaze. "I think I'm old enough to make the decision."

She sighs, brushing a hunk of hair from my eyes, quiet for a long time. Finally, she says, "I hate to admit it, maybe you are. Okay, if it's so important, I won't forbid you to go."

"Thank you, Mom." I hug her.

"Wait, Evan. I don't intend to make this easy. If you insist on going, it'll be your responsibility to pay your own way."

"But Mom, it costs like two hundred bucks! Where am I supposed to get that kind of money?"

"You're a smart boy. You'll find a way."

"Well, I have some birthday cash I could put toward it."

"Fine."

"And I've got money in the bank."

"Nice try. You are absolutely not to use your savings."

"Okay, okay."

I'm thinking of Gran and Gramp as she says, "And don't even think about hitting up your grandparents for the money. Understand?"

It's like she can read my freaking mind. There's always Reg and Ro.

"Or your aunts, either."

Dang! She's too good. "All right, I'll just have to find a job."

"I suppose, but I don't want your schoolwork to suffer."

"Don't worry." I kiss her cheek, something I haven't done in a long time. She looks pleased—and a little embarrassed. "Now that you mention it, I've got homework to do."

I head down the hall, brain in word problem mode. Encounter's in six weeks. I've got $26 squirreled. That'll cover my nonrefundable deposit, but where can I get the other $174? All right, that boils down to $29 a week. With that, I could provide enough cornmeal, oil, and salt to feed a Guatemalan family for nearly three weeks. I immediately feel guilty for having just blown $12.69 on frozen beverages. Okay, I'm getting off track.

One hundred and seventy-four dollars. Not a fortune, but let's face it, that's a mess of returnable bottles and cans. If it were summer I could mow lawns. Shoveling? God, I hate shoveling. Anyway, there's no guarantee of a steady weekly income shoveling. I need a real job.

Maybe I can sell Mochakoolas instead of sucking them down. I decide to head to the mall again after school tomorrow. This time with a mission: Evan Galloway, Employee.

I put on headphones—Suicide Songs—and crash on the bed with my *Human Anatomy and Physiology* book. I'm supposed to highlight Chapter 28, the male reproductive system. Oy.

Instead, I stare at page 117, an illustration of the brain, seeking that auxiliary lobe. I finally settle on the amygdala. Small, almond-shaped, it's tucked within the white matter of the temporal region. The text says its primary concern is survival: heightened emotion, adaptive response, fight or flight, blah-blah. "Interpreter of stressful sensory input, THE AMYGDALA identifies emotional need, instantly initiating a protective response." Bingo! I've located Falsehood Central. I ring the tiny cluster in red, cross out "fight or flight," and pencil in "lie or die."

Closing the book, I glance at my Mystery Machine alarm, another Aunt Reg gift. Only 8:15, but I feel like I've slogged through a month since lunch. I shut my eyes. John Denver sings something about "Living and dying" being our "intimate friends."

Creepy, yet comforting. Shoving my backpack to the floor, I shut out the light.

They say, "**When the student is ready, the teacher appears.**"

Hopefully the same is true of employers. Planning to hit the mall after school, I wake with purpose. I also have a stiff neck and Schnauzer breath from sleeping with headphones on, psycho food binge residue in my teeth.

After a blistering shower and lengthy tooth-brushing, I itch to conquer the world of retail. But I'll have to survive Sebastian's first.

School's blissfully ordinary, at least compared to yesterday. I pass Mr. Pettafordi in the hall; he nods mechanically and presses on. At least he made eye contact.

At lunch, I tell Lex about my encounter plans.

Ever helpful, she says, "Oh man. Encounter? Kiara Landreth said they beat you 'til you cry, that it's like emotional zip-lining."

"Funny."

"I don't think she was joking."

After school, I head straight to Foundry Hill Commons, an ironic name for a mall built in the giant crater on the site where they demolished the old iron foundry. I make my way around the consumer utopia's top floor, doors slamming in my face. Figuratively. No store has an actual door, but I'm told repeatedly it's the worst time to look for work. "Christmas rush is over. Things are dead."

On level one, I fare better. At Country Candle, Bella, Mrs. Bottaro's cousin, tells me they won't be hiring 'til May. But she says they're looking for someone at Body Barn.

Less than thrilled at the prospect of hawking lotions in green coveralls and a gingham apron, I mutter, "What the hell, it's worth a shot."

Glade, the assistant manager, stifles a laugh when I request an application, pointedly asking if I have experience with "aromatherapeutical essences."

I lie. "A little."

"Because we're very committed to what we do here. It's not just about smelling nice."

"Obviously."

"There's a whole Body Barn philosophy our employees need to embrace."

She's so earnest as she flips back a sheet of ginger hair, I'm intrigued.

"Tell me."

"Well, obviously all our products are completely natural—never animal-tested!—and our packaging is Earth-attuned. You have to love that."

"Absolutely."

"Plus, we've got the most kick-ass combinations. Our wheat grass and pomegranate pore reducer is a miracle."

"No kidding?"

"Seriously. There's such stress in the world," she makes a pouty face, "but we're doing our part to alleviate the bad, through beauty and wellness."

As she talks, I bask in Glade's serenity.

She touches the back of my hand with petally fingers and says, "Our goal is to accentuate the nature aspect of human nature."

I'm sold. I drift, thinking, *How did her eyes get so green?*

We're lying in a field. Glade braids forget-me-nots into my organically coifed locks. Sipping beet tea, I dab geranium toner on her cheek, nearly drooling as she discusses the benefits of Body Barn's potions. It all sounds so right; I can almost see each word float from her perfect lips, rimmed in mango gloss.

Then I do drool. My leg does this involuntary flinch; I realize I've been dreaming. Glade seems not to have noticed. Lit from within, she's still reciting the Body Barn philosophy. I crash back to reality as she says, "Mother Earth aches to share her secrets. Our ultimate goal is spiritual. Fulfillment, self-realization through devotion to botanicals. It's goddess-oriented. Open your mind to possibility."

"Huh?"

"I need to know if you're prepared to join us. Are you ready to become one with the Body Barn family?"

I'm unsure how to answer. What does it mean, "becoming one with the Body Barn family"? Does it require a vow? I scan the store. The employees seem to glide toward me, smiling. Serenity's definitely morphed into something else. And Glade's eyes suddenly look a little too green.

I stammer, "Uh . . . I'm . . . Catholic. We don't really go in for the whole goddess thing. Besides, I'm mostly just looking to make some cash."

Glade's expression sours. She snaps her leaf-embossed interview binder shut. "That is just so WRONG! Disrespectful. Body Barn is not about *making some cash*. We're promoting a path to wholeness. A solution." She clasps the binder to her chest and tsks. "I'm sad for you, closed-minded, little boy."

I feel awful—and a little relieved. Sure, I've offended her, but what kind of freak show are they running?

"Glade, I didn't mean to . . . "

"We're through," she spits. Color rising, she stalks off.

I notice the other employees; they're still advancing on me—no smiles. "Well, bye."

Fleeing the chamomile-infused air, I nearly mow down a pregnant woman at the Body Babies display. She's eyeing a tube of Boisenbaby Butt Balm "guaranteed to lift your newborn to a higher realm."

I whisper, "Get out while you can."

Dashing, mindless of destination, I picture a fragrant mob in pursuit. God, I'm losing it! I'm finally stopped by the lump of dripping chicken thrust in my face. A sample-pusher. I'm not sure whether he's from Teriyaki Jack, China Gourmand, or F&D BBQ. But it's no mystery I ended up in the food court. Once again, the human spirit seeks salt and grease in times of confusion: Mighty Cholesterol, Balm of the Soul.

Ogling the prefab buffet, I remember I've only got $1.16 in my pocket. I'll skip the junk munch, grab a seat, plot the rest of my job search. I refuse to leave 'til I'm hired.

I study the mall map, drawing thick Xs through rejection stores. Flipping the brochure to check other options, I notice it. In classic fine print, bottom left corner, it says, "All potential employees of Foundry Hill

Commons are required to undergo mandatory drug testing. Minimum age for employment: 16." SIXteen? SHIT!

That's it. My employment plans just joined the rest of my life in the crapper. I may as well admit defeat, tell Mom I'm bagging encounter. Resign myself to growing bitter in my bedroom, a pasty middle-ager in suspenders and horn-rims, who lives with his dilapidated mama.

Freaking Dad, all embalmed and cozy; screw Mom and me! He had no right to do this. I wish he'd taken us with him. Double murder/suicide—that's the ticket. At least in my own little drawer I wouldn't have to deal with this shit.

Wow. That must be what they mean by teen angst. Well, before I head home to take a plunger to the septic clog that is my existence, I can at least score some sample chicken. As Gramp would say, "It's cheap and filling."

I approach the Teriyaki Jack guy, authentically Japanese, startlingly blond. I barely make eye contact, and he's jabbing a toothpicked chick-chunk at me. "Very fresh! You'll love!"

It's really quite good, tender with a tangy zest. I give it an 8.5. I'm a little guilty just walking away without ordering. Oh well, tough nuts.

Next stop: China Gourmand. This time a pimply, red-haired dude, defiantly non-Asian, is handing out samples. I hesitate; the chicken's as greasy as his face. His apron's filthy; fingernails match. I nearly pass; then I think, *Who cares? It's not like I have anything to look forward to. So what if I check out early from E. coli?* I eat the chicken. Not half bad.

I walk toward F&D (Fred and Darla? Fat and Dumpy?) for my next chicken hit. There's a commotion. Some geezer's arguing with the sample handler, letting her have it. Something about "substandard slop"—as if slop should have standards.

Way past caring, she's ditched nicety. "Listen Hemorrhoid, I'm just tryin' to earn my minimum wage. You don't want to try the chicken? Fine. Bend over, I'll give it a proper burial."

"No, you listen, you representing the food service industry! You should be proud. Give you customer respect. Not peddle you garbage, with you nasty face!"

This looks like a potentially interesting scenario. I hang back to avoid the inevitable flying BBQ. They're evenly matched in vehemence, if not physicality.

The guy's short and scrappy in a white shirt and pinstriped pants. From my vantage point, he looks like an unstrung marionette, all spindles and joints. His hair cups his skull like a misplaced Scooter Pie.

She's about a foot taller, outweighs him by at least ninety pounds. Plus, she's armed with a bowl of toothpicks. Beginning to fear for the old guy, I consider going for mall security but notice a guard nearby, smirking at the spectacle.

It's about to come to blows when a woman sweeps to the rescue. She's around thirty, with a Subway bag and a bemused look. It appears she's done this before.

"Pop, can't I trust you for a minute?"

Taking his elbow, she maneuvers past Chicken Girl, giving her a "What can I say?" shrug. The Fowl One's jaw loosens, but I still wouldn't turn my back on her. As they settle at a vacant table, I notice two things. One: The old gee is Mister Alberti. Two: He's waving.

I wave back, feeling awkward. I can't pretend not to have seen his near knockdown. Then I figure, *Well, I guess we're even*. After all, last time I saw him, Mom and Gran were going toe to toe and I was delivering the world's worst singing telegram. I shudder at the memory.

"Evan, she called me a hemorrhoid!" He's beaming. "What you think of that?"

"Well, Pop, you are a pain in the ass." She kisses his forehead. "How you doing, Ev?"

"Don't mind Angela, Evan. She's got a mouth just like her mother, God rest her."

"And Mom wouldn't approve of you wrestlin' girls at the mall, neither."

"That was no girl. And the crap that *balena* was dishing out, I think it was squirrel."

Their conversation is rapid-fire, animated, very Italian. I struggle to keep up.

"I'm fine."

They both pause, look at me, doubtful.

"You don't look fine. You haven't been eating that chicken?" He laughs. "You want real food, you come by the restaurant. I'll fix you such a cacciatore, you'll want to make love to it."

"Pop, you're embarrassing him."

"It's okay. He does make great cacciatore. It was my dad's favorite."

They exchange a look, then Angela says, "Well, he's embarrassing *me*. Always pickin' fights. I swear he's got a death wish." Awkward moment number three. "Oh jeez, Evan, I can't believe I said that."

I start to say "Don't worry" but Mister Alberti stops me.

Clapping a bony hand across his daughter's mouth, he says, "Angela, she has a runaway tongue, but she means well. How is you mother?"

"Okay, I guess. This past year's been pretty tough on her."

"Is she here at the mall with you? I'd like to give her my regards."

"Um, no. I came straight from school."

By now, Angela's managed to pry her face free from his grip. She gives me a guilty smile and says, "How long you been driving?"

"I don't. I walked here from school. It's only about a mile."

"In this weather? Well, you're not walking home. Pop and I'll drop you off."

"No that's okay, really."

"Angela's right. You ride home with us. Are you through with you shopping?"

"Oh, I'm not here to shop. I need money for a school trip. I'm looking for a job."

"Any luck?"

"Yeah, all bad. Turns out I'm a year too young. They wouldn't even trust me to hand out squirrel nuggets."

Mister Alberti laughs and puts his hand on my shoulder. "It's no coincidence, Angie."

"What's that, Pop?"

"Wasn't I just saying we need somebody to help at the restaurant?"

"Were you?"

"And young Evan, he shows up just like that. Our Lady, she provides."

Angela rolls her eyes. "Yeah well, no disrespect to your celestial employment service, but traffic's honestly been pretty slow at the restaurant, now the holidays are through."

"You start tomorrow."

"Jeez, Pop. Give the kid a chance. Maybe he doesn't want to schlep pasta." She grabs my hand. "And he's a miserable boss, Evan. He never stops talking!"

I can't tell if she's serious; I think it's just part of their act.

"Nonsense! If Alberti's was good enough for the father, it's good enough for the son."

"What do you mean, sir?"

"You call me Zio. That means uncle. Zio Joe, all right? That's what you father used to call me when he worked at my restaurant."

"I never knew he worked for you."

"Even a genius can't know everything, Evan. But you keep you ears open, Zio Joe will teach you a thing or two before we're done."

We shake on it, his hand surprisingly warm in mine. They drop me in front of my house, a fine sleet falling. As I negotiate the slick walk, I remember that saying: *When the student is ready, the teacher appears.* I wave to Mister Alberti, watching from the car.

School's in session.

There was something unsettling about seeing Judas with my father's ears.

The Bad Disciple had Dad's whole face, but those ears really rocked me.

It's Saturday night; just hung up with Lex. She leaves tomorrow for her annual winter break at her Great Aunt Bert's. I've learned not to envy her.

Sure, Citrus Streams' average winter temp (60.2 degrees) sounds appealing, but according to Lex, that's the single draw of Manatee Village. Their website says "This picturesque adult community was named for its resident wildlife: the largest herd of these delightful, endangered marine mammals in the Sunshine State."

Lex insists the place got its name because most of Aunt Bert's neighbors look like lumpy sea cows lured ashore by monthly perms and Canasta. She says watching them pilot their Cadillacs and walkers and oxygen tanks through the moss-draped trees is like witnessing some disturbing migration ritual, and that the only things worse than the humanatees are the leeches in the nearby Withlacoochee River, "big as yer freaking arm—and feisty."

Even though she complains, I think Lex secretly grooves on life among the Ancients; she's like the Jane Goodall of the Elderly. Last year, she organized a low-impact, midmorning stretch to the Captain & Tennille. It could not have been a pretty sight. All I know is she came home with a load of great stories and some mighty unattractive vacation pics.

Her week's bound to be an adventure. But this year, I've got Lex beat. Working at Alberti's, I've already developed a huge repertoire of Italian swear words—*Scassacazzo!*—and a palpable garlicky aura. Plus, Mister Alberti wasn't kidding about teaching me a few things. I've learned how to stuff ravioli, sculpt foil into a decent replica of Italy's boot, and when to duck to avoid flying prosciutto. Tempers flare hot and often in the Alberti kitchen.

They're your basic, everyday family, but louder and with more sauce. It's usually just me, Angie, and Mister A in the kitchen, but you'd swear there's a crowd when they get going. Oh, and there's this other guy who never talks. Angie's mother's second cousin, Lupo. Angie says he's "straight from the old country, and none too bright." He mostly makes antipasto and scrubs the sauce pots. I've never seen him smoke, but he always has a cigarette behind each ear.

The past three days have been a whirl. I reported for my first shift on Thursday, right after school. Had no choice; Angie was idling outside Sebastian's. She chauffeured me home, waited while I changed, then drove me to the restaurant. It was a little odd, sitting next to her in the car, like an ill-advised blind date. But once I realized she'd do all the talking, I relaxed.

"So Ev, how you like school?"

"It's okay. I've been—"

"That's good. 'Nothing like an education,' Pop always says."

"Yeah, I've started—"

"Then again, Pop says lots of things. You'll find that out soon enough."

"Oh, yeah. My Gramp is—"

" 'Course, when I wanted to go to NYU for acting, that was a whole 'nother story. College was good in theory, but no daughter of his was about to waste money on some pipe dream."

"Wow, that's too b—"

"But it don't matter. I know he had my best interests at heart, so. Anyway, I can't picture doin' anything 'sides what I'm doin' now. The restaurant's like my skin. And you don't change your skin. Unless you're a snake, am I right?"

"Uh right." By the time we arrived, I'd perfected a system of grunts: "Uhnuh, hmmph."

I found out right off Mister Alberti's not so easily appeased; conversing means exercise. He asks my opinion on everything, refusing to accept "Uhmwwhm" in reply. Whether discussing the whacking of a white ball (he was village Ping-Pong champ back home) or the eternal essence of the soul, Mister A seasons each topic with a perfect mix of formality and humor. He'll amaze with tales of his favorite saints, Anthony and Jude, then ask which one I think would win in a game of lawn darts. I laugh, but he says, "No, Evan. It'sa no joke. You tell me tomorrow."

It's extreme, how he savors every word, and disconcerting being focused on so totally by an adult. He doesn't half-listen, like Dad did. His concentration's intense and it sort of makes me reach, like I'm stretching for thoughts stored on a top shelf. I'm expressing opinions I never knew I had. On topics I didn't realize I care about.

I went home that first night exhausted—I'd spent most of the evening bussing tables and delivering fresh bread—but energized, too, like Zio Joe's priming my mind for what's next.

Friday was noon dismissal. I struggled to nap before work, but the journal hijacked my mind. I'm waiting 'til encounter to read more, to really steep myself in the Dad Experience, but sprawled on my bed, I couldn't help replaying everything in my head, imagining these crazy scenarios for what's next. I finally dropped off just as the alarm buzzed.

Mom dumped me at the restaurant. Literally. I'd barely cleared the car as she sped off, splashing plow juice. She's sour on this whole Alberti thing, probably because of the brunch debacle. It took, like, UN-level negotiating to talk her out of the idea I was somehow trying to become

Dad. She finally agreed I could take the job, provided I quit the minute I earned my encounter money. She also *forbid me* to "get attached to that Zio character."

I met Angie on my way in. She'd clearly thrown in the towel. As she yanked off her apron, I waited for her to throw that, too.

"I've had it with him today! Nothin' I do is good enough!" She shoved past me.

Mister A was in the dining room, sipping espresso, a bottle of Sambuca and his feet on the table, shoes off. He waved me over.

"That one, like a locomotive! Clear the tracks, boy."

Angie shouted from the kitchen. Thanks to my enrollment in *Neapolitan Swearwords 101*, I understood most of what she yelled before the back door slammed. Yikes.

"Should I go after her?"

"No, Evan. She'll be back. Friday's a busy night. She just needs to blow off some steam. You want some?" He jiggled the bottle.

"Um, no thanks. I'm fifteen, remember?"

"Come on. I don't try to get you drunk. Be a sport." He poured, pushing the brown cup my way. "Salute."

I sniffed the drink, eyes tearing. "I'm not sure about this."

"Ah, your father used to tip a mug with Zio. The talks we had! He was a good boy, Evan, like you. A good man, too. And a *great* artist."

I sensed movement onto vital turf, the Sambuca an initiation. Bracing, I gulped.

Apparently, I have much to learn where liqueur-based rituals are concerned. For instance, I was perplexed by the slippery pellet glued to my tonsil. Attempting to hack it up, I discovered my gag reflex, numbed, was incapable of expulsion.

Oblivious to my universal-choking-symbol gesture—hand clasps throat/tongue lolls—Mister A regarded me calmly. "Minda the coffee bean."

As I tried to recall Miss Delateski's Heimlich demo, a firm backslap dislodged the obstruction. Launched from my gullet, it skittered across the tabletop, glistening spit.

Cousin Lupo hunched behind me: my silent hero. I managed a weak, "Thanks."

I would have said more, but a huge, black-Twizzler-scented belch rose like an eruption in the dining room. The Lupester plucked my spewed java nut off the table and, tucking it into his apron pouch, shuffled wordlessly back to the kitchen.

Grinning, Mister Alberti squeezed my hand and said, "Sip, don'ta gulp."

Picturing Mom busting in, waving a breathalyzer and an arrest warrant, I slurped. No bean distress. And the stuff wasn't half bad. I patted Mister Alberti's wrinkled cheek and burped again. Shaking his head, he laughed.

"I'ma show you something, Evan, something you father left behind."

Wobbling, I ran my hand across chair backs as he led me to the infamous banquet room, site of the Bereavement Brunch Follies. The décor was dinge-based, dark-paneled, and stuccoed, the floor worn to an uneven sheen by generations of dress-shoed gatherings: christenings, funerals, rehearsal dinners. You could almost smell unclaimed emotional leftovers—celebrations, mournings. I'm sure ours wasn't the only fête to end badly. Melancholy hung as thick as the faded burgundy drapes covering the far wall.

Mister A steered me to a booth, cupping my elbow with his leathery palm. He reminded me of a rickety Webelo working on a merit badge. Sitting across from me, he fiddled with a foil noisemaker, remnant of some New Year's party. His hand trembled.

"Evan. You father, he wore a coat of sorrow." He let out a sigh that shriveled him. "But he always knew to come to Zio Joe. He told me things, secrets."

"Tell me."

"I can't, not yet. But I can help you find you answers, when you're ready."

"I am ready, Mister Alberti. Tell me."

"Zio. Call me Zio."

"Yes, Zio. I'm ready to know the truth about my father. Please tell me."

"You think you ready, but this old man knows better. You're not ready to bear his weight, Evan. Anymore than he was."

His eyes—moist, round—held something between sorrow and fright. If I could swim those orbs, like a diver in an underwater cavern, I'd find treasure. But somehow, I knew not to push it—enter slowly, don't splash—for fear I'd scare off what waited in the grotto.

"What is it, Zio Joe? What did he leave behind?"

"You father worked for me, Evan, when he was a little older than you. He spent hours here, cleaning up, making salads. School vacations. Weekends. Sat with me and shared a plate. This was before Lupo showed his ugly puss."

As he continued, I recalled what Angie said: Mister A could talk your ear off. Waiting for him to get to the point, my mind flooded. He detailed Dad's preference for fresh pepper on buttered bread, how he'd always yawn after a good meal.

I began to feel I'd taken a wrong turn in a sunken cave. Air running out, Mister Alberti's words were white noise, surf slapping my ears. Staring, I tried to find meaning in the shapes his mouth made.

Whether from the booze or some ancient Italian hoodoo, my chin skimmed the tabletop. Feeling a twinge, I lifted my head to find a crab twisting the skin above my watchband. About to slap it away, I noticed its wedding ring. Realizing the crustacean was in fact my boss's veiny hand, I looked from fingers to face several times before grasping his words.

"Will you finish his wall, Evan? Will you finish you father's wall?"

"Hwubaah?" was all I could manage in reply.

For once, Zio didn't press for a lucid response. He stood and solemnly left the table.

I panicked, knowing I'd blown my chance at revelation. Jolting up, I toppled my chair. How to stop him? I grabbed the noisemaker, blew a sharp burst. But the feeble, damp blat had no impact on Mister A's steady progression. I was screwed; he'd reconsidered.

Stooping to pick up the chair, I said, "Fine. Skip it. I'll just go."

Riled disappointment sobered me faster than coffee could have. Knocking over the chair again—this time on purpose—I turned to leave.

Behind me, Mister A cleared his throat. Just above a whisper, he said, "Pick up that good-for-nothing chair and come over here, already. I have something to show you."

He hit the dimmer switch, and flame-shaped sconces winked into faux-flicker. I felt I'd finally surfaced, cleared the water. As I stepped tentatively toward him, he lifted one bony arm. "This is what you father left for you." With a magician's flourish, he drew back maroon velvet.

I gasped. Honestly, this giant gulp of air, like an actor in a slasher flick, or a telenovela. I'm not sure what I expected behind curtain number one, but this was not it. The thirteen figures at table spilled gold, the painting somehow illuminating the restaurant's dim recesses. I just stared, floored. My dad had truly painted this? I'd never seen him so much as doodle.

"It'sa the Last Supper."

"I figured."

He pulled back the drape, revealing the entire mural, the wall's length. It was painted in the style of some Old Master, not that famous Da Vinci version, Tintoretto or someone. But my father included modern details. Through the archway behind Jesus' head was Saint Anne's steeple. I could also just make out the gas station on the corner of Hart and Branch. And beside the chalice was an Alberti's menu.

There was a familiarity to the faces, too, just out of reach, not quite recognizable. Painted with something beyond skill, emotion palpable as technique, each was a study in reverence, humility, wonder. The apostles appeared mesmerized as Jesus broke bread. My father had captured the colossal awe they must have felt witnessing a miracle.

Then I noticed Judas and gasped again.

At first, it was like seeing my reflection, only a bit older, in Bible wear. But I often have this momentary confusion when I see his old pictures, like it could be me. I'm a passable Dad clone. But the ears, they were Evan Senior, all the way.

He sat to Jesus' left, the most sorrowful Judas, eclipsed by this anti-aura, an absence of that glow. Instead of looking at the miracle, he studied his own expression in a water glass. The Eucharist eluded him, not like he was unworthy of salvation—worse, that it was a fraud. Seeing that face, I had a hint of the despair my father must've felt at the end. His eyes transfixed me.

Mister Alberti broke the spell. Arm around my shoulder, he said, "So, what you think?"

"He was twice the artist I'll ever be. I never even knew he could draw, let alone paint like this. Why didn't he ever show me? I mean—"

Stepping closer, I pressed cheek to wall, touching fingertips to tiny brushstrokes my dad made a lifetime ago. I swear I could feel his pulse through the wall, his soul layered with pigment. I wanted nothing more than to enter his mural like a Mary Poppins sidewalk drawing and seek out its creator.

But, as persistent as a cough, Mister A disturbed me back to reality.

"Pretty good, huh?"

"Beautiful."

"He worked on it after college."

"Un-huh."

"Never finished though." He gestured to a large section where the mural fragmented into washes of color and vague outline. "See, this whole part's just . . . what'd he call it?"

"Underpainting."

It was Angie. In my fugue state, I hadn't heard her come in.

"Pop, what in the name of—Him," she pointed to the central figure, "are you doin'?"

"Tap-dancing! What you think I'm doing, Angie?"

"You promised you wouldn't pull this. I can't believe, the minute my back is turned, you drag the kid in here!"

"I show the boy, maybe I help him figure things out. Where's the harm?"

"It's like a sickness with you!"

"*Basta*, Angela! Enough! He's going to finish his father's masterpiece. It's about time, too. I'm tired of these shitty drapes."

"Don't listen to him, Evan. He hired you to help in the kitchen, not to be a painter."

Corralling Mister A toward the main dining room, she stage whispered—I assume, for sensitivity sake. Still, I heard every word; subtlety is not an Alberti trait.

"Pop, you are so friggin' gauche. Are you *trying* to scar the kid? You got no right springin' this on him. You ever think it might be painful for him dealing with his dead father's artwork? It's no picnic for me! And what's next? What're you planning?"

Mister Alberti plugged his thumbs in his ears and left the room, singing "Beautiful Dreamer." His voice wasn't half bad.

Angie pounced like a pit bull on a veal parm. "Look Evan, my father had no right to put you on the spot. He gets these screwy ideas. I apologize if he made you uncomfortable. You should forget this whole mural thing."

"I'm going to finish it."

"No! No, listen. Don't think you need to please him. He means well, he's just—*un uomo anziano pazzesco*—a crazy old man."

I channeled my inner ballsy Italian. "*You* listen. I'm finishing that mural, Angie, whether he pays me or not. I won't let you talk me out of it. So don't bother trying."

Her face was a mixed sky: grin-tilted lips, eyes overcast.

"Okay, Ev. If that's what you want. But as for my father, take him with a grain of salt, understand? Don't get too wound up in his stories. He just likes the sound of his own voice."

"What is it, Angela?"

"What's what?"

"What don't you want me to know?"

For the first time since I'd met her, Angie was speechless.

"Nothin', Ev. I . . . I better get back to the kitchen."

Once she was gone, I returned to the mural. Staring into my father's Judas eyes, I remembered a passage from the Gospel—Saint John, I think—about how, after Jesus gave the piece of bread to Judas, Satan entered into him. "And it was night."

Was that how my father saw himself: betrayer, bringer of night? Was the self-portrait some screwed-up symbolism, a message? Or even back then, did he know what his end would be? Did he live knowing one day he'd follow Judas to the tree? Maybe Mrs. S-B-C was right when she said there are worse things than not knowing.

"Why Judas?" I whispered. The wall gave no answer, not yet.

Sleepwalking through the rest of my shift, folding napkins, filling water glasses, my mind was in the back room, and I kept finding reasons to join it.

Finally, Mister Alberti took me aside and said, "Evan, you knock off a little early. It's slow, anyway. Come tomorrow morning. Don't forget you brushes."

I was about to call Mom when Lupo materialized. Wish they'd tie a bell on him, so I'd know he's coming. Jangling Angie's keys, he jerked his head. I followed him through the delivery entrance, night air instantly crisping my nose hair. In his black parka, hood tight around his face, there was something eerily familiar about him.

Opening my door, he waited 'til I was inside, then shut it gently; I'd half-expected him to buckle me in. I tried giving directions, but he unfolded what looked like a treasure map, my house marked with a big, red X. Angie must've made it. As we rode in complete silence, I realized who he looked like in that black hood: The Ghost of Christmas Future was my driver.

At one point, I switched on the radio; Lupo didn't flinch when Angie's CD, "Teenage Dream," blared, max volume. He stared straight ahead as Katy Perry wailed.

Hopping out in front of my house, I said, "So . . . thanks."

Lupo just made this hand motion, and I realized he had it rough. Not speaking English must be isolating. But as he drove off, I heard him belting, "Baby, you're a firework!"

"How's the wrangling this year, Lex?"

"They're puckered and leathery as ever, but enchantment's in the air. I'm helping stage a musical review, a sort of geriatric *Fantasia*, set to classic '70s tunes. We're calling it *You're So Veined*. I promise it's like nothing you've seen."

"I'm sure. So the humanatees have accepted you as a juvenile herd member. Doesn't that make you a calf?"

"You say the sweetest things."

It's Monday night, no Tuesday—1:58 A.M. I tossed for over an hour, trying to purge Lupo's anthem and Dad's Judas face from my brain.

Somehow they've melded into Judas/Perry Pavlov response, my new nightly ritual: I close my eyes and—BAM!—Dad's face/that tune echoing.

I suppose total Last Supper immersion doesn't help. I arrived early Saturday like Mister A suggested, art box in hand. Angie's reception was only slightly less chilly than the outside temp (a balmy 14 degrees), but that's okay. When I'm performing my regular duties—bussing tables, filling waters—she's all business. And I'm basically out of her way while I work on the mural.

Okay, "work on" is a stretch. So far I've spent most of my time just staring at the wall. Saturday I made a few sketches, took measurements. Sunday a baby shower commandeered the room, restricting me to kitchen duty: salads, bread, the usual. I did manage to glimpse behind the maroon swags as we doled pastries and punch, but it was basically a wasted day.

Tonight, paint finally met wall. Nothing major, beyond the challenge in matching his brushwork. I roughed in some clouds. I'm avoiding the figures for now, afraid to screw them up. The other key factor is it's damn depressing, Dad staring down at me. I'm not sure whether Mister A requested a Last Supper, but I know I would've preferred something a bit cheerier. Dad as singing gondolier? Winking elf? But no, I'm stuck with Jesus and the Boys.

So after quilt-wrestling from 12:00 to 1:00, I flipped through *Gardner's Art Through the Ages*, hunting all the Last Suppers for inspiration. Now my synapses won't stop crackling. The restlessness is part mural anxiety. Can I do him justice? But it's more than that.

"Are you still there? And why are you calling me in the middle of the night?"

"Lex withdrawals."

"Dunderhead. Seriously, what's up? How's Alberti's? Any big revelations?"

"Just this: My dad betrayed Christ."

"Okaaaay. Should I be worried?"

"No, I'm just being dramatic. See, there's this unfinished mural at Alberti's. My dad started it like twenty-something years ago. It's the Last Supper. In it, he's Judas."

"Yikes."

"So . . . Mister A asked me to finish it."

"Cool." She gulps a yawn as she says it, and I wonder if she's up to listening. But it's Lex, so, assuming I rate higher than sleep, I press on.

"I'm a little freaked, Lex."

"Why, Ev? You're a great artist."

"It's not that. I just . . . I don't know. God, I wish you were here, Lex. I mean you should see his work . . . it's incredible, but . . . "

"What?"

"I don't think I can do this. It's . . . "

"What?"

"Looking at it . . . his face . . . it's too much. His expression. It's like he had nothing to live for. But I guess he didn't, did he?"

"Don't be stupid. He had everything to live for. He had you."

"This was before, Lex. Way before me. It seems like he just wasn't ever happy. You see it in grade school pictures even, that wounded look. I wish I knew what it was."

"Well, maybe finishing his mural will be a way to figure it out."

"Maybe."

"And there's one more place you might find answers."

"I know. I know, the journal. Lex, I told you I'm waiting to read it 'til encounter."

"Yeah, explain that again, okay? Because it sounds like classic avoidance."

"That's crap."

"Oh, right. Mustn't disagree with Lord Genius."

"That's not what I meant. It just has to be *my* decision when to read more."

"Whatever. Look, it's late, and I really need sleep. I'm meeting someone for breakfast. It's cool about the mural. I can't wait to see it. I'll call you. G'night."

She's about to hang up, and I've got a wad of dissatisfaction in my throat. I definitely didn't get what I need from this call; I'm unsure what that even is.

"Lex?"

"Huh?"

"There's one other thing."

She sighs. "What?"

"The spring formal, remember we talked about doing a just-pals thing? Well, I wondered if we're still on, because—"

"Oh."

I wait. All that's coming from the phone is extended silence, generally not a good sign. I visualize her scrambling for a way to turn me down, consulting a website, Letemdowneasy.com. Shouldn't have asked. Didn't need more disappointment tonight. And judging by that "Oh," disappointment and I are hurtling toward a head-on.

"Well?"

"I'm . . . uh . . . not sure. I think I might have a *real* date."

"Oh." What I mean is *OUCH.*

Dead air. Finally, "I should've mentioned this sooner, but I didn't want you getting the wrong idea. Tyler's here."

"What?"

"Tyler Wattrous. He's here. I mean, not *right* here. He's visiting Manatee Village, too. His grandfather moved down last fall. Isn't that strange?"

"Yeah, like *two-headed kitten* strange. When'd you find out?"

"On the plane. We were seated next to each other. He was semi-freaking. Never flew before. So I . . . kept him company. I guess we bonded over a barf bag."

"Delightful."

And then, something so foreign, so anti-Lex, it must be a joke: she giggles. A genuine crush-afflicted, girly-girl giggle followed by, "So, we're kind of hanging out. He's helping with the review. But don't mention it to anybody. He'd die if the team knew."

"And he's taking you to the dance?"

The giggle, technically a titter this time, repeats, and she says, "I'm just saying it's a possibility. He's really pretty charming away from those track apes."

I'm unable to formulate a speakable thought.

Lex bursts my stupor. "Evan? Are you still there?"

"You're right. It's late. I'm tired too. When you see him at breakfast, could you maybe ask Tyler not to try flushing my head down the toilet anymore? I'd appreciate that."

I hang up fast, to avoid an excuse, a justification, or worse, more silence. She doesn't call back. Why would she? What've I got compared to the good looks, athleticism, and razor wit of Wattrous the Great? A morose nature and genetic predisposition to self-destruct? What a draw. I finally sleep, cell beneath my pillow.

Jerking awake at 5:34, I instinctively grab the phone, but the ringing's in my head. I try to recall the brief-yet-crushing Lex exchange, but other images intrude, specters of a dream: Winter beach. A dark figure glides toward me. I can't see the face, but I know it's Dad. Closer, his eyes shimmer like sea glass. He works his jaw, trying to talk, but there's no sound.

I go to speak, but his icefingers press against my mouth. Teeth clenched, he goes, "sssssssssssssssssssssssssssssssssssshhhhhhhhhhhhhhhhhhhhhhhhhh," and bends me in a tight embrace.

Folded to his chest, I scan the horizon beyond his shoulder. A shadowman, larger than Dad, looms, a wolf crouched alongside. I try to yell, to warn my father; again, he shushes. Then, releasing me, he floats back, his lips parting to speak.

Instead, a rope spools from his mouth, coiling his neck. I tear at it, but—eyes bulging, face black—Dad's hoisted, ripped shoeless, dragged into clouds. I scream after him 'til hoarse I fall on my knees. On the ground with his loafers is the journal, splayed to February 27th, 1976.

Rubbing my eyes, I shift in bed. Picturing the dream dizzies me. Leaning to place the phone on the nightstand, I notice it, open on the blue-coiled rug: the journal. Either it dropped from the sky, like in the dream, or I sleepwalked again. Reaching for it, I lose balance, topple to the floor. I lie, face pressed to page, Dad's words a close-up smudge of looping blotches.

Peeling my cheek from the spit-damp page, I study the date, the same as in my dream. I drag a pillow from my bed, clutch it to my chest, and begin to read.

2/27/76

Dreamed it again last night. Can't even look at Tony. Luckily, he's been avoiding me. Something's going on.

Worse than last time. It started out with Melody again, but as soon as she took off her clothes, SHE WAS HIM. He came at me. Suddenly we weren't in the gym. So strange. I can't figure out where—someplace else. Tony whispering, calling me his special . . . something. Then I woke up.

March 1, 1976

Had it again. But this time, Father Fran was there.

The more the f**kin' merrier.

But *that part*, with Father. Different somehow.

NOT a dream? A MEMORY?

I can hear his voice. Real soft. He's stroking my hair. Saying, "It's okay, Evan. I'll always take care of you. You're my special boy." We're in the rectory at Saint Anne's and

I turn the page, eager for what's next. A blank sheet. And another. It goes on for pages—the only mark a scribble across each—reminding me of a flat-line EKG, like when the patient dies on a medical show. Maybe it's a code.

As I reexamine the March 1st entry, something happens. An audible crack; the binding loosens; a section slides onto my lap. The part with the scrawl. Running my finger up the gap in the spine, I see a chunk's been cut from the book. The flat-line section's a glued-in replacement for the missing pages, the ones that held answers.

"Crap!"

I'm about to fling the book across the room, when a voice in my head says, "Look again." God, I'm sick of these IMs from the Great Beyond. I miss being oblivious. Minding the voice, I open the journal. With the blank piece removed, the book flops to the last page: final entry.

March 21, 1976

Journal—I've learned a lot these last months. All SHITTY.

Sorry to slice you up. Thanks for sacrificing the pages.

I was afraid to have those poems and stuff in here.

In case Mom found you, found out. Couldn't risk it.

So I put them someplace safe. It'd be interesting some day to read you again, like when I'm thirty. Maybe I'd even laugh. Somehow I don't think that'll happen. It was the right decision. It's too much.

Having you on encounter helped me figure things out when all that was happening. I really think I'm over it now, okay? That's why I wanted to write it all down, like barfing up a mess.

I gave Reggie the painting. I'm not sure how long it'll take her to look inside, or even if I want her to, but it feels better getting it out.

If Reg ever DOES find the package, they won't be OUR secrets anymore, but it won't matter THEN, will it?

Looks like this'll be my last sign off. Thanks for listening.

Evan Frederick Galloway

I can't believe this. He's screwed me again—from beyond the crisper. How can a section be missing? It's just like him to withhold crucial info, Mister No-Suicide-Note. But what'd he mean about Aunt Reg "looking inside the picture"? What package?

Well, it's obvious my day begins at—glancing at the clock—5:51, because there's no getting back to sleep. It's okay; I'm eager for dawn. I have a good idea where the day will take me.

"Well, we weren't _Waltons close_, but sure, we talked."

Aunt Reg's condo: 7:20. I stalled as long as I could, arrived unannounced, hoping surprise would work in my favor. Said I was "in the neighborhood"; feeble, really, considering she lives two minutes from our house. We're at her breakfast table, chatting over soup-bowl-sized cocoa mugs.

I'm looking to delicately bring up the picture, to get as much info as I can without red-flagging her. My life's starting to resemble some lame detective show.

"So, he'd confide in you?" I feign passionate interest in a wicker placemat.

"Evan?"

"Yes, Aunt Reg?"

"What do you want to ask me?"

Staring at the moon rising on my thumbnail, I search for words. It seemed so easy in rehearsal; reality's different. Not only is the topic sensitive, but how do I raise it without spilling what I know—and how I found out?

I decide to tell her about the mural, and not a moment too soon. Aunt Reg is getting antsy watching me watching my thumbnail.

"You heard I'm working at Alberti's?"

"Yes. Congratulations. How's gainful employment?"

"Great, I'm learning a lot from Zio Joe. That's what Mister Alberti said to call him."

"Naturally."

For just a second, her face shifts, giving the distinct impression she's not too fond of Mister Alberti. I can't explain why; it's just a feeling.

Then she says, "I'm not too fond of Mister Alberti." Disregarding my dropped jaw, she continues. "He's not a bad guy, Ev, just a tad pushy for my taste. But your father was crazy about him. I'm sure you've heard he worked at Alberti's, too."

"Yeah, I found out the day Mister A hired me."

"I suppose you've seen the mural."

This is almost too easy.

"It's amazing! Zio asked me to finish it."

"Holy smokes!" Now she's hoisting *her* chin off her lap. Clearing her throat, her forehead creasing, she says, "I'm not sure that's a good idea."

"Why not? Cash for painting! How cool is that?"

"It's just—you're named after him. You go to Sebastian's. You've got a job at Alberti's. And now you're finishing his painting? It's a bit much.

You can't bring your dad back by becoming him. We all miss him, Ev, but be careful about following in his footsteps. That's a dangerous path."

She's been talking to Mom. "Please, Aunt Reg. Don't go all Intro to Psych on me, okay? I'm not trying to resurrect him—I get it. I was there when they sealed the crisper drawer."

Saying this, I know, is flat-out nasty. I wait for her to play the respect card; threaten to call my mother; execute some typical, disappointed-adult display.

Of course, my aunt's anything but typical. She laughs.

"You're too much, Evan. Crisper drawer? Oh my Lord!"

"Sorry, Aunt Reg. I didn't mean—"

"Listen, it's okay, you say what you need to. And you better know you can always say it to me. As for Mister Alberti, be wary. He's got this Svengali sway over the Galloway men. Don't take him too seriously."

It was like she and Angie read the same chapter in the *Big Book of Cautionary Tales*.

"Okay. But I'm revved about the mural. Not for some goofy, symbolic reason, just . . . it'll be cool to have a piece of work out there . . . and . . . yeah, it makes me feel closer to Dad."

"Well that's a good thing, right?"

"Sure. And the reason I brought it up—it's . . . like, three weeks ago, I had no idea my father was even an artist and now—it's just strange. I don't understand why he hid it from me all those years. His talent, I mean."

"I'm not sure. I guess he basically shut himself off artistically after—" She takes a gulp, gets up, and crosses to the kitchen sink.

"After what?"

"Oh . . . after he got married. I guess he thought it was time to get practical. A shame, really, he had definite talent."

Now I'm totally fishing. Running a finger around my mug rim, I speak ultra-casually. "So, you have any of his artwork?"

Aunt Reg's brows skid into a furrow. She'll need Botox after this visit. Managing a passable smile, she sits. "I have a few small woodcuts, some illustrations from *The Quill & Barb*."

"Anything else?"

"Um." I imagine I hear her cranial sprockets whir as she weighs a reply. "As a matter of fact . . . yes. I have a painting he did years ago. It was odd. He gave it to me when he left for college, asked me to hold onto it for him."

"What's it look like?"

"Believe it or not, I have no idea. It was mummified in paper and duct tape. I got the feeling he didn't want me to see it. So, I tucked it away, basically forgot it. Then, years later, just after you were born, he showed up, asking if I still had it."

Nonchalance is getting progressively difficult.

"Oh, really? So you gave it back?"

"No. He didn't want it, just wondered if it was safe. I teased him, asked if he'd stashed loot inside. He got all pissy, like, 'Put it away somewhere, Regina.' I knew he meant business. He only called me Regina when he was serious."

"What'd you do?"

"Well, I debated tearing in, ripping off the back to see if there was something inside. But I figured that was silly—and pretty damn nosy—so I did what he asked."

"Stored it away?"

"Since he wanted it hidden, I put it in a true low traffic area: my exercise room closet."

I follow Aunt Reg to the basement. It's tricked out as a passable home gym: stationary bike, rowing machine, magenta free weights, most of it coated with a skin of dust.

"Convenient having the laundry across the hall." She sweeps a tangle of bras off the Cardio-Glide. "I'll just run this upstairs. Back in a flash."

Staring at the louvered doors, I envision Dad crouched within the dark closet, arms outstretched. Ah, the blessing of a creative mind.

Breathing deep, I open the closet, triggering a video avalanche: *Glutes of Gold, Absolute Abs, Eat Bad/Look Great.* I'm squatting in the heap, trying to hide the mess, when she returns.

"Hey, sorry . . . had a little mishap."

"Don't worry. I've been meaning to reorganize those." She hands me a cruller. "So, I sense you're eager to see it."

I blush.

"Scooch over, will you? Let me in there."

With a loud cracking of knees, Aunt Reg squats. Shoving videos aside, she excavates the jumble of holiday decor and fitness devices. First, she hauls out Gran's old tree—it's fully decorated with crocheted elves and reindeer. A stray ThighMaster bobbles as I catch it.

Another landslide: plastic bins (silk flowers, willow wreaths, scrapbooking supplies) flood the room. Abruptly diving atop the pile, she pitches stuff out. Cupids and pilgrims, bunnies and leprechauns mingle on the carpet with Suzanne Somers and stacks of Deal-A-Meal Cards.

Then she strikes gold. Jammed against the back wall, the bundle's about 3' × 4', swathed in craft paper and loads of duct tape. Not quite able to reach it, even stretched out on her belly, she does this ungainly breaststroke, dragging forward a few inches, and grabs the painting.

"Pass it to me."

"I can't."

"Why not?"

"I'm stuck!"

"What can I do? Should I call someone?"

"NO!"

I enter the closet gingerly, planning to clear debris and unwedge her. Aunt Reg yelps as a box topples, sending hundreds of plastic eggs cascading. I freeze.

Gasping for breath, she says, "Ev, step away. Slow. You're my only hope. Pull me loose!"

I back out carefully, the only casualty a ceramic leprechaun that makes a sickening crunch as my foot smashes it.

Having escaped the closet of doom, I firmly grasp my aunt's ankles and, an obstetrician delivering the world's biggest breach baby, haul her to freedom. Happily, the giant newborn has an equally strong grip. She's held onto Dad's painting.

Laughing, she says, "Success!" and shoves it toward me.

It weighs a ton. And that's merely the physical heaviness. I shudder slightly, anticipating the emotional heft in store.

Before I can say anything, Aunt Reg hugs me. "Well, I'd better survey the damage to Ye Ole Storage Center. I'm guessing you'd prefer to look at his work on your own."

"If you don't mind."

She winks and says, "As long as you split the loot with your old auntie."

"Deal."

Upstairs, we wrap the painting in trash bags to protect it on the walk home. After I zip into my winter gear, Aunt Reg hugs me again. This time, no wink/no laughter. She has tears in her eyes as she reminds me to be careful, to call if I need to talk.

I bungee cord the painting to her old toboggan and pull it along the frozen drive, turning back to wave. Aunt Reg blows a kiss, a cruller in her hand, worry on her face.

Duct tape: man's most durable creation.

I slide my fingers under and tug, but it's clearly not meant to tear. Stretching, it rolls on itself, nearly cutting my palm. I ease my art box from under the bed and use my X-ACTO to slice the tape, careful not to carve into the picture beneath. Peeling back a corner of the yellowed paper and bubble wrap, I hesitate. You'd think, by now, I'd have shaken this peeper's guilt.

I know this frame. An antique, gold-leaf thing, gloppily ornate, it's an exact match to one in Saint Anne's rectory, behind Father Lessard's desk. That one borders a routinely gruesome rendering of Sebastian. Tree-bound, he gazes heavenward, perforated by arrows. I always pictured him sipping water and gushing, sprinkler-style, like in a *Tom and Jerry* cartoon. Obviously, I never mentioned that to Father; it's definite grounds for a spiritual ass-whupping.

All right, no more stalling. Mom will be home soon; better get on with it. I squinch my eyes like a kid birthday wishing, then eager for the big reveal, strip the remaining wrap. Eyes snapping open, I flinch at movement within the frame: Pupils stare back. Squinting for focus, I realize the eyes are mine, reflected by mirror shards. Still, I'm creeped by the image.

It's another self-portrait, not Judas this time, but maybe more disturbing. I can see why this never showed up over Gran's sofa. My father's painted himself at about age eleven. The painting is acrylic on board with collage elements. Along with bits of mirror, he's included old typewriter keys and what look like real oak leaves, cracked and brown.

The work obviously owes a debt to Sebastian imagery. My father stands naked, alone in a field of burnt grass, hands cupping his groin. A larger hand reaches in, covering his mouth. It bears a stigmata wound.

His scrawny body's too much like mine; I concentrate on the landscape. Beneath deepening skies, the field's littered with branches, gum wrappers, and—in exceptionally gross detail—piles of dog shit, likely from the beast at Dad's feet. It's visibly male, some type of shepherd maybe, splayed on its back. Dirt-sprawled, tongue swollen and hanging, its paws are tinged red. I follow the stain trail from the dog's feet to its source: a blood pool on the grass.

Looking at my father, avoiding his face, I check to see if the blood is his. It's not, but I realize that, like Sebastian, he's tethered. The collar around his neck's attached to a leash that winds his torso, binding him to a thick, gold pillar. Blood flows down the pillar, pooling at his feet.

A microscopic inscription wraps the column's base. I can only read what curves around front: "is in memor." Touching the words, I feel a bolt of recognition. On the altar with Father Greg, holding the cup, I read the words circling its base. "Do this in memory of me." It's not a pillar my dad's lashed to, but a giant chalice. Why?

Scouring the portrait for clues, I forget my real objective: the pages within. I stare at the typewriter keys. Scattered throughout the composition, they're seemingly random. But they must contain a message. Top-to-bottom, left-to-right, it's gibberish:

L – C – O – N – H – Y - U – V – E – A – T – N – N - O

I'm tempted to pry them up, rearrange them on the rug. But I just can't mess with Dad's image. Grabbing a charcoal pencil from my art box, I scribble on the floor.

T H E N O U N C A N—I doubt it's a grammar lesson.

C A N Y O U N O T H A V E—Shoot! Only one A.

C A T L U V H O N E Y—Plain stupid.

Swiping coal marks, I smear out C A T and scan what remains. A few minor shifts, and the letters start making sense.

Not HONEY. HOLY. And if I add U and N it becomes UNHOLY A definite possibility! But unholy what?

What's left? C – V – E – A – T – N – N – O

UNHOLY N E A T O C N V—Doubtful.

UNHOLY V A N E C O N T?

A N T C O V E N—Nasty, an ant coven on teeny broomsticks. Hold it. Ant. Coven. I flip the words. Insect witches become something else: COVENANT. That's it,

UNHOLY COVENANT!

"My God."

For an instant, I'm confused, convinced I spoke aloud. Then it dawns: It wasn't my voice. Mom stands in my doorway, gaping at Dad's painting. Taking advantage of her stupor, I slide the journal toward me, tuck it into my waistband.

"Um . . . you're home early."

Moving mutely, eyes glued to the image, she nearly lands on the art box as she crouches. For an eternal minute, she's frozen. With her behavioral track record, anything's possible.

Mom finally speaks through a fist. "When did you paint this? And who else has seen it?"

I'm not sure why I lie.

"In the fall. I only showed it to Lex."

"Evan, what does it mean?"

"I don't know." That's the truth.

Her whole body shakes. "I think we should talk over these feelings, honey, because you're frightening me."

"Mom, it's not like that."

"Don't try to tell me this is normal, Junior."

I frown at the nickname.

Noticing, she corrects herself. "I'm sorry. *Evan.* I just don't get what you're trying to prove. If this is some sad attempt to identify, to climb inside his pain or something, I can tell you it's not healthy."

"Mom, listen—"

"No. You listen." Now she *is* crying, and I can see where we're headed. "This," she jabs a finger toward the painting, "is not the product of a normal fifteen-year-old. You expect me not to worry? I find you scribbling on the floor, gawking at a picture of yourself being tortured. Am I supposed to ignore the strap around your neck? For God's sake, what are you thinking?"

So she thinks it's a *self*-portrait; Dad did whittle the ears a bit. I aim for damage control. "It's a painting, Ma. Mister P showed us this religious art, asked us to do a portrait inspired by one of the images. It doesn't *mean* anything. Lex did one too—she painted herself as Joan of Arc at the stake. That doesn't mean she's intending to spontaneously combust."

"Well I think I need to speak with Mister Pettafordi. This seems terribly inappropriate."

"NO!"

Rocked back on her heels, she nearly tips from the force of my response. Guess I could have scaled it down a few decibels. Steadying, she moves toward the painting.

"What're you going to do?"

"I'm taking it."

"Mom, you can't do that."

"Watch me." She reaches for the frame. "And you can forget about encounter and working at Alberti's."

About to lose it, I snap. "I swear to God, you touch it, and I will make you sorry."

She's never seen me like this; doesn't know what to say.

"If you're so afraid of me doing what he did, why are you pushing me to it? Take that picture from me, and I swear I *will* hurt myself."

Hands to mouth, she smothers a moan. Hugging the painting, I run from the room, down the hall, to the garage. Dad's Tahoe's still there, silent since he died. I climb in.

Painting cradled across my lap, I replay what I said about hurting myself. The scary thing is, in that moment, I think I meant it.

Last time I felt this bad in the backseat of a car, I was nine.

Aunt Rosemary took Lex and me to Hammonasset one Saturday, stuffed in the steaming interior of her VW Bug, with a cooler of Dr. Pepper, Oreos, and egg-salad sandwiches. The beach was a blast, but bouncing home over hilly Route 16—windows sealed, AC whimpering—I hurled.

I guess three sandwiches was overkill. I'd turned to Lex to say, "What melon insists on a church wedding? Give up? Cantaloupe. Get it, *can't elope!*" but only got halfway. The joke was Dad's—and lame—but I'm sure Alexis would've preferred his dorky punch line to my stomach smoothie. My puke made her puke, which made Aunt Ro veer off the road, jumping the curb and blowing out the right front tire.

While Aunt Ro changed the flat, Lex and I rinsed the VW with ice melt from the cooler. It was a fairly unpleasant ride home. I don't think I've eaten egg salad, or cantaloupe, since.

After multiple shampooings, Aunt Ro sold her Bug that fall, and Lex still does a fake gagging routine whenever I tell a joke. Just recalling that trip conjures a scent memory to make my stomach cartwheel. Bad as that was, this is worse.

At first, I expect Mom to bust in with Father Brendan and a team of doctors, bent on performing a combo exorcism/psychiatric throw-down. She doesn't. Maybe she's calling Crystal Hills to book me a room.

I should just go quietly; it's crazy pursuing this. Then I close my eyes, and the dream replays: Dad ripped away, his journal on the sand. Suddenly aware of the corner biting into my waist, I remember it's concealed there. Hitching my jeans down, I remove the journal and place it on the seat next to Dad's painting.

I climb in front, pop the glove compartment, and snag the mini toolkit I gave Dad one Father's Day. Squeezing back between the seats, I flop beside the picture. Staring at my father's image, I wonder about UNHOLY COVENANT. Am I doing the right thing trying to figure this out, or should I let the dead rest? Studying his eyes, I vow to continue. I owe him that.

Turning the portrait facedown on the seat, I examine the stapled cardboard backing. Gripping a screwdriver, I work the head beneath a staple, pry it up, then glance toward the house, half-hoping Mom will appear. Coast still clear. The metal pulls loose with a tiny squeak, and I go at the others. When some stick, I lose patience, yank the cardboard, ripping off sections.

Soon my lap's covered with corrugated strips; mounding them on the seat, I turn my attention to the center of the board. Taped there is a padded envelope. This is it: the message to Aunt Reg. I hesitate. Now that I know it's real, I'm afraid to look inside.

After some deep breaths, and the sign of the cross, I peel off the tape holding the envelope. The package is lighter than I'd expected. I'm not sure why I thought it'd be heavier, maybe because of the contents. Secrets? Answers? Or just more questions?

Hands trembling, I flip the envelope. More staples and tape cover the flap. Whatever's inside, he was determined to keep it sealed. I whisper an Our Father as I tug at the tape. Reaching in, I remove a thick packet of paper and say the last words of the prayer, "deliver us from evil. Amen."

Still no Mom. Unfolding pages, I'm surprised when something drops out, luging to the car floor. Papers in my right hand, I feel beneath the driver's seat, just brushing the object's edge. It's out of reach. Stretched to my limit, I circle fingers around a flat rectangle. I fit my pinky into the notched wheel: a cassette. Another song selection?

Pulling my hand out, I study the tape. The label bears Dad's inked inscription:

Reg, I'm giving you this because you'll know what to do.
Listen where no one will hear. Keep it safe till after.
Counting on you. So sorry, Evan (May 24, 1976)

"Jackpot." Looking from the papers in my right hand to the cassette in my left, I feel like Alice when the caterpillar gave her two pieces of mushroom, one for growth, one for shrinkage. Where to start? I think of my dream with Father Brendan on the giant 'shroom. "Answers lie within your chest (plip)."

So I should start with the pages . . . or not. I mean, Dad bothered making this a multimedia event, so maybe I should go straight to audio. Wriggling up front, folding down the driver's visor, I brace for disappointment. But when I feel inside the pouch, it's there: Dad's spare key. I slide it into the ignition, turn to accessories. It'll never work; the car's gone untouched for almost a year. So when the radio blares, I nearly piss myself like some Stephen King character.

I hit the eject button. The player expels a CD, and the sweet tones of the B52s mercifully end, replaced by some radio doc counseling a caller. Fascinating as these phone-in relationship woes are, I press the function button 'til the green cassette light glows. Then I inhale a lungful of courage and push tape into slot.

For a moment, there's no sound, just a low static buzz like a distant toilet flush, 'til he clears his throat and emits a Darth Vader sigh. When he speaks, I literally rock back at the sound. I'd expected him, so it's eerie hearing the words in a voice so much like mine. Of course, Dad was barely older than me when he recorded this. Drawing knees to chest, I listen.

Reggie, if you're hearing this, I'm an excellent judge of character. You really are as nosy as I suspected. Knew you'd take the bait. If you're NOT hearing this, I apologize.

I applaud your self-control. *Clap. Clap.*

Either way, this is something I need to do—telling.

Mostly, so I can work on forgetting—again. Thought I'd done a decent job—forgetting. But now it's all seeping back "like shit up a clogged pipe," as Dad would say.

In my case, it's like a bad dream, or that's what started it: the dreams. Remember February? Figured you would.

It's not every night your brother appears by your bed shrieking like some mental defective, huh?

Thanks for letting me stay in your room. I needed to feel safe. I know I'm too old to act like such a Sissy Mary.

I owe you big time for not laughing. Not telling.

I lied about what was wrong. Yes, I had a nightmare, but not about that Amityville book. This was way worse than bleeding wallpaper or red eyes at the window.

I wasn't even sure whether the dream WAS a dream or something else, an echo or a . . . memory. But the more I thought about it, the more real it got and that scared me, Reg, because it was worse than any movie, no shit.

And after encounter I was sure. I wish to God I'd never gone, but I did, and now there's no pretending.

I don't know if it's even fair to dump this on you. It's okay if you never say a word. That might be better.

It's just, I'm afraid if I don't get it out, it'll eat me up.

I know that sounds stupid, but . . . it's murky, so . . . sorry if my narrative thread is tangled.

Miss Solomon's always on my back about that.

He attempts a laugh, a crackle of sound, like twigs snapping, one of the saddest things I've ever heard.

I must've been ten, maybe, when it started. We went to Feinsmith's. Father Fran had complimented that poster I'd made for Catholic Schools Week. Remember they hung it for the special Mass? I think Ma still has it up in that cabinet in the attic. Anyway, he said, "Think what you could do with decent supplies."

I told him Dad wasn't thrilled about my drawing, how he said art was for girls. Father said, "That's a shame, Evan, a sin. Talents are from God. It's your duty to use them."

So he took me downtown, bought me a box of pastels and some drawing paper and this book, *Anatomy for the Artist.* I told him Mom'd kill me for looking at a book with actual naked people, but Father said not to worry. It was our secret. He said he'd keep it at the rectory and I could look at it there, bring my supplies and draw.

I was so excited about private art lessons. When he dropped me home, I told Father it was the best gift ever. I hugged him, and I noticed the muscle in his jaw twitching like worms under the skin. He just looked at me, coughed a couple times, and said real low, "I'm glad."

We'd spend hours drawing, first from photos in the book, then posing for each other. He said it was okay to be shy, but there was nothing wrong with my body. It was God's greatest creation.

Still, it was strange seeing him in only a pair of shorts—even stranger to sit in my underwear while he drew. But I got used to it, and it was Father, so it had to be okay.

He called it our special time.

Some Saturdays we'd just drive around town. It was cool when he'd slide me next to him to steer. He'd put his arm across the seat back, his fingers hovering, tickling my neck. He'd always say to watch the road, but sometimes I'd catch him, looking at me smiling.

We'd drive to the park and sit, looking at the baseball diamond, talking, sometimes saying a rosary. I remember being there once, just before they flooded it for skating. Father was distracted. Kept forgetting which mystery we were on. Finally, he started "Descent of the Holy Spirit" for the third time, and I said, "What's wrong, Father?"

He asked if I ever told anyone about our lessons. When I shook my head no, he said, "Atta boy," ruffling my hair. "If you do, we'll probably have to stop being friends."

I got so upset, 'til he said, "Don't worry, Evan. I was teasing. God brought us together." Then he smiled and said, "I've got a special surprise. You like dogs, don't you?"

I hit stop. This is creeping me out. Not just the story, how he's telling it. Almost sounds like three people on the tape. There's Evan, age sixteen, narrator. But his voice sounds deeper when he's quoting Father Fran. And it's younger somehow when he says his childhood parts, like he's reliving it. I consider ejecting it; instead, I hit Play.

> **We drove for a while, toward the country, past the town dump. Finally, he turned the station wagon into a driveway with this small sign that said B.A.R.K., Beacon Acres Rescue Kennel. As we parked, I saw high, chain-link fencing in back. Father said his friend Carole worked for B.A.R.K. "She said stop by anytime. Gave me a key."**
>
> **As we closed the car doors, I heard this unearthly howling.**
>
> **"That'll be Kaspar," Father grinned, putting an arm around my shoulder. "Close your eyes."**
>
> **I couldn't help peeking as he guided me down a path. The fencing turned out to be a row of cages. I sensed frantic movement as we passed. Finally stopping, he whispered, "Eyes closed?" I nodded and Father said, "Good, now give me your hand."**
>
> **I squirmed as sticky warmth slicked my palm, but Father's grip was strong. Chuckling, he said, "Open your eyes."**
>
> **I did, seeing the source of the slobber—and that crazy yowling: the biggest dog I'd ever seen. On his hind legs, claws grasping the fence, he looked like a monster from some Saturday horror flick. But his face was sweet with a shaggy bison beard, one pale eye, and a hollowed knot of fur where the other eye should've been.**

"My God." I look at the dog in the painting. Studying its face, I notice it for the first time: a single eye, light blue. It's him, Kaspar.

> **"He likes you."**
>
> **This made me nervous. I hoped he wasn't talking about the slimy pink thing sprouting between Kaspar's legs.**
>
> **Father either read my mind or followed my eyes, because he said, "Don't be embarrassed, Evan; it's only natural. He's excited about our visit, that's all. Down, boy!"**

Then he unlocked Kaspar's pen and led me in. The dog immediately rolled on its back whimpering, tail beating the chain-link.

"Atta boy!" Father knelt, roughing the spiky coat. Starting at Kaspar's neck, working downward, his large hands moved toward the animal's groin. I stood numb, as he rubbed and squeezed, murmuring, moving in rhythm.

In a few minutes, it was finished. Father wiped his sticky hands through the dog's fur, stood and grinned.

"All right then. Now he's calm enough to take for a run."

When I didn't answer, Father laughed and said, "It's okay, Evan. Remember, Genesis says God gave man dominion over the beasts."

He coughs, then there's a click, as if he's stopped the tape. That's followed by silence until the player buzzes.

"Shit!"

Sure the tape's broken, I nearly press Stop, but then he resumes. At first it's garbled, like he's underwater, then a crackle, and his voice comes out clear.

... going to B.A.R.K. every weekend, only taking Kaspar out if no one was there. Otherwise, we'd walk other dogs. When it was just us, Father'd take me right to Kaspar's pen for his ritual. Sometimes he'd ask me to join him, saying "Don't fret, Evan. I'd never ask you to do anything wrong."

One day I said okay.

Father hugged me, then took my hand. When we touched Kaspar that way, it was like watching a movie, unreal. I felt scared, but kind of excited, too.

After, on the path, I knew something had changed; Father wouldn't look at me. I started crying, and he rubbed my shoulders, said, "Evan, if you want, I'll take you home and we won't come again."

I nodded, wiping my face on my sleeve.

Then he went red, saying, "Naturally, you'll need to return your drawing supplies. And when we get to your house, I'll speak with your parents." He scared me, the way his fingers dug into my shoulders, his face . . . and now, bringing up Mom and Dad. I asked, "Why Father? Why do you have to talk to them?"

Tapping a Winston from his pack, he lit it, took a long draw, and said, "I have to explain why we can no longer be friends. I need to tell them what you did." Smoke poured from his nose, like a dragon's, as he spoke. "What you did with Kaspar was wrong, Evan. Evil. Your parents deserve to know."

Crying again, spluttering, I yelled, *"NO! YOU WANTED ME TO DO IT! I WAS ONLY TRYING TO MAKE YOU HAPPY!"*

He slapped my face, dropped his cigarette, ground it out with his shoe. Then he hugged me, stroked my hair, said, "God has asked me to test you, Evan. He considers you a special soul, but you must be purified. And I'm to help."

I asked what he meant. Father stared into my eyes for a long time. "Evan, a special soul meets unique challenges. You've been chosen by God for great things. But there's a darkness that feeds on exceptional grace. It's as if you have a demon within. Today, praise God, we've identified it as a demon of lust. And that is the first step toward victory. Do you want to vanquish the demon, Evan? Do you want to serve the Lord?"

"Yes, Father."

"Atta boy, Evan, good. But you cannot do it alone. And you won't have to. You see, God has brought us together that I might help you achieve all He has planned. You must rely on me, Evan. Will you do that? Will you put your faith in me?"

I shivered. He wrapped his coat around me, gave me a piece of gum, placing the mint strip on my tongue like a communion wafer. In the car, I said, "I trust you with my life, Father."

"With your very soul. But you must promise not to breathe a word about the things we'll do. If you tell, if you break this trust,

it will be a grave betrayal to God. You'll be just another Judas then, and He'll punish us both for your weakness. Understand?"

All I really understood was I'd done something wrong, and I was about to lose Father. So I said, "Yes, Father Fran. Please don't tell my parents. I'll do everything you say."

"You bastard." I lean against the car window, stare out; the garage swims like the windshield's rainy. I stop the tape. I can't process what I've heard. How to reconcile this poor, betrayed kid with the guy who taught me to tie my shoes, tweezed out my slivers?

I haven't recalled that stuff for so long—the goofy rhyme he sang to help me make a bow, how he'd distract me with multiplication tables as he loosened a splinter—and now every thought of him's linked to this freakin' painting and what I've learned. I hammer a fist against my thigh, masking emotion with physical pain.

Pages of his words go with whatever else is on the tape, but I can't take anymore. Mister Alberti said I'm not ready to carry his weight.

"You were right, Zio Joe." I grimace saying it, wiping my nose on my sleeve, too gouged to reach for a glove compartment napkin.

A sudden realization: Mister Alberti knows. Dad must've told him about Father Fran. Maybe I should bring the tape to the restaurant, ask him. See if he can tell me what happened on encounter. But first I need to hear the rest, read his pages, exhume his misery. There's no going back; God, I wish I could.

After that, things changed. We still got together most Saturdays, but stopped going to B.A.R.K. Usually we'd stay at the rectory, or ride in his car. A couple times we went to the movies.

Dad was pissed I wasn't around to help at home, but Mom said it was good I spent time with Father. She said he was "so good to take an interest in the kids like he does." No one noticed his special interest in me, or questioned when he'd pull me from class to "help with a little rectory project." Or when he'd give me presents: Wrigley's gum, comic books, religious medals.

His voice starts to break. I can't tell whether it's emotion or the crappy tape. I lean close to the speaker.

Reggie, I don't know how to say the worst. Some of it's locked in this drawer in my head I don't dare open. Because what I do remember . . . let's just say it's . . . um

His voice gets even quieter.

. . . it's real bad.

There's a long silence then; all I hear is faint crying. I crank the volume to MAX; static fills the Tahoe, crackling dead air. I'm thinking that's all, when his voice blasts, reverbing in my head. I twist the knob to normal and freeze as I hear,

I thought of killing myself. The stuff he did . . . I get flashes. The journal poems, that's mostly what they are, images: the pinprick pattern on the ceiling of Father's station wagon. I'd count dots as he . . . I, I can picture diamond shapes on the hall runner in the rectory. I see it in dreams, but worse, when I'm awake . . .
   He used to lay me on that rug and he'd . . . he'd put his hands and . . . mouth . . . on me. He'd say not to look, to keep my eyes closed or study the stained glass Saint Agnes and her lamb. Sometimes I thought I'd hear her whisper, "Sweet boy, be still," but really it was him I heard.
   The worst part is . . . there were times I liked it, Reg, the way it felt. And I know God will never forgive me for that.

He's crying again—not faint now, bawling. I join him in his fear and shame. When he starts talking again, his voice is different, mechanical.

He gave me wine, "blood to seal our covenant." I needed it, Reg. It helped blur time. After, in the confessional, he'd make me

"unburden myself," describe things we'd done. Sometimes as I talked, I'd hear him breathing, and I knew what he was doing.

Reg, so many times I wanted to just let it gush out to you or Mom. I even came close to telling Ro once. But I was so scared.

Father said we'd go to hell if I told, but if I stayed the course, my reward would be great. He said, "Each time we partake of the flesh, we're closer to conquering the demon, nearer God."

He said we were "purging my evil urges by acting on them." When I told him I'd never had those urges, he said the demon was trying to destroy our progress.

So I decided it must be God's will. And if He allowed it, so should I. Sometimes during Mass, when Father's hand would stroke mine as I handed him the chalice, I wanted to scream and scream. But I never did.

Exhausted, I hit Function: AM radio, low and out of tune. I rub my forehead, glance at my watch: 11:54. Amazing how much shit you can slog through before lunch. I can't believe I'm spending winter break huddled in a freezing garage, reliving the freak show that was my father's childhood. I'd have preferred Cancun. I laugh despite not having experienced anything remotely humorous in, oh, eleven months.

Catching my reflection in the rearview, I'm puzzled. I'm laughing, right? So why's my face that sick gray shade? And what's with the purple splotches where my eyes used to be? I look like laughing crap, Dorian Gray in reverse. Somewhere a portrait of me is looking GOOOOD. I laugh again; the sound makes me stop. Too much like Dad's taped laughter: hollow, humorless.

Suddenly starving, reaching for the center console, I lift the lid. It's stuffed with typical Dad debris: napkins and sporks, thumb-smudged sunglasses, about fifty ketchups. I dig beneath crumpled sweetener packets, empty Funyuns bags, and a blank 1997 day planner. Pay dirt: half a pack of Hubba Bubba and an unopened Slim Jim.

Always jerky-averse, I shuck wrappers, jam in three gum cubes. They're powder sweet/rock hard, cold or old; not sure which. Beginning to work them, my jaw aches as they soften. Glancing left, I realize I've chosen the passenger seat, like I'd half-expected him. I'd offer him the last piece of gum; he'd spot the lump in my cheek and say, "Can you spare it?" Mourning his absence for the millionth time, I rummage again, face the fact: Jerky's my only relatively edible option.

My wrapper inspection reveals no expiration date. Gambling that "hydrolyzed gluten and mechanically separated chicken" probably *can't* spoil, I peel the plastic sheath. Raising the zesty stick, I salute the painting. "This one's for you, Dad." Shifting gum-gob to my cheek, I gnaw jerky, gathering pages. I lift the book, open to the sliced section, and reinsert the sheaf. The cut edges match perfectly. Swallowing the salty, processed animal, I read,

I'm ten years old.

It's my second dose of pay dirt: no missing pages. This picks up right where the chopped entry—

We're in the rectory at Saint Anne's and

—left off. I continue.

I remember hanging at the rectory drawing. Who knows why I'm dreaming that—so long ago. Maybe because Tony's acting so weird about Father. Still, there's something else, a feeling. And a smell: Wrigley's spearmint. And some dog. God, I'm going nuts. We never had a dog like this, just that beagle when I was little. This is a big, hairy thing—Wolfhound? Mental. Must sleep.

March 3, 1976 (middle of night)
Just woke with the raunchiest image: that dog, it only had one eye. I'm sure of it. And I think it was called . . . Cat (?) No that's asinine. Who'd name a dog Cat? I still can't remember who owned it. Why do I keep thinking it was Father Fran's? Guess I could ask him about it after class tomorrow. I wanted to talk to him anyway, about Tony.

126

"Don't, Dad!" God, I'm like those people who yell at the screen during a slasher flick.

Cripes! My head hurts. Wonder if I should risk sneaking to the kitchen. Mom's got an open bottle of Fontana di Papa in the pantry. Tastes like horse piss, but if I choke down a cup, it helps me sleep. Mom'd brain me if she found out, but it's not like I haven't been drinking wine since I was—Whoa! I almost said "since I was ten." But that's crazy, isn't it?

So he didn't remember it. How's that possible? Some kind of shock or repressed memory? I wonder what brought it back on encounter. He said something happened there that made him realize his dreams were real.

"Got room for an old man in there?"

I scramble to hide the journal pages as Gramp climbs in the car. He doesn't notice me shifting the stack of paper under my butt cheek.

He avoids looking at me; probably thinks I'll freak. Wonder what he's heard from Mom. As he messes with the auto compass on the dash, minutes pass; finally he prepares to speak.

I brace for the force of his words. There's melancholy in the clearing of his throat, in the slight clack of dentures as he does a slow exhale. "You *tryin'* to kill the battery?" He turns the key to OFF. "Amazing there's any juice left. When's the last time you started 'er up?"

Not what I expected. Then again, when it comes to communicating, Gramp makes Dad look like Mister Sensitivity. I decide to pass on car chat, get right to it.

Mimicking his abbreviated way of talking, what I call Gramp-speak, I say, "She call you?"

"No, I'm a friggin' psychic. 'Course she called. And she was none too happy to have to."

"Sorry."

"Least your mother was able to save a little face. She didn't have to get past my guard dog. Lucky thing Cerberus is on one of her bus trips."

I always laugh when he calls Gran that; she usually does, too, before smacking him.

"So, what's this all about?" He seems uncomfortable asking.

Feelings are foreign territory for the old guy. He's shifting in his seat, wearing an expression like somebody trying to pass a stone.

"What did Mom tell you?"

"What do you think?"

"I think this would go quicker if you'd stop answering my questions with questions."

During the silence that follows, I seriously expect him to cuff me. Instead he asks, "You sure about that?" a sly grin crinkling his lined face. Then he does cuff me, but in a playful grizzly way. Twisting me into a headlock—the closest he'll get to a hug—he spots the painting.

He stares, color sapped from his jowls. A sweat pearl slips from under his cap, coming to rest in the crease above his eye. He doesn't blink, just sits, fixed on the painting, face white as his hair. He's starting to spook me; I hope this isn't how a stroke looks. I'm about to remind him to breathe, when he says, "Where in hell did that come from?" his voice missing its gruff vigor.

Then he coughs, a series of phlegmy lung-rattlers. I'm torn between ducking for cover and calling for backup.

"You okay?"

He waves me off, rummaging in the glove compartment. Hawking an alarming glob into a napkin, he says, "He painted that in high school."

"So you've seen it before?"

"Not the finished product, but I caught him working on it in the attic. He tried to hide it from me. Guess you can see why."

"Well, I suppose it is a little disturbing."

"A little? That's soft-pedaling, don't you think?"

"I guess."

"Son of a bitch painted one hell of a nightmare."

"I think that's just what it is."

After glancing back toward the house for just a moment, he looks at me carefully and says, "You sound pretty certain. What makes you think so?"

I know not to underestimate him. Gramp does an award-winning bumpkin act, but there are no flies on him.

"I don't know. It looks like a dream, you know? I mean it can't be from real life. Right?"

It might just be imagination, but he seems reluctant to look me in the eye.

"I'd say it's some kind of allegory. Looks like he's telling a story. Not one I'd like to hear, I'll tell you that."

"So, when you 'caught him' working on it, you didn't ask what it meant?"

"Hell no, but I did tell him to be damn sure his mother didn't see it. Your gran would've blown a goddamn gasket. I'm guessing that's what your mother did today, huh?"

We both grin in spite of ourselves as I say, "I guess she did."

"I won't ask where you got it, but how exactly did you explain that to your mother?"

"I told her I painted it."

"Shit, boy! Why'd you do that?"

"Well, she assumed it was a self-portrait, and it seemed easier to just let her."

"Whooboy. No wonder she was riled. She says you been acting out. That you been 'distant,' whatever the hell that means." He studies his hands. "Junior, she says you been acting . . . like him."

He gestures toward the portrait, gaze lingering. I ignore the *Junior* (bigger fish) and count to ten before I speak. "You said he painted it in high school. Do you remember anything about that time?"

"Like what?" It's the tone he usually reserves for liberals.

"I don't know, did he seem upset about something?"

"He was always upset about something. Your father was that type of kid. *Sensitive*." He says it like a dirty word. "Your gran didn't help. Always asking how he was feeling."

"What about you?"

His sharp stare's followed by a grudging, "What?"

I don't back down. "Did *you* ever ask how he was feeling?"

He hesitates; when he does answer, I can tell the words grieve him. "Not my job. I was his father, not his friend." His lip curls, an anti-smile. "Besides, he had someone to talk to."

"Father Fran?"

Judging by his expression, Father's as appealing as a rat omelet. Gramp glowers, his reaction involuntary, instantaneous. Silent.

Ignoring his disgusted look, I repeat my question. "Was it Father Fran?"

"Was it Father Fran," he parrots in a pinched whine that sounds nothing like me.

Face flushed, I reach for the door handle. I'm about to spring the latch and jump, when he clears his throat and touches my shoulder.

Quickly sleeve-swiping his eyes, he says, "Sorry, Evan. I really am a nasty bastard."

"You really are." I'm relieved when he smiles. "So, I get the feeling you weren't a big Father Fran fan." I resist the urge to say that three times fast.

"Hardly."

Trying to project disinterest, I shrug. "How come? Did he do something?"

Lifting his cap, he scrubs at his forehead with the balls of his fists. He's about to divulge something big. Not that it'll be a surprise after what I've learned.

"It's nothing specific, Ev. It's just . . . he always had that not-of-this-earth attitude. Drove me nuts. And your grandmother! He just about pissed holy water where she was concerned."

"Gramp?" So much for disinterest; I'm shaking.

"Yeah, Evan, what is it?"

I'm so close to telling, it's not funny. Why shouldn't I? Who am I protecting? Besides, he said it himself. He wanted them to know. I'm about to punch the Function button; blast the cassette. Then Dad's face flashes in my head and, like in the dream, he says, "Sssssssssssssssssssssssssss ssSSSSSSSssssshhhhhhhhhhhhhhhhhhhhhhhhhhhhhhhhhhhhhHHHHHHHHH hhhhssssssssssssssssssssssSSSHHHHHhhhhhhhhhhhhhsssSSSSSSSSSSSSsssssss shhhhhhhhhhhhhhhhhhhhhhhhhhhhh."

Snapping back to myself, I realize Gramp's shaking my shoulders, leaning into my face, calling my name, "Evan, speak to me, Evan," like in some old movie. All I can think is *He must have had salami for lunch. I hope he doesn't slap my face.*

"Ouch!" I rub my cheek. "Did you have to smack me?"

"What just happened? One minute you're asking me something, the next you're having an episode! What's the matter with you, Junior?"

This time I can't ignore it. "DON'T CALL ME THAT!"

We're both shocked at my sudden rage. I've never yelled at him before.

"I'm sorry, Gramp. I just . . . do you know how it feels to always be compared to him? It's like . . . everyone's picking me apart looking for pieces of him."

"Nobody expects you to be like him, Evan, but there's no denying you're his spitting image. I guess maybe you're our second chance—and we're afraid of blowing this one too."

"Great. So you're waiting for me to self-destruct. Or worse, you expect me to redeem the Galloways, like it's my mission to restore the family glory. Well, either way, it's not fair. It's like . . . just being me is never good enough."

He just looks at me, no response.

"Oh forget it. I'm not making any sense. It's just . . . I know what made him do it."

The air's sucked from the car, like a plane cabin losing pressure. It's not 'til I look at Gramp that I remember to breathe. He does too. We take big gulps, like we're about to dive.

He's first to speak. "Who told you about him?"

"No one exactly told me." I'm afraid to mention the tape or journal, feeling guilt for spying on the dead. "I just found out some stuff."

He grabs my wrist. "Your gran best not have told you," his green eyes—a senior version of Dad's—probe my own, "because we agreed to honor your parents' wishes. They never wanted you to know."

My brain lurches, realizing Mom knows about Father Fran. And my wrist is starting to hurt; he's not going to let go 'til I answer.

"No, Gran didn't say anything."

"Was it that snoop Alberti? He never could keep his trap shut!"

"I said nobody told me! Jeez, what's the difference how I found out?"

I pull my hand away; the skin's Indian-burn red. Waiting for what's next, I don't expect him to say, "Let's drive."

Before I can respond, he hits the visor button, opening the garage door, and we're backing into the driveway. Gramp clips the holly hedge with the passenger mirror, spilling a powdery curtain of snow.

"Where are we going?"

"To pay our respects."

"The cemetery?"

"Yep."

We pass the space where Mom's Outback was parked. She must've bailed after calling the cavalry. I'm relieved not to have to face her.

I dread this; I have zero interest in a crisper pilgrimage. Wish he'd skip it. Opening my mouth to say so, I really see him: eyes cemented to the road, hands clenched so tight his knuckles threaten to split the skin.

He reminds me of this statue. We went to Gloucester, Massachusetts one summer, and there was this huge figure of that guy from the fish sticks box, gripping a ship's wheel for dear life. That's how Gramp looks now, like he's steering through a squall. Only the squall's inside him. If I break his concentration, I think he might capsize us, send Dad's SUV off the road. However much I don't want to visit my father, it seems Gramp needs to even more.

Wish I could turn on the radio to break this tension. But, afraid to draw his attention to the cassette, I don't dare. So we ride mute. It's a relief when I spot the cemetery. At least I'll get to vacate this freaking car.

"Hey," I tap his arm, "you missed the turn."

"What?"

"The cemetery. You passed by."

He looks at me, features askew with focus and puzzlement. Then he says, "Leave the driving to me, Junior. I know where I'm going."

Heading left at Saint Anne's, straight onto East Main, he keeps going past the plaza. I notice the Applebee's sign; used to be Burger Shack, where Mister P freaked out at lunch. The Card Shoppe's still there. Clerk's about a hundred; probably the woman from his journal.

He turns onto Colonial Ave. I'm afraid to ask where we're headed. That look on his face—spooky. I try convincing myself it's one of his crazy "shortcuts" that take you miles out of your way.

We're leaving town now, past the old Tri-bury Drive-in. He slows the car, and I gasp, "Omigod." There's a faded wooden sign to my right. It says B.A.R.K.

"Why are we here?"

He snaps, "I said, let me do the driving." Then he looks at me and adds, "You okay? Look like you seen a ghost."

About to answer, I see he's making a left onto Avalon Hill. He'd just been waiting for an oncoming car. But I mean—HOLY SHIT!—it's the place. I have to ask.

"What'd that mean, B.A.R.K.?"

"Oh, like the sign said, it was a humane society place. Stray dogs, mostly. Your father volunteered there Saturdays—de-crapping kennels and stuff—with Father Fran. Couple of regular Assisis, those two."

He slows the car again, and I guess we're here. There's an iron gate set into the stone wall. The sign says Avalon Hill Memorial Park. As Gramp drives through the gate, he heaves a mondo sigh that turns into a sequence of coughs, forcing him to pull over. He opens the window and hacks one into the snow. Then, he says, "Ready?"

I nod, but my gut's a bowling ball of second thoughts.

We climb twisty hills, the car occasionally fishtailing on scuds of ice. Trees overhang the narrow road, branches weighted down.

I've never been in this cemetery before, even though it's only a few miles from town. The Galloway relatives are in All Saint's, Home of the Crisper. I look out over rows of headstones half-buried in snow, wondering who's here.

In answer to my unasked question, Gramp eases the Tahoe partway off-road, into crusted snow, and says, "Here's the place."

I wait for him to cut the engine, but he just points. "It's about twenty yards straight beyond that big tulip tree. You better take my jacket, or you'll freeze." Twisting to shuck his coat, he winces at bursitis in both shoulders.

I shrug into warm flannel, breathing its Gramp smell. "Aren't you coming?"

He's focused straight out the windshield, but I can still see tears as he replies, "I can't."

Stepping into bitterness, I slam the door. My feet skid on frozen slush. Still, I can't resist heel-punching the skin of puddle ice near the car. It makes that seal bark shatter. Then, picking through deeper snow, I hear the automatic window. Gramp leans toward the passenger side. For a second, I think he might tell me to forget it. I wish he would.

He struggles to speak; I strain toward his voice as he says, "Evan, there's an angel on the headstone. A baby angel."

"I told the girl no onions. Do you people need written instructions?"

The woman brandishes a forkload of slimy rings like a challenge.

"I just deliver the friggin' bread, crotchety bat." That wasn't meant to go beyond thought stage. But either she's a major clairvoyant or I blurted; the lady looks pissed.

She drops her fork. Onions fly. "What did you say?"

Her dining companion, pin-striped, fiftyish (nephew?), eyes me with panicked wonder. Did I pick up on his secret name for Auntie? Maybe I'm the psychic.

Thinking fast, speaking slowly, I overdo enunciation. "I'll . . . just remind her what you said. Sorry 'bout that."

It's a classic TV-style verbal diversion, but it seems to work on manners-impaired patrons. She triple-dabs, like she's applying a smile with her napkin, anger deflating.

"Oh, all right then, dear. No harm done."

Swapping bread basket for offending salad, I escape. Back in the kitchen, I lean against the walk-in, wishing I could live inside. Leaving the world behind, I'd wallow in frosty solitude and chocolate torta.

But the restaurant's a nuthouse. I haven't had a minute to think, or stop thinking, since Dad's car. My brain's on overload: the journal, the tape, the fear there's worse to come.

And Gramp's bombshell. After my cemetery revelation, I think Father Fran may be a dead end. It was so long ago.

"Hey, Renoir! You going to just stand there, or bus me some tables?"

Since I started on the mural, Angie's been on this famous artist kick, like, "Will Matisse kindly water table two?" or "Yo, Vincent, step away from that bread knife!" It's about a seven on the irritation scale, somewhere between bleeding gums and SATs.

"Sorry, Ang'."

I feel guilty for hiding out. Time check: twenty-five minutes gone. Whoa, these gaps are out of control. Maybe I'm a werewolf; they're always losing time. I growl at my steel-door reflection. Yeah, I'm overtired.

In the dining room, the crowd's finally thinned. Only Onion Lady, her escort, and two other couples remain. Lupo and I start the nightly ritual. It's barely 9:15, but with luck his vacuuming/my table wiping will hint the stragglers out, and I'll be home by 11:00.

Mister Alberti hates when we rush the customers. He says a good meal's like a Mass; it's wrong to chase people out before the final blessing. Of course, he also claims his peach gelato's "sweeter than a virgin's tit" and "breaking wind is the body's way of praying."

But tonight, Angie's in charge. She persuaded Mister A to take a night off. She said he's been rundown, and since the *History Channel*'s running a Mussolini bio, she convinced him to stay home, put his feet up, and jeer.

It sucks, majorly, him not being here. I'm desperate to discuss what I've learned: Pettafordi, Father Fran. Why I'm really not a junior. Maybe tomorrow; I can't wait to just collapse tonight.

I called Mom earlier, apologized via machine; figured it's my only hope of avoiding a scene later. Wise move, because I'm not sure what I might say.

Even though my discoveries have slammed me, they've also made me feel bigger somehow. Wiser. Like knowing's given me this magic energy: the strength of not caring. It's bizarre, everyone hiding the truth from me for so long. What for? They thought I'd break?

I mean, sure I've felt like my guts are on the outside since hearing Dad's tape, and yeah, I heaved at the cemetery. Curse you, Slim Jim! But that was just physical. Mentally I'm okay.

I'm not saying it's *not* a big deal. The shit my father went through will provide nightmare fodder for-like-ever. And what I learned at the cemetery, I can't deny it's changed everything.

But despite all that, nothing beats knowing. It's the next step that's tricky. All I'm sure of is encounter is crucial. It was obviously his turning point. On the tape, he said everything came back to him *after what happened on encounter.* I have to go, learn what that means. It matters. Even though it has the capacity to detonate what's left of the Galloway brood, I need to know. Maybe that's selfish, but—

Lupo hauls a loaded dish bin to the kitchen. I scan the dining room. Our noisy housekeeping's driven out the lingerers. It's just past ten. I know I should put in some mural time while they finish shutting down, but somehow I just can't face Dad—even in painted form.

It's so tempting to redo his Judas face: shrink the ears, add a nose ring, anything to make him less Dadlike. But I don't think it's the right thing to do. Now that I understand it's an illustration of his betrayal, code for what Father Fran did, I guess I should leave it alone. Let it stand as a sort of memorial to Dad's pain. Still, it's hard to look at.

So is the painting in the backseat. When Gramp dropped me here, he promised he'd put it in the Tahoe's wayback, under the old picnic blanket. I know Mom won't look there, which is good; I'm afraid to think what she'd do with it. I need to protect it, like evidence. Maybe I should give it back to Aunt Reg. She kept it safe all these years.

What about Aunt Reg? Do I tell her what I found? The cassette was meant for her ears, not mine. Would she be pissed, or hurt, that I listened to it?

"—okay?" Angie touches my forehead, checking for fever, I suppose.

"What? Yeah, fine." I swat her away.

"Well, you don't look fine. Your face is whiter than Lupo's apron. Course, that ain't sayin' much. Remind me to bleach that rag."

"Hey look, if you don't mind, I'll just bag the painting tonight. I think you're right. Maybe I'm coming down with whatever your dad's got."

Her eyes puddle. "I don't think so."

"What is it, Angie? What'd I say?"

"Nothin'. I'm okay. It's just . . . my dad. They think it's Alzheimer's, Ev. Don't it figure? He's about to stick me with this friggin' place, and he won't even realize what a great job I'm doing runnin' it. Ah well, that's nothin' new. Bastard never appreciated me anyway."

She breaks, and I hug her; her fist's a tight ball against my chest. We're still pressed close when the sleigh bell on the front door jingles. Our heads snap toward the sound.

Mister Alberti's like a spectral version of himself. He stands in striped pajamas and corduroy slippers—no coat, no gloves. His comb-over's undone, the slack brown fringe plastered to the side of his head, hanging below his ear.

The three of us stand for a minute, speechless. Then, realizing she's still in my arms, Angie clears her throat, moving away. She's about to speak when Mister Alberti launches like an elderly attack dog. He must've misinterpreted our embrace, because he's yelling at Angie, alternating between calling her a *puttana* and saying, "Theresa, how could you do this?"

It's scary; there's this fire in his eyes as he yanks her apron, swings her away from me, nearly flinging her into the specials board.

He comes for me next. I shield my face as spindly arms wheel and strike. He packs a wallop for an old guy, but more painful is the look on his face as he says, "Evan, you betrayed you Uncle Zio. My Theresa. *Voi fatti lei sporca.*"

Finally, Lupo runs in from the kitchen. Embracing Mister Alberti carefully from behind, he hums softly in the old man's ear, until Mister A's breathing returns to normal. I recognize the tune, "You Are My Sunshine."

Singing along in Italian, "*il mio soltanto sole,*" little by little Zio returns, that odd flame flickering out.

Once he's quiet, Angie goes to him, strokes his cheek, and lifts the flap of hair, smoothing it into place.

"Pop, you feel better now?"

"Theresa?"

"No, it's Angie, Pop. Theresa's . . . gone," she looks at Lupo, "up to bed."

"Oh, sure. Sure. Angie. Did they deliver the chianti?"

"Yeah, Pop. No worry; everything's set."

"You're a good girl, Angie. A motormouth, but a good girl."

She turns and whispers to Lupo. Kissing her father's forehead, she says, "Okay, Buster Brown. Time to close shop. Lurch here will bring you home. I'll catch up later."

He just stares, hands beginning to shake.

"Did I say something wrong? Where are my shoes?"

"Don't worry, Pop. You were just sleepwalking, that's all."

"Sleepwalking? Mama mia, like a baby!" Squeezing my hand, he says, "You take care of her. Promise me?"

I look to Angie for guidance, and she nods slightly, so I say, "Yes, Zio. I promise."

He hugs me 'til a sob shakes his brittle frame. Choking it off, he lets go. Even before he speaks, I see he's the real Mister Alberti again. Hand to heart like a pledge, he says, "He was just a kid then, you father. I shouldn't have said the things I did. Forgive a pigheaded old man?"

Before I can answer—or ask him to explain—Lupo herds Mister A toward the back door. I'm left in the empty dining room, spluttering like a stalled car, my brain in overdrive.

What's next? Is my father's face going to appear among the to-go menus and scat sing a belated suicide note? Will I discover Kaspar's head newly mounted behind the desk in Mister A's office? Or will Angela levitate above the cash register, dispensing after-dinner mints from her butt? I swear nothing would surprise me.

Speaking of Ang', where the heck is she? I check the stairwell to the basement office. No lights, no sign of her. She's not in the banquet room either. That leaves the kitchen. Heading toward the swinging door, I hear water running in the ladies room. I wait outside. Anxious, I press my ear to the door. I hear muffled sobs—and swearing—inside.

My hand's on the knob when it swings open. Everything I'd planned to say evaporates at the sight of Angie, her face a waxy mask, streaked with mascara. I finally manage, "So."

She doesn't acknowledge me, just shoves past, toward the dining room. I trail her as she checks oils and vinegars. She's plainly not planning to speak to me. I don't care. I'm through letting people decide whether they want to deal with me. I stick to her like a shoeful of gum.

Finally, admitting I'm here, she turns, blasts me, "What? What do you want from me?"

Once my head stops echoing, I answer, "I just wanted to make sure you were okay." All right, that's not the-whole-truth-and-nothing-but. Still, it seems like a safe reply.

"BULLSHIT! You be straight with me or get out of my face. I got work to do."

I expect her to plow through me again, but she doesn't. Instead, she stands, arms crossed, defying me to speak. So I do.

"Who's Theresa?"

Her nostrils pulse, and I get the distinct impression she'd rather deck me than continue this conversation. Then she says, "Theresa's my older sister," and slips around me and heads for the oak buffet where they keep glasses and stuff.

I follow. I know she can see me in the mirrored buffet back. Catching her eye in the glass, I say, "I never knew you had a sister."

"Why would you?"

"I . . . it's . . . just odd your father never mentioned her."

"Yeah well, he mentioned her tonight, didn't he?"

"Um, he did, yeah." I'm thinking about him calling her *Theresa* and *whore*; I'm sure she is too. "What was that about?"

She smacks her hand against the buffet hard enough to clink glasses. "It's about time you stopped asking questions!"

"Okay, sorry."

I'm halfway to the coat room when she says, "No . . . look . . . Ev, I'm the one who's sorry."

She's crying again, but I don't care. As I duck into the alcove— thwack!—something hits me hard in the back. Ready to fight, I spin, pick up Angie's makeshift weapon, a jar of crushed red pepper. I'm tempted to wing it back, 'til I really see her.

She stands pole-straight, yet somehow seems slumped. Defeated. I can't muster anger. Instead, at the nearest table, I pull out two chairs. We sit.

Angie stares as if trying to melt my face with her heat vision. "God, you look so much like him it's scary."

"Yeah."

Suddenly blushing, she says, "I had such a crush on your father when he was young."

"Did you two ever—"

"NO! Jeez, I was a kid when your dad worked here. Besides, he only had eyes for her."

Sure of the answer, I still ask, "You mean Theresa?"

"Uh huh."

"So they dated or something?"

It takes her too long to reply. And her voice trembles as she says, "Something."

"Angie, please tell me. What'd my father do? That thing your dad said, '*fatti le sporca,*' what does that mean anyway?"

I expect her to yell again, but she doesn't. She doesn't say a thing. And her eyes, they're like pulled shades. Blank. Whatever Angie knows is locked behind amber eyes.

Defeated, I hit the coat room, grab my jacket, kill the alcove light, and stand in the dark.

From behind me Angie says, "You done her dirty. *Voi fatti lei sporca.* You done her dirty."

I'm struggling to reply when she whispers, "I better drive you home, it's getting late."

She's Lupo-quiet on the ride. I wrack my brain for some way to get her to talk. I'm desperate to know, sick with possibilities.

"Angie, please . . . I just want to understand all I can about him. If you're trying to protect me—or his memory—I'd, I'd rather hear the truth."

She chews her lip, wrestling tears, and says, "Ask your mother."

It's ringing.

After Gramp's surprise and the scene at Alberti's, not to mention Dad's hellacious book-on-tape, I needed to reconnect with my True North. So the minute Angie dropped me off, I dialed Florida.

Even though things were a tad strained last time we talked—meaning I was a complete douche—I know Lex'll be there for me. My flip side.

Still ringing. Hmm, I doubt she's out this late. From what she's said, Manatee Village shuts down at dusk. I must've dialed wrong. I hang up and try again, extra careful with number selection.

It's ringing again. Once. Twice. Maybe Lex is still pissed, avoiding me via caller ID. I'm about to give up when she answers.

I try for normal, but the words gush. "Hey, Philomena! God, I'm glad you're there. Things are out of control. I really need to talk . . . Lex?"

"She's um, a little busy right now. Can I tell her who's calling?"

The troglodyte tone is unmistakable: Wattrous. I'm thrown, can't imagine what he's doing there. No, that's the problem. I *can* imagine; that's why I suddenly want to gag.

"Hello? Are you still there?" It's Lex.

"I'm . . . uh," my voice grinds like damp gravel. I clear my throat. "Sorry to bother you."

"Evan, is that you? You sound strange. What's wrong?"

Knowing it's no use lying to her, I do anyway. "Nothing. I'm fine. Look, you're obviously busy. Call me if you feel like it. Tell Tyler I'm sorry to interrupt."

Before I can hang up, I hear her say, "Don't be a freak, Ev—"

I sit, surveying the room. The blue of the lava lamp illuminates Lex everywhere: photos, artwork, stuffed animals.

Climbing from the bed, I cross to my desk, avoiding the telltale floorboard. No way I want to wake Mom. Couldn't believe my luck when I got home and she was asleep.

Snatching Lex's card from my memo board, I read it aloud, "Two peas forever" like bitter spit on my tongue. God, it seems like a million years ago.

I drop the crumpled pod in the trash and fall on my bed, mentally scrolling through options: I could make some mural sketches, do some studying. Or maybe sneak to the garage, retrieve the cassette and journal. Listen. Read.

Amazingly, I'm asleep minutes later when the phone rings. I'm tempted to play the screening game myself. Caller ID flashes Florida; I can't resist.

"Howdy."

"Do I need to fly up there right now and step on your throat?"

"What, and miss out on Tyler Time?"

"Would you give it a frigging rest? Ever since I told you he's here, you've acted like a major shit heel."

The way I see it, I've got two choices: 1) Hang up, in which case we're back at square one; 2) Apologize; so no one's more shocked than me when I go for option 3) Cry like a wussy.

"Evan, please tell me what's wrong! You're freaking me out."

"I'm sorry, Lex. I don't mean to spoil your vacation. It's great, you and Tyler getting together, really. I was just surprised to find him there so late. I didn't realize things had got—"

"Okay genius, listen. I'm only saying this once. Yes, I like Tyler. He's a total hottie. Now brace yourself, I'm about to share the intimate details of what we were doing when you called."

"Lex, no!" I nearly drop the phone. "I really don't need to know!"

"Tyler and I have spent the past four nights together—listening?—rubber-cementing sequins onto thirty-six pairs of support hose. It was slightly less romantic than you'd imagine."

"You're joking."

"I wish. We tried hot glue, but it literally melted the freakin' hose. I think I have like third-degree burns on my wrist. Live and learn, I always say."

"Since when?"

"Okay, just stop. You're doing that thing."

"What thing?"

"Minimizing."

"What are you talking about?"

"You, my friend, are a minimizer."

"You mean like a teeny cheap person?"

"Not funny. And you know exactly what I mean. You call me, all whacked out, and then, when I ask what's the matter, you say everything's peachy."

"I never said peachy." She's not laughing. "Alexis?" I think I've blown it.

Sighing, a faint sign of life, she says, "Talk to me."

"I'm not sure what to say, where to start, what you'll think."

"Now I'm pissed. Since when do best friends edit for content? It's Alexis, Evan. Tell me what's wrong."

"The more I learn the worse it gets."

"Tell me!"

"There was this priest and Mister Alberti has another daughter, and my grandfather showed me this gravestone. I don't know, Lex, I—"

"Slow down. You're not making sense."

I know she's right, but how can I make her understand what I can't?

"I want you to take a deep breath and start over. Tell me everything."

"Okay," I inhale through my nose like Miss Lubeck taught us in Intro to Drama, letting it out through my mouth, I begin. "Aunt Reg had this painting my dad did after encounter . . . "

Throat dry, I glance at the clock; it's 1:53, and I haven't even gotten us to the restaurant. Lex hasn't said more than "Wow" and "Uh huh" for forty minutes. That's got to be her sustained silence personal best. Maybe she's asleep.

"You still there?"

"Of course. So, are you okay? I mean . . . it's a lot to find out."

"And I haven't told you all of it."

"I want you to."

"I know. But it's hard. When I was listening to that tape—the stuff with Father Fran—all I could think was *how did he not kill himself then?* I mean, how'd he survive it in one piece?"

"He didn't."

"What?"

"No one does."

As her voice fades, I see her so clearly: Smurf nightshirt, knees hugged to chin, alone in Aunt Bert's guestroom. Lost.

"He's gone, Lex. He can't hurt you anymore."

"He doesn't have to *be here* to hurt me."

"Lex, are you okay?"

"Yeah, it's just . . . I was thinking. I can almost understand your dad not wanting to live with the memories anymore. They're always there, you know? Like an oyster."

"What do you mean?"

"It's like . . . an oyster takes this grit, this dirt inside, and covers it over and over, coating it to mask the irritation. It creates this lustre, but at the heart there's just muck."

"And?"

"And it's the same with these memories, Father Fran, my stepdad. They're the nasty secrets our minds try to wipe clean. But instead of soothing it over . . . instead of a pearl . . . it's like," her voice wilts.

"What, Lex?"

"Instead of a pearl, there's only a seed, this black seed of shit and shame, and you'll try anything to cough it out. Some people drink, some starve themselves. Some even try to get rid of it by planting it in someone else. They're the worst. Finally, you realize it's always going to be there—so you settle for fooling people."

"Fooling them how?"

"Pretending mostly. That you're the smartest, the nicest, the funniest. That you're *just a little eccentric.*"

"Lex, you are all those things."

"See, I've fooled you, too. Sometimes I even fool myself, Evan. For a little while. But it always comes back, the guilt, the fear. You can't escape it anymore than you can change your fingerprints or your blood type. It's always there, because it's who you are."

"You're so much more, Lex—"

"And you know the only way to get rid of that filth is to cut it out, but you can't. It's rooted so deep in your soul, without it you'd be like a shucked oyster, dead empty."

"So what do you do?"

"You just accept it, learn to act as if."

"As if?"

"As if you're normal, as if you're not damaged goods. Some days it's easier than others."

"Do you think it was the same for my dad? Maybe that'd explain—" I can't say it.

"Explain what, Evan? Why he killed himself?"

My voice wavers. "Something else."

"What is it? Tell me; maybe I can help you figure it out."

"I know . . . I just . . . I'm not even sure. It's Mister Alberti's daughter, Theresa. He did something. Mister Alberti said he 'did her dirty.' "

I ignore her gasp.

"And that's all he said?"

"Pretty much."

"What about Angie? Did you ask her about it?"

"I did."

"Well, what'd she say?"

"The worst possible thing. She said I should ask my mother."

"So? Did you?"

"Are you nuts?"

"The jury's still out on that. Don't tell me you're not going to."

"No way! She'd probably descend on Alberti's, attack the old guy, burn the place down, who knows what."

"You owe it to her, Evan."

"I don't owe her anything. I thought you understood the way it is with her, Lex."

"Look, Evan. Don't take this wrong, but I think your perception's a bit skewed."

"What's that supposed to mean?" It comes out louder than I intended.

"It's like you think you invented grief. Give your mom a break. He was her husband."

"Well then she shouldn't have driven him out of his home."

"Maybe if you really talk to her, she'll surprise you."

"You're the one who's surprising me, Lex. What is this 'Kumbayah' crap?"

"I just think you owe it to both of you to try."

She refuses to get angry, which is making me mad. "That's easy for you to say from a friggin' thousand miles away! You don't have to deal with her."

"Are you really mad at me, Evan? Are you?"

"No."

"Because all I'm saying is, you've come this far, isn't it worth taking the next step? It's just a question."

I surprise myself by saying, "I'm not sure I can live with the answer."

"Can you live *not* knowing?"

I want to argue; instead I say, "Why do you always have to be right?"

"We all have our crosses to bear, I'm just glad I get to be yours."

"Ha ha."

"So, when are you planning to ask her?"

"I . . . don't . . . know."

"Well, no time like the present and all that. Why not do it now?"

"You *are* nuts!"

"So you've told me."

"It's quarter to three!"

"Evan, some things transcend the constraints of timeliness."

"What's that supposed to mean?"

"It means, do you honestly think there will ever be a *good* time to have this conversation? Personally, I have my doubts."

"So what are you saying? You just told me I need to ask her. Now you're saying I shouldn't?"

"Cripes, sometimes it's like talking to a hairbrush. NO! I'm not saying you shouldn't. I'm saying it's NEVER going to be easy, but it's important."

"I can't do it."

"Well, you'd better. Or else."

"What?"

"I'll do it for you."

"Yeah, right. What're you going to do, call her?" Even as I say it, I picture her singing in Mister Pettafordi's office. "Oh, God, you're serious."

"Evan, I swear, you call me back in one hour with details of your conversation, or I'm calling her myself."

"Why would you do that? I told you it's a bad idea to talk to her. She'll just go ape."

"Listen, Galloway, you got a whopper of a brain there, but that doesn't mean you have all the answers. Sometimes it takes someone just outside the bubble to see what's going on inside. Trust me. Talk to her. And remember, you've got one hour."

She hangs up, the dial tone a siren in my ear.

"Tell me about the baby."

I'm as shocked by the question as she is. It's not what I'd intended.

Her breath comes in a weak shiver, and I brace myself for Mom volume. But when she starts to talk, it's soft, like a bedtime story.

"We never wanted you to know . . . "

"What? That I was the replacement?"

"Evan, that's preposterous."

"Evan Take Two?"

"It wasn't like that."

"Baby Do-over?"

Bingo. She's ticked.

"It is nearly three o'clock in the morning, and you have no right barging in here to accuse me." Standing by the bedroom door like a hostile Walmart greeter, she waits for me to leave. When I don't, she sighs. "I am not having this conversation."

I sit on the edge of her bed and say, "Yeah. I think you are."

"We didn't raise you to be so disrespectful."

I've had it. "What has being respectful ever done for me? Made me invisible? Easier to deceive?"

"What are you talking about?"

"Do you not get that it matters to me—that you and Dad lied to me all these years, never told me I had a brother? You called me JUNIOR for God's sake!"

"You didn't need to know."

"How can you say that?"

Crossing to the bed, straightening the comforter, she sits beside me.

"We were just trying to protect you."

"Well you did a pretty sucky job."

"ENOUGH!"

That had to hurt. Can you fracture a tonsil? It takes a minute—and several labored swallows—before she continues.

"Okay, fine. We've failed you as parents. Where do we go from here?"

God, not the self-pity card. I roll my eyes.

"I asked you a question, Evan."

"What, 'Where do we go from here?' Well, I guess my answer is back to bed. Talking to you is pointless."

I'm halfway down the hall when she calls out. There's a quality to her voice I recognize immediately. It's how she used to sound when I was little and got too close to the stove, the curb, the stranger. Panic.

Peering into her room, I expect to find her still on the bed. She's not; for an anxious moment, I'm stumped. Is this a joke? An ambush? Is she lurking under the bed like a Boogeymom?

The closet light's on. I find her inside, perched on the stepladder at the back. As she climbs down, I see the photo album pressed to her chest.

"Want to see?"

In that instant, she's a seven-year-old offering her art project. Her whole face trembles as she approaches, like her features are going through a random shuffling. The album's thin—about half as thick as the phone book—but the way she carries it suggests significant weight. I take it. In that moment of transfer, her face settles into a single expression. It looks like gratitude.

She emerges from closet shadow, and the illusion implodes; she goes from grammar school to geriatric. Instinctively taking her arm, I lead her to the bed. We sit side by side, neither of us daring to speak or look at the album between us.

Finally, as headlights span the bedroom wall, she lifts memory's cover and—careful not to look inside just yet—she speaks. "They weren't bad people, Evan. Just ill-equipped." She sighs. "It's taken a lifetime to understand."

"Who, Mom?"

"My mother and father. They were supremely unsuited for parenthood."

"Oh."

"Kind of ironic, isn't it? I mean, I'm sure you think your dad and I have ruined your life, and here I am about to tell you how my parents ruined mine." She laughs, looks ashamed. "I'm sorry, I shouldn't be telling you all this."

"No, it's okay. Maybe you need to."

"Maybe I do." She brushes her hair back, and I notice how bare her hand looks without the ring. "It was a sad, brief ride being their child. They just never seemed interested, Ev. They gave me the basics: food, bed, great clothes. But the real basics, attention and affection, were in short supply. In kindergarten—I remember my parents laughed about the note—my teacher was alarmed to find my imaginary friend wasn't interested in playing with me. Pathetic, huh?"

"Well . . . it is kind of . . . odd, I guess."

"But it was what I'd been taught: Be quiet, keep occupied. Stay out of the way, because there was no room in their relationship for me."

It seems really important to her that I understand this.

"My father never wanted a child; my mother was one. I have very few childhood photos, because they didn't care to take any. But you could paper a room with their vacation snaps. Oh, I'd get an occasional postcard at school. Always 'Having a nice time' but never the rest."

Realizing she's squeezed my fingers blue, she gives me a shamed look, loosens her grip. "You know I was sixteen when their plane went down."

"Yeah." It was one of the few crumbs she'd ever offered about my missing grandparents.

"But what I never told you is," her voice breaks, and she puckers into an odd smirk, "I was relieved." She busts out crying.

"Mom, are you okay? Do you need something, a drink of water?"

She shakes her head. I grab the Kleenex from the nightstand, hold the box out to her, and wait. Finally, she snatches a handful and blots the clump to her face.

"I never thought I'd have a child. I was terrified of the idea. Sure I'd repeat their mistakes. That my child would hate me."

"I don't hate you, Mom."

"No?" She looks genuinely surprised.

Have I really acted like I do? "Of course not. But . . . sometimes."

"What?"

"Never mind."

"Please, tell me."

"You make it really hard to love you."

"Oh, honey, you're right. I guess I got so used to having people pull away I never quite wanted to give as much as I should. Does that make sense?"

"I think so."

We sit quietly, looking just past each other, both afraid we've said too much. Afraid to promise we'll do better. Not sure we could keep that one.

Finally, she clears her throat and, with colossal effort, hoists the album onto my lap. "This was your brother."

I suppose I expect a mini-me, or a diapered version of Dad, but I see something else.

It's one of those first-day hospital shots. The baby's got the mandatory bead strand on his sausagey wrist, his hand raised in a wee gangsta salute. Eyes slightly crossed—chalky, unfocused slits, poked deep in massive cheeks—his head's a vague cone shape, crested with strawberry fuzz. I can't stop thinking guinea pig.

"He's beautiful."

Mom actually laughs. "You think? I was a bit shocked when I saw him. Clearly, it was a rough trip down the birth canal."

When I blush, she says, "Sorry. I suppose you don't want to hear about that."

"Not really."

"Turn the page. He gets better."

I do; he does. I flip slowly, studying photos of Mom and Dad and Baby Evan. Their firstborn. Once his head settles into human shape, he's sort of cute. There's a shot of him curled on a blanket wearing this tiny Mickey Mouse shirt. And a first Halloween picture of him dressed as, what else, a pumpkin.

They have pictures of me at this age, too, frames full. Visualizing them now, I connect the dots between our dual babyhoods.

On the next page, there's a shot of Dad holding him; the baby's about a year old. I'm not sure why at first, but I feel almost dizzy looking at it. Then I realize it's the take-one version of a picture on the living room mantel: Dad and me.

In both, my father stares into the camera, holding a year-old Evan. They wear the same sweatshirts. Dad's says The Old Block; both babies wear a shirt that says Chip Off The Old Block. And in each, father and son wear matching Red Sox caps.

I'm a little angry, realizing they dressed me in dead Evan's clothes. It just feels wrong. But that's not what upsets me about the photo. It's Dad's expression. Unlike the version with me, in this one he looks happy.

His chin's glued to the kid's head, like he'd never put him down. Our shot's different. Dad sort of bobbles me on his knee, like I'm wired with explosives. He doesn't seem magnetized to me like he was to my brother. God, it's peculiar thinking that—my brother—like I ever had one.

"Mom, tell me about him."

From this mask of fear, she says, "What do you want to know?"

"Everything."

She clears her throat and begins.

"We were kids, Ev. But your dad, there was something solemn, sort of a film over him. Even then. An emptiness in his eyes, sometimes. I think it was part of what first drew me in, fragility where you'd never expect it. I suppose I thought I could fill that void."

As she takes my hand, a tiny static shock makes her pull away. She slides over to her side of the bed, and I swing my feet up, leaning back against Dad's pillow.

"We met junior year at college. I was in the basement laundry when these legs appeared. He'd locked himself out, was trying to squeeze through the tilt window. Well, he got halfway in when it just sort of gave. There was this huge POP as plate glass smashed to the floor. Scared the life out of me—I nearly maced him. But his dopey grin won me over. We were squatting, gathering shards, when I noticed this big sliver stuck right in his butt cheek. I didn't think twice, just yanked it out and—oh my Lord—the blood! So, our first date was to the infirmary. He made me go with him to keep pressure on the wound. After that, we were a couple."

Pausing, she reaches for the glass on the nightstand. As she lifts it to her mouth, I catch the sour scent of leftover wine.

"The following October we learned I was pregnant, and . . . this is hard. I wanted an abortion. I was just so scared. But your father, it was his finest hour. He said we weren't just two people anymore, that I'd never be without a family, ever again."

"And so, we agreed to be together, the three of us, whatever life brought. And, God, that made me brave! We moved in together—your gran loved that. Set up house, finished school, and graduation robes make everyone look pregnant anyway. And when the baby came, well, suddenly that film, it lifted. Your father was a shaft of light. When I said I wanted to name our son after him, he cried and cried. I got scared, Ev, he cried so hard. And you know what he said? He said he was crying because God had given him a second chance. He said this new Evan Frederick Galloway would erase all the smudges from the first Evan.

"God, that first year was like a dream. We lived in this tiny apartment above Jade Palace. Everything smelled of fried rice. I was teaching night classes at the Continuing Ed Center, your dad was freelancing, and your brother," her voice cracks, "your brother was like a fourteen-month-old fireball. God, that little acrobat!

"One night, in the middle of an English as a Second Language class, your grandfather appeared at the door. He was gray. I knew, Evan. I knew right then. I didn't say a word to the class, not that they'd have understood. I just ran, left my purse in the desk drawer, and ran."

She goes silent, closes her eyes. I wait a minute to ask, "What did he say?"

"Your gramp's a good man, Evan, but not much of a communicator. He drove me to the hospital without a word."

"When I walked in, your father . . . he was like a ghost. He wouldn't look at me. Just kept saying, 'I sang to him, Kat. That song he likes.' "

Closing her eyes, she starts to sing, a tear slipping down each cheek.

"I left my baby lying here,
Lying here, lying here
I left my baby lying here
To go and gather blackberries.

Hovan, Hovan Gorry og O
I've lost my darling baby!"

Voice trailing, she opens her eyes. Sighing, more of a shudder really, she blows her nose into the wadded tissues and prepares to go on. I want to stop her, go back to my room, pull the covers over my head, pretend we never started. But I can see it in her expression: she needs to tell the rest.

"Your father'd fallen asleep at his drawing board. He was working on a cover illustration. It was a huge break; he had a killer deadline. He'd just dozed off, you know? And the baby, he got hold of the curtains. It's absurd. They warn you everywhere nowadays: 'Don't put the crib near the window.' But we were stupid, and young. Mostly just young, I'm afraid. And our baby, our boy . . . your father found him with the cord twisted around his neck.

"He lived for three days before we took him off all those damn machines. There was no brain activity, so. We said goodbye. Or I did. Your father, he just kept singing that awful song."

Before I can say a word, she's off the bed, album in hand, heading for the closet. Still facing into it, she says, "Evan, your father and I did love each other. And we had our happy times, but at the heart of it, I'd say our relationship was based on grief. That seems like a powerful bond, but in the end, it just didn't make for a marriage."

Then she's done, and I think I understand, just a little, what it's been like for her. To have lost them both. To be terrified I'll be the next Evan to go.

And for a second, I know why Dad did it. Not just because the baby died, or because of Father Fran, or their marriage disintegrating, but because—

"Evan, are you okay?"

"Yeah, Mom. I just . . . "

"What is it?"

"I love you, Mom."

"I love you too, sweetheart."

"I won't ever leave you. I promise."

Her features do that liquid dance again as she tries to keep from crying. Before she can speak, I say, "I'll skip encounter. I don't need to go."

She stuns me with, "No, Evan. I want you to go. Maybe it will be good for you."

Back in my room, I realize I never talked to her about Mister Alberti's daughter, or shared what I know about Father Fran. Maybe it's best if I keep his secret for now.

I shoot Lex a quick text: *L, mission accomplished. talk soon.* I don't have the energy for details.

Guess I could've skipped the berries.

After last night, I felt like we'd made a breakthrough, finally understood each other a little better. Closer.

So I got up early to surprise Mom with her favorite: stuffed French toast. The recipe's in this cookbook from a B&B where they stayed before I arrived and their marriage imploded. Dad always made breakfast on special occasions: anniversaries, Mother's Day. Convincing myself there's nothing creepy about fixing your mother a big morning-after feast, I went all out.

I even used that little plastic tool and carved her apple into a flower shape. Now I'm faced with the consequences of eating double everything: French toast, bacon, yogurt with berries, fruit cup, coffee, OJ. Oof.

As I approached her bedroom with the breakfast tray, I saw a sheet of flower fairy stationery on the hall table. She'd chosen the Forget-me-not Fairy, a blue-petaled infant, nested in a bed of leaves. The fairy tot was certainly cuter than either Evan baby.

The note said:

Ev,
   Had some paperwork to clean up. Gone to office.
   Fresh box of Special K in pantry.
   Called Aunt R; she'll drop you at work.
   See you tonight.
   x. o., Mom

Surprise. Guess it'll take more than one night for her to adapt to interacting like real people. I sat on her bed, studying my brother's baby book, and polished off everything on her tray. Looking at the pictures seemed to make me hungrier, so I went to the kitchen, ate the rest. At this rate, I may end up the subject of a reality show: Ten-Ton Teen.

At the counter, I reread the note, with its tiny x. and o. (who punctuates a kiss and hug?), and say, "Well, it'll be nice to see Aunt Reg, anyway." Then I spread Mom's note in the sink and trickle bacon grease on top, watching how it blooms across the page, darkening the flower babe's cheeks, smearing Mom's words.

I soap the dishes. The water's extra hot; I hold my hands under as long as I can, like a test. After flopping on the couch in my pjs, I veg to cartoons. A couple mind-deadening hours later, I realize Aunt Reg'll be arriving anytime to taxi me to Alberti's.

I'm barely through showering when the doorbell rings. Pulling on yesterday's clothes, I yell, "One sec!" From my bedroom window, I spot Aunt Ro, not Reg, on the stoop, tinged pink with cold. I prep for her gardenia chokehold, the inevitable interrogation: "How do you FEEEEEL, Ev? Okay? Have you asked your little friend out? Do you want to talk about your dad?"

I open the door.

"Hey, Aunt Rosemary."

"Evan," she pushes into the living room, "have you eaten? You look so thin!"

I burp in reply, then add, "I'm fine Aunt Ro. We better get going." Scooping my backpack from the closet, I pull on my coat, flip up the hood to protect against her laser gaze more than the cold.

The second she starts the car, I switch on the radio—great, AM oldies—hoping to deflect her concentration, praying for clear roads and quiet. We pull from the driveway and head slowly up Madison. I feel her watching me from the corner of her eye, sense her emitting waves of urgent compassion. I hum along to "Love Potion Number 9."

She pushes a button on her steering wheel, the audio commandeer, I think it's called, silencing the radio. Under other circumstances this would be a mercy (remember, it's "Love Potion Number 9"), but Aunt Ro's like nature, only instead of vacuums, she abhors silence. I brace, press my feet to the floor like a nervous driving instructor working the phantom brake.

"So, your mom tells me you've gotten a job."

"Uh huh."

"Care to tell me about it?"

Now she's deliberately *not* looking at me, like Grand Duchess Nonchalant. Obviously, she knows all about Alberti's. *She's driving me there for cripe's sake!*

"Didn't my mother already fill you in?"

"Weeeeell," she stretches the word to about six syllables, annoyed by my smart-ass tone, "I was interested in hearing it from you, but since you're feeling so put upon, skip it."

I swear she's Mom's sister, not Dad's. She's got that whole rigid vibe down.

"Sorry, I didn't mean to be pissy. It's just . . . can't we please cut the crap?"

"I don't appreciate your attitude, Evan."

"Yeah, fine whatever. Obviously you already know about the mural. Right?"

"Your mother may have mentioned it, yes."

"So you know I'm finishing it. You probably also know Gramp told me about my dead brother. Can we stop pretending I'm two years old and need protecting? I'm sick to death of it!"

"Okay. I see how it is: Rosemary as Emotional Whack-a-Mole. What else is new?"

Jabbing a lacquered nail at the wheel, flicking on the radio, she clacks her tongue against her teeth. "Hound Dog" plays, slightly off station, but she makes no move to change it.

I'll never beat her in a battle of seething. Besides, I have been sort of a prick. I lower the volume and my hood.

"Look, Aunt Ro, I'm sorry. I shouldn't take it out on you. I appreciate the ride."

She doesn't respond; keeps her eyes bolted to the traffic light; rapidly nail-taps the wheel. We finally get a green, and turn onto Aurora, her rhythm slowing.

"So, work's okay. The Alberti's are wild, like the anti-Galloways: all noise and big emotions. Funny as anything. With the fireworks in the kitchen, it's remarkable they serve a single meal, but—"

"They should've told you."

"Excuse me?"

"About the baby. I always felt they should have told you."

"Thanks."

Then, as I'm about to bring up Father Fran, a slab of ice hits the windshield. Aunt Ro shrieks, pumping the brakes. We fishtail into a snow bank, back bumper whumping crusted snow. As I jump out, a couple kids, probably fourth or fifth graders, skid around the corner.

Aunt Ro joins me on the sidewalk to inspect her Saturn—no damage. I grab my stuff and give her a quick hug. Alberti's is only a block away; she seems relieved to be rid of me.

At the front entrance, I sense something's wrong. The closed sign's still up. I slide on ice by the kitchen entrance. It's wide open and I can hear Angie yelling inside.

When I walk in, she and Lupo are toe to toe, like they're about to slow dance. I hesitate for a second, 'til Lupo embraces her. Afraid to witness some icky, cousin-on-cousin action, I clear my throat. They turn. Silence. Normal for Lupo. But a speechless Angie cannot be good.

Something's up. The kitchen even smells off. It's obvious! Nothing's cooking. I stammer into the odd tension.

"Hey, uh. Sorry I'm late. Mom left early this morning. Had to get a ride from my aunt. *That* was a fiasco; some kids nearly put an ice grenade through her windshield."

I pause for some reply, but they just stare, and I realize Angie's been crying.

She says, "You'll need to get a ride back home. Lupo and I are leavin'."

Lupo nods, actually starts to speak, but Angie stops him with a yank on his apron.

"Oh—everything okay?"

"Fine."

It's a three-way staring match. Angie's got this you-can't-make-me-talk look; I just plain don't know what to say; and Lupo, well, he's just Lupo.

I'm starting toward the dining room for a quick look at the mural, when Angie suddenly comes to life, grabbing my wrist.

"What do you think you're doin'?"

"I wanted to check the mural before I go, get some ideas. I'll only be a minute."

"We don't have a minute. Go!"

"Angie, you can't just throw me out. At least tell me what's going on."

She loosens her grip and says, "We need to get to Saint Luke's, okay?"

Quick-scanning for visible signs of kitchen injury—sautéed forehead, missing thumbs—I ask, "The hospital? Jeez, what's the matter?"

"It's my dad."

As I glance at Lupo, he looks away, head shaking slightly.

"Is he all right?"

She just looks down, twists her gold bracelet.

"Angie, is he all right?"

"I don't know! Evan, Lupo found him this morning in the yard. In his pajamas again, all tangled in this plastic tarp. I think he was tryin' to get at my mother's roses. He had the pruning shears out—in the middle of winter! He don't know what he's doing anymore. God knows how long he was out there, practically froze solid."

"But he'll be all right?"

"They're not sure. He's unconscious. He opened his eyes in the ambulance, tried talkin', but he wasn't making no sense. Not just screwy the way he gets either, the words were all mangled, like he couldn't remember how to talk. I hope to God it's not a stroke on top of everything else."

"Well, we should get down there. I'll go with you."

"I don't think that's a good idea."

"Why not?"

She purses her lips so tight they're rimmed white. "Just NO. Okay?"

Before I know what's going on, Angie's Honda's gone, and I'm solo on the sidewalk.

The car shrinks to nothing as she coasts through the intersection and heads downtown. I begin walking after them. Shoving hands in pockets, I count the change there. Down the block, I duck into a bus shelter. Won't be long before one comes; I'll thaw on the way.

It reminds me of a sports venue—or a casino.

There's a preponderance of marble; the escalator's gigantic, like something from Ancient Rome. I half expect Christians and lions to descend in tandem. Comfy chair, though, like sitting in a giant catcher's mitt. Of course, I've never seen a catcher's mitt in lavender.

It's a pastel oasis, everything muted to uniform value. Muted = soothing, soothing = good. I guess. But this intentional quality—this forced calmbience—makes me nervous.

I mean, I know color theory. Hit me with cool gray-greens, hints of placid blue, a dollop of beige, I think, *Okay. You want me sedate.* And that makes me freakin' nervous.

Or maybe the situation's got me frazzed. After waiting sixteen minutes, I was chanting, "Hurry! Hurry! Hurry!" when the bus appeared. I was the lone passenger, and the driver went out of his way to be nice, apparently enjoying the company. He kept asking: Was I warm enough? Did I want a mint? Was the radio too loud?

I wanted to yell, "Drive the f@*king bus, already!" but, figuring that was a mite rude, I just clenched him a smile. He finally dropped me at the stop closest to the hospital.

Bolting off, I heard him call, "Have a sparkling day!"

But now, after nearly breaking my neck running the last icy block, I've stalled in the lobby. Scared, I suppose. I doubt Angie will welcome me; plus, I'm not sure what I'd hoped to achieve by coming. But I needed to—just in case. I'd hit the chapel, but I forget where it is.

Incredibly, I'm hungry; it's been a while since mega-breakfast. I consider paying a visit to the mauve-and-beige vendor cart; it's like a snack Xanadu at the foot of the escalators. You can get warm pretzels, ice cream bars, and cappuccino. They also offer organic treats and sugar-free diabetic options. This is a hospital after all.

I decide against purchasing for two reasons: 1) I'm flat broke (the bus ride did me in), and 2) I'm a little shell-shocked. So I just sit, reluctant to leave my cushy chair embrace for the soothing-shade-of-green info desk. What would I say? "Good afternoon, tranquil-hued volunteer, can I get the room number of a patient I've been told not to visit?"

Yeah, that'd go over big.

This is really not how I'd envisioned today. Wonder what Lex and Tyler are doing—yish!—best not go there. Instead, I focus on the people sharing my serene digs: A group across the lobby, circled in their own pleather mitts, converse in animatedly hushed tones. Their demeanor screams support group—but quietly.

To my left, a procession of fretful relatives. Shoulders shaped like worry, they glide toward an arch marked (uh oh) Oncology. I'm relieved when they hesitate, change course, pass through a door etched Rheumatology instead. Better chronic than terminal.

On the wall opposite the info desk are two doors. One bears the universal men's room sign. To its right is another, marked Hospital Chaplain. I briefly mull approaching one, but I'm not sure which I need most. I'm recalling Gran's horror stories about hospital restrooms—"germ incubators," she calls them—but the chaplain's door has visible cobwebs. I stay put.

"Inertia, thy name is Galloway." Crap, I said that out loud, judging by the faces of the support circle, anyway. Embarrassment urges me toward the horseshoe-shaped counter.

"Can I help you?"

I hear Mrs. S-B-C's voice in my head: *I don't know; CAN you?* I resist flaunting my grammar skills. I mean, the old lady's just trying to help. Can? May? Who cares?

Her nametag says Iris in jiggly cursive. She's taken obvious care matching the ink to her earrings and eye shadow, all a suitable-to-the-pastel-environs blue.

"Um . . . yes, I . . . I hope so. I'm here to visit a patient."

"Name?"

"Evan Galloway."

"One moment." Twisting in the violet rolly-chair, she scans her monitor, apparently finishing what I interrupted. About three minutes in, lower lip pooched like a tiny, pink diving board, she says, "Sorry, there's no one by that name. Maybe you want Bradford."

"What?"

"Hospital. Maybe you want Bradford Hospital," she wrinkles her nose in distaste, "the *other one*. Across town."

I just blink, positive Angie said Saint Luke's, then I repeat, "What?"

Huffing, sliding her glasses down her sizable nose, she glares over pale lilac rims. "Young man, I have no one named Ethan Gallaghan on the patient database." She seems to savor the words "patient database" on her tongue.

I'm wondering if she's an escapee from the idiot ward, then I realize I'm the one having a brain stutter. "Oh, sorry! *I'm* Ethan Gallaghan." It's best she doesn't know my real name.

Her lips tighten into a perturbed o.

"When you said, 'Name?' I thought you wanted *my* name. But you meant the patient's name—obviously."

"Obviously."

Ignoring her withering tone, I say, "Right, the patient's name, Giuseppe Alberti."

Immediately efficient, she tabs down her screen. "Alberti? Like the restaurant? Okie-doke. Just gimme a sec. Yep, I've got a Joe Alberti. He came in around eight this morning, through the ER. He's in ICU. You're family?"

I don't hesitate; thanks, amygdala. "Yes. I'm his grandson."

Her eyebrows stretch to their upper limits. "Gallaghan?"

"Yeah," I match her snippiness quotient, "my mom's his daughter, Theresa Alberti *Gallaghan*."

"Okay then. You'll find him on nine. Down the hall. Take the Father McGivney elevator to three, hook a left past the cafeteria. Then take the Pierpont elevator. You can't miss it."

"Thanks."

I sprint down the hallway, surrendering to the urgency that's been nibbling my brain since the restaurant.

"He wouldn't want you here, Evan."

Six words with the power to deflate. I pause long enough for Angie to shove me backwards, into the hall, outside Zio Joe's curtain corral. He doesn't have a real room; no one does in ICU, just these plastic, floor-to-ceiling drapes partitioning each patient from the others. I try to slip past, reenter the little rectangle where Mister A floats in his metal bed. Angie blocks me like a vicious goalie.

"But Angie, I—"

"No buts! Except maybe butt out, okay? My father is dying, kid, and whether or not he knows who the hell I am right now, I intend to be with him 'til he goes—ALONE."

As she says it, Angie jerks the drape shut in my face. She reminds me of Mister Alberti pulling back the curtains to reveal Dad's mural. Or a really angry magician's assistant. If not for her furious expression, she could be performing some magic back there; I'd vote for making all those tubes and machines disappear.

I was only with the old guy for about ten minutes before Angie returned (probably from the ladies' room) to eject me, but from what I saw, things aren't good. He just lay there, machines huddled around the bed, tubes in both arms, this snorkely thing in his mouth. His hair was off to one side on the pillow, but he was in no shape to care.

He looked like a husk, what's left when a beetle molts its skin: an exoskeleton. I remember finding one on the windowsill when I was a kid and trying to get it to walk, or fly, before realizing it had nothing inside. God, why was I thinking of that?

The curtained pen lacked a chair, so I sidled up, half-cheeking it on his waffle-blanketed mattress. I felt like I should say something to Mister A, in case he sensed me there. Fingers trembling across his pillow, I tried to reposition his comb-over. As I did, I whispered, "It's me, Zio. I promise you'll be out of here soon. And when you come home, I'll have the Last Supper finished."

I'm not sure he heard me, but right then, as I made an impossible promise, his eyes fluttered open, meeting mine. I swear he tried to say something; the hand nearest me flopped on the blanket like a speared fish.

I leaned toward him, asking, "What do you want to tell me?" like he could form a word with that vacuum hose in his mouth.

Then Angie appeared, to catapult me from their lives. As I stand, staring at the beige barrier, I begin to realize she's probably right; Zio *wouldn't* want me to see him in this condition. I remember at the restaurant how he hugged me when his brain rebooted. He seemed desperate, ashamed even, of being so out of it. Safe to say he'd be humiliated to be seen this way: feeble, drugged, and tubed.

I feel guilt for even coming here. What was I hoping to do, pump him for some deathbed revelation before he went? Nice. I finally understand this isn't about me. However much I've convinced myself I'm a member of the clan—and despite what I told Info-desk Iris about being Theresa's son—the Alberti family really doesn't include me.

Backing down the hall, past the Ladies Auxiliary gift shop, I poke my head into the family waiting room, the perfect brooding nook: dimly lit, vague piney aroma, dilapidated sofa. I'd hoped to find Lupo here, but no sign. Maybe he's in the cafeteria. Or else Angie sent him to notify the rest of the family about Mister A. That'd be interesting. I picture relatives cross-country, jiggling silent receivers, asking, "Lupo, that you?"

I think about calling Mom or one of the aunts for a lift, but can't face another Galloway Gal car ride. Walking out the main hospital entrance, I taste snow in the air. Luckily, Grandmother's house isn't really over the river and through the woods, because I've decided to hoof it.

"More pie?"

I've already had two pieces, but the tart goo somehow soothes. Gran hoists another meringued slab onto my plate, then heads back to the kitchen.

I guess it's ironic, ending up here with the Queen of the Galloway Gals, after nixing the lure of a warm car ride to avoid interacting with one. But, post-hospital, I craved familiarity—the comfort of brown linoleum, that faint mothball scent, a no-questions-asked hug, and dessert. Major dessert.

I was really looking for Gramp, hoping to clear up some stuff about the dead Evans and the whole "you done her dirty" thing, but Gran said he's "at the depot." That cracks me up, like he's living this second life as a conductor, when really he's at *Home* Depot, probably salivating over dangerous power tools.

Gran's back, leaning over the coffee table with her big ceramic cow pitcher. I never understand why she can't just serve milk from the carton like normal people.

She fills my glass, claiming, "That crust's a little on the dry side."

There's this slight buzz in my head, and I can barely keep my butt on the couch. I'm ready to bust. Not just from pie either—it's Alberti stress, and of course, Father Fran. Gran, perched on the La-Z-Boy, seemingly oblivious to my agitation, grins across her coffee cup. Emboldened by sugar, I plunge.

"I'm going on encounter, but I—"

Making this exaggerated, stick-out-your-chin face, she leans across the table, dabs me with a dishcloth.

Through the damp fibers, I continue. "I need to talk to you about something."

"What is it, Jun—?" She catches herself, "Evan?"

An image of cliff divers pops into my head as I say, "I was hoping we could talk about Father Fran."

Bracing for the dropped cup, the hurled pie server, I expect her to scream. Faint. Something. But she just looks at me with a strange nonexpression and says, "That's odd."

"What is?"

"Your grandfather brought him up just last night."

"He did?"

"Yes, and it's not like we talk about him that often. Such a good man." She winks. "And so good-looking, like a television star."

Eeeuww. "Father Fran was Dad's art teacher?"

"That's right. But even before, when your father was maybe nine or ten, he recognized your dad's talent."

I suppress a cringe. "He did?"

"Yes, your father made a poster for Catholic Schools Week. Oh, I was so proud they chose it to hang on the altar."

"That's great."

"Father complimented his artwork—your dad was an altar boy then—and asked if he could treat 'the budding artist' to some supplies. Well, I knew your Gramp would never allow it, but it seemed like such an opportunity. Private lessons! So I agreed it'd be our secret."

It's killing me to not just blurt what really happened during those lessons. But what good would that do? What could I hope to achieve other than making her feel as bad as I do? Worse, because obviously she'd blame herself.

"So, he and my dad were close?"

"Well, yes, Evan, they were. But how'd you find out about that?" She looks a little puzzled, nothing dramatic.

I risk gliding on half-truth. "I found some pictures in Dad's trunk."

"Wait a second." She crosses to the corner curio. From the bottom shelf, where it's sandwiched by Hummel figurines, she pulls a brass frame: a yellowed photo of Dad, altar-robed, next to a priest. "This the picture you found?"

"Uh . . . yeah." I feel dizzy, staring into the eyes of my father's monster. He does look like some actor—really tall, broad shoulders, the dad in that old '60s Disney movie, *The Parent Trap*.

"And what else did you find?"

"Nothing much. Bubble gum cards, cassettes, junk like that."

"Junk? Too bad. I was hoping you'd find something good."

Scooping a final lemon gob, I prod the last hunk of crust and push my plate aside. "So, whatever happened to him?"

"Hmm?"

"Father Fran."

"Oh, he passed."

"When?"

"Just after you were born."

"Must've been tough on Dad."

"Now you mention it, it was. Your father took it surprisingly hard. It'd been years since he'd seen Father. Of course, they had been close."

"Why hadn't he seen him for so long?"

"Well, priests, they have no control over where they're sent. Father Fran was reassigned out West when your father was in high school."

"Did they keep in touch?"

"No, and that puzzled me. I remember your dad was very upset, like he'd lost his best friend. It was only natural, I suppose. It was sudden. And he'd really come to rely on Father. You know, for a time, I thought he might follow in Father's footsteps."

"How?"

"Well, he confided in me he was considering becoming a priest. I think it was mainly that he and Father had become so close. He was a wonderful influence on your dad."

I stifle a shudder.

"What is it, Evan? You look a little green. Was three pieces too much?"

"No." I worry my cheeks may split from the effort to smile. "I'm okay. What do you mean 'a wonderful influence'?"

"Well, your father could be . . . " She struggles, twisting dishtowel fringe as her eyes pool.

"You okay, Gran?"

"Yes, honey. It's just . . . it's hard to talk about." I nearly do a Pettafordi spit-take as she finally says, "Your dad could be a little moody." She spots my eye roll. "Okay, you're thinking that's a bit of an understatement, right?"

"Sort of."

"Look, Evan, you never exactly got the best your dad had to offer, but," stopping herself, she picks at coffee table crumbs, "that's not what I mean to say."

"Gran,"

"No, let me finish. He gave all he was capable of. I'm sorry it wasn't quite what you deserved."

"It's okay, Gran."

"You're a good boy, Ev. And I guess the father he was is the father you were meant to have. But if you could have known him," her voice weakens, "before."

"Before the baby?"

Biting her lip, she smoothes my hair. "I'm not sorry your grandfather took you to the cemetery, Evan. We always felt you had a right to know."

"Thanks."

"Did you ask your mother about it?"

"Yes."

"And did she talk to you?"

My voice comes out papery. "Yes, she showed me some pictures."

"That's good. She was very strong when it happened, stronger than your dad. But it's something no one should have had to go through." She inspects the porcelain server. "Finished?"

When I realize she's talking about pie, I nod. Gran scoops my fork/glass/plate and bolts for the kitchen in one quick movement. We pretend the running water masks her sniffling.

Joining me on the couch, she clears her throat and says, "He was never really the same after. I'm afraid you got sloppy seconds."

"I always felt a bit like I *was* the sloppy seconds. I guess now I know why."

"No, honey. You mustn't feel that way. He really did love you."

"Okay."

"But even when he was a child, it was almost like there was another world inside his head."

"How do you mean?"

"Well, he was a very gentle boy. Your Gramp was always worried there was something wrong with him, that he was weak."

"But Dad was this big sports star. How could Gramp think that?"

"This was before, when he was a skinny, little kid. But I always knew. He wasn't weak, Evan. He was special."

"Special how?"

"It's hard to explain. Sensitive. Kind. He'd cry over little things. We had, I don't know how many, road kill funerals when he was five or six. And he worried about people. I remember, when he was eight, he didn't want to keep his Christmas presents."

"Why?"

"He'd seen a TV program about orphans and he wanted to send them all his gifts. Said we all should. Well, Rosemary, she was furious, thinking she'd have to give up her Chatty Cathy."

I can't help laughing. She joins me. "I know, it was priceless." Then we look at each other, wondering if laughter's okay.

"Was he *ever* happy?"

"Sure he was. And when he was happy, he glowed. People stopped and smiled wherever we went, drawn to him like moths. Even though he was shy, if someone paid attention a light switched on. He could be so . . . articulate and, I guess you'd say, charming."

I try to steer the conversation back to Father Fran. "And talented."

"Yes, he was that. I always encouraged his artwork, even though your grandfather had misgivings. We did projects together: paint by numbers, decoupage. Sweet times. How we'd talk! But your Gramp said I babied him, made him soft. He was never one to talk about feelings."

"You're kidding."

"I know. The more things change . . . but your father craved—now what's that Oprah word?"

"Validation?"

"That's it. He needed a reminder that he was loved, was worthy. And the artwork seemed to give him that—it was like food. But I guess your Gramp had a point."

"About what?"

"He claimed your dad was too attached to me. Maybe I *was* a tiny bit overprotective."

Just not when he needed you. I nearly say it. Instead, I swallow hard. Stomach lurching, I almost feel the words congeal in my belly with her lemon pie.

"Not that he was a mama's boy—I always hated that term. But it was time for him to stretch a little. That's why his friendship with Father was such a godsend."

I will not scream.

"I'd prayed for it, for someone else to recognize his gifts. And Father Fran was just what that sweet boy needed."

Could she have really been so blind? It's almost a joke. How else to explain her tickling the edges of what really happened? I've stopped listening; I picture her skimming this sparkly surface, a Great White coursing just below.

"Sorry?"

"I said, it's not nice, but I wanted God to give your Gramp a big, fat I-told-you-so."

"And He did."

"Yes, He surely did. Your Gramp resented the time your dad spent with Father Fran, not that he'd admit it. He'd just complain about your dad 'gallivanting whenever there was work to do.' Of course, he didn't know what was really going on. We said your dad was volunteering. Your grandfather never would have gone for it if he knew what they were really doing at the rectory."

I can't take it. I don't know what's worse: that she was totally, freaking oblivious to what he suffered, or that everything she says is sick with double-meaning. She's like some horrible stand-up. Next she'll say, "Father really knew how to make that boy smile," and then I think I'll have to stab her in the neck with the pie server.

God, what is my problem? Am I mad at her because my father was too good at keeping secrets? Because she was too stupid to see what was going on? I need to change the subject. She's clearly a dead end. And I've got to leave it alone, say my goodbyes, get out of here.

"Gran, I found Dad's journal in the trunk."

Once again, I seem to have propelled a grandparent toward cerebral hemorrhage; I'm becoming dangerous to know. Gran's face is slack. Fidgeting on the couch, she picks up a magazine. Replaces it.

"Gran, I said—"

"I heard you."

Okay, she's not stroking out. Still, like a cuttlefish, her color wavers, white to pink to purplish, as if she's attempting to blend with the afghan. She opens her mouth, but no sound emerges. Then she literally runs for the kitchen.

Indecision bolts me to the couch. When I finally follow, she's slumped against the sink, a soaking rag to her forehead.

"Gran?"

"It's not true."

"What?"

"Whatever you read in that journal. It's not true."

"Have *you* read it?"

Glaring like a cornered animal, she twists the dish rag. Her knuckles are bulgy-white, like baby onions. "I never saw it, but I know what it says."

"How?"

"You better go now."

"Did you know, Gran? Did you know?"

"I said GO!" Snatching a plate from the sink, she raises it high, ready to, what? Attack?

"Gran?"

She slides the plate back into the sink. Then, buckling, she leans against the counter and moans, "My God, my God!" I reach for her, but she shoves me back, slouches onto the telephone chair. "I would have done anything to protect him!"

My only hope is to calm her. "Yes, that's what mothers do."

She takes a monster breath, exhaling quick huffs as if she's in labor. When she looks toward me, she's eerily calm, like in a trance. "I can't."

"Yes. You can. I need you to tell me what you know, Gran."

"I never wanted to believe it. I prayed it was just a dream."

"What?"

"He came to me once. In the middle of the night. He'd always sleepwalked, but—he was about ten—he'd started wetting the bed. Your Gramp would've been furious, so we kept it between us. I figured he'd just outgrow it, you know?"

"Uh huh."

"So I took him to the bathroom to clean up, and he was very upset. He kept saying he was bad. So, so bad. I held him, and I said, 'It's okay, sweetie. You're still my special boy.' "

"And then?"

"He started crying, and he said, 'That's what Father Fran calls me.' "

"Can you remember anything else?"

"I wish I could forget. I said that was nice and then . . . "

She won't look at me. Her hands flutter near her collar, seeking out the tiny crucifix at her throat. Lips moving silently, she twirls the silver cross. I realize she's praying.

"Gran, what else do you remember?"

"His eyes got so wide, and he said, 'It's not a sin if Father loves me.' "

Shaking, she coils the phone cord around one wrist, no longer aware of me. I approach slowly, afraid to startle her. Kneeling, I untangle the cord and take her hand. She pulls away, as if I've burned her, starts to rise from the chair, reconsiders.

"I said maybe I should have a talk with Father, but he begged me not to." She barks out a wet sob, and I rock her in my arms, noticing her sharp angles, her doughy smell. I try to pull back, but she won't let me; she speaks into my shoulder. "He said, 'Without Father, the demon will take me.' "

"What did you do?"

"I couldn't face it. God forgive me, I told him to stop talking nonsense and go back to bed." She brings my face close, her eyes pleading.

"Did you tell anyone about this?" I already know the answer. I try not to hate her for it.

"I couldn't."

"Why not?"

"So many reasons. Your grandfather might've done anything. Everybody loved Father Fran, me included. I was afraid to know. Maybe it was just a dream. That last one—I needed to believe that, Evan. And I honestly thought it was best if he did, too."

Her lip quivers. I try to see past the gray fold of chin, her sour breath.

This question's the hardest; still I need to ask. "But if you suspected something, why?" I hold her gaze. "Why did you let him keep going with Father Fran?"

She's quiet for a long time; tears plink in her lap. "The next morning when he woke up—it was Sunday, he was scheduled for 9:15 Mass—I told him I didn't think he should serve anymore. That maybe he needed a break from Father Fran."

"What did he say?"

"It was the strangest thing. He seemed to have no memory of the night before. And he was so upset at the thought of not seeing Father. He said, 'Father Fran is helping me be holy.' "

"So you let him go?"

"I let him go," she studies her hands, "and I prayed for it to not be true. It was all I could do."

"It wasn't enough."

Rushing to the refrigerator, she takes down a magnet frame with a picture of Dad and me at Disney. She holds it out like an offering. Or a shield.

"Remember this? He said he already had his own Mouske-ears."

I ignore her diversion. "Did he ever talk about it again?"

She doesn't answer. Her arm hovers before dropping to her side.

"Gran, did he?" My voice breaks.

Slapping the frame back, she speaks to the freezer door. "Only once, just before he died. I think he was trying to bring it up. He said, 'Don't blame yourself for what happened when I was a kid.' "

"What did you do?"

"I did the only thing I knew. I pretended not to know what he was talking about. And, God bless him, he let me."

We stand voiceless for a long time, not sure whose move it is, or what to say. I want so much to love her like I did an hour ago, but I don't know if I can. Finally, I whisper, "I'm sorry."

"What for, honey?"

"For making you face it."

"Well, it looks like letting the dragon out of the cave hasn't killed me after all."

"No, but I wanted to ask a couple more questions."

She folds her arms. "Are you *trying* to put me in a pine box?"

"I'm sure Gramp'll spring for the heavy gauge steel."

She raises one eyebrow. "Okay, listen. If we're going to continue the twenty questions, I've got to piddle first. Remember, I'm an old lady."

When she returns, she goes straight to the hutch and pulls down the owl jar. "Cookies?"

"Just one."

"I guess you mean business."

I take a pecan sandie, wolf it in one bite. The dry lump tastes like authentic sand. Back in the living room, we take our places: Gran on the La-Z-Boy, me on the couch.

"Fire away."

I'm not sure where to start now that subterfuge is no longer necessary. "Uh, Dad's relationship with Father Fran went on through high school, right?"

"Yes."

"And he was, like, this amazing artist?"

"That he was." A short answer steeped in regret.

"So how come he stopped?"

She sighs. I'm not sure whether it's sorrow or relief at the new topic.

"I think it was too hard after the baby. He blamed himself, blamed his painting, like it cost him your brother. I guess he thought it was too dangerous to care about something so deeply. He just slammed that door. I always felt it was a shame—especially when we recognized your talent. That was something you two could've shared."

"Yeah, well, it's too late for that."

"Maybe not."

"Well, unless you're planning a séance, I'm afraid it is."

"Oh, that's right. You inherited his sarcasm too, didn't you? I'm talking about the mural. Your Aunt Reg tells me you're working on it. That's a way to share your art with him."

"I guess. But I'm not sure what'll happen with the mural now that Mister Alberti—" I can't finish; there's a lump in my throat that has nothing to do with stale cookie.

"What's the matter, Evan?"

"He's in the hospital, Mister A. They think he had a stroke on top of Alzheimer's. I just came from there. I don't think he's going to make it." Suddenly the levees burst.

"Evan, honey, it's okay. He's a very old man." She doesn't seem particularly broken up. Maybe she shares Aunt Reg's opinion of Zio.

"I know. I only . . . he's been telling me things about Dad. And now— it's stupid—I feel like I'm losing another link to him."

Gran shifts to the coffee table; I meet her gaze. She's turned her high beams on. "So what'd he tell you?"

"Nothing, just stories, stuff about when Dad worked there."

"Stories?"

"Yes."

We sit there in mongoose-versus-cobra pose for a moment. "Evan, make me a deal. I've been honest with you. And I'll continue to answer you truthfully, but only if you'll do the same."

"Okay."

"Did Mister Alberti say why your father started working for him, back in high school?"

I can't see what this has to do with anything. "No. I figured he needed money. For a car, maybe."

"He wasn't saving for a car."

"What then?"

"Your father'd gotten in trouble, Evan. He'd—" Crossing to the back door, she moves Gramp's soggy boots onto the mat. "Your grandfather would have this place looking like Tobacco Road if I didn't keep on top of things."

"Gran, what kind of trouble?"

"This is still embarrassing, all these years later. It wasn't like him, Evan. Even after, he'd never say why he did it."

"What did he do?"

"He vandalized the painting studio at school. Tore up canvases, smeared paint all over. He even threw a metal easel through the window. He caused over $500 worth of damage."

So this is what Mister P meant when he said Dad had *gotten disruptive*. "My God."

"I know. I was humiliated. He'd never done anything destructive before—or after—thank God."

I almost say, *well, he did hang himself.*

"They were going to kick him off the team, expel him. Until Father Brendan intervened. He said, if your father apologized and made full restitution, they'd forget the whole thing."

"Really? I'm surprised Father B was so easy on him."

"I know, even then he had a reputation as a disciplinarian. We expected him to come down hard on your dad."

"And he wasn't angry?"

"Not really. In fact, I remember thinking he seemed as shaken as we were. It was clear he wanted to protect your dad. He insisted no trace of the incident would ever appear in your father's permanent records."

"Wow."

"So, your Gramp was in the Elks with Mister Alberti, and they arranged for Evan to work at his restaurant to pay the debt."

"When did this happen?"

"Well, I guess it was right before Father Fran left."

"And after encounter?"

"Yes, about a month afterward."

"Something happened on encounter, didn't it? Something bad."

"I think so, honey. But I don't know what. Your father came back different—closed off, angry, keeping to himself. He hardly spoke to anyone but Father, and even then . . . one time I heard him yelling at Father on the phone. Terrible."

"What was he saying?"

"I can't remember exactly. 'I won't! Not my friend.' Something like that. When I confronted him, he said it didn't matter, they weren't friends anymore."

"Did he mean Tony?"

She looks a bit startled as she says, "Yes, his best friend was named Tony. How'd you know, another footlocker picture?"

"Sort of. And I know Tony is Mister Pettafordi. I already talked to him. Mister P said the same thing: Dad acted strange after encounter."

Eyes narrowing, she says, "God, Evan, you're a real detective. What else do you know?"

"Mister P told me Dad completely shut him out after encounter. Any idea why?"

She actually blushes. "Your father said . . . Tony had developed inappropriate feelings. He said they couldn't be friends anymore . . . because Tony was in love with him."

"Why would Dad say that? Pettafordi insisted they were just friends. He flat-out said, 'I was never in love with him.'"

"I'm only telling you what your father told me. Then, when he did what he did at school—"

"Trashing the studio?"

"Yes. After that, everything else seemed less immediate."

"So he came back from encounter, went Hulk on the art studio, ditched his best friend, and started pasta-based community service."

"Very concise."

"And that was the only trouble he caused?"

"Evan, how long have I known you?"

"Um, my whole life. Why?"

"Because I know when you're fishing. What else has Mister Alberti told you?"

"Nothing."

"Wrong answer. Remember, you promised to be honest."

"Okay, he mentioned something about Dad and his daughter, Theresa."

"Son-of-a-bitch!" She's way past startled, officially furious. "That whole thing was a misunderstanding. It became crystal clear when her baby was born."

"Whoa, what baby?"

"Maybe it's not right, telling you all this." She crosses herself—eyes heavenward. It's such a classic Gran gesture I almost smile, 'til she says, "She accused your father."

"Of?"

"He was a good kid, Ev, but in high school . . . he was so handsome, he got a little wild with the girls. Things just got out of hand."

"Out of hand how?"

"He had all these girls and trouble keeping track. I told him it was disrespectful, he was getting too big for his britches. I suspected he might even be," she blushes again, "having sex."

"Okay, this isn't uncomfortable at all."

"That was another reason I thought encounter might do him good, but afterward, things got worse, with the vandalism and all." She leans forward, straightens the *Family Circles*.

"Gran, what did she accuse him of?"

She sighs. "Your father started hanging around the Alberti girl."

"Theresa."

"Yes, and Mister Alberti encouraged it—he'd come to really like your dad. I thought it was a bad idea, mixing business and pleasure. And her, almost twenty, for goodness sake!"

"So was he in love with her?"

"I think so. Even when he went to college, he came home to see her every chance he got. At least at first."

"What happened then?"

"I'm ashamed to say, he behaved like a typical male. He stopped calling Theresa, started spending all his time with this new one."

"You mean my mother?"

"And then the girl, she ends up pregnant."

"Mom?"

"No, Theresa."

What was he, the freakin' Johnny Appleseed of sperm? "Was it Dad's?"

"No, that's the thing. I don't even think they'd been . . . intimate. He came home to break it off with her once and for all. I think he'd realized he had a future with your mom. But Theresa wouldn't let him out of it."

"What do you mean?"

"She tried to seduce him, to *make him* have sex. He said he was sorry, he'd fallen for someone else. She went to her father, told him your dad forced himself on her. When that man showed up at our house, I swear, he wanted to kill your father."

"So, what'd Dad say?"

"He said he loved Theresa and he wanted to do right by her."

"Marry her?"

"Yes, and this when he hadn't even finished college and with another girlfriend he supposedly loved. He wanted to provide for her and the baby. But I knew something was fishy."

"How?"

"He was my boy, that's how! I could tell he was lying. And then about a week later, she disappears, and don't you know, the Chang boy goes missing too."

"Okay, you've lost me."

"It turns out Theresa was two-timing your dad. She was carrying on with Jimmy Chang from Jade Palace the whole time your father was away at school. They ran off, and about a year later, Netta—Mister Alberti's wife, rest her soul—she shows me a snapshot of Theresa's baby. Unless your father had some recessive Asian genes, there was no way that child was his."

"This is like a freakin' soap opera!"

"No, Evan. This is life. Sometimes there's more drama than you think you can stand. Mostly, it just is."

"But wait, why'd Dad say the baby was his? I mean, he had to know it wasn't."

"Evan, it was like with the Christmas presents."

"How do you figure?"

"When I asked why he offered to marry her, he said, 'Ma, I don't matter so much. I just knew I had to protect her.' He was afraid her father might kill her. As it is, I don't think Mister Alberti ever spoke to Theresa again. I swear Netta died of a broken heart."

"So he didn't 'do her dirty' then?"

"Oh, Lord. Is that what that old fool told you?"

"Um, yeah. But he was pretty far gone when he said it, Gran. I'm not sure he even knew who he was. And he apologized after he came back to himself. He said Dad was a good kid."

"Well, I'm glad, because he truly loved your father. In a strange way, I think the whole Theresa fiasco really sealed the deal. He said your father had acted honorably."

"By defending her?"

"Yes, too bad he wasn't half as understanding of his daughter. But blood's funny."

"I guess."

"Oh, jeez, look at the time! I'd better throw supper together. Your Gramp'll be home any minute. And he's always hungry like a bear when he gets back from that depot. You want to stay? I'm making meatloaf."

"I should head home."

At the door, she grips my sleeve, this look of panic in her eyes. "Evan, don't hate me."

"Gran, I—"

"I'm sorry. I don't mean to be melodramatic. It's just I'm not ready to discuss any of this with your Gramp. Or your mother. It's going to take me some time. Okay?"

"Gran, I haven't thought much about how this'll affect the rest of the family, and I honestly can't worry about that. I need to be the selfish one right now."

She looks down, and I nearly apologize for the emotional sucker punch, but can't quite manage remorse.

Pulling me into a stiff goodbye hug, she whispers, "He'd be proud of you. Just be careful. Encounter, and all this . . . information. I hope it's not too much."

"I'll be fine."

She closes the storm door. I look toward the front walk, feeling a tiny bit lighter knowing Dad didn't "do her dirty." The phrase makes me picture Mister A, pasted back in that hospital bed. I tap on the glass; Gran opens the door a smidge.

"Say a rosary for Zio, would you? Things look pretty bad."

She presses her palm to the glass.

At first, I think it's flour on his hands.

Then I notice his smeared forehead, the tip of his nose. His blotched work pants. And I detect this smell, familiar somehow.

It's Saturday morning. Figured I'd give Angie a day to decompress before showing my face. Lex is due back this afternoon; rather than counting seconds 'til her plane arrives, I thought I'd do some painting.

I've convinced myself no news is good news on the Zio front. When I called Alberti's yesterday, I wasn't surprised to get the machine. I'm sure Angie's still keeping vigil.

But Lupo's another story. I couldn't imagine the cubicle was big enough for both; with Angie's temper, he'd probably end up in a metal bed, too. And besides, Saturday morning's delivery day at Alberti's. So I was betting he'd be here.

When I walk in, I see I'm right. First off, I'm *able* to walk in: the kitchen door's ajar. Crates from Barbetta's sit on the floor. Eggplant glistens in one wooden cage; romaine frills peek through the slats of another.

But that chemical odor.

"Lupo?"

For some reason, the empty-kitchen echo throws me into panic mode. I bust through the swinging doors.

Hunched on a barstool next to the register, Lupo pinches an unlit cigarette between thumb and forefinger. He stares at it, about an inch from his nose, lips moving slightly. Setting it on the counter edge, he rubs a fist across his brow. That's when I spot his hands—dredged-looking— and his white-spattered hair, face, clothes.

I make some movement that catches his attention; he's suddenly wide-eyed. Slipping the cigarette behind his ear, he drops from the stool. As he does, I notice the bucket at his feet.

My stomach flipping like I've crested a Ferris wheel, I fly past Lupo, bark my thigh against a table, and stumble into the banquet room. I don't even need the lights to know. In here, the stench is unmistakable: KILZ. Gramp used it in Aunt Reg's old room to cover the Elvis portrait she'd painted above her bed.

"PleaseGodnoPleaseGodnoPleaseGodno God Please PLEASE!"

Yanking the cord on the maroon drapes, I breathe in rough hiccups. The clink of curtain rings seems magnified in the dim room. I study the mural: Jesus' liquid gaze; the feathery brushstrokes in Peter's beard; Judas's haunted look. It's phenomenal. But it's all just an afterimage, like a camera flash leaves. Because the painting's gone.

My father's masterpiece has been covered over with a thick coat of foul, white primer.

I just stand there, forgetting to inhale. Then, desperate to uncover Dad's picture, I swipe my sleeve across the wall, hoping to salvage this last scrap of him. But the KILZ has dried.

Lupo must've worked all night to get such perfect, even coverage. It probably took hours, but he's succeeded in obliterating my father's Last Supper. My mouth's gone dry and a blue mist edges my vision. I have a burnt foil taste in my mouth, like that time I fainted in line for the log flume. The world's going dim.

And then I howl.

My art box is on the floor. I pick it up, the hefty metal cool against my palm. Swinging wild, I bash it into the newly painted wall, gouging the white. The latch pops; brushes, paint tubes, pencils, blades fly.

"Hey!"

Lupo's behind me. He flips the switch and candle bulbs lick the darkness.

Before I know what I'm doing, I'm on him, punching Angie's cousin in the chest and shoulders. Then I claw at his ears, shredding the cigarettes, screaming, "Why? Why did you do it, you bastard? Why?"

I'm not sure Lupo even understands me, and he makes no move to shield himself—God knows he could snap my neck if he wanted to—just takes it, softly grunting as I hit him repeatedly.

Finally, exhausted, I slump to the floor to gather brushes. I'm arranging them by size, when, thinking, *what's the point?* I snap them in half, hurl them at the blank wall.

Then I'm bawling, not caring about Lupo or Angie or anything except losing another piece of Dad. Crawling to the wall, I run my hands across it like Helen Keller. I notice a tiny area Lupo's missed. One of Judas's ears is partly visible through a thin layer of KILZ. I press my lips to the wall in a whisper-kiss of goodbye, sobbing even harder. I didn't cry this much at his funeral. As a matter of fact, I didn't cry at all; Aunt Ro was "very concerned" about my "total lack of emotion." No danger of that today.

I barely notice the squeak of Lupo's Keds; suddenly he's squatting beside me. He rubs the back of my neck with one rough hand and says, "*Perdonarme*, Evan. Forgive me. Angie, she make me do it. She say, 'It'sa for the best.' "

"Sorry I hit you."

He cries too. Swabbing his face with his apron, he says, "I sorry I ruin you father's picture. Maybe you paint something new there one day. Something happy."

"I don't think so."

Lupo hesitates, glances toward the door, as if Angie might overhear, even from Saint Luke's.

"What is it, Lupo?"

He exhales, searching for words. "She want to hurt you, because she hurt. She's angry at the old man for leaving, but one day she come around."

I don't say anything, just rub my eyes. Angie's made it clear I'm no longer welcome.

Lupo seems to sense what I'm thinking; he smiles and says, "You don' believe Lupo. He just the dumb cousin from the old country. But it's true. Angie like you."

"Look, I'd better go. I'd better not be here if she comes back."

I finish gathering supplies. With one last look at the bare wall, I turn to leave. Lupo tries to speak, but I won't listen. Instead, I say, "You missed a spot."

In front of the restaurant, I try to decide what to do; maybe I'll head to the mall. As I contemplate the frosted sidewalk, Lupo sticks his head out the front door and whistles. I take a couple steps toward him, knowing I'll never set foot in Alberti's again.

Coming outside, Lupo takes my wrist and says, "Look in you art box, Evan. There's something inside for you."

Perhaps it's self-control borne of a good Catholic education. I mean, I'm practically conditioned to raise my hand before speaking. And I spent K through eight waiting single-file to use the toilet—once a day, right after lunch, whether I needed to or not. That sort of heightened self-discipline can't help but make an impression.

So maybe that's how I'm able to duck temptation—walk home, small talk with Mom. Her reaction to the mural news: "I know you're upset, but really, it may be best, the mural being gone. From what I remember, it was a bit much."

I skip dessert and head to Lex's house—all without looking in the box.

We're sitting on the couch, eating dry cereal. Mrs. Bottaro's gone to book club; Lex insisted, even though it's their first night together since Florida.

She said, "Really, Joyce, we can't have you skipping a shot at meaningful interaction."

Lex's mom just shook her head and said, "My name's Denise, remember?"

"Well yeah, but you've always struck me as more of a Joyce."

Mrs. Bottaro laughed as she put on her coat and called, "Be good you two."

This nature show's on, and we ignore the uncomfortable silence sharing the sofa. A pair of snow monkeys gets busy, and Lex looks at me. "Have you finished the journal?"

"I'm saving it for encounter."

"Ah yes, the better to recreate his experience."

"I guess."

I nearly aspirate Lucky Charms when, out of nowhere, she says, "So, what's in the box?"

Finally catching my breath, I answer. "Not sure."

"Yeah, right, you're not sure? You have the most organized art box of anyone I've ever met. You could probably tell me, without looking, what's in every compartment."

"Not tonight. I don't know what's inside. Seems like the whole Alberti gang's got a thing for surprises. Lupo told me there's 'something for me' in there."

"Ooh, I love a mystery."

"So I've heard."

I fill her in on Zio, how he's in the hospital. I can't help choking up. Lex puts her arm around my shoulder. Feels like old times—pre-Tyler. Maybe even pre-Dad. How's she do it?

Then I tell her about Lupo's demuralization project, and *she* starts crying. "How could they do that? They had no right!"

That's another thing I love about Lex: you can count on her for righteous indignation.

"It's like stealing, or . . . or vandalism! God, it's a . . . a desecration!"

"It's okay."

"No! It's not, Evan. It was one of the few things left. And I never even got to see it!" Somehow she seems most upset about that.

"Are you okay?"

She does this fluttering thing with her hands, like she's drying nail polish, and catches her breath. "I'm sorry. I didn't mean to get all mental. It's just dumb."

"What is?"

"I miss him too."

"My dad?"

"Yeah. Your father was . . . " Trying to hold it together, she takes this huge gulp of air, which makes her burp. Neither of us laughs, and she continues, " . . . he was . . . the closest thing I had to a dad of my own."

I hadn't considered, didn't realize she'd felt that way.

"Remember, after my mom threw the stepbastard out—*like, the week after*—school held that stupid Father/Daughter Dance?"

"Pretty bad timing, huh?"

"Well, he offered to take me."

"My father did?"

"Yes."

"How come I never knew about this?"

"I guess you don't know everything after all. And we didn't end up going."

"Why not?"

"Well, for one thing, my mother thought it was a little freaky, him asking. Her perv radar was, like, off the charts at that point."

"Small wonder."

"Yeah, unfortunately, it'd been on the blink for three years while Mister Wonderful was prowling."

"So Dad didn't take you to the dance?"

"No. Your mom had finally convinced my mom it was okay. Your dad was on the up-and-up. I was planning to go. I'd gotten a dress and everything, but then . . . I don't know. I felt like everyone would be staring, like they all knew. I guess I stood him up."

"Oh."

"So he brought the dance to me."

"He what?"

"He came over anyway." She blots her eyes with a napkin. "Brought some tunes he liked: Van Morrison, Fogelberg. I think Mom was just as happy to have me where she could see me. He and I danced right here in the living room."

I'm trying to picture it—Dad and Alexis dancing in this very room all those years ago.

"Anyway, he was so sweet. Told me to keep the records. That was the start of my collection. And he told Mom and me, if we ever needed to talk he'd be glad to help. And . . . "

"What?"

"He said he understood what I'd gone through."

"Wow."

"He told me some day it'd get better. And to . . . " she starts crying again, "to have faith. Obviously, I didn't know what he was talking about then. But I guess we do now, don't we?"

"Yeah, I guess we do."

We don't say another word, just sit holding hands. The TV suddenly gets extra loud—some guy screaming about a citrus-based cleanser—and the bubble breaks.

Lex releases my hand, says, "Want popcorn?"

"Sure."

"Okay, give me two minutes and thirty seconds." She starts toward the kitchen, turning back to say, "That should be enough time for you to see what's in your art box."

I surprise myself by saying, "Why don't *I* make the popcorn?"

"Huh?"

"And you can open the box."

"Really?"

Nodding, I head to the kitchen. The Jolly Time's in the cabinet above the microwave. I pull out a bag. Punching the microwave buttons, I lean against the counter and wait. As the first kernels explode, I hear the squeak of Lex lifting the lid.

Returning with buttery carbs, I find her sitting Indian-style on the floor. Crying again. I put the popcorn on the leather ottoman by the loveseat. Lex flips the TV off as I join her. Spread on the berber in front of her are the new contents of my art box.

"He looks just like you."

"That's what they tell me."

Fanned out in front of me are half a dozen Polaroids, each dated. Lex has arranged them chronologically. In the first, Dad looks about sixteen; must be right after he started at Alberti's. He and Mister A (a Mister A with a shock of wavy, black hair!) stand in front of the restaurant shaking hands. Dad seems a little shy, smiling for the camera. There's another shot of him looking utterly beat, beside a mountain of dishes.

"Look at this one," Lex slides a picture across the carpet. "It has to be Theresa."

Dad's wearing a green graduation cap, standing between the Alberti gals. He's got his arm around Theresa's waist; she's turned toward him, whispering in his ear as he laughs. To his right, little Angela, maybe ten, squints at the camera.

The last picture's the hardest. Dad must be twenty-ish. He's in the banquet room, doing the classic artist pose: arm out, thumb extended, one eye closed. Grinning like an idiot. He must have just begun the painting; there are ghosty figures sketched across the wall. At the table next to him, my infant brother sleeps in a restaurant high chair, a baby beret on his head. I turn the photo face down, unable to look at this tableaux of loss another minute.

Just then, Lex says, "There's this, too."

I'm almost afraid to look, but when I do, I see she's holding an envelope. My name is on the front, scrawled with red marker in Angie's vigorous hand.

"Open it."

Lex gives me an are-you-sure? look, and I mouth "yes," volume failing. She tears it open. Lifting out the contents, she says, "It's a letter."

"Read it."

As she unfolds it, a clump of bills drops out. Lex picks them up, starts to smooth them.

"Lex, read it. Please."

Clearing her throat, she begins.

Evan,

Okay, it's a given you hate me. But think. Why'd you want to remember your dad like he looked in that painting? Whatever made him paint himself like that, I'll never know. See, it wasn't meant to be—you taking over for him. That was just one of Pop's crazy ideas. But it wasn't good for any of us, you being here. It just brought everything back.

After what happened with your dad and my sister, nothing was the same. I don't blame him, Evan. Or your mother, really. Theresa was no angel. But when she took off, well, that was the end of my mom. Anyway, this is old blood, best left buried. Or whatever you do with old blood. That's what I tried to tell Pop.

Course, when did he ever listen to me, right? And now he can't. They said he'll probly never be more than a vegetable, Ev. Not in so many words, but I got eyes . . . So. I thought you'd want these pictures. Pop squirreled 'em away. I think he meant for you to have 'em.

And the money. I remember when we first ran into you at the mall—God! That seems like a million years ago!—you said you needed $174. Well, here it is. And there's an extra $100 for all the shit we put you through. Okay, I said more than I meant to. I better seal this up before I change my mind.

Be good, Rembrandt,
Angie

Lex and I stare at each other for a minute, then she says, "What now?"

I just shrug. If I had any integrity, or pride, I'd go back down there and throw the money in Angie's face. But this is it: my ticket to encounter. I look at Lex and, despite my continuing ride on the anguish coaster, I crack a smile and say, "Popcorn?"

✠

It's 3:55 Friday afternoon, and I've officially overpacked.

It's not the clothes either; I've got the bare minimum, which according to Mom means five pairs of underwear for a two-night stay. Not sure what she's thinking. I mean, I've heard encounter can get messy; still, I don't intend to soil myself.

Besides abundant briefs I've got the basics: sweats, jeans, socks, toothbrush, paste, deodorant. Journal of angst. Cassette of horrific narration. And for extra motivation, a copy of Dad's Sebastian self-portrait; I snapped a shot of the painting and printed a copy. Those last three add impressive heft to my duffel. And I've found his anguished face to be a great motivator. Prolonged staring causes emotional numbness, which makes it easier to contemplate actually going on encounter.

Because, now that it's a reality—and one that begins tonight—I'm freaking out. It's almost comforting pretending I have a choice, like there's a chance I'll listen to that tiny, sane portion of my brain whispering, "Don't go." But I'm ignoring it; no way am I turning back.

Since last Saturday, when Angie paid me off, my plan's ratcheted into high gear. I spent the rest of the weekend compulsively counting: three fifties, six twenties, four singles, a neat stack. Thirteen bills. Hope that's not an omen. Poor thirteen, supposedly its history as unlucky goes back to the Last Supper—Jesus and the Boys numbered thirteen. And we all know how that played out.

The week's flown. Usually the first days back from break drag; not this time. Between getting into the swing at school and obsessing over encounter, Lex and Tyler, dead baby Ev, and Father Fran, my brain's in overdrive.

I haven't heard from Angie; I doubt I will. I took a chance, swung by the hospital Monday after school. Lex offered to come with me, but I figured I'd have a better shot as a lone intruder. I talked her out of coming and she seemed to understand. I, however, instantly regretted it. As she rode off with her mom, I almost chased the Blazer, begged her to join me.

As it turned out, Lex or no Lex, the trip was pointless. In ICU, they told me Zio's condition "necessitated transfer to an extended care facility." That's hospital-speak for lost cause. They wouldn't even give me the name of the place; the nurse said they couldn't release that information to just anybody. Ouch.

I phoned Lex the minute I got home, but she was on another call and "couldn't really talk." I knew it was Tyler. We planned to meet Tuesday in free period before Spanish, but she showed up late, so we didn't have much catch-up time.

I'm trying to be understanding, even happy for her, but I have to admit: without Lex, I'm rudderless. And even though she's back—and the other night felt almost like old times—things've changed. Example: Our standing lunch date's pretty much been toppled.

That became clear on Tuesday when she broke formation in the caf and headed to Tyler's table, "just for a sec." I ended up eating solo, keeping an eye on her backpack.

I guess I've got no right to be jealous, but somebody should tell that to my guts. They pitched uncontrollably as she sat three tables off, giggling with Wattrous and the gang. At least Spiotti's been scarce. He has some major league detention or something—who knows why? He's been spending most of his time in Father Brendan's office. That's a mercy. If the Wattrous party included Lex *and* Randy, it might kill me.

Anyway, after today's incident, I'll be lucky if Lex even speaks to me when I get back.

The rest of Tuesday was pretty typical. We saw each other in Father B's class, met in the stairwell twice. And we sat together in study hall. It was silent study, but Mrs. Koothrappally was monitor, so we managed a bit of whispering. I told Lex my plan to reschedule encounter.

"I figure there's no point waiting 'til late March now that I've got the cash. I'll stop by the office after homeroom, see if Mrs. Teague can make the switch. If there's an open space, I can go this weekend."

Alexis fidgeted and bit her cheek. "So this is it, huh?"

"I guess."

"What'd your mom say?"

"I haven't told her."

"Oh." She stared past me then, eyes wide, unfocused. Then she looked at me like I'd just told her my execution date.

"What is it, Lex?"

"I don't know. Nothing. I'm just . . . I'm a little creeped out about this whole encounter thing. You don't think it's a giant mistake, do you?"

"Great. Thanks. That's just what I need."

"No, don't get mad. I know it's important to you. I'm sure it's nothing. My premonitions almost never come true."

"What premonition?"

She tried to smile then, but her eyes were uncooperative. "Um, I got this image of you just now, kind of like a vision . . . You were really crying."

"That's fascinating, but I don't think you're ready to join Psychic Friends just yet. What are the chances I'll go on encounter and NOT cry? They practically guarantee it."

"I guess you're right. But . . . be careful, okay?"

"Yes, Madame Fortuna."

She had to leave then; her mother was picking her up early—some appointment. As she stood to go, she squeezed my arm and said it again, "Be careful."

She spooked me. Honestly, I was happy to be left alone. In homeroom, I kept folding and unfolding my permission form; tracing Mom's signature; checking my pocket for the envelope of bills. When the bell finally rang, I fought the crush of bodies like an eager salmon, elbowing my way officeward.

As I spread my creased form out on Mrs. Teague's desk, she said, "What is it, Evan? Did you have a problem with the application?"

"Not exactly." I fanned out the money on her blotter, like a royal flush. She smiled as if it was a Valentine's gift.

When I said I'd like to attend encounter this weekend, the Teaguester gave me a that's-impossible-on-such-short-notice frown. I countered with my patented, son-of-a-dead-guy pout. She made some quick calls and got things straightened out. Scooping my cash into her little lockbox, she plugged me into the last remaining slot and sent me on my way.

I sprang the news on Mom at supper. It's becoming a tradition with us, the kitchen table debate. But she reacted with atypical calm. She agreed it might be good for me to go sooner rather than later, "especially with the added stress you've been through lately."

I assume she was talking about Mister Alberti, though she never truly talks about him, just hints around the edges. All in all, it was a successful day, and as I lay in bed Tuesday night, I tried not to think about Lex's premonition.

Wednesday was an almost-normal high school day. The highlight reel would look like this. Standard classroom scenario: Long, boring stretches, moments of extreme disinterest, occasional disrespectful outbursts. Oh yeah, and Mister Pettafordi pointedly NOT looking at Lex and me.

Anyway, I came straight home after school and dove into homework. Miss Delateski laid it on thick: four chapters to read and annotate.

After supper, Mom and I watched a movie. I think we both craved a slice of normal with all that's been going on. So we carefully chose a title devoid of meaning. Finally picking a Marx Bro flick, we kicked back for an hour or so. It's been a long time. I kissed her good night and headed to bed around 10:15. I swear I conked while shutting off the bedroom light. And, mercifully, I drifted dreamless 'til morning.

Yesterday, Lex passed me a note in Father Brendan's class. It said:

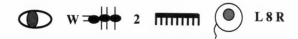

She almost got me in trouble, because I sat trying to puzzle it out 'til Father B said, "Mister Galloway, am I disturbing you?"

"Sorry, Father."

After class, I grabbed Lex in the hall and said, "What's with the hieroglyphics? I want to comb balloon?"

"It says, I WANT TO COME OVER LATER!"

"So balloon means 'over'? Poetic, but kind of vague."

"It's not a balloon. It's an ova—Jeeesh. Did you *not* read Chapter 29 last night?"

"Oh."

"So, can I?"

"Come over? Of course! What's up?"

"Tell you when I get there. So how do you like it?"

"What?" I knew exactly what she meant, and I *didn't* like it. But I'd decided not to comment, in the old, "don't say anything at all" tradition.

"The hair, doofus! How do you like my new 'do?"

"Oh. Fine. Very . . . becoming."

"Wow, thanks for the rousing endorsement."

"No, it looks nice. I'm just used to it being long and, sort of . . . well, frazzly. I always thought that look suited you."

"Well, thanks."

Just then, Bethany Breton and a couple other girls we used to call "track sluts" sidled up. Bethany tugged Lex's sleeve.

"Oh hey, Beebs. Be right there." Turning back to me, she whispered, "Okay, I'll stop *ova* after supper." And then she was gone.

As I wandered the hall, I tried to convince myself her whisper wasn't for their benefit, so they wouldn't know she was coming to my house. It didn't work.

But by the time the doorbell rang, I was past it; just glad to have Lex over. I figured it'd be nice to spend encounter eve with my best friend. And I was happy thinking she understood what it meant to me. It set my mind at ease, like we really were okay.

So it was a bit disappointing to find Mrs. Bottaro on the stoop, Lexless. She was struggling with a big, cardboard box. As I opened the door, she nearly fell inside.

"Where's Alexis?"

Mrs. Bottaro's voice always goes up about two octaves when she's nervous, and she was definitely in soprano territory. "Hey . . . I know . . . you must be surprised to see *me*, huh?"

"Sort of."

"Listen, Lex can't make it. She called me about an hour ago. Some 'thing' came up with one of her girlfriends—can you say boy crisis? But she asked me to bring you these." She hoisted the box into my chest, nearly knocking me over.

"Thanks."

"Can't say I'm sorry to see these go. Okay, *hasta la vista!*" And she skidded down the front steps, looked back over her shoulder, and fake-whispered, "I've got a date!" As she waved from the car window, I couldn't help thinking how much she looked like Lex.

I recognized the box immediately; I'd seen it in Lex's room a zillion times, but why'd her mother bring it here? I dragged it down the hall to my room and opened it on the oval rug. Inside was a sizable share of her record collection: several Neil Diamond albums, some Carpenters, *The Very Best of Gordon Lightfoot*, Simon and Garfunkel, most of her faves.

Closing the lid, I set the box in my closet on top of Dad's footlocker. Before going to bed, I checked if Lex was online, to ask what this was about. But near her name on my buddy list was a little snoozing icon. I figured I'd try to sleep too, and catch up with her at school.

At lunch, I asked about the albums; she shrugged it off, promised to talk later. Later was free period. After Modern Lit, we slipped back to the choir cubes. I could tell she was reluctant to go there, so I promised I'd "control myself" this time. That made her laugh.

Now, shivering on the curb awaiting my habitually late grandfather, I replay this afternoon for the hundredth time and savor that laugh. It may be the last time I hear it.

After we closed the cube door, Lex sat on the piano bench and started plinking keys. Then she smiled and said, "So?"

"So why'd you give me your records?"

She spun back to the keyboard, but before she could continue playing, I closed the lid, sat next to her, and said, "Why, Lex?"

She let out an exasperated huff, saying, "God, Ev! I've just outgrown them, that's all."

"I don't understand."

She wouldn't look at me, and she used this voice I'd only ever heard her use on her mom. "I'm listening to newer stuff now." She shrugged. "Tastes change."

"Tyler doesn't like them?"

Her complexion replied. Before she could say a word, her face went deep pink. Knowing it was futile to lie, she still soft-peddled.

"Well ... no. He's not crazy about my collection, but it doesn't matter. I really like his music anyway. He's going to take me to hear this band, Penalty Box. They're cool. He saw them with his cousin in Boston. They're playing an all-ages show next month at The Lizard. It's a double-bill with Cloth Mother Monkey. Tyler's really excited—we may get backstage passes."

"How awesome." All of a sudden I thought I might cry. I'm such an asshole.

"What's the matter?"

"Nothing, I'm glad for you. I'm just surprised. Those records always meant a lot to you."

She avoided my eyes. "Honestly, I think those old songs were more of an ... affectation than anything. Like a love-me-I'm-quirky type of thing. I don't need them anymore."

"Why not?"

"Because! I don't *need* to be different. I don't *want* to be different anymore! I have a boyfriend. I mean, he's popular, Evan."

"And you're afraid of?"

"Nothing!" She stood, moved toward the door.

I blocked it; no way was I surrendering so easily. "Well, I think you are. I think you're afraid to tarnish mighty Tyler's reputation by being too different. *Too weird.* I think maybe he even told you that, didn't he Lex? Didn't he?"

"NO!"

I just gaped, because I knew she was lying. And if we were still playing by her rules, that was the only unforgivable offense.

Finally, she ran her hand through her new hair (courtesy of Tyler's criticism, obviously) and, just above a whisper, said, "Okay. He might've said that ... some of his friends thought my taste in music was lame."

"And?"

"And? What?"

"Why should that matter? You never cared what those morons thought before! He's screwing with your mind, Alexis! Is he screwing more than that? Is he? Are you and Tyler—"

She smacked my mouth before I could finish. I'm not sure which of us was more shocked. For a second I thought she'd apologize; maybe we'd even laugh about it.

But then her eyes narrowed to slits and she said, "What if we are?"

"Just don't catch anything. I doubt you're the only one."

Now she looked like she wanted to cry. "Why can't you understand? For the first time in my life, I have friends!"

"Oh."

I guess she realized how that sounded. "Evan, I didn't mean—"

But it was too late. She reached for my hand, but I slapped hers away.

"Forget it. I don't even know you anymore. I hope you're happy." And I walked out.

It would've been better if I'd just slammed the cube door and kept going. But she'd started crying, and I couldn't leave her alone like that. I turned around, stepping back inside. I swear I intended *Sorry*, but then she actually smiled and said, "I knew you'd come back."

For some reason, that made me madder than anything, as if she had a right to know anything about me now. So I looked at my best friend like she was less than a stranger and, in a dead monotone, I said, "And I don't want your records. I've always thought they were stupid."

Then I left her sitting there in the silent music box and went to my locker.

I resisted calling her as soon as I got home. I mean, what's the point? Now all I can think about is what Mister P said, how he was too efficient when it came to saying hurtful things. When did I get to be like that?

I sprint up the walk into the kitchen, check the phone one last time. "You have no messages." I'm staring at the flashing red zero when the horn honks. After sticking my Post-it to Mom—"See you Sunday! Love, E"— on top of the answering machine, I run down the walk to the Bonneville.

Gramp cracks the window, peers out. "You sure about this?"

"Nope." He just looks at me, waiting for the rest. "But take me anyway."

"All aboard."

I slide in, and we head for the school lot to catch the bus that'll take me to answers. Or at least a weekend of emotional thrills and chills.

"Your grandmother and I are going away next week."

"Atlantic City?"

"Yup. You're on mail duty."

"Okay."

"So, make sure you come back from this thing in one piece."

"I'll try."

I clutch the duffel to my chest, picturing Dad's face, voice, words inside. Gramp spares us further interaction, and I'm nearly asleep when we get to school.

In the lot, he gives me a shove and says, "Last stop: Rowayton." Maybe he really does have a second life on the rails. I kiss his cheek and jump out. Tooting, he drives away minutes before the red Blazer pulls into the lot.

It feels like we should be blindfolded.

We've been lurching over dark roads for what seems like days, country station blasting on the radio. The retreat house is apparently like some covert destination; I swear the bus circled for the first half-hour to throw us off. According to all the handouts, Holy Family Merciful Wisdom Center should only be about a forty-minute ride from Sebastian's. I check my watch; we've been on the road nearly two hours.

I take a furtive peek at my fellow passengers: varying stages of zombification. Some are asleep; most blankly stare at their reflections in the frosted windows. The mood is less than celebratory.

Then again, it's not like this is the monorail at Disney. I think everyone's anxious about what to expect, what's expected. This is it. Encounter. We've all heard the stories. You're grilled about every bad thing that ever happened to you. You pray 'round-the-clock, bunk with strangers. Sometimes you have to stare into another guy's eyes for a full thirty minutes—no talking. It's like Guantanamo, but with stained glass.

Adding an extra layer of awkward: guys from other schools will be here too. We're expected to bare our souls for total strangers. As if "sharing" with fellow Sebastianites isn't daunting enough.

They say this kid named Allan went crazy at HFMWC, tried to burn the place down. Supposedly, he was taken away in an ambulance and never returned to Sebastian's.

I have to keep reminding myself why I wanted to come, refocusing on the reason I'm doing this. It's a Journey of Dad (not self) Discovery. Eyes closed, I prep for what lies ahead, forcing myself into rhythmic breathing. It's almost working; I start to feel relaxation enter my brain. Then Lex's voice intrudes. "I think you need to put it behind you," and I'm right back in the school lot, ambushed.

Gramp had just driven off, leaving me with no bus in sight. Guess I shouldn't have made a point of being here at 4:30 for a 5:15 departure. The lot was mostly empty, except for two cars parked in the bus lane: other early birds, but with the benefit of warm cars.

As Lex's mom approached, I regretted telling Gramp to go—I was cornered. They pulled into a spot and, before the Blazer even came to a stop, Lex jumped out and ran toward me.

"I'm so glad I caught you!"

"Hey."

"I couldn't let you leave that way . . . with us fighting, I mean."

"Yeah, I'm sorry for what I said."

"Me too."

We took a step toward each other; Lex did a "one potato," bumping my chin with her mittened hand. Suddenly it was just us: no Tyler, no Mrs. Bottaro idling twenty feet away, no long, yellow bus pulling up to the curb.

Then my big, fat mouth joined us. "So. I'm in love with you."

Silence. Lex tipped her head back, stared up at the thickening gray.

"Aren't you going to say anything?"

"Looks like snow."

"That's it? You're going all friggin' meteorological on me?"

"What do you expect me to say?"

"Nothing. I'd better go." I stomped toward the bus.

"Ev!"

I didn't turn around, didn't want her pity. "What?"

"Your bag."

Spinning, I walked right up to her, and said, "It makes me sick to think you're really with him." It was a total blurt; even I was stunned I'd said it out loud.

Praying Lex would just let it go—the way she ignores it if Mrs. S-B-C spits on the desk while reciting the Bard—I tried to "two potato" her, to salvage the moment.

But Lex batted my hand away and said, "I like him. He's fun to be with, which is more than I can say for you lately."

"So that's why you'd rather be with him than me? Well, excuse me for not being my usual bag o' laughs. Learning about my dad's molestation's put a bit of a dent in my sense of humor. I thought you of all people would understand." I bent to pick up my duffel.

"Look, Evan. What your father went through was horrible, and I *can* relate. But it's not like it happened to you, okay? I think you need to put it behind you."

"Now you sound like my mother: 'Get over it.' Yeah, that's great advice."

"That's not what I meant."

"Bullshit! That's exactly what you meant. You think you're in love—or whatever—so all of a sudden everybody's supposed to just . . . ta da! . . . get happy?"

"Don't be stupid!"

"Well, no matter what you say, it *is* like it happened to me. Because the things that pervert did to him left a mark, broke him somehow. So Father Fran didn't just fuck *him* over, he fucked *me* over, too. He left me with half a dad. And finally with no dad at all. So forgive me for having a little trouble 'putting it behind me.' "

She tried to grab my arm, but I pulled away, yanked my bag off the sidewalk, and banged on the bus door. The driver looked up from his magazine and gave me a "hang on" look. I could practically feel Lex's eyes drilling into the back of my head. Couldn't she just leave it alone?

"Evan, wait."

"It doesn't make a difference. You're better off with Tyler anyway. It's obvious I can never make you happy like he does. Just forget it, Lex."

When the door finally folded open, I vaulted onto the bus; sat on the other side from where Lex was standing; put up my hood. Suddenly there was movement on the stairs. I looked up expecting her, but it was just some kid getting on the bus. As remorse registered, I understood how bad I needed her to come after me. I also knew she wouldn't. Looking out the window, I watched her stalk across the lot and disappear into the Blazer. Mrs. Bottaro backed out of her space, and I slouched to avoid Lex's gaze—not that she was looking at me anyway.

So that was roughly two hours ago. My butt's gone numb from sitting here, and I'm doing my best not to interact with anybody onboard. It's not exactly my dream group.

The driver's toothless and stubbled, his eyebrows obscured by this knit cap, a jingle bell suspended from one long piece of yarn. He's like an escapee from *Canterbury Tales*: "The Man of the Bus's Tale." Jolly-bawdy, it'd relate how he heartily drove as the rowdy teen pilgrims squabbled and swore and listened to iPods, while one traveler stared out the window wondering just what kind of crusade he was on.

This burly supporting character, Sir Novack, Knight of the Track and Field, would chuckle at their antics and say, "You shut yer piehole when I'm talkin', Randy!"

Whoa, that's hardly Chaucerian. Didn't I mention Spiotti's here? No doubt that was intentional. I've been trying to will him off the bus ever since he boarded with that shitbag grin and "accidentally" stepped on my foot walking up the aisle. He's alternated between whispering my name, burping "loser," and pelting me with candy wrappers for the last fifteen minutes.

Finally, he pegged Novack with a half-eaten Chunky and got sent up front, just behind Old Jingle Cap. Every few minutes he turns, sneers, makes this hand gesture, a finger-prongs-to-eyes thing. Not sure what it means exactly; fairly certain it's not friendly. Novack's plugged into a pair of headphones—either doesn't notice or more likely doesn't care.

So I guess encounter will be a weekend of torture, basically. Even worse than expected. It's not fair; they should let you see a list; tell you who else is attending before you sign up. I'd probably have waited 'til it was a non-mortal-enemy situation.

Hey, maybe we'll bond. Yeah right, the only way I'd ever bond with Spiotti is if those track goon pals of his crazy-glued us together as a joke. Oh shit! What if we end up together? I'm sure there's no choosies when it comes to roommates, and it seems to be my destiny to be stuck with this guy. That's it; we're bunking.

I contemplate the tilt-out window, wondering if it's large enough to facilitate escape. I've almost convinced myself to leap from the bus and crawl home, when we hit a huge pothole and the vehicle shudders. Looking out, I spot a silver marker that says Holy Family Merciful Wisdom Center. Hoopla.

Jingleman hits the brakes, and we exit the interstate, just as the snow resumes. The bus shimmies sideways. No one else seems to notice our slide toward the guardrail, just me and The Capped One. He steers into the skid like they teach you in driver's ed. Holding my breath, feet jammed under the seat, I brace for impact. It's almost a letdown when none comes.

Mister Jingle succeeds in straightening the bus and, as our eyes meet in the rearview, he winks me a toothless grin. Taking it a mite easier as we head down this big old hill, he hooks a slow-mo left into the entrance.

The driveway's long, straight, lined with perfect rows of sculpted evergreens. Softly haloed by an occasional streetlamp in whirling snow, they're like winter saints lighting our way.

The bus slows more as we approach the circular portion of the drive, and there's a collective inhalation as the outline of the Center emerges from the snow gloom. I'm not sure whether anybody else knew what to expect, but I certainly didn't think it'd look so much like someplace the Wicked Witch might call home.

As we get closer, the sinister impression fades. Still, the place literally looms out of the dark. I'm really beginning to regret signing up for a weekend here; it's not exactly Motel 6.

We skid to a stop. The main building looks like your classic stone fortress, complete with Rapunzel-ready turret. Wide, stone steps lead to a pair of massive doors. Above them hangs a giant steel sculpture of the Holy Family. It's done in this semi-abstract, '70s style. Looks like something the Bradys might've had, if they were into oversized religious iconography.

And speaking of oversized religious icons, I'm thrilled when Father Brendan appears in the doorway. It's a relief to see a familiar face; hopefully, with him here, Spiotti'll be on his best behavior.

We trudge up the stairs, totally silent, Mister Novack bringing up the rear. Miraculously, even Randy seems respectful as he climbs toward Father Brendan, head slightly bowed. Then I notice he's giving me the finger behind his back.

As the fourteen of us cluster outside the doors in the night chill, Father speaks. "Good evening, gentlemen." He pauses, waiting.

Coach Novack clears his throat, and we reply in unison, as if we've rehearsed, "Good evening, Father Brendan."

Father raises his arms in blessing. "Let us bow our heads in gratitude for your safe arrival here tonight."

We do.

He launches into a major prayer medley as we huddle on the steps. This sense of reverent unity seems to settle over the group as we stand there, backpacked, duffeled, waiting for the big finish. He ties it all up with a sung Hallelujah—the old guy's got a very decent baritone—and then gestures us inside.

Novack closes the doors behind us. Everyone stares at the cavernous interior, taking in the stained glass, the rose-stone walls, the statues. As Father B makes his way to the base of the staircase across the foyer, we instinctively gravitate toward him, in horseshoe formation.

"This weekend represents a great opportunity for you as young Catholic men. In coming here, you make a covenant with Our Lord and Savior Jesus Christ."

I love how he says it, like one word: ourlordandsaviorjesuschrist. The word *covenant*, however, has new significance thanks to Dad. My stomach rolls at the thought.

"In the spirit of the Holy Family, we shall embrace one another."

A vague muttering comes from the back of the group—the Spiotti cluster. Novack shoots them a look; the noise dies out.

"Over these next two days we shall become a spiritual family." Father scans the crowd as if cataloging faces. "A family, a collective, is, however, still made up of individuals. And as individuals, you have each been called here for a specific reason. Some, perhaps, are here out of longing, a deep hunger for God's intimate love." This is met with snickers from the rear. "Others hope to quell doubt." His eyes narrow as he looks at the track boys. "Some of you were brought here for atonement."

He looks directly into my eyes then, as he says, "And, naturally, you seek answers."

Eeeeee! How does he do that? He holds my gaze momentarily, his gray eyes penetrating mine. I shiver. Finally, he looks away and continues.

"Regardless of the nature of your personal need, you will find fruition only through faith, prayer, and self-examination. Coach Novack, do you wish to add anything?"

Novack's not prepared for this. He spins his wedding ring distractedly, looks at the floor. "Uh . . . like Father says . . . keep your eyes on the prize and . . . uh . . . remember," his face blanks, like he's mentally fishing for pocket change, "there's no I in team."

Well, that was inspirational.

Spiotti says, "Yeah, Coach!" and the goons start a chant: "No-VACK, No-VACK!"

The coach seems to be enjoying it, until he glances over at Father Brendan, who looks less than amused.

"Sorry, Father." He makes a slashing motion across his throat. "Enough, guys."

Father B nods as if to say, "Indeed it is," but instead, announces, "The other students have already arrived. There are a total of fifty-two fine, young men from Saint Bernard's, Assumption, and Holy Ghost Academy. We will be celebrating Mass with them shortly. Please proceed to the library for registration and to receive room assignments."

"What about dinner?" It's Novack, stroking his gut like he's comforting a sleepy toddler.

"You'll have to make do with spiritual sustenance, Coach Novack. As I said, Mass is about to begin. It's unfortunate you missed dinner—the shepherd's pie was exceptional. But we expected you over an hour ago."

"The driver got lost. So that's it? Your plan is to let these poor kids starve?"

"I assure you they won't starve. Besides, fasting and abstinence are pleasing to the Lord."

"Sure, Father." As we climb the stairs, Novack hangs back, waiting for Spiotti; leaning toward him, he whispers, "Got another of those candy bars?"

"Sure thing, Coach." Randy slips Novack a Chunky. Then he looks at me and says, "What are you staring at?"

Novack pockets the contraband, says, "Move along, Galloway."

I do only too gladly. Catching up to Father Brendan, I follow him into the library. A long table is stacked with plastic packets: our paperwork, standard devotional literature, schedules, that type of stuff.

A priest sits behind the table. He hardly looks older than us. He's wearing wire-rim specs and a pin that says "I'm lovable!" I'm first to reach the table.

He hands me a packet, says, "Welcome to the Center. I'm Father Calvin. And you are?"

"Evan Galloway. Glad to meet you, Father."

"Call me Cal. Let's see, you said, 'Galloway,' right?" He's scanning his list for my name.

"That's right. Evan Galloway."

"Odd."

"What is?"

"I don't seem to have you on the list." He looks at Father Brendan.

"It's okay, Calvin. I'll vouch for this one," he claps me on the back. "He was a late addition. Should be a note from Mrs. Teague."

Father Cal flips through his pile. Clipped to the last page is an index card; there, in red pen, is my name. Next to it's the number 214; must be my room.

"Okay, here you are: Evan Galloway, Room 214. You're going to take a right down the hall, past the reconciliation rooms, and up a flight of stairs. Then, go left and you'll run straight into the 200s.

"Thanks." I hesitate for a second. "Um, what about a key?"

"Key? Oh, no. Locks are unnecessary, Evan. They're a symptom of the barriers we put up between ourselves and God. We've no use for them here, though the administrative offices are sealed tighter than a grave."

"Oh, sure." I get this sick feeling imagining Spiotti with total access to me and my stuff. Although, if we had keys, his would definitely fit my lock, since I guarantee we're both in 214.

Father Calvin says, "Anything else? We need to get the rest of the boys checked in."

I glance back toward various degrees of boredom and apprehension. Leaning elbows onto the table, I whisper, "I was just wondering who I'll be rooming with."

Father Cal flips back a couple pages. Clicking his tongue, he scans the sheet. "Hmm, Room 214, Kevin Geragosian. Isn't that funny? Evan and Kevin."

Yeah it's a real scream. "Kevin who?"

"Geragosian."

"Kevin Geragosian?"

"Yes, he's from Saint Bernard's."

"So . . . *not* Randy Spiotti?"

Father Calvin has begun to look at me with exaggerated patience, like I'm maybe a tad slow. "No, Kevin Geragosian. This Spiotti boy is one of your classmates, I take it?"

"Yes, Father."

"Well, that would be against policy. I'm sorry if you're disappointed, but we don't allow friends to room together. This isn't summer camp."

I don't bother explaining that Spiotti and I couldn't technically be classified as friends. I also don't click my heels together, though I definitely feel like it. I have *so* dodged a bullet regarding roomie assignment. *Amen. Hallelujah!*

"Thanks again." Shoving the plastic packet into my duffel, I head for the library exit.

This brother standing at the door says, "Not so fast, Sport." He holds a basket out to me. In it are piles of buttons: M&M-colored disks with "I'm lovable!" stamped in white. I fish in the basket, pick a brown one, stuff it in my pocket. The bro shakes his head.

"What is it?"

"You've got to *wear* it. All weekend. Here take another."

He puts the basket down; pulling an orange button out, he bends back the pin and blithely jabs it onto my sweatshirt. "There you go."

As he pins me, there's a flash of light. Through silver fog, I see a teeny nun with a humongous camera. She chirps, "That's a keeper," and gives me a thumbs up before going in search of her next victim. Holy paparazzi, Batman!

I tip my head down, chin-to-chest, to look at the button. "Wow, thanks."

"You are, you know."

"Lovable?"

"Yes, lovable. So don't forget it."

"I'll try."

I'm about to hook a right out of the 'brary and scout my room, but Father B gestures. He's lining kids up in the hall. "We'll be processing directly to chapel. Just bring your things with you. Plenty of time to get acclimated after services."

There's a bit of grousing as we slog down the hallway. "I'm starvin'," "Mass already?" "Wonder if they got Wi-Fi."

Novack herds us to chapel, looking none-too-happy at the thought of Mass. He wipes Chunky schmutz off his chin; it's a given he's thinking about shepherd's pie.

Kids from the other schools are already seated. As I walk to the first empty row, I simultaneously groove on the surroundings—stained glass, stone floors, oak pews worn to a mellow gloss—and try to size up the group, pick Geragosian out of the crowd.

I'm so absorbed with examining backs I miss my chance to slip in among the harmless: three drama clubbers and a pair of Lex's choir friends. Instead, I land in a track cluster. I suddenly find myself caught in a Spiotti/Nealson sandwich.

They sit a little too close. Kenny swings his backpack, which smells oddly of liverwurst, into my shoulder. "Oops." Dropping the leg of the kneeler on my toes, Randy thuds onto it, crosses himself, and grins.

I'd always assumed it was just an expression, but I see literal stars; they blur as my eyes brim. Gnawing my lip, I stifle the scream Spiotti craves. The result's a sore lip to go with my throbbing toes.

Thankfully, as Father Brendan and crew file in, everyone stands, and I'm able to extract my foot from under the kneeler. Still, distracted by imminent hurt, I find it hard to follow along. I've never felt such unease about the sign of peace. I just hope my metacarpals heal by spring. The music consists of your typical, warbled hymns, until Father Calvin and that miniscule nun bust out guitars and launch into some classic Bette Midler and—interesting choice—"Rainbow Connection" during the offertory. In a true stroke of luck, Spiotti carries the wine. Taking advantage of his absence, I give Nealson the slip and shift back a pew, safe among the artsy.

During communion, mini-sis sings "Eagle's Wings." Dad always loved that tune, and she's got the voice of an angel, so I can't help crying. One hour of encounter, and I've already lost it twice; wonder if that's a record.

Father gives the final blessing: "The Mass is ended. Go in peace to love and serve the Lord." The "Thanks be to God" seems particularly loud and especially heartfelt.

But as we prepare to leave, he moves to the podium and says, "Please take your seats."

There's a communal shoulder slump, like, "Now what?"

"Before we recess, I shall introduce a special speaker. To you who attend Sebastian's, he needs no introduction. A valued member of our faculty, as well as a distinguished alumnus, he has served our school exceedingly well.

"If you have come this evening from another of our excellent Catholic schools, it is my great pleasure to introduce him to you. He has agreed to be here tonight to discuss the impact encounter can have on a young man's life. Please join me in welcoming Saint Sebastian's Instructor of Art, Mr. Anthony J. Pettafordi."

There's a distinct "cricket-cricket" moment. Nobody's quite sure how to join him in welcoming Mister P. Then Father begins to applaud, meaty palms echoing. Everyone takes his cue and begins to clap as Pettafordi enters stage left and approaches the podium.

"Thank you. Thank you so much. Your warm welcome is especially appreciated on such a blustery February night. I, for one, was tempted to stay at home in the company of a heavy quilt and a steaming vanilla chai—the drink of champions." He regards us with this expression of anticipation that sinks into an "is-this-thing-on?" look.

Was that a joke? Yikes. Just then, camera-nun scurries up the aisle and snaps a really unflattering candid of Mister P mopping his upper lip. He clears his throat and, in this gesture I've seen a million times, his "I've-lost-them" tell, he flattens his necktie with his thumb and forefinger, running them down the edge three separate times. Then, just like he does with art history slides, he dispenses any attempt at human connection and proceeds to talk at us, eyes focused just above our heads.

He tells us how he went on encounter senior year. "I wasn't exactly popular then. And I was unhappy at home." His face clouds as he says, "My father was a bully and a tyrant. But I had one friend who meant the world to me."

Oh jeez no.

"I'll call him Everett."

How creative.

"He was all that I aspired to: popular, handsome, a terrific athlete."

I will myself to dissolve into the pew, wondering if there's a patron saint of invisibility.

"Everett," he says it like he's teaching a new word to his pet macaw, "attended encounter the year before I did. We'd gone through a rough patch, grown apart. When he returned from encounter, it was clear our friendship was over. Then Everett got into some serious disciplinary trouble at school. He—"

Father Brendan coughs once—loudly—and Mister P glances toward him. This odd current jumps between them for a moment; I'm probably the only one who notices. Then Pettafordi shuffles the pages on the podium and continues.

"I came on encounter for all the wrong reasons. I wanted to prove something, not just to myself, but to my lost friend. And to my father. What that was, I'm not quite sure. Perhaps that I was worthy of respect, that I had value."

He's looking from face to face now, searching. Finally his eyes land on me, and I'm unable to look away; it's like he's working some kind of hypno-ray.

"But the main thing I brought on encounter—as sure as if I'd packed it in my Samsonite—was anger. Anger at Everett," his eyes bore into mine, "at my father. And yes, anger at God."

The audience is fairly attentive. I mean, we're a roomful of teen guys; we know anger.

"And I won't insult you by claiming I was 'washed clean of that anger,' that it vanished."

Well, that's good. I'd have to protest if you did. I've seen it firsthand.

"But what I discovered on encounter did change me. It tempered the anger." He smiles at his own ironic word choice. "What I discovered was love."

I anticipate an audible groan, but the chapel remains mostly silent (except for Kenny Nealson, who can't help oofing when Spiotti elbows him in the ribs).

"And that love, the wonderful truth is it was here," he cups his left pec, lingers slightly too long, "all the time. It is the love of God, and it lives in us all. Recognize it, allow yourselves to feel it, for believing you are worthy of it can truly illuminate your lives."

I expect him to launch into a full-on version of that Whitney Houston song—and he probably would too—when he pauses just long enough for Father B to step to the altar mic and say, "Thank you, Anthony. Your reminiscences are deeply felt and much appreciated."

I'm guessing Father's subtext is "Cross this nut off the motivational speaker list."

Pettafordi sort of gulps, looking a tad stricken. Gathering his many, many unread pages from the podium, he shoves them into his Monet folder and shakes Father Brendan's hand. Then, wishing us a successful encounter, he vacates the altar.

We process from chapel in a less-than-orderly fashion. I overhear some kids in Holy Ghost letter jackets laughing. One says, "What was with that art teacher? He was whack!"

I should come to Mister P's defense, but they're gone before I can think of anything to say. Besides, I'm not so sure I disagree.

Wandering down the hall, for the moment, I'm blissfully Spiotti-free. He and Kenny disappeared into the john right after Mass. Hopefully there's a smoke detector in there.

Passing the reconciliation rooms, I start upstairs, looking for 214. I'm actually eager to meet Kevin Geragosian; who knows, maybe he's a cool guy.

Can't believe I got the bottom bunk.

This blows. It's lame, but I'd visualized myself up top where I could disappear; pretend I was in the penthouse; be invisible. Instead, I'm wedged below, counting mattress stripes an inch above my face. Okay, at least three feet, but still. With every move, my roommate sags. I'm seriously expecting 300-plus pounds of furry Geragosian to come crashing down. Still, I'll take death by flattening over rooming with Spiotti any day.

I caught a glimpse of that particular circle of hell earlier, in Room 206, just down the hall. I have to remember to say a Divine Mercy Chaplet for the poor dude bunking in that fun house. I passed their open door earlier, on my way to the toilet, and heard the following:

"Did I *say* you could get down?"

"No, but I thought you were asleep."

"Well you thought wrong. How do you expect me to sleep if that light's shining in? Get back to your post."

"But I—"

"But nothin'! When you stand on that chair, your head blocks the moon. What don't you understand?"

"Can't we please just close the shade?"

"Do I really need to re-explain the spiritual benefits of physical suffering?"

"No!"

"No what?"

"No, sir."

"Good, it's a pretty basic concept. Now up you go."

Poor kid; he's the tester Evan. Guess I should be thankful Kevin's just a thyroid case. The guy's huge, but there are worse things than rooming with a giant. Actually, Bigfoot—that's what I've taken to calling him in my interior monologue; he's the hairiest human I've seen; I'm talking alpaca-hairy—has turned out to be decent. I mean, he's only said about ten words. Twelve, really: "Hey. Plantsfield. Nope. Yup. Vanilla. Not really. A sister. Nope. Good night."

But, mercifully, he's a gentle Sasquatch—lucky, because he could easily dismember me if he wanted. And he gets extra credit for sleeping like a dead guy. Sure, he shifts every minute or so and, yeah, I went into panic mode the first couple times, expecting to be squashed, but the bunk's endured. He doesn't even snore. Nope, other than his massive, shifting weight, his tectonic plate-ishness, you'd never know he was there.

And I don't think I could disturb him if I tried. I bumped into the nightstand a while ago as I was rummaging through my duffel—sent the alarm clock crashing to the floor—and he never moved.

It's 12:44, way past lights-out, but since I've pretty much embraced the nocturnal life, I'm up, listening to Dad's Walkman. I've replayed most of what I heard the other day. It wasn't any easier to take this time.

I'm not sure how much more there is, but I definitely need a break before continuing. Throwing off the covers, I swing my feet over the bedside and move to the window. The snowy grounds look like pewter in the moonlight. Eyes soft and unfocused, I scrape with my fingernail, etching the frosted pane.

When I glance back at the clock, I discover I've been at it for nearly half an hour. I've scratched an image into the ice film: Dad and me from that dream. I'm screaming, he's being sucked to the sky. Charming. Breathing warmth onto both palms, I press the glass, smear off the picture. Feeling cold for the first time, I wonder if that poor kid's still standing on a chair in 206.

"Okay, Evan. You're stalling." I glance over at Kevin—still asleep—then get under the covers. Suddenly freezing, I slip the headphones back on, press Play and hear,

I wanted to scream and scream. But I never did.

After that, there are more Father Fran details, places they went, stuff like that. At one point he mentions,

. . . his cheek against mine.

He sounds regretful, almost like he misses it. That makes me even colder. Now there's just muffled noise, as if he's breathing too close to the microphone, then,

Shit!

followed by a series of clicks, a grinding sound (a drawer closing?) and really distant, muffled, I hear,

Okay, Ma! Gimme a sec.

The tape runs blank for a full five minutes, cuts out. When it starts up, there's all this noise: paper shuffling, a TV in the background. He says,

I wrote a poem. Want to hear my poem, Reggie? It's a sonnet.
   This love has chewed a canker in my soul;
   it rips me raw and pulls me to fierce fire.
   You say this touch will save us; make us whole,
   preaching trust, you foul,

he's struggling

infectious

clearing his throat, he repeats,

infectious

it comes out "infeshus"

**liar! Anyway, it goes on from there. You can read it yourself soon
. . . uh . . .**

losing it, he breaks down, shifting from laughter to sobs. The tape's all garbled; battery's probably getting low. I'm about to turn it off when he suddenly gets louder, clearer, and says,

Sorry, Reg. I'm a little wasted. Been sneakin' again, since encounter. I graduated to Dad's Seagram's—altar wine doesn't cut it anymore.

More laughter, ending abruptly in a cough; then his voice gets deeper, cold somehow.

I used to do it when I was a kid too . . . once Father started givin' it to me and I saw it helped . . . Ma kept that bottla wine in the pantry. Anyway, helps calm me down. And . . . promise not to say anything.

He laughs again, a bitter croak this time.

How stupid am I? It'll be over by the time you get this. Y'need to know I did it to catsh him, make him shange. Father, I mean. So he couldn't get away with it anymore. People will think I was crazy or, or just . . . bad . . . but, you'll know the truth. So, if I go through with it, I'm counting on you to tell.

The sound goes all funky again. I notice the warmth of the Walkman against my chest, can feel it, even through the covers. I hit Pause/Play/ Pause/Play. His voice comes on again, super clear, and he says,

. . . been sneakin the pills for a couple weeks and after I wreck the place I'll take 'em all . . . and . . . then when they come to the art studio, expecting to find me and Tony . . .

Pause.

I can't believe it, drunk or not, he's talking about wrecking the art studio, then killing himself. But why's he bringing up Tony? They weren't even talking at this point. Okay, he was able to pull off Part A, trash the studio—over $500 in damages—but why didn't he go through with Part B, trashing himself?

Rewind/Play.

. . . and . . . then when they come to the art studio, expecting to find me and Toooony theeere waaaitinnngGGRE-EEE-EEE-EEE—EEEEE-ck-ck-ck

Yanking the headphones off, I stare at the Walkman. Inside the plastic window, I can see tape unwinding, beginning to shred.

"Shit! Shit! Shit!"

Repeatedly hitting Eject, I try prying open the little door; the Walkman's hot. I flip it over, pop the batteries. The whirring/shredding stops, but it's no use. When I finally get the lid open, the tape looks like melted confetti. Despite valiant respooling efforts, it's clearly unsalvageable.

I launch the Walkman into the wall and it explodes, shards flying. Kevin lets out the tiniest whimper, farts grandly, and rolls over. Jumping from bed, I crawl on the floor, gathering plastic scraps.

Unsure how to proceed, I just dump the little pile of plastic and wires in the garbage. The acoustic portion of our program has officially ended. I almost feel like giving up, giving in. I certainly don't give a crap about tomorrow's "official encounter activities."

Climbing into bed, I cover my head. The journal's under my pillow, filled with unread pages: poetry, entries. But I don't think I can face them. Determined to will myself to sleep, I clamp my eyes. I'm picturing page 117 of my *Human Anatomy and Physiology* book, mentally labeling sections of the brain: cortex, cerebrum, medulla. Highlighting each, I will it to sleep. It's very soothing, meditative. And it's not working.

Sitting up, I switch on my book light, blinking as my eyes adjust. "So, let's read some poems." The envelope's tucked into the journal. I slide the pages out; train the tiny beam. Each poem's on a single journal page, five in all. The first one's called:

Some Things I Remember
 coarse gray,
 fur-mingled scent
 spearmint/smoke,
 constellations of holes:
 pin-patterned ceiling
 above me, your
 face: pearling sweat,
 hot cheeks rocking
 over throat-wafer,
 rectangled white;
 pushing me down,
 bitter taste of oak
 leaves and worse
 behind my trembling
 lips, shrieking black

Frantic sketches fill the margins: eyes, smears of smoke, the snarling face of a dog. God, it's like a study for a Bosch painting. Stomach tight, I'm anticipating a bad-to-worse progression in the series, so starting this bad has me worried. I flip the page; it's the sonnet from the tape.

TAINT
 This love has chewed a canker in my soul;
 it rips me raw and pulls me to fierce fire.
 You say this touch will "save us; make us whole,"
 preaching trust, you foul, infectious liar.

You take me as you slickly moralize,
with whispers of salvation, gently urged.
And I, your meek disciple, swallow lies;
my innocence and pain—twins sepulchered.

And each time that you come, my will is bent,
in threads of black and ritual enrobed.
The water and wine: UNHOLY COVENANT
that you name "Penance" and a "debt we owed."
The wooden Savior, hanging silent, weeps;
as watchful eye of God above me sleeps.

"Oh my God, Unholy Covenant, like the painting." I can't believe this is his work. I mean, I can; I do. It's just . . . a tear splots the page, rippling ink. Blotting the paper, I leave a faint, black mark on the pillowcase: my own taint.

As I fold pages back into the envelope, I say, "Why couldn't you have just put it out there? Had a gallery show of abuse paintings? Published an illustrated book of poetry? Told somebody. Done something. Anything other than what you did. Shit, Dad!"

I'm barely aware I've gotten out of bed and begun pacing. "I really can't do three more pages. This is too much." Why can't I get desensitized, develop an emotional callous?

I collapse into the desk chair, its legs scraping across the floor. Staring at the window, I try to believe my reflected face is his against the moon. Anything to feel like he's with me. Shivering, I go back to the bottom bunk, fall in. Face the wall.

I'm memorizing cinderblocks when there's a sudden grinding sound. Bigfoot hangs over the bunk edge. "Hey, kid?"

I snap off the book light.

"I'm sleeping."

"You okay, man?"

"Yeah, I'm fine."

"Oh. I, uh, thought I heard you crying."

"Me? No, you must've been dreaming."

He lets out a mammoth yawn. "Impossible. I never dream."

"Well . . . I'm sorry I woke you."

"You didn't. I been awake most of the time anyway, just playing possum."

"Are you serious?"

This is beyond embarrassing. I mean, I've been carrying on: crying, reading out loud, throwing stuff, like I had not just the room but the whole planet to myself.

"Yeah. I'm kind of an insomniac. So, want to talk about your dad?"

"It's awful late."

"Yep, it is."

"I better get some sleep." I roll over, slip the journal beneath my pillow, close my eyes.

The whole room shakes as he drops to the floor. I turn to find Sasquatch sitting next to me; my mattress groans in protest. I can feel warmth off him like a giant baked potato. He's too big to comfortably fit under the top bunk rail, so his head sticks out, beyond view. I'm talking to shoulder rather than face.

"Look, Kevin, it's nice of you to offer. Really. But I seriously don't want to talk now."

Even without seeing his expression, I feel like he's smiling as he says, "Maybe not, but you *need* to."

"You're right."

He climbs back up the bunk, a silverback returning to its nest. Once settled, he says, "So, tell me about him."

"Okay."

Recounting the tale takes exactly one hour and fifty-eight minutes, including backtracks for clarification, and energetic pacing. Throughout the saga, Kevin remains placid, sprawled on his perch. He asks minimal, yet insightful, questions showing he really is listening, but offers no opinions. He'd make an excellent therapist.

Finally, at 3:28, I've started to feel exhausted and decide to make my way back to bed. Twisting the covers around myself for warmth, I say, "Thanks."

His only reply's a nasal grunt; I realize he's snoring.

"Pleasant dreams, furry one."

Bigfoot has left the building.

I hate to say I'm happy, because, obviously, someone going mental and being forcibly removed from HFMWC is not a good thing. And after last night—the way he listened—I'd started to think of him as a friend. Potentially, anyway. I mean, he seemed to care. And the best thing was he knew not to bring it up in the light of day.

Nope, this morning he seemed to have no recollection of last night, didn't moon over me or act too careful. Instead, he just pushed by me heading for the bathroom; edged me out of line at the urinal; took the last towel. It was nice—like he wasn't afraid I'd break. I sort of miss him.

But I have scored the top bunk as a result of his expulsion. And the back hair quotient in 214's way down. I'm trying to focus on the perks of having the place to myself. I've got Dad's pages lining the top bunk right now. I'm considering this my reading loft, and I plan to sleep on the bottom. I'm accustomed to it. Plus, now that there's no longer 350 pounds overhead, I can relax in burrow-like coziness without fear of a cave-in.

"The Incident," as they're calling it, occurred at breakfast. We got a loudspeaker wakeup at 6:45 with orders to report to chapel for morning Mass. It was mercifully uneventful. I managed to avoid Spiotti, losing myself in a clump of Holy Ghosters.

After Mass, I caught up with Bigfoot in the dining hall. I decided to join him; figured it'd be wise to show solidarity with the largest guy here. Hoped it might keep Spiotti at bay. And I wanted to get to know him better, to bond a bit over muffins and eggs. Still, I tried hard to limit our conversation to talk of the small variety, give us both a break before the day's relentless soul-baring.

He seemed to appreciate my casual topic menu: TV, favorite cereals, that old standby, the weather. I was hitting all my marks, 'til I introduced a subject I couldn't have known was taboo: pets. It went like this:

Evan (careful to use his real name): "So, Kevin, got any pets?"

Kevin (going purple, coughing out eggs): "*What* did you say?"

Evan (stupidly repeating): "I asked if you have any pets."

Luckily, by this point, the two brothers serving breakfast noticed the disturbance at table nine. As Kevin lunged across the oak surface, a brown-clad savior grabbed each arm and led him out of the caf. All heads pivoted toward the swearing for just a moment, 'til the double doors swung shut. Then there was a collective shrug as everyone went back to eating.

This little guy one table away went "Pssst!"

I looked up, and he waved me over. Leaving my tray—which now contained a mouthful of my attacker's chewed eggs—I joined him.

Evidently, not all Catholic schools have a dress code as strict as ours; this kid's personal style would definitely not fly at Sebastian's. Even allowing for the hour and probability of bed-head, he had a seriously wild coif: a question mark shaved over each ear, his brown hair, switching to Kool-Aid orange, stood up five inches off his head. He wore an Urban Care Bear tee and a lobe-stretching disk in each ear.

Offering his hand as I sat, he said, "Hi. I'm Lovable."

"Aren't we all?"

He smirked. "Debatable. I'm Jeffrey."

"Hey. Evan."

Flash! Roving nun winked.

I smiled and said, "I'll take twenty wallet-size."

Looking puzzled, she giggled in a squirrelish way, then took off.

"So, what the freak did you say to Kevin, man?"

"You know him?"

"Sure, we go to Bernie's together. He's a real nut."

"I noticed."

"So, what'd you say?"

"I was just making conversation. He didn't seem bothered by weather talk, or game shows, or even my running debate over flakes versus loops."

"Those *are* pretty hot button."

"Then I asked if he had a pet and—"

"Oh, shit, man! You didn't! What've you got a death wish?"

"Huh?"

"He almost got sent to Quaker Lane for beating up his old man."

"Quaker Lane? Isn't that like a special hospital for juvenile offenders?"

"Yup."

"Well . . . why'd he do it?"

Jeffrey sipped his juice, trying to build suspense. "Bastard shot Kevin's Yorkie."

"What?" I don't know whether I was more shocked that Kevin's father had killed his dog or that the Sasquatch had owned a toy breed.

"Yeah, apparently Corky puked on the sofa once too often. Broke the camel's back."

"So, when did this happen?"

"Couple months ago. Kev' was out for a good two weeks."

"That's terrible—about the dog I mean. His father must be a real psycho."

"Not particularly. I mean, I saw him get in a screaming match once at a ballgame, but they seemed like decent people. Guess you never know what's going on inside someone's family."

This line of conversation was making me nervous. I mean, I'm sure people said the same thing about the Galloways. "Well, I guess it's nobody's business why."

He grinned, picking at a corn muffin. "What're you kidding? This is encounter, dude! It's like open season on family secrets. So what're *you* in for?"

Jiggling the salt, I shook my head. He seemed a mite overeager for my story. "You first."

"You name it: abandonment issues, low self-esteem, an affinity for self-destructive behavior. Nothing major with that last one. I just pull out my toenails sometimes." He hoisted a flip-flopped foot onto the table for proof.

"Eeeuw."

"I'm a frequent flyer—the folks bought a season pass."

"Well, I can't top that."

"I don't know, Death of Parent is pretty major. I think you get bonus points for suicide."

"What did you say?"

"Your dad. He killed himself, didn't he?"

"How did you know that?"

"Oh, hey . . . sorry, I didn't mean to upset you."

He gulped, nervous, like he expected me to follow my roomie's lead and dive over the table. I thought I might.

"Who told you?"

Returning his creepy nail-free foot to the floor, he said, "Your friend Randy."

"Yeah, well, I don't have a 'friend' named Randy."

"Well, I have a roommate named Randy," voice dropping, he looked over his shoulder, "whose only break from tormenting me was talking about you."

"Great."

"Yeah, it was some night."

"So you're the human window shade?"

He laughed in spite of himself. "I guess so. Look, I'm sorry. I should've kept my mouth shut about your father. Obviously, Randy was setting me up. He told me to ask you about him."

"What for?"

"I really don't know. But I didn't feel like I had much of an option not to."

"I know what you mean."

Just then, I spotted them across the caf, obviously tuned into our table: Nealson, bright red, snorted behind a copy of the *Saint Hubert Herald*. Spiotti glared at me with that intense-Malamute stare. I was about to embrace prey mentality, seek shelter in the nearest thicket, when Father Brendan's voice boomed over the PA.

"Amen. Amen. Good morning, gentlemen. Pleasure to see you at Mass this morning. I'm delighted to welcome you to day one of our spiritual journey. We've a fine group in attendance, and I assure you the incident which occurred moments ago has been resolved and will have no bearing on our time together."

"Resolved? Wonder what that means," I whispered.

"Oh, it's not that unusual. They probably just locked him in the dungeon."

"Are you serious?"

"Uh . . . no."

Father continued, "I would ask that you join me in a moment of silent reflection for one of the Saint Bernard lads who has reconsidered taking part and will be leaving shortly"—brief bowing of heads—"Now, on to today's activities. Father Calvin."

A shrill warble as they shuffled the microphone, then Father Cal's mellow tone. "Today, our focus will be trust-building through a series of explorations. All activities begin in exactly forty minutes. We'll split into three groups. Group one will experience rigorous reflection as Brother Cyrus leads an outdoor rosary walk through the Stations of the Cross. It's a beautiful devotional exercise; the stations, larger than life, are set into the hills. Those wishing to participate should meet in the foyer. Be advised the trails are unplowed and it is quite chilly. Dress accordingly. Those suffering respiratory ailments are strongly discouraged."

Spiotti and Nealson practically fell over each other racing out the door; several other jockish types followed. I guess they were into the allure of the frigid hike.

Jeff and I looked at each other. Eyes rolling, he said, "Chilly AND unplowed? Tempting."

"I know. I wonder what our other options are."

Father Calvin continued, "We're also offering a lecture and stream-of-consciousness writing with Father Saint Martin. It is entitled 'The Dove Within: Seeking Inner Peace through Self-Love.' There was a wave of snickering, probably set off by the term *Self-Love*. "This superb event will be held in the auditorium."

Some of the more artsy types left their tables and filed from the hall.

Jeffrey was shaking his head. "Been there, done that. Boring AND freaky."

"Finally, a mirror exercise, called 'Soul Search,' in the solarium. I will be facilitating this activity, and look forward to working with all those interested."

"Mirror exercise?"

"Yeah, it's pretty easy. Two people sit at a table and basically try to communicate without talking. Something like that anyway. It involves a lot of staring."

"Sounds fascinating."

"I think I fell asleep last time."

"I'm not surprised. What's the point?"

"It's supposed to encourage the stripping away of the masks we all wear. They say that's key to uncovering the truth within."

"The only truth within me right now is I truly need to whiz before I hit the solarium."

"Me too."

At the urinals, we stuck to the established, eyes-forward policy. Jeffrey was, however, a john-talker; it did nothing for my already reticent bladder.

"Want to be my partner?"

"Uh . . . "

"I'm talking about the mirror session."

"Oh, that. Sure."

"Great, let's go."

"Right. Look, I'll catch up, okay? I just need to stop by my room for a bit."

"No prob. Solarium in twenty?"

"Got it."

Once he left, I was finally able to pee instead of just standing, thinking liquidy thoughts. Then I practically ran to my room, climbed up to the reading loft, and broke out the poems.

It almost feels wrong to read this stuff in the light of day, but after today, I've only got one more day here. Bus leaves for home at 4:30 sharp tomorrow, Sunday. So far, I haven't made any big strides in Dad knowledge, so I have to keep on task.

The first poem's called "Lazarus Eyes." Cool thing is it's a work in progress. He's annotated the page with little notes to himself in the margins.

Lazarus Eyes
  Were they still
  death-clogged   *death-clouded, death-smeared, death . . .*
  when he sat up, shambled free
  of his tomb? And was the crowd
  polite; did they overlook his stink;

excuse the traces of rot? Oh!
But HE wasn't putrid anymore;
Christ undid HIS death. I wonder,
will I be as lucky, or will I always
bear the stain, our sin-rot, decaying   *of us (or soul-decaying)*
deep within these Lazarus eyes?

What if I show these to Miss Solomon—yeah—I could leave them in her mailbox before I do it.

Holy shit, he was planning to share them with Mrs. S-B-C. Wonder if he ever did. I hear a tap on the door; it's Jeffrey. Rushing to hide the poems, I fold them into Dad's journal.

"Hey, you better hurry. The exercise starts in five, and they hate it when we're late."

Slipping the journal under the covers, I jump down. "Okay, let's play the mirror game."

"Just don't call it a game in front of Father Calvin. He takes this stuff very seriously."

Walking to the solarium, I take a moment to admire the surroundings. The stained glass lining the hall is astonishing; with the sun streaming in, it's like walking through a kaleidoscope. My mood's noticeably brighter too. Just knowing Spiotti and Crew have left the building has lifted my spirits. I picture them struggling through waist-high drifts, yelling for help. I suppose someone would be sent to look for remains if they disappeared on the snowy trails. Still, I can dream, can't I?

I will not blink first.

That would be a fatal error, an admission of weakness. Of defeat.

Six minutes have passed. My eyes feel on the verge of bleeding. I never knew it was possible to keep from blinking this long.

I try to imagine a less comfortable situation. Orthodontist chair, melon-fisted Dr. Hanrahan wrist-deep in my mouth. Movie with Tyler and Lex:

"Ty, could you take your hand off Lex's boob and pass the popcorn?" Unpleasant scenarios, for sure, but rosy compared to reality. From the minute he got on the bus, I've been expecting something like this.

We're at a little table near the window, just the two of us. Spiotti faces me, seated directly beneath this larger-than-life crucifix. It's the post-resurrection type, where Jesus sort of hovers in front of the cross, arms outstretched. From where I sit, it appears He's coming in for a landing on top of Randy's pointy head. Hope He's heavy.

Jeffrey and I got to the sunroom just in time. Father Calvin was about to explain Soul Search. Because Jeff's been through it before, I guess he seemed like the perfect demo partner.

Father Cal took his arm as we walked through the archway, led him onto this platform near the French doors overlooking the courtyard. As he talked us through the exercise, he and Jeff demonstrated. It looked a little like this Harpo Marx routine: the pair face to face, Jeffrey following Father Cal's every move, mirror-style.

After a few minutes (and about seven shots by Sister Shutterbug) you couldn't tell who was leading; I guess that was the point. They'd keyed into each other. When he explained that was just the warm-up, there were groans from the group.

Father Cal said, "Come on, now, bear with me. Jeffrey, you know the drill. Ready?"

Jeff said, "Sure, Father," and they sat at this table facing one another and just stared.

It went on like that for about five minutes before Father said, "Okay, you get the idea. Team up, warm up, grab a seat. Really study your partner's eyes—they don't call 'em windows to the soul for nothing. Embrace the experience. You may be surprised what you learn."

Just then, the door at the end of the room banged open, blasting us with icy air. Brother Cyrus stomped in, snowy boots pounding flagstone. Spiotti and Nealson, wearing their penitent choirboy looks, tromped behind him.

"These bozos are *your* problem now, Calvin! I'm through! We no sooner got to the first station than I caught them making a snowman near the path—an anatomically correct snowman."

Some of the guys laughed and, behind Brother Cy's back, Spiotti did a WWE pose.

Father Cal caught it and said, "All right, enough. I'm glad you brought them in, Cyrus. This will do them a world of good." Turning to Randy, he said, "We're about to begin. You'll need a partner."

Before Spiotti could suggest Kenny, Father Cal grabbed Nealson and said, "You'll be paired with Jeffrey here." Then he put his hand on Spiotti's shoulder and, as every nerve in my body fired, pushed him toward me, saying, "And you will team with Mister Galloway."

Randy smiled in a way that can only be described as Grinch-like and said, "Perfect."

It's just typical I'd get paired with Spiotti for an activity called Soul Search—as if he has one! So we're supposed to silently stare into each other's eyes for a full thirty minutes.

So far about 360 seconds have elapsed. I know because I've been counting Mississippis in the face of Spiotti's glare. Oh, and there's a clock next to giant Jesus.

It's gone from spiritual exercise to battle of wills. Neither of us has changed expression, looked away, or blinked since this started. He's like a sphinx, only meaner; doesn't blink, doesn't move. His upper body remains perfectly still, betraying none of the movement beneath the table.

First, I think it's an accident as his boot presses on my slippered toes. I flinch, just slightly, and move my foot away, like you do when someone stands a little too close in the checkout line: a minor adjustment.

But when it happens again, I know it's deliberate, can almost see his foot seeking mine on the nubbly stone floor. There's more pressure as he grinds my foot beneath steely treads.

I will not blink. Will not speak. I allow myself another shift, this one larger. Lifting my foot, I drape it across the other leg, my eyes never breaking from Randy's hate-filled gaze.

We study each other like gunslingers. Then his boot connects with my shin, and I buckle in my chair, releasing a sharp chuff of air. Bending, I rub the egg already blooming from the blade of my shin. When I look back up, Spiotti's grinning.

"Sorry, Gal'."

"No talking." It's one of the monitors, some brother I don't recognize. They tend to meld, in their dull brown robes, like a flock of giant sparrows.

Spiotti looks at Brother No-name and, innocence embodied, says, "I kept telling him to be quiet."

Taken in by Randy's saintly expression, the bro says, "That's fine, son." Then he turns to me, frowns, says, "See it doesn't happen again. The spiritual benefits of this exercise truly depend upon your silent cooperation. Understood?"

Hand clapped to mouth, I offer a serious, slow-mo nod. The brother, satisfied, moves on.

When I face Spiotti again, his eyes are crossed, mouth slack: personification of "Duh." God, I hate him! I'd love nothing more than to reach across the table, grab his lolling tongue, and yank it clear off his face.

Instead—in what proves a seismic shift in the nature of our relationship—I uncross my leg, ratchet my foot back like a slingshot, and ram my heel squarely into Spiotti's balls.

For a second, I'm not sure I've connected. Randy just sits there: no reaction. Then his eyes widen and all color drains from his face. Slumped onto the table, he emits a tiny, wounded-kitten mewl. Hand over his mouth, he retches softly.

I feel a ripple of guilt, not to mention fear. I certainly didn't consider the consequences. I'll be lucky to make it out alive. Glancing over my shoulder (mostly to map an escape route) I notice Kenny Nealson looking our way. Awesome.

In attempted self-preservation, I whisper, "Look, I'm sorry. Are you okay?"

Randy speaks with great effort. "Don't . . . pretend . . . you're . . . sorry."

"No, I am!"

"Bullsh . . . it." He manages to gain his breath, sits a bit straighter in his chair. Pointing a finger in my face, he says, "Okay, I had that coming."

"But I—"

"Just shut up. I'm letting it slide."

"Really?"

"Really. But you tell anybody about it, I'll *kill* your ass."

"Deal."

The brother glides by our table, and we go into limpid pools mode. All I can think is, *It's a good thing this is a silent process.* What if we had to talk to each other? I glance at the clock; we're halfway through—another fifteen minutes.

My eyes keep focusing and unfocusing (maybe I should get checked for astigmatism) as I stare into Randy's. It's probably a defense mechanism, since I'm seriously not into the idea of seeing past his surface. And it could only be a bad thing to allow him access to my deeper self.

Hmm, I never noticed that. Spiotti's got a hairline scar looping around the tip of his nose; it sort of skids off his left nostril, forming a pucker on his cheek. Wonder what it's from. I'm staring at it, instead of looking into his eyes. Randy must notice; he lifts his hand from the tabletop and hooks his index finger over his nose, covering the scar. It's funny; I think I've seen him make that gesture before.

I look into his eyes again and see something totally foreign. Could it be? Vulnerability? It scares me, but now I can't look away. Not because of some battle of wills, but because I'm stunned. Is there really more than just another layer of evil beneath Spiotti's mask?

He blinks and—Holy Crap!—a single, perfect, chick-flick tear slips from the corner of his eye, trailing down his face. When it hits the glitch on his cheek, it changes direction, meandering onto his upper lip. Very slowly, Spiotti's tongue emerges to receive the tear, guiding it into his mouth.

I know better than to react, and Randy's expression never changes.

"Time's up," says Father Calvin. He's on the little platform, looking at a stopwatch.

Everyone sighs and stretches. You'd expect noise—talking, laughter, something—after thirty minutes of intense silence, but the group remains quiet. There's a sense of fatigue.

"Okay, everybody stand up. Shake it off."

Now there's a cacophony of chairs scraping the stone floor, feet stamping, chatter.

"Next we verbalize. I'd like you each to get a couple sheets of paper and a pencil. You'll find them on the monitor table. Once you've gathered supplies, return to your seats and record your impressions of the previous thirty minutes."

A hand shoots up; it's a track dude. "What do you mean impressions?"

"Thoughts. Feelings. Insights you had into your partner."

"Are we being graded on this?"

Father Cal looks a tad miffed. "No. You won't be graded, but I expect you to take this seriously. You'll be sharing these thoughts in group. Now gather paper and pencils, and spend the next twenty minutes writing."

A traffic jam forms at the supply table. I almost miss Jeffrey, but then some kid steps aside and I spot him. He looks haggard; probably the result of his extended Nealson workout.

"Hey!" When I tap his back, he jumps. The relief's visible when he sees it's me.

"Hey yourself." He shoves up his sleeve to show me his wrist. It's scarlet, classic Nealson Indian Burn. "You go to school with these psychos? How do you survive?"

I don't have a chance to answer; Father Cal interrupts. "Please take an extra pencil and paper back to your partner, Evan. It seems he's had a little breakthrough."

I look at Spiotti sitting head down, face buried against his forearms.

"Wow. Break*down*'s more like it. What'd you do to him?"

Remembering Randy's warning, "I'll kill your ass," I shrug and say, "Nothing."

"If you say so." Jeff grabs a sheet of paper and, shoulders slumping, he heads to his table.

Snagging pencils and paper, I rejoin Spiotti. A brother—Lucius, according to his name tag—squats next to Randy's chair, checking on him. Praying I haven't been ratted out, I sit down.

Brother Lucius smiles, says, "Good work, boys," and leaves us.

We spend the next twenty minutes writing. I'm honestly at a loss, especially knowing I'll have to read it out loud. Finally, I manage to fill a page with stuff like: "Focusing on someone else enabled me to find a quiet inside myself," "It felt like floating in a peaceful place where I truly understood God's love for me," and assorted other groovy stuff I'm sure they'll love.

Randy seems to have no such issue with writer's block. He's filled two pages front and back, and just before Father Cal calls "Time," he asks if he can use my extra sheet.

"Sure."

I slide the paper across the table, hoping he's not detailing what it felt like when my foot made contact with his tender bits. Maybe that's his plan: get me in trouble by telling the whole group I attacked him.

We spend the next hour listening to people's Soul Search musings. Mercifully, it's a voluntary situation; we're not required to read our stuff out loud. Naturally, I opt out.

Father Calvin invites Jeff to begin, saying, "You've been through this before, and always seem to have such great insights. Feel like sharing?"

Jeff declines, barely looking up from the table, and I notice Kenny smirking.

Surprisingly, several people volunteer. The hour is filled with amazing testimonials: an even mix of touching and horrific. I'm stunned at the level of risk, the willingness to reveal darkness, speak the unspeakable, like Soul Search has woven this safety net of trust. One guy tells how his father repeatedly humiliated him in front of his Cub Scout troop. Another kid, Rickie from Holy Ghost, confesses the relief he felt when his brother finally died after sixteen months in a coma.

"All I could think was *Now we don't have to spend another Christmas in this hospital.* " Rickie can't stop crying and keeps asking, "What's wrong with me?"

Father Calvin guides the session beautifully; he knows just how to talk a kid down, when to ask him to delve deeper. He's like some incredible umpire of grief. Just as the hour's coming to a close, Father C asks if anyone else wants to speak. To my horror, Spiotti stands.

All eyes are on him, and I'm sure they expect some wise-assery; he's already gotten a rep. Nealson and the rest of the track apes start chanting, "Ran-dy! RAN-dy!" 'til Novack yells, "Cut it!"

Spiotti clears his throat and begins. "Uh. I just wanted to say a couple things." He shuffles his pages, brings them close to his face. He's never exactly been an eager reader. "I didn't come here by choice. Me and some of the other guys pulled some shit at school. Sorry, Coach."

"No sweat, Randy. Just watch the language."

That was obviously for the benefit of the robe-wearers. Novack's language has been known to dissolve eardrums.

"Sure. Anyways, I'm glad I did. Come on retreat, I mean. And this activity, even though I thought it'd be total BS at first . . . "

Laughter from the crowd, even Father Cal.

"Wait, but it wasn't. It was sort of cool. My partner was Evan Galloway, this kid from my school."

I feel sudden heat in my face.

"We've never really been friends." He looks up from the pages, an apparent departure from what's written. "Actually, I've always been a dick to him."

When Nealson laughs, Coach Novack cracks the back of his head with his clipboard.

Spiotti continues, "But sitting here staring in his face, I guess I realized something. I stopped seeing him as this weak, doofy, little brainiac brownnoser." *Wow, I'm touched.* "I started seeing just another kid." Folding his papers, he's about to sit back down.

I'm thinking, *That's it?*

Father Cal must sense Randy has more to share. In this soft voice he tells him, "Go on."

And—BINGO—he does!

"Just . . . I've always been kind of . . . people look up to me. And that's great, but . . . sometimes, like I said, I'm sort of a dick—sorry—a bully. And this Soul Search made me see a little better why I act like that. And now I feel like, maybe, it's time I change. That's it."

The room's silent. I spot Nealson; he's wearing this queasy look, like he's discovered pudding in his jockstrap. I feel my own jaw slightly unhinged in disbelief and, closing my mouth, look across the table at Spiotti. He smiles and offers his hand. It's a real Hallmark moment.

Father Cal leads the applause that engulfs the room. Then we break for lunch. It seems I've become an object of curiosity; no doubt, due to Spiotti's little interlude, everyone's eager to get a look at the brainiac brownnoser. Happily, there's no sign of Spiotti himself. Small favor.

As we tuck into our Sloppy Joes and baked beans (only later, in the confessional, will I question the wisdom of serving such flatulence-inducing fare to a herd of teenage guys), Jeffrey still looks shell-shocked. Head down, he rocks slightly, keeps rubbing his wrist.

"Are you okay?"

He looks at me—eyes sad, red—but he only shrugs. "Just tired. Listen, we got almost an hour 'til confessions. And I'm totally wiped from Soul Search. I think that Nealson scumbag may have extracted mine somehow." This foggy look returns, but when I clear my throat, he offers a smile and says, "I think I'll grab some Zs."

"Okay."

Somehow, watching his back as he trudges down the hallway starts me thinking of Lex. I briefly consider breaking rule #1—no outside contact—and giving her a call. Instead, after dropping my tray onto the waste conveyor, I decide to spend the free time reading. But I don't feel like sitting in my room; I plan on the chapel. It'll be quiet there, and private.

I've gathered some stuff from 214. The journal's in my hoodie pocket and I'm heading to the chapel when I happen to glance out the big glass doors overlooking the back hill. This glorious valley view glints through bare trunks, the ice stained like fruit sherbet by the waning sun.

Staring out, I imagine I can see my house from here (like I know where *here* is). A pop of red catches my attention as a cardinal shoots from a pine, landing on a half-buried stone wall. The movement draws my eye to a figure huddled against the wind, partway down the hill. Thinking it's a brother—he's got that shapeless-brown-lump quality they share—I tap the window. No response. Curious, I put my hood up and step out, feet sinking, toes instantly damp.

As I approach the brown-clad form thinking, *Why am I out here in slippers?* he turns. First thing that registers: the buttons, his robe's really a corduroy trench coat. Then I see the cigarette. I'm close to an about-face when he calls me.

"Galloway!"

Terrific.

"Hey, Randy."

"So, if I embarrassed you before . . . sorry."

I've begun backing toward the double door. "No big."

"But . . . it is."

I'm almost to the doors when my heel catches the ridge of snow-caked walk and I topple. Luckily, the drift buffers my head as it hits stone.

"Hey, you okay?"

"Fine."

Randy tries to lift me, but I shake loose of his grip.

"I said I'm fine!"

Standing, I get my first good look at his face, and can't help asking, "Are *you* okay?"

Snorting a last clot of smoke, Spiotti flicks his butt into the snow with a tiny *sizzz*. "I'm great."

Unsure why I even care, I pursue it. "You don't *look* great."

"Yeah, well, I been thinking."

"What about?"

I shudder when he says, "You, me. We're not that different you know."

"Gulp." Oops, didn't mean to say that out loud.

"What's that supposed to mean?"

"Sorry. Just a joke."

"Whatever. Look, I been realizing we have some shit in common."

"What type of shit?"

"Your old man, my mother."

"What about your mother?"

He starts downhill toward this stone gazebo. Ignoring my better judgment, I follow.

"Wait up."

I join him in the gazebo. He clears snow off one of the benches— these big, carved granite slabs—and sits, head hanging, hands between his knees. I shove the snow, like a big, white sheet cake, off the bench opposite him and sit.

"She . . . uh . . . bailed on us. Just like your father."

"Wait, you mean she killed herself?"

Staring at the painted gazebo ceiling—Blessed Mother, serpent crushed beneath her heel—he sighs. "Might as well have. She's dead to me."

"Oh."

"The bitch walked out on my old man and me when I was six." The way he sneers, like he's auditioning for a movie, he almost convinces me he's angry, not hurt. I wonder, has he convinced himself?

"That's rough."

"Yeah. Actually it was the day before I turned six. Some birthday, huh?"

"Wow. I'm sorry."

He stares at me for a long time, puzzled. I'm beginning to feel like a specimen in a museum case when he finally says, "Shit, you really are, aren't you? Sorry."

"Well, yeah."

"Why?"

"Uh . . . I guess . . . I just feel bad for you. That must've been—"

Suddenly he's looming. "Who are *you* to feel sorry for *me*?"

I try to stand, but he pushes me back onto the bench. Certain he's about to hit me, I sink in defensive posture, hands over face, shoulders hunched. I'm cringing for a good thirty seconds, braced for contact, when I hear it: a blubbery exhalation.

Slowly opening my eyes, I'm stunned at the sight of Spiotti hunkered on the far side of the gazebo. He's crouched, leaning against the bench, face pressed into the remaining snow. His whole body shakes, like an elastic stretched to snapping.

"Randy?" Stepping closer, fawn approaching rabid wolf, I ask, "What is it?"

He mumbles something I can't quite understand. When I put my hand on his back, he tenses as if I've delivered an electric shock. I pull back.

"I said, just go!"

"Maybe I can help you."

"No! I don't need your help. And if you don't go now, I'm afraid what I might do to you."

I have a horror movie flash: this guy transforming into a werewolf warns his friend to run. He's snarling, "Save yourself," and just like the friend, I'm stupid enough to refuse.

"Just talk to me."

"Evan, I swear, you better get away from me right now."

But he's shaking as he says it, and I sense a part of him, at least, wants me to stay. I sit next to him on the icy stone floor. He's clenching and unclenching his fists; I honestly believe he might pummel me. But I see something else in his face, something new. His lip trembles as he talks, and I realize what that new thing is: Spiotti at six. Motherless. Broken.

"I'm scared, man."

"Why?"

"This shit! All this 'I'm lovable' bullshit. How am I supposed to accept that? How does that apply to me? If I'm so lovable, why didn't my own mother think so?"

I truthfully don't have an answer for him, but I realize he's not really expecting one.

"Oh forget it! This is all homo bullshit anyway. What's the point? Like any of this shit applies when we get back to school on Monday."

"Maybe."

"What, you think things will be different because some friggin' celibint—"

"You mean celibate?"

"Celibate, right. Some celibate asshole sticks a pin on my shirt and all of a sudden everything's perfect? Bullshit! You think that pin will bring my mother back? How 'bout your father? Some pin on your shirt going to bring him back to you?"

I'm pissed, but manage a monotone, for safety. "I don't think that's the point."

"Then what is?"

"Maybe just the fact that you and I are talking to one another like human beings, maybe that's reason enough to have come."

Randy's about to answer when we hear the siren, faint at first. I almost believe it's just passing by. But then I see the ambulance speeding up the drive, lights flashing among evergreens as it draws up to the Center's front doors. Spiotti and I look at each other, then back to the building. There's a commotion, a cluster of bodies in the hall, just visible through the glass doors.

We freeze, uncertain. A part of me wants to stay in the gazebo, pretend nothing's happened. Then I picture Jeffrey, eyes empty, as he said, "I think I'll grab some Zs."

With a twinge in my gut, I run for the building. As Spiotti and I reach the double doors, I notice most of the guys clogging the hallway are from Saint Bernard's.

I shove through the group to the center of the hall, wet slippers skidding. I'm about to ask what's going on, when two EMTs round the corner. They push a stretcher, leaning to talk to their passenger. I see his face, pale, waxy; his Kool-Aid hair's like a pumpkin nest on the pillow. The last thing I notice as they push Jeffrey past is his bandaged wrist.

They must have a written procedure.

It went that smoothly. And given the level of efficient cool with which they handled the situation, I'm guessing attempted suicide's not exactly rare in these parts. Not that I'm surprised. I mean, take the emotional issues of your average teenage boy; multiply by sixty-six attendees; mix in the stressors of forced intimacy and dorm-style accommodations; sprinkle generously with bullying cliques; and stand back. Somebody's bound to blow.

Seriously. In spite of the soothing poster selection—rainbows, doves, loads of smiling Jesuses—and the "man-who-stilled-the-water" musical stylings, this place is an emotional crock pot. It's impressive we made it all the way to Saturday afternoon before EMTs were summoned.

Rolling past on the gurney, Jeff swam in and out of awareness. Still, I wanted him to know I was there. Trailing the paramedics, I called his name. As his eyes rolled my way, I said, "It'll be okay."

He didn't answer, just lifted a gauzed wrist and, hand-to-ear in a phone gesture, mouthed, "Call me. "

When I tried to follow them out the front doors, Novack pretty much body-checked me back into the lobby. He said, "Leave this to his folks, Galloway."

Following his stretcher's bumpy progress down the stone steps, I saw them: Jeff's parents, at the curb. They didn't rush to meet him or get in the ambulance; just waited alongside for the guys to load him in. Then they got back in their car and tailed their son's emergency vehicle down the drive.

I had barely a minute to process it before we heard Father B. "We will convene in the chapel in ten minutes for a brief prayer service. Please proceed in orderly fashion."

I expected a major change of plans: an announcement that buses would be coming to take us home; cancellation of the rest of encounter; at the very least, suspension of the remainder of today's activities. Didn't happen. Instead, we said a rosary in honor of "young Mister McAlister." Funny, I hadn't known Jeffrey's last name, even though I'd begun to consider him a friend.

Then, after a brief free period (during which I did a little reconnaissance work, with some promising results), it was on to business as usual, though the Bernard boys had the option of calling their folks and leaving right after the prayers. I was surprised none of them did; then again, Jeff didn't seem particularly close with any of these guys.

Confession came next, and it was a "Bless-me-Father" blur. I seriously can't even recall what I said. I was just relieved it was some priest I didn't know. I'd been dreading getting Father Brendan. It's impossible to withhold anything from the guy, and I really didn't feel like divulging everything I've been going through these past few weeks.

Now we're back in the cafeteria, and suppertime brings a small concession to the awful events of this afternoon. Father Cal clinks a spoon against his water glass, wedding reception style, and stands to announce, "In order to lift our spirits, and get encounter back on a positive track, you'll be receiving your palancas a day early."

Apparently this is a big deal. Father explains the strict protocol governing dispersal of palanca letters. They're traditionally handed out on Sunday afternoon after the Promise Ceremony, prior to closing Mass.

"But," he says, "I think Jeffrey would want us to forge ahead with spiritual growth, to recapture joy. And one way to do that is to hand out those babies. A palanca," he explains, "is an act of sacrifice: fasting, abstinence, or prayer. The letter or gift is NOT the palanca; the letter or gift is a physical representation of the sacrifice. The palanca means someone has promised to join with you spiritually, to partner with you through prayer. The palanca shows you are not alone; you are part of a community."

He says we should head back to our rooms, promising we'll find the "physical representations of sacrifice" there. Wow, I'd have settled for a mint on the pillow.

We file out of the cafeteria. When I enter 214 it's apparent the encounter elves have indeed made a delivery. A cardboard box sits on the desk with "Galloway: RM 214" scrawled on the side in black Marks-A-Lot.

Hefting the box, I swing up to the top bunk. When I pop the lid, I discover a bunch of envelopes inside. I can tell who most of them are from just by the size, color, and handwriting.

- Flower Fairy: Mom, obviously;
- Neon green, SpongeBob sticker: Aunt Reg;
- Large manila, Little Sisters of Infinite Hope logo: Aunt Ro;
- Plain, white #10 utility: Gran and Gramp;
- Purple craft paper, silver ink: Has to be Lex;
- Square, green vellum: Could it really be Mister P?
- Heavy buff with an S B C monogram on the back flap.

It feels like Halloween, dumping my pillowcase, surveying booty. All in all, a decent haul. I decide to open the Anonymous Three first. One's just a folded and stapled sheet of pebble gray paper. I pull the staple free, drop it in the trash. Unfolding the page, I see the return address: Office of the Archbishop. Printed in laser jet script below, it says,

Dear Candidate,
    A Mass is being offered in your honor. Wishing you success in all you encounter this weekend and always.
    May God bless you,
    Archbishop L. J. Donaldson

Great. Nothing like the warm fuzzies that come with a form letter from the archdiocese; ". . . success in all you *encounter*," who knew the Archbish was a punster?

The next one's from Mrs. Teague—really, Mrs. Teague! I expect another form letter, and it is. It says she's dedicating her daily prayer to the intentions of the young men on encounter. Very nice. But at the bottom, she's written a personal message. In her precise hand, it says,

> **Evan,**
> **I know a bit about what you're going through. My older sister took her own life in college. You never quite get over it, but in time, you will find some peace. I'm praying this weekend helps you do just that.**
> **Love & Blessings,**
> **Mrs. T.**

"Oh my God." I'm not sure why this hits me so hard, but I just sit for a few minutes, my stomach souring. Who'd have guessed we had such a weird connection?

The third envelope contains two sheets of paper. I unfold them, and a prayer card and "I'm lovable" bookmark drop on the bed. It's a rate-your-encounter-experience survey. Quick-scanning, I see questions like, "Was support staff approachable and receptive?" and "Did you find any elements overwhelming?" Ugh. Wondering if Jeff will get one of these, I toss it aside.

Okay, on to friends and family. I put Lex's envelope aside; whether because I'm saving the best for last, or out of fear of what's inside, I'm not sure. I start with Mrs. S-B-C.

> **Dear Evan,**
> **You're a smart kid and, too often, brains and sensitivity don't cohabit. In your case, you've got perhaps too much of both. Your father was a special kid too, and I can never shake the sense that I failed him. Come see me when you get back. We have some things we should talk more about.**

I wanted you to know I'm praying especially for you this weekend and, in your honor, I'm limiting my reading to the Psalms. Some would say I'm doing this simply to avoid freshman comp papers.

While there may be some truth to that, I want to focus my prayers and energy on you, Evan, because—corny as it sounds—you deserve it.

You are lovable.

All good gifts!

Mrs. Solomon-Baxter-Coombs

What could she mean by "I failed him"? It must have something to do with those poems. What if he did show them to her, like he said in the note alongside "Lazarus Eyes"? Would she have reported it—or did she fail him by not telling?

Pettafordi's palanca's next. I carefully fold back a vellum flap and examine the contents. It's like a riddle. After repeated readings, I'm still not sure whether he's trying to be philosophical and enlightening, or just plain confusing.

He's sent four postcards: each a famous image. He's numbered them. First up: *The Annunciation* by some Flemish Master. I remember it from Art History—the badly skewed perspective of Mary's tabletop, Gabriel's shiny wings. On the back, he's written: Miracles must be measured in contrast with the ordinary. Knowledge resides in the small things.

Card two is a Hopper painting, that famous one of folks in an all-night diner. Night Owls? No, that's wrong. I check the title: *Nighthawks*. This time he's written: The human heart is capable of both extraordinary love and uncommon loneliness.

The third one's a Muppet parody of Botticelli's *The Birth of Venus*, but with Miss Piggy on the half-shell. Bizarre. And I have no idea what the notation's supposed to mean: There is beauty in all, that which is given and that which is taken away.

Finally, card four shows a huge waterfall. It's a black-and-white shot by that famous photographer, Ansel Adams. On this one, Pettafordi's written: And your tears shall purify you. Fascinating, but I'm getting a major headache. I tuck his philosophy flash cards back in their packet, wondering what he was smoking when he crafted this little care package.

Next, I open Aunt Rosemary's. This I'm prepared for. An enormous Mass card from the Little Sisters, it looks like a diploma folder. The outer cover's sky blue leatherette. Inside is this poem: "An Encounter Prayer." She must've done some major searching; it's the perfect accessory.

An Encounter Prayer
  I'm praying for your precious soul,
  That God will make it soar.
  And raise you with His gentle hands
  To guide you through love's door.

  The time you spend with Him today's
  A special time for you.
  And as you pray and talk and share,
  Please know I'm praying, too.

  I'm praying for your wisdom, that
  It blossoms like a rose;
  I'm praying for your doubts and fears
  That you'll be healed of those.

  But if dark thoughts should come your way,
  Like clouds to make you blue,
  Just think of me at home in prayer,
  For God to see you through.

Copyright 1998 by Jaqueline Joakitis for The Little Sisters of Infinite Hope
Published by Saving Son Ministries, a division of Perpetual Life Publications

Opposite the poem, a page details my enrollment in The Little Way Society. She's also written a note on the bottom: "You will be remembered in their daily Masses—in perpetuity. Love, Aunt Rosemary."

"Wow, perpetuity." That's a long time. It's sweet, especially knowing how important she considers that stuff. It'd be like Gramp enrolling me in the Young Republicans, or the Elks.

Thinking of Gramp leads me to the next envelope. I know it's from them; it's the type Gran uses for coupons. They buy them in bulk at Big Box. Probably have a case of 20,000 in the pantry next to the twenty-gallon jug of mustard.

The writing on the front clinches it: Personal for Evan G. Galloway, Junior, Saint Sebastian's High School—DOB: Jan. 22. Yup, that's Gran. Nothing if not thorough. I'm surprised she didn't list my shoe size. Opening the envelope, I slide out a sheet of lined paper. In Gran's slightly irregular, sloping script, it says,

Evan,

Honey, I can't believe how grown up you are. My God, you look so much like your dad! Gramp and I hope you know how proud we are of you.

They told us to be sure and say you're lovable. Like I need to be reminded! Besides, you know that, don't you? I hope you do. You are my world, honey. You've lifted so many clouds.

The talk we had the other day was a long time coming. Even though it hurts, it's for the best, knowing the truth. Thank you for helping me face it.

We're leaving for Atlantic City, and you can be sure that car ride will be spent in prayer, sweetie, sending you so much love!

Okay, your grandfather wanted to say something too, so I'm turning the pen over to him. Xoxoxoxoxo, Gran

BUDDY BOY,

DON'T LET THE TURKEYS GET YOU DOWN. LEFT THE HOUSE KEY WITH YOUR MOTHER. TAKE CARE OF THINGS WHILE WE'RE GONE.

GRAMP
P.S. LOVABLE, MY ASS. HA HA

He's too much. I laugh out loud. Then picturing him in the Tahoe, stone-faced and struggling, I stop, refold the page, and slide it back into the envelope.

Aunt Reg is next; let's hope the message is in keeping with the Sponge on the front, because I could use a laugh. This whole palanca thing's a bit twisted, like a premature eulogy. It's nice in theory, to know how people feel about me, but what'll it be like seeing them? Will we treat each other differently now that they've revealed this stuff in print? Then again, I've always known they love me. Well, except for Mrs. Teague. That was a surprise.

Aunt Reg's envelope has a center bulge. When I open and tip it upside down, a Reese's Cup falls onto the bedspread. It's a little worse for the wear after its journey, but I don't let that stop me. I pop it in.

Candy + laughter = near-death-by-choking. She Photoshopped her face onto a picture of the yellow fry cook. Above it, a banner says, "Our Main Ingredient Is LOVE!" The rest of the card's set up like a menu:

- Breakfast Saturday: fat-free chocolate chip muffin, ¼ cup raw almonds; sugar-free Swiss mocha gourmet coffee
- Lunch: turkey Reuben, baked chips (sour cream/onion), large Diet Birch Beer, mixed berry FF frozen yogurt
- Snack: bag low-fat Cheesy Puffs, caffeine-free diet cola
- Dinner: chicken enchilada combo from Señor Pablo's, cinnamon sopapillas, diet raspberry soda
- Dessert: nonfat carrot cake ice cream with caramel topping
- TV snack: pudding cup (fat-free devil's food)

As evidence of the deep love I have for you, I'll be foregoing some of my favorite things (see menu above) as I FAST all day Saturday in unity with your spiritual quest. You'd best appreciate

it, pal. It's only Friday night and I'm already regretting this decision.

No, seriously, love you buckets, Evan-bo-bevan. And I hope encounter brings you peace and clarity. ((((((Evan)))))) = BIG, SQUISHY HUG!!!! Aunt Reggie

Two to go. Not sure which I'm more nervous over, Mom's or Lex's. Ordinarily, Lex would be the safe bet. But based on our last exchange, I'm leery. I weigh an envelope in each hand. Mom's has a plumped-out quality, a bit like Aunt Reg's, but I doubt there's candy inside. Lex clearly took a lot of time on hers, so chances are she's overlooked my stupidity and there's no anthrax inside.

Okay, no more delay. I opt for Mom's, pull out the card. It's a Lily of the Valley fairy kneeling in a prayerful pose, gazing up at a stalk of the tiny white bells. A rubber band around the card secures it to a small manila pouch.

Pulling the band free, I read the card, the briefest palanca note so far.

Ev,
   There are no words.
   No way to tell you how proud I am. ~ x. o. ~ Mom
   P. S. I'm praying so hard. And believe me, I won't sleep all weekend. I hope that counts as a sacrifice!

Well, that was pretty painless. I turn the pouch over, see a note on the front:

Don't know if you'll remember this, but thought you should finally get to see it.

Tearing open the pouch, I squeeze it in my hand and look inside. A mini plastic bag holds a bubble-wrapped lump. This wave of unease makes me hesitate. The packet has a familiar weight, like a memory, in my palm. I carefully unwrap it, surprised when a thin, gold chain slips out, swinging between my fingers.

Last time I saw the locket I was about six; I've never seen her wear it. I remember:

On tiptoe in front of her chest of drawers, exploring forbidden territory, looking for Dad's garnet tie clip. We're going to Gran and Gramp's anniversary dinner. Opening Mom's jewelry box, I see it, shiny against green velvet. The shimmery oval's marked "K" for Katherine.

I lift it from the drawer, hold it to the light. Just then, her bedroom door squeaks. Mom sees me; starts to speak; notices the locket.

It's like she flies across the room.

She grabs my wrists, practically lifting me off the floor. "WHAT ARE YOU DOING?" Instantly, I'm crying. When I drop the locket, she dives to rescue it, then shoves me out the door into the hallway. I hear her sobbing as I slam my bedroom door.

Blood pounds my ears at the vividness of the memory. Holy crap. Why'd she send me this? Turning the locket, I use my thumbnail to pop the latch. It accordions out like a teeny road map, revealing a tri-fold frame.

Each segment holds a baby picture. On the left is Infant Dad, all dimply smile and those ears. The center frame holds Evan Jr. It's one of the pictures from the album; his head's still vaguely bullet-shaped. In the right-hand frame I see the last Evan, the sole survivor, me.

I stare at this trio for a long time as that line from *Hamlet* "Good night, sweet prince" echoes through my head. Folding the locket shut, I bring it to my lips, to kiss it like an icon. Then I hook the chain over my head and drop it inside my sweatshirt, to dangle near my heart. I gather the rest of the letters and, wrapping them in a T-shirt, place them in my duffel.

Only Lex's remains.

It's sort of a shame to open a Lex present; she takes such care wrapping. This is no exception. She's handmade the envelope from glittery, purple stock. I picture her slender fingers creasing these perfect folds. The back flap's sealed with a mini photo-booth sticker of us wearing haloes and wings. We must be eight-ish. Right around the time her life began unraveling. I peel the sticker, careful not to rip it, knowing we'll never be so close again.

Dear Evan,

It's true what they've been telling you all weekend: YOU ARE LOVABLE!

I love you, Evan. More than you know. You are my greatest gift.

SO ... Yes, I guess "SO" is sort of like "BUT" ... And I promised to keep my big butt out of this! Sorry, that was lame.

The things you said before getting on the bus really made me think (for one thing, I thought, "Hmm, I'm not used to Evan having such a potty mouth"). But seriously, I guess I owe you an answer.

I suppose I've always known you felt that way about me (even before the music room), but hey, what's not to love? And I'd be lying if I denied having feelings for you, because in a lot of ways, I do feel the same (see above).

But, Evan, I can't ever "BE WITH YOU" that way. Even the thought of it makes me a little queasy—no offense.

Doctor Lindquist says I may always have "intimacy issues," that letting people close might never be easy, because of what the stepmonster did. She says it's a trust thing. (Picture me doing air quotes. She does that—ugh.)

And the physical stuff—I'm afraid part of me will always think of it as ugly, scary, dirty. And I couldn't stand it if I ever thought of *you* like that. So, I just can't see dragging you into my mess. You're too important to me. What I'm trying to say is: If I was ever truly able, ever capable of really being "in love"—in a real relationship—with somebody, it'd probably be you. But I'm afraid that'll never happen. Not meant to be.

Catch you on the flipside, Bud. (Besides, you'd probably get sick of me, anyway. I'm always saying annoying stuff like, "Catch you on the flipside.")

Well, I've basically disregarded the whole protocol here (which Sister Dorothy explained in excruciating detail during Palanca 101), that being to avoid hot-button topics; offer complete support; be positive and reassuring. I hope you can forgive me. I've never been great at following rules, as you may have heard. But I figured I should be honest. I thought it was important to clear things up.

However, they may intercept this and screen it for subversive content, so I shall now include some official palanca-speak . . .

I pledge to join with you in spirit during encounter weekend. In support of your spiritual journey, I've vowed to say three rosaries each day, and to attend special Saturday AM Mass being offered for encounter candidates. This sacrifice of morning cartoons (which, in all honesty, were never my thing anyway) is a gift to you and a testament to my belief in your walk with Christ. How's that?

Peas 4-ever,

Alexis

PS: The average guy has roughly 8.4 serious girlfriends in his lifetime, but you can have only ONE REAL, BEST FRIEND. I'll *ALWAYS* be yours.

I'm not sure what to feel. I've just received a "Dear John" palanca. But wait, there are at least three separate points where she admits having feelings for me. Of course, she also says the thought of being with me makes her queasy. Not exactly encouraging.

Thing is, though, that doesn't really have anything to do with me. It's because of her past. So . . . she's seeing a therapist . . . maybe things will change. Never say never; I've got a shot.

Except she's dating Tyler. So apparently, "physical stuff" is only "ugly, scary, dirty" when it involves me. Terrific.

Why does "best friends" seem so suckish right now?

"Crap." I jump off the bunk, add Lex's palanca to the pile. "Crap. Crap. Crap!" Well, this is a suitable journal-reading mood, I suppose. Bring it on.

Climbing up top, I lean against cinderblock, open Dad's journal. I'll cut to the chase, skip to the encounter pages. They're in the chunk he excised from the journal. Thumbing through the lost excerpts, I find my way to:

March 12, 1976

Hey, J.

Got to Holy Family Merciful Wisdom Center an hour ago. Nice place. All that's missing are suits of armor. I'm in Room 316 with some guy we creamed in the semis last year. He's pretending not to remember me. It's strange, I didn't know what to expect from encounter,

That makes two of us.

but I didn't realize there'd be so much personal attention from Father Fran.

Uh oh.

It's kind of nice. He joined me after introductions, helped me settle in. We said a rosary together—oddly familiar. I guess we must've prayed together when I was an altar boy, but still . . . Yeah! They just announced dinner!

I guess his first night wasn't bad. He sounds pretty gung ho.

March 12, 1976 Continued, 9 P.M.

Okay, this is going to suck. First off, the food tasted like horse shit, then we had a 2-1/2 hour Mass. Why am I here? Right, Father Fran invited me personally. Okay, maybe it won't be so bad. At least I'll have a chance to find out about that dog. It's been driving me nuts.

I did ask him about it earlier, but we got interrupted before he could answer. I'm waiting for him now. He's supposed to come get me so we can talk. He said there were some things we need to discuss.

He had the funniest look on his face when he said it. If you didn't know him, you might even think it was creepy. Anyway, we're going to his office after he's done prepping tomorrow's activity. Hope he comes soon, lights-out is at 10:00.

Be careful what you wish for, Dad.

He's here—later journal,
   E.

I'm afraid to turn the page; this has to be it, the big whatever happened on encounter.

March 13, 1976 Middle o' night
   Hey,
   Swore I'd just forget about this. It's obviously just me misreading things. But Father seemed really screwy before. I tried, but sleep just won't come. So I figure I'll write for a while and maybe then my brain will shut down. Unfortunately there's no Fontana di Papa here.

He's close. I see him crossing a river; piranhas roil the water. He teeters on a mossy log.

I followed him down to his office. This tiny room, down a hallway, past the chapel, no windows or anything. His one "luxury" is a pay phone in the hall. He didn't say a word 'til we'd gotten inside and shut the door.
   I started talking. I asked him about the dog again, and he said something about it being "a sign" for him.
   When I asked what he meant, he murmured, mostly to himself, "I've been wondering if it was the right time. I asked God to send me a sign. And He has, through your question."
   "A sign? For what?"
   He answered my question with his own, "What do you remember about this dog?" When I hesitated, he said, "Close your eyes. Meditate on it."

Eyes closed, I tried to see the dog. Father whispered, "What do you see?"

I told him, "There are trees, a fence, no a cage. We're inside with this big dog. Is his name Cat or something like that, Father?"

"Kap, I called him Kap, short for Kaspar."

I opened my eyes then—couldn't help it—and yelled, "Thank God, it IS real! I thought I was going crazy!"

I was surprised to find Father kneeling right in front of me. I didn't even hear him cross the room. He said, "What else?" and I really tried to remember more, but that was it.

Father frowned for a second. Then he said, "What's troubling you, Evan?"

I got the feeling he was talking about Tony, so I said, "Well, you know Tony and I've been going through a rough patch."

His face changed then: tightened. He seemed to listen to a noise I couldn't hear. Then he said, "We're not ready to talk about him just yet."

I was confused—he'd asked what was wrong—but I said, "No sweat."

Then Father touched my shoulder and said, "You're a special boy, Evan, always have been." That should have made me feel good. But it just reminded me of that dream, and I kind of shrank in my seat.

He hugged me then. That smell—what was it? Old Spice and . . . something. He said, "Off to bed! They'll have our heads if we break curfew." At the door, he whispered, "This'll be our secret, Evan."

Here I am, hours later and I can't shake that feeling. But tomorrow's (crap, it's already tomorrow) another day and F. F. promised he'd make time for us to talk, just us.

G'night, Evan

God! Is he dense, or what? This is killing me. It's like a movie, some bad *Lifetime* saga Lex'd memorize.

3/14/76

Journal,

What a day—nonstop activities starting with Mass at sunrise. That was pretty cool. Father Fran chose me to be altar server, like old times.

There was a strange moment during Mass where he zoned out. (Hope he's not getting senile. He's too young). When I handed him the chalice, he sort of stopped and stared into my eyes. I don't know if anyone noticed.

Didn't see much of F. F. after Mass. Father Brendan led my small group. He's cool—even though he can be scary in class— he's like a monument come to life, not even sure what I mean by that, just . . . solid I guess.

Anyway, we did this activity called Soul Search—ACK!— Had to sit and stare into this guy's eyes for nearly an hour. I had this dork whose eye meandered. Made it a little tough to stare into. I know he couldn't help that, but the steady nose-picking was way too much.

I have no clue what the point was, but halfway through, I just lost it. Totally humiliating. I started bawling like a friggin' two-year-old. I asked Father B to be excused. He said okay, but followed me to the men's room and said, "Don't be ashamed, Evan. Introspection often reveals painful memories. If you'd like to talk, I'm here."

I said, "Father, I really don't know what it was about," and he said, "Perhaps you're not ready. But my advice is to offer your burden, whatever it is, up to Christ." I said, "Sure, sure. I'll do that," and he left.

As I finished at the sink, Father Fran came in, all bugged. He'd seen me leave the sunroom. He asked, "What've you remembered?" His face was super weird, but when I answered, "Nothing," he looked normal again and said, "So you didn't mention anything to Brendan?" I said, "Nope," and he said, "Don't forget, I want to see you tonight, around 11:00. I'm busy 'til then with paperwork. Come to my office. I've got a surprise for you."

10:45. I'm heading down the hall even though it's lights-out.

Shit, this must be it! God, what I wouldn't give to time-travel back there and save him.

OH GOD! OH GOD! OH, SHIT! Shit, what am I supposed to do?

I don't know how to wrap my head around this. It's all changed. Everything.

We were in his office and it was fine. Then . . . it . . . wasn't. He wasn't. He was smoking. He used to smoke. I didn't remember that. He asked did I want to have a private drawing lesson, "like we used to."

At first, I just looked at him, like, how strange that he'd bring that up now, when I'd just been thinking about it after so long.

He said he'd draw first, so he sat me on the floor, in front of a bookcase. He asked me to take off my shirt. I felt weird, but I didn't want to hurt his feelings. He sat behind me at his desk, sketching.

It was unreal, sitting half-naked with Father sketching as he talked, real quiet, about stuff: my latest art project, the team's record, shit like that.

Then his voice turned raspy, like a hand was around his throat. I started to turn, to check if he was okay, but he said, "NO! Don't move. Hold the pose." There was a shuffling. Then he cleared his throat and said, "You've really grown since last time, Evan. You're quite the man." When I didn't answer, he said, "Enough for now. You must be tired. Let's take a break."

I started to put on my shirt, but he said, "Wait. Just let me look at you." I should've just left. I was about to. Don't know why I didn't.

You couldn't, Dad. He knew how to control you, like you belonged to him.

I guess it was because he said, "You wanted to talk about Tony?"
I nodded.
Father lit another cigarette. "You and Tony are very close, aren't you?"
When I said, "I guess so, but we've been fighting," he laughed. But there was no humor in it. Then he said, "Fighting . . . that's natural. Young boys have so much," he grinned, "energy. What else do you and Tony do together . . . to blow off steam?"
I started to get pissed. It was like he was saying . . . well, what some of the guys joked about sometimes—that Tony and me weren't just friends.
I couldn't figure out what to say. So I just sat there.

Closing the journal, I jump from my bunk. "Oh God. I can't read anymore." I pace the room, trying to walk his words from my brain. It's no use. I pull the journal down, crawl into the bottom bunk, a frightened animal in a cave.

Father came close, took his hand out of his pocket, and said, "Want a stick, Evan? It was your favorite." I put out my hand, but he just smiled.
Unwrapping the gum, he held it to my lips, waiting. Finally, I opened my mouth. He touched the stick of Wrigley's to my tongue.
I must've closed my eyes then. I started seeing things that weren't there, like flashbacks: Woods, the dog on its back. Me and Father rubbing its fur. It was surreal. Even the taste of mint changed into something else. The diamond shapes on the rectory rug, the station wagon, Father's breath hot on my neck. I felt him pushing me down. GOD!
But when I opened my eyes, I was still sitting on the chair in his office. Father perched on the edge of the desk, watching me,

eyes shiny like coins. He said, "You still like it. I'm so glad." My head pounded as he leaned close, starting to touch me, saying, "I've missed you, Evan."

I couldn't speak. Random thoughts still flashed in my head: the confessional, the taste of altar wine. Refocusing, I realized he was talking about Tony. ". . . attractive boy. Softer, the Pettafordi boy. Perhaps we should include him, open our little circle to your friend?"

I gagged then, on the sticky sweetness of the gum, ran out, shirt in my hand. Stumbling down the hall, I found Father Brendan's office, banged on the door. I had to tell him. Finally my pounding woke the brother next door. He poked his head out, said, "Brendan's been called to administer Last Rites. He'll return tomorrow afternoon. What did you need?"

I just shook my head. Came back here. Fell into bed. My roommate never knew. He's still snoring like a chainsaw. I don't know what to do. It's 3:45, and I still can't sleep. Every time I close my eyes they start. Now I KNOW they're not dreams. Oh God. The things we did. God, forgive me.

And now he wants Tony too. I can't let him do it. I won't.

"Attention: We'll be meeting in chapel for nightly prayer and reflection in ten minutes. Remember, this is NOT an optional activity. All candidates are expected to attend. Thank you."

Great! The last thing I want right now is to put the journal down and freaking mingle. But I have no choice. Hopping down, I look in the mirror—UGH. I head to the bathroom, splash some water on my face. Then I gargle with hot water and antibacterial soap, attempting to rinse away the imagined taste of spearmint.

As I step out of the bathroom, I catch Spiotti coming from my room. He hesitates for just a second, a stutter-step; then he continues toward me.

"Galloway, I was looking for you. Thought we could walk down to chapel together. Since we both lost our roomies."

My old sensors kick in, but he seems sincere. "Just a sec. Let me . . . turn off the light." It's a lame excuse, but it'll have to do. I scoot into 214, quick-scan for damage. Looks okay. The journal's still open on the bottom bunk. Folding loose pages together, I slip it into my duffel.

When I turn around, Randy's standing behind me. "What's that?"

"Nothing important. Just some notes I've been writing to myself."

"Like a diary?"

"I guess."

"Cool." As we walk down the stairs toward chapel, he says, "Some weekend, huh?"

I smile and nod, thinking, *This is too strange.*

At the bottom step, Nealson appears, running in the wrong direction, heading *up*stairs. Randy stops him. "What's up?"

Kenny pauses, looking at me, then he says, "Forgot something."

"You better mojo."

"Yup."

Randy sits with me in chapel. I can't help thinking, *Is this real?* or wincing instinctively whenever he shifts in the pew. But after a few minutes, I allow myself to visualize a life where Spiotti is NOT my mortal enemy.

During the closing prayer, Nealson slips into the next pew. Breathing heavily, he grins, flashing Spiotti a thumbs up. Randy turns to me; rolling his eyes, he mouths, "What an a'hole," just as Brother Lucius bids us a "restful good night."

I'm finding this transformation hard to accept, but no matter. It's not like I'm shopping for a new best friend, regardless of the state of things in Lexland. Besides, if I was, Spiotti certainly wouldn't make my short list, metamorphosis or no.

He lingers with Kenny when prayers end, and I quickly return to 214. There's a moment of abject horror when I see Dad's journal on the desk and realize someone's been rummaging.

Snatching the bag and journal, I do a rapid inspection. Everything seems to be intact, but I'm sure I didn't leave it out. I examine the rest of my stuff, but nothing's missing. Well, if it was Nealson snooping, he didn't steal anything. Still, it's a good case for installing freaking locks.

It should've just said SECRETS.

The sign really read, STAFF ONLY, but I suspect that means DEEP, DARK STUFF HIDDEN HERE.

I'm night-wandering again. Only now, freed from the constraints of Casa Galloway, I've got the entire Holy Family Merciful Wisdom Center to explore. I spotted this door tonight after chapel. We had a free period before lights-out; well, officially, it was for silent reflection, but nobody said we weren't allowed to reflect while prowling. I'm headed back there.

I was initially attracted by this giant potted tree—a fig, I believe. It seemed to call to me like Moses's burning bush. I didn't hear an actual voice; I'm not that far gone. But it sort of glowed, in a shaft of February starlight. As I approached, I half expected to find an orangutan or lemur scaling the trunk. A sloth maybe. No wildlife was evident, but something did seem odd: the tree was shoved into the middle of the hallway. Like a roadblock. The only thing missing was a sign saying, "I'd turn back if I were you."

Peeking past it, I saw three doorways, and I got this immediate sense I'd found it: the entrance to Father Fran's old office. Judging from its nearness to the chapel, it had to be.

I was about to take a closer look when this brother emerged from a heavy wooden door down the hall behind the fig. He looked over his shoulder in a "coast clear?" way; then he double-checked the lock. He didn't notice me drop into prayerful pose beside the tree, forehead to windowpane. He passed right by.

So anyway, Fig Tree Hallway seemed ripe for exploration. I waited about thirty minutes past lights-out to flip the bedside lamp back on and try to do some reading. But I kept having this creeping sense the fig was calling.

Now I'm in full Hogwarts mode—well, minus the Invisibility Cloak— sneaking through darkened stone passageways in search of answers. Making my way down to the first floor, I'm zeroing in on Fig Hallway now.

It's mine-shaft dark with just the moon and exit sign aglow; when they say "lights-out" they mean it. Kaleidoscope Corridor's gone dank, and the moon's casting grotesque shadows through the stained glass. Pale saints, distorted, stretch up the wall like tie-dyed ghosts.

I heard sporadic sleep murmurs as I slid by the other retreaters' doors, but here on the main floor it's almost perfectly silent. I toe-heel past the chapel and reconciliation rooms. The fig shimmers ahead like that heat wiggle that comes off the road in summer.

It feels like I've been walking for hours, but the tree's no closer, like the hall's stretching with every step. I imagine a team of tiny monks laying a stone path to infinity. Then, as I'm about to speed to a trot, I hear it—sudden, shocking in the hollow quiet—a guttural howl from behind the massive fig. My mind jumps to Kaspar, but that's not possible; he'd be, like, forty years old. Besides, it repeats, and I realize it's more human than animal. Just barely.

Skin prickling, eyes bulging, I stop, feeling the stucco wall for a light switch. No dice. I'm debating running to my room and burrowing beneath the covers when—*creeeeaaa*—the STAFF ONLY door swings slowly inward. My jaw clicks as I grind my teeth, twisting my pajama shirt into a knot at my waist.

Alarmingly, though I should bolt back to 214, I glide forward 'til I'm nose-to-bark with the fig. Before my brain can question the wisdom of proximity, my feet carry me past the braided trunk, the canopy of waxy leaves. In the entry, shivering lightly, I face the forbidden door. Ajar, flickery yellow light visible within, it looks even less inviting.

I continue toward it, like I'm magnetized or caught in a riptide. I can hardly feel my bare feet skimming stones.

There's a door on each side of the hallway. The one to my right has a pebbled glass window and plaque reading OFFICE, but there's a table in front, barring entry. It's stacked with hymnals and pamphlets. A sheet of paper's taped to the glass: Water Damage. Do Not Use.

The door across the hall—door*way* really—is just an alcove. Inside's a metal chair, and the pay phone Dad mentioned, mounted to the wall. I have an overwhelming urge to call my mother, blurt into the receiver, "Mommy, come get me. I'm scared!" But then I remember I'm not five years old; this isn't a sleepover, and I don't generally carry coins in my pajamas.

Instead, I pause at the table. Not that I'm especially interested in new reading material, it's just, suddenly I'm less than eager to look behind door number two. I grab a booklet, glance at the front, nearly drop it when the Jesus on the cover turns to look at me. Laughing tensely, I realize it's a hologram.

"Okay, enough," I whisper outside the door.

It's only open a fraction of an inch, but I can hardly believe it. I was expecting locked. Now I have no choice but to keep going.

Leaning against burled wood, I press my palm to the door—just above the brass faceplate—and tilt my head, squishing one ear to the wide panel. The door seems to throb against my cheek; really it's my heartbeat, pulsing in my head.

Gripping the knob, I tighten my fingers around it. Eyes closed, I can almost read the filigree pattern like Braille. The handle's so chilled I shudder, feeling urgency fire up my spine.

"Is someone there?"

I nearly scream when I hear the voice, soft, fearful. It's a minute before I can answer.

"Yes, it's me, Evan."

Pushing the door, I reveal a room, maybe 10 × 10 feet, windowless. A candle burns on the small oak desk, near the bed. These are the only pieces of furniture. Above the bed hangs a large, wooden crucifix, the candle flicking liquid shadows onto Christ's anguished face.

I hesitate; touch one foot to the stone floor, like testing water. The temperature inside the cell seems even chillier than in the hallway. I expect to see my breath.

"Come in, come in. I've been waiting for you."

Taking the smallest steps possible, I venture in. Fully inside, I keep eyes fixed to floor, to candle, anywhere but the form on the bed.

"Close the door and sit, so we can talk."

Never one to defy the Ancient, I comply. The door squeaks in reverse— *aaaeeeerc*—and as the candle spits, casting silent-movie shadows, I look for a place to sit. I'm momentarily baffled by the lack of a chair.

Then the figure says, "Here," patting the mattress with one clawed hand.

I have this flash of absolute stranger-danger clarity. Then, almost as if observing from afar, I'm aware of myself dropping onto the bed.

"It's good to see you again."

So far, I've avoided eye contact, but now I engage. I study the leathery face. Candle sparks against the tortoise-rimmed lenses obscure his eyes.

"Sorry, have we met?"

He just chuckles—this dry husk of sound that prickles the flesh on my neck. I mean to get up, to bolt, but I'm bound to the mattress by curiosity and fear.

"How are you enjoying your stay with us, Evan?"

"Um . . . it's . . . fine . . . I'll be glad when the weekend's over, honestly."

"And why is that?" He seems to have gotten larger (closer?) in the moment I've sat here, like a balloon inflating. But that's just nuts.

"I . . . uh . . . I learned some things."

"Troublesome things?" He grins, and I notice how yellowed, somehow dangerous-looking, his teeth seem by candlelight.

"Yes."

"Yes, Father."

"Yes, Father."

"That's better. I'm here to listen. Share your burden with me. Lay your burden down."

"Like the song says?"

"Yes, Evan, just like the song."

"Um . . . I think, maybe, I should get back to my room."

"Nonsenssse! You've only just gotten here."

"I know but—"

"Our party's just beginning!"

"Party?"

He laughs again, that dry rasp, and says, "A joke. Forgive an old man his amusements."

"Oh, sure. Look, I should really go."

"Yes, I suppose you *should*, but you won't leave me just yet, will you?"

I'm not sure why, but I say, "Not yet, Father."

"Good, good! Splendid!"

He pats my knee, his nails thick, yellow-gray, like the talons of a hawk. When his fingers tighten just above my knee, it's like static shock. I can't help jumping as the current pulses through my leg.

"How is your mother?"

The question throws me. Before I can answer, he says, "Maureen was always a fine, a godly, woman. And a trusting friend to me."

I'm about to say, "Maureen is my *grand*mother," but he continues.

"She was instrumental in bringing us together."

He's beginning to skeeve me out. For one thing, I realize his hand is now on my thigh.

"Look! I don't know who you are—"

"*Don't you?*"

I shove his claw away and stand, "Or who you think *I* am."

He rises too and, like some creepy CGI effect, he's taller than I thought, fuller. His face twists into a vulgar pout; voice deeper than before, he says, "You're hurting my feelings. Would you deny me, like some Simon Peter? You're my special boy, Evan. My own special boy!"

"Father Fran?" His head snaps back in laughter. "But Gran told me you were dead!"

He advances. The room's so cramped, I've no place to go. He presses into me, jamming me against the door, and I cringe at his breath—smoke/mint/rot.

I try to scream, but he claps a palm to my face, silencing me, his other hand pinching my nostrils. When I open my lips to gulp air, he removes his hands, presses his eager mouth to mine. His tongue, rough as a parrot's, probes my mouth like a feeler, pushing deeper, filling my throat.

I choke. He throws me onto the low, wooden bed, my head cracking the cinderblock wall. Screaming, I thrash on the filthy mattress. He overpowers me. As I continue to fight, his face appears/disappears above me like a neon skull, partially obscured by the metal rim of the top bunk.

"NOOOO!!!!"

Large hands shake me, gripping my shoulders. "Evan!"

"NOOOO!!!!"

"Evan, wake up!"

Opening my eyes, I see his flushed face, plaid pajamas . . . the age-spot Rorschach . . . it's Father Brendan. I begin to weep, fighting my way out of the nightmare.

Father B keeps repeating, "It's all right now, Evan. It's all right, lad."

I'm vaguely aware of figures in the doorway.

Father says, "Back to bed, Mister Spiotti, Nealson. Show's over Mister Dunham."

There's a general murmur as they leave. I finally catch my breath, but disorientation's tougher to shed. I insist I met Father Fran. Finally, a mix of frustration and concern, Father B agrees to investigate the room behind the fig.

It's hours 'til dawn. He doesn't want to wake the troops by turning on lights, so we travel with just my book light as a guide. No doubt, Father could navigate these halls blind.

He's silent until we reach the corridor opposite the fig, then he says, "Nearly there."

The tree looks smaller; though it's in the middle of the entry, it's not quite the obstacle I recall. Flipping on a light in the phone alcove, he fumbles for a key.

I say, "It's not locked."

Looking slightly perturbed, Father B jiggles the handle. It refuses to budge.

As he continues searching for the key, I say, "Forget it."

"What's that?"

"I said never mind. I'm obviously off my nut. Sorry I wasted your time."

He doesn't correct me, but I see by his eyes he doesn't think I'm certifiable. "Here it is." Opening the door, he leads me inside. It's not the room I was in. Or, if it is, it's undergone a rapid renovation.

"It's a storage closet?"

"Yes, it is. Now."

"But it wasn't always?"

"No, it was once an office."

"Father Fran's?"

"Come with me." He leads me to his own office, probably the very door Dad banged on all those years ago. "Tell me exactly what you saw."

I recount the whole thing. By the end, I've started calling it a dream because, obviously, it was one. Thank God.

When I finish, he's silent for a good five minutes before saying, "How much do you know about Father Fran, Evan?"

For a second, I consider dodging; evasion's been my tactic since I first discovered the journal. But—whether out of exhaustion or trust—I tell the truth about the journal and most of what I've learned since finding it. I end by saying, "So you can see I know quite a bit, Father."

"Yes, I guess you do. And I think your experience tonight was more akin to vision than a simple dream. I think perhaps you've a bit of a gift."

"Yippee."

"The room you saw was, in fact, once Father Fran's office. And I can only presume some of the evil he perpetrated against your father, and likely others, occurred there."

"Whoa."

"Whoa, indeed. So, as you said, you know quite a bit. My question is: How much would you like to know?"

I don't expect him to ask that. Before answering, I stare into his eyes. They're so kind, so incredibly sad.

"I'd like to know everything."

He nods slowly, letting out a sigh. "None of us can know everything, son. And I'm not sure it would be good for you to know all I know anyway."

"Please."

"I'll tell you what I can, given the limits of the confessional."

"Oh." I hadn't considered that. Anything he learned during the Sacrament of Penance is off-limits.

"Your father was a very special young man, Evan."

"Father, wait. If one more person tells me that, I think I'll scream . . . I'm sorry. It's just. If he was so special, why didn't God protect him?"

He looks like I've hurt him personally, just for a second. Then he says, "Ah, yes. The big questions: If God is all-powerful, why is there evil in the world? Why does He allow bad things to happen to good people? I'm disappointed, Evan. Haven't you been studying your catechism?"

I blush. "Well, sure, I understand on an intellectual level, but . . . this is my dad."

"Of course. Perhaps it will help clarify things if I tell you what I found particularly special about your father."

"What?"

"Forgiveness."

"Why forgiveness?"

"Let me explain. As you've learned, Father Fran's acts were especially grievous—"

"He was a sick bastard. Forgive my language, Father, but he was."

"I'm not so sure."

"How can you say that? If you'd read the journal . . . understood everything he did!"

"Sickness can surely cause a man to do horrible things, Evan, but in Father Fran's case, I believe we were dealing with something else." He picks up a Holy Family snow globe, shakes it, causing a captive storm.

Silent, he studies the globe 'til I say, "What, Father? If not sick, what?"

"Evil. Father Fran was evil, plain and simple. And there is a sharp distinction between sickness and evil. I only wish I had recognized that at the time. Perhaps then, I'd have dealt with him in a more suitable manner."

"What do you mean?"

"Your father came to me just after encounter, and told me Father Fran had hurt him. It was extremely difficult for him to confide in me. And—" Removing his glasses, he pinches the bridge of his nose.

"What is it?"

"My greatest failing, Evan, is that I did not take him more seriously."

"What are you saying?"

He just looks at me, his color rising. "The things he was telling me, I think my own arrogance prevented me from believing him. I felt if I were right with the Lord, Father Fran could not have deceived me."

"Deceived *you*? So your pride was more important than my father? Than the truth?"

He has no answer for that, can't even meet my gaze.

Flashing with rage, I see myself punch him. Instead, I push back my chair, stalk to the office door.

"Evan, wait."

I stop, exhausted. When I turn around, I really see it: He's just an old man.

"He came to you?"

"Yes."

"And you didn't help him?"

"No. I did not." His eyes finally meet mine.

As if he's punched me in the gut, I steady myself, sink back onto the chair. "What did you tell him, Father?"

He doesn't struggle, just says this flat out, maybe because he's had years to mourn these words. "I told him he must have misunderstood."

"And what did he say to you?"

"I'll never forget it. He said, 'Father, I forgive you, for you know not what you do.' It was more than a clever paraphrase, Evan. It was the essence of who your father was."

"And then what?"

"He vandalized the art studio. And then I was convinced. By Father Fran's reaction, partly. But also by the corroborating evidence Miss Solomon offered."

"My father's poems?"

"The poems. May I assume you've read them?"

"I wish I hadn't."

"Well. They say 'the truth shall set you free,' but often it feels like a burden, no?"

"So you knew. Mrs. S-B-C knew. On some level, Gran even knew. And no one helped."

"Father Fran *was* sent away. At that time, it was the protocol. He received counseling and a reassignment."

"And then he died?"

"Yes, he did. Around the time you were born."

"Good. And I hope he's rotting in hell."

"You mustn't say that, Evan. He may well be in hell; his sins were very grave. But our Lord is merciful."

"And what about my dad? Who had mercy on *him*? Why didn't anyone make sure *he* got counseling?"

"Your father came to me privately. He apologized for his actions in the art studio, saying he just wanted to 'put it all behind him.' He was very convincing. And," he lifts the globe again, taps it with his finger, "I suppose I wanted to get past it as well. It was Saint Sebastian's fiftieth anniversary gala. I was hoping to avoid any unpleasantness."

"I see."

"I'm not proud of that, Evan. But, at the time, I felt I was doing the right thing for all involved."

"Did you know about Tony . . . Mister Pettafordi?"

Frowning, he gives the snow globe a sharp swirl. "Evan, your father did make some unfortunate remarks about Anthony at the time. He seemed determined to discredit, if not destroy, his friend. I'm not sure why."

"You mean, you don't know?"

"If you're referring to Anthony having feelings for your father, I—"

"No!" He's surprised at my reaction. "I'm sorry, Father . . . to cut you off. It's just, that stuff about Tony being in love with Dad, it was like camouflage."

"Camouflage?"

"Yes, my father made it up. And, after what I read in his journal, I think I understand why."

"And would you care to share this information?"

"He was trying to protect him. At least, I think so."

"Protect whom?"

"Mister Pettafordi. My dad was trying to protect his friend from Father Fran."

"Protect him? I don't see how he intended to protect him by claiming—"

"In his journal Dad said Father Fran was after Tony. He was pressuring my dad to . . . recruit him, include him . . . in the things they did together. He wanted him to invite Tony to 'join their circle.' That's what he said."

"That filthy son-of-a-bitch!"

After all I've heard lately, you wouldn't think anything could surprise me, but *that* I do not expect.

Father B clears his throat and says, "Beg pardon."

"No argument here."

"This does answer some questions. It couldn't have been an easy thing for him to do. He and Anthony were very close."

"Well, I guess he figured Tony's safety was more important than their friendship."

"Yes, it was a substantial sacrifice."

"So you honestly never knew about Father Fran's interest in Tony?"

"I had no idea."

"Then did you know my father intended to kill himself in the art studio?"

After a protracted pause, he says, "Not until Miss Solomon shared his note."

"Note?"

"Along with the poems, he'd left a suicide note. Thankfully, Miss Solomon found them sooner than he'd anticipated. That's how she was able to catch him in the act."

"The act of trashing the studio?"

"Yes."

"So, you *knew*—and *she knew*—he was suicidal."

"As I explained before, he was very convincing when he came to me. He said he'd never really have gone through with it."

"Well, we know that's not true."

"Yes. I suppose we do know that now, but at the time—"

"You had a gala to focus on!"

"Evan, I do appreciate your frustration, but—"

"I'm sorry, Father. I really am. I'm just trying to understand why no one helped."

"But we did try. When I suggested holding a conference with his parents, he begged me not to tell them."

That I can understand.

"And after the business with the art studio, after Father Fran left, he truly seemed to put it all behind him."

"Yeah, he seemed to. Just like he seemed happy about having a wife and son. I guess he was good at convincing everybody. Except himself."

"Well, that's sometimes the hardest task, isn't it? Convincing oneself. The only thing that may be harder is to forgive oneself."

"What do you mean?"

"I said before your father's special grace was an ability to forgive. He displayed this quality many times. He forgave me for my blind inaction. And he forgave Father Fran as well."

"What?"

"Yes, when Francis was diagnosed with lung cancer, he contacted me. I was unreceptive. I told him I found his belated remorse pathetic. His apology struck me as a desperate attempt at spiritual whitewashing. It reeked of death row conversion. I doubted its authenticity."

He twirls the snow globe.

"But he swore he was sincere, he'd changed. He begged me to put your father in touch."

"And you did?"

"I spoke with your father after Mass one Saturday. He'd returned to Saint Anne's by then. He was our star lector."

I smile at the image of Dad at the podium.

"I expected him to be upset at the mere mention of Father Fran. And he was, but after explaining Father's illness, and his desire to apologize, I told your dad to take a day or two to think about it. And do you know what he said?"

"What?"

"He said, 'I don't need to think about it, it's God's will. It's always been in my heart to forgive him. I've just been waiting for him to ask.' He called Father the next day. And he forgave him, Evan. He even promised to pray for him. Do you understand what a powerful grace that is?"

Father Brendan's on the edge of tears. I'm way beyond the edge. I'm blubbering.

"He gave Father Fran a great gift: the mercy of a victim soul."

"A victim soul?"

"Yes, when Father Fran preyed on young Evan, he exposed him to hideous possibilities. He introduced the corrupting force of evil into his life. People don't wish to talk about evil these days, Evan, except in a vague political sense: Neo-Nazis, terrorists. These are undeniably evil. But the capacity for evil exists in us all. It is a real force; it lives and breathes. We must be vigilant against it."

He's starting to freak me out. I feel like Frodo to his Gandalf.

"And your father could easily have succumbed to evil in his own life, steeped in it as he was by Father Fran's wickedness. He could have become the next Father Fran. But there is a force stronger than evil. And we believe that it will inevitably triumph. That force is—"

"Love?"

"Exactly. And your father displayed an immeasurable depth of love in forgiving, in praying for, Father Fran. The prayers of the victim soul are very powerful."

"But not powerful enough to save himself."

Father Brendan shuts his eyes, sits back in the chair, like he's in his pre-class trance. Finally, he says, "I'm not sure any of us has the power to save himself."

"I'm still confused. If he was over it—could forgive Father Fran—why did he kill himself?"

"We're on spongy turf here. I cannot betray the sanctity of the confessional, but I will tell you he was never able to grant himself the same clemency he offered to Father."

"So, he wasn't able to forgive himself for being molested? But that's crazy!"

"The molestation and . . . other losses . . . weighed heavily on his mind."

"My brother?"

"I didn't realize you knew. Yes, I believe he felt responsible for his son's death."

"So that's why he did it?"

"Evan, you ask too much. One, because I cannot break the vow of the confessional, and two, because none of us really knows. It's like the snow globe here." He raises it gently without disturbing the flakes. "Still, settled, it is peaceful. It appears stable. But look," he shakes it, "see how the smallest disturbance stirs up sediment?"

"Yes. I see."

"Life is like that. Everything may appear settled, still. But one slight nudge—a memory, an unkind word—can cause that calm to shift, scatter. And you must realize sorrow is cumulative. Father Fran, your brother—who knows how many layers it took to undo your father? Or why that particular Easter it all became too much."

"So you're saying it doesn't matter?"

"I'm saying you'll probably never know for certain. May I ask a question?"

"Of course."

"Why do you need to know?"

I don't expect to have an answer. I'm hoping he'll say, "You needn't answer, just think about it," like he sometimes does in class. But suddenly it's clear.

"I just want to know it wasn't me. I want to know he loved me."

Father Brendan smiles and says, "You needn't question that any longer, Evan. And I shan't betray his confidence telling you this. Through all his doubts and fears, the anger he expressed, there was one constant in your father's life. It was you."

"Please retrieve all carry-on baggage as we touch down to relative normalcy."

Walking through the doors at Sebastian's, I imagine this flight attendant announcement. It sounds a lot like Father Cal.

Sunday was a total smear. After talking with Father Brendan, I staggered back to 214 and plowed through a grand total of two hours sleep. Then—GOOD MORNING, CANDIDATES!—it was time to start all over again. Prayer/bad cafeteria food/prayer/bad cafeteria food/Mass.

Then we had the closing ceremonies. No doves were released, but we did each get an encounter certificate: an angst diploma, showing we'd survived. Everyone had these satisfied smiles. It occurred to me at Mass: Most likely, I wasn't the only one going through some big-ass drama. Kind of interesting to think sixty-plus diverse dudes had struggled through and were all now officially certified: Grade A Lovable.

The bus ride wasn't even torture. Seemed everyone had taken love-thy-neighbor pills. Either we'd all been replaced by kinder/gentler clones, or encounter really worked. Tackling demons, facing fears, sharing troubles, and wearing snazzy buttons really did make for happy Catholic boys. I know it's a little naïve thinking it'll last beyond the weekend, but so far so good.

Randy and Kenny sat across the aisle and, instead of assaulting me with snack packaging, Spiotti offered me a candy bar. Then, when I slipped exiting the bus, he caught my elbow, kept me from falling. When I thanked him, he shrugged.

"Least I could do. Guess I owe you an apology."

I asked, "What for?"

He said, "The last three years."

So, progress has been made. They told us the real test would be applying the lessons we'd learned—and remembering we were lovable beyond the buttons—in everyday life. And so far that hasn't even been so bad.

Mom met me at the bus, and it was the first time in . . . let's see . . . since I was fitted with a newborn ID bracelet . . . we were both genuinely excited to see one another. She invited R & R to a supper of all my favorites.

It was a nice time, though we were all prone to spontaneous crying fits and declarations of deep affection. For my part, it was definitely encounter honeymoon; I think they were just hormonal. Father Cal warned us about this phase. He said we might "feel more deeply" for a few days and advised us to "go with it," but to "be prepared for mixed reactions."

Mom had invited Alexis, too, but Lex couldn't come. She called, though, to welcome me home. That was a little tough, not because things were awkward (they were a bit), but because she was the first person I consciously didn't love bomb. Judging by her reaction last time I professed my feelings, it seemed inadvisable. But, really, I think things will be okay with her.

I thanked her for the palanca, and she said, "I meant what I said, Ev."

When I told her, "I understand. And I respect your feelings," she seemed pleased with the response, though I'm not sure exactly what I meant by it.

Last night, I got the best sleep, possibly, of my entire life. And there's going to be a spirit rally this morning in the gym. I'm looking forward to it. I've been to them before, but never on the receiving end. It's like a pep rally, but instead of being sports-focused, it's a rollicking welcome home for the retreat group. The whole school attends.

Mom beeps as she drives off. We had a nice ride together, stopped for a quick bagel. As we pulled up to Sebastian's, she surprised me by leaning across for a hug. As I unbuckled my seatbelt, she smiled and said, "Your dad would be so proud."

The lobby's bustling in typical Monday mode, but looks brighter, cleaner. I doubt it's Mr. Moriarty's maintenance; more likely, it's altered perception, courtesy of encountered eyes.

The place buzzes with excitement. It seems everyone's been choreographed into place; they're practically in step. Several people wave to me. Two cheerleaders walk past and smile; it's like I've wandered into a Teen Channel Original Musical.

Heading to homeroom, I pass this board, decorated in our honor. Beneath the words "Welcome Back!" are the names and photos of all the guys who lived through encounter. I'm a bit bummed they've used my freshman orientation photo, complete with mouthful of wire.

Post-homeroom, the whole student body—minus our group of returnees—reports directly to the gymnasium. We're told to line up outside Mrs. Teague's office for our grand entrance. Peeking through the doors, I scout for Lex. I finally spot her; she's already up in the bleachers with Tyler. When she sees me, she waves like a maniac. Tyler salutes.

The gym's mega-festooned. It's an explosion of school color: green and gold streamers, signs everywhere. We make our entrance, to echoing chants of "LOVE-A-BULL! LOVE-A-BULL!"

Coach Novack leads us single file to a grouping of chairs at center court. Father Brendan sweeps in, microphone in hand, and I have this Ringling Brothers moment, expecting him to yell, "Laaadies and gentlemen, turn your attention to the center ring!"

Instead, he says, "Amen. Amen." His mic makes this insane feedback squeal, and everyone groans, quieting as he says, "My dear family of Saint Sebastian, it is my distinct pleasure to present this group of fine young men. I can attest they have given their all this weekend in their quest for a deepened relationship with our Lord."

Judging by the reaction, you'd think he announced free Rolling Rock in the cafeteria. There's a gush of cheers and foot-stomping. It's pretty glorious to realize it's partly for me.

The next thirty minutes are an I'm-lova-blur. We sing the school song, "Archers Aiming Straight Are We"; the cheerleaders do a "Gimme an L/ Gimme an O/Gimme a V" routine. After a while, Father B quiets the crowd, and Mister Novack steps up, takes the mic. At least this time he's semi-prepared.

"I just have to say I'm real proud of you boys! You gave 120 percent back at the retreat house and, well, I'm just real stoked is all. I had my doubts about the whole encounter thing, but, I guess you could say I've seen the light."

He hands the microphone back to Father. I notice Mister Pettafordi in the front row of bleachers, looking like the last pick in a kickball game. Father B does not offer him the mic.

Two freshmen wheel in an AV cart, and the big screen descends from the gym ceiling. The Sebastian community has always embraced this "Let's put on a show" mentality. I suddenly picture Photo Nun and can't help groaning, "Oh no. We're in for it."

Randy leans across Kenny, grinning, and says, "No, this is going to be great."

The music starts—an "Amazing Grace" instrumental—and the lights dim. Projected on the screen is an exterior of the Center. Must've been taken in spring because forsythias are in bloom. Across the bottom of the screen it says "Holy Family Merciful Wisdom Center: A Place of Heart."

As songs continue to play—easy listening inspiration—images flash on the screen. In one, Brother Lucius and Father Cal pose with celery stalks hanging from their mouths like walrus tusks. There's a shot of Spiotti with about a hundred "I'm lovable" pins on his T-shirt. It's captioned, "Ain't he, though?" This earns appreciative laughter. Randy and Kenny verge on hysteria.

Pictures of more reverent moments are included too: Father Brendan, arms raised in blessing; a couple shots of Jeff and Father Cal doing the Soul Search warm-up. I have to look away at that point.

When the picture of me getting pinned comes on, Nealson says, "Nice shot, Ev!"

I can't help joining as they laugh. Randy turns back to the kid at the projector. I think he's a sophomore; they must know him from track.

The slide show runs for a good fifteen minutes and—in a cool touch—features snippets of dialogue mixed with the music. We hear quotes from some of the attendees: " . . . such a sense of peace . . . " " . . . friends I'll never forget." There's a segment from one of Father B's sermons, even a dash of Pettafordi's speech, ". . . that love, the wonderful truth . . . God . . . lives in us." I watch Mister P in the weak light, staring at his shoes.

I notice Randy gesturing to Projector Guy. I crane toward the cart, too, as Spiotti nudges Nealson and whispers, "This is it." The brief, skittery clicking on the audio sounds like the sophomore's switching discs.

Turning back toward the screen, I join the communal gasp washing over the gym. Above our heads, pixilated and slightly blurred, is my father's painting. I sit in shock as the entire school population stares at my father—obviously thinking it's me—naked and bound.

I never would have believed the image could get anymore horrible. But somehow, suspended in the gym on a 12' × 12' screen, horrible stretches to mythic proportions. Plus, there's the caption. Scrawled below the picture, it says, "Evan's Secret."

Beginning to shake, I'm unable to pry my eyes from the screen. Above muttering and laughter, I hear someone scream, "OHMYGODOHMYGODOHMYGOD." I barely realize it's me. Then I hear something else, a fake-lispy voice that's barely recognizable as Spiotti's:

Father's breath hot against my neck.
I felt him . . . GOD! OH YES!
He said, "You still like it. I'm so glad."
It was throbbing . . . as he touched me . . .
softer than you, the Pettafordi boy . . .

With a huge crash, Coach Novack sails into the AV cart. The sound cuts out as the projector flips backward. For just a second, my father's naked body's still a faint shadow against the corrugated ceiling. Then, just as Novack pulls the plug, the lights come on. The first thing I notice is Pettafordi's face. He looks like he's just returned from a guided tour of Dante's hell.

Finally able to move, I scan the bleachers; a thousand eyes burn into me. Just before Novack grabs him by the collar, Spiotti steps forward and says, "Hope you liked the show."

Afraid to collapse in front of everyone, I run for the doors. I'm vaguely aware of Father Brendan yelling, "Wait, Evan!" but I can't stay here another second. Shoving through the crowd that starts pouring onto the gym floor, I race for the exit.

The last thing I see before crashing through the steel doors is Lex. She's standing at the top of the bleachers, crying. Tyler's stroking her hair, her head against his chest.

It's like wading through ink, chilled ink.

Groping in the attic, I search for the pull cord. I came here straight from school. Once I cleared the gym, I didn't look back, didn't stop for my coat or anything, just sprinted out the front doors and ran.

While Gran and Gramp are away, I'm on mail and paper duty. So I've got a key. I doubt they expected my access to include the attic. Far as I know, no one's come up here since they found Dad, but the minute I fled Sebastian's this was my destination.

"Got it!"

I bat the hanging metal washer, grab the twine, and yank. The bare bulb glows; swinging, it casts crazy shadows across the raftered space.

"This is it," my voice comes out brittle and overloud in the murk, "scene of the crime."

I try to act all cool and procedural, like a TV cop, but there's this thudding pressure at my temples, like my heart's about to make its external debut.

"Why?"

It's a colossal why; I'm not even sure what it has to do with anymore. After what I learned on encounter—he tried to protect Mister P; he forgave Father Fran—what he did in this attic makes even less sense. At the same time, I think I grasp how he felt. It's like Father B said, "sorrow is cumulative." I'd say I've developed a sufficient understanding of that concept.

So I guess The Why has to do with me now. Like, why, God? Why'd I need to go through these past weeks? What's the point? Did I seriously believe answers would bring some sort of closure? And was I truly stupid enough to trust Randy Spiotti?

I move toward the metal cabinet, stooping so I don't whack my head on the joist. The door makes this mournful whine, releasing a mousy smell, as I open it.

Inside are boxes and shopping bags stuffed with papers, books, holiday decorations. Hauling them out, I stack them on the floor. I spot a cardboard tube, pull it from the cabinet, and examine the label: Evan's Poster ~ C.S. Week, 1970.

Bringing the rolled poster to the center of the attic, I kneel on plywood beneath the bulb, twist off the cap, and peer in. A sharper smell comes from inside. When I touch the roll of paper, it feels faintly damp, fleshy. As I unroll the coil, a small, tissue-wrapped bundle drops out. I lift it, carefully placing the poster on the floor.

The tissue swaddles a plush bunny rattle and faded terrycloth bib. Unfolding the bib, I read, "Baby's First Easter." Lifting it to my face, as Dad might have, I conjure my brother's powdery scent. Tucking the bib in my pocket, I unroll the poster, carefully flattening it, but the paper curls back, the result of forty-plus years of coiled storage.

I reverse roll it, scanning the attic. Taking four books from beside the cabinet, I place one on each corner, smoothing the poster with my palm. Then I look at it.

"Damn good for a ten-year-old."

It's big: about 4 × 6 feet, a mix of paint and cut paper. Across the top, it says: LEARNING AND LOVING—FRIENDS IN CH IST. The R's missing. Below is a picture: A boy—he has very large ears—standing with a priest. I try to ignore his resemblance to Father Fran.

The boy reaches toward the priest, holding an apple. Father's hand hovers above the boy's head, giving a blessing.

So this is the poster that helped make him *Father Fran's special boy*. The thought comes in Spiotti's voice, mocking lisp included. I picture Randy's face in the gym, the way he laughed as everyone stared at me. Guess I shouldn't be surprised at not being angry, not crying. I haven't felt anything since running out of there. I guess this is how I'll be from now on: alone in the dark, devoid of feeling.

I picture Lex just standing, clinging to Tyler, as the rest laughed. Was she ashamed? Studying the image like an entomologist with a pinned butterfly, I'm all detachment. Part of my brain still insists I should react, muster a tear, like that'll help. But I've dried up.

I focus on the poster; it's a decent painting, a hint of the artist he'd become. But something's wrong with the kid's face. Bending, nose-to-paper, I sniff. Mold. A powdery film scums the boy's forehead, cheeks, his chin peppered with blotches. Brushing it away, I notice cuts, rough scratches like you'd make scraping a nail or paperclip back and forth, nicking the surface. They cover the boy's eyes and mouth. See no evil, speak no evil?

And something else: his body is marked with red pen, tiny numbers at his neck, chest, crotch. They're dates. What was he doing, cataloging the abuse? And when did he do this? Maybe it was one of his last acts, up here, before.

Even in my dulled state, I find this disturbing. Standing up fast, I bonk the bulb, pitch it into a wild swing. Reaching up to steady it, I notice them. Chafed into the rafter, unmistakable: rope prints, and deeper gouges that can only be the gashes Gran made cutting him down.

I'm transfixed. Stretching on tiptoe, I run my fingers across marked wood. A wave of calm floods me. In a weird way, I've never felt closer, like I finally understand him—connected. And I realize there's only one way to really, truly know my father.

Crossing to the corner where they keep the Christmas decorations, I shove the tree box aside and open the giant bin of lights. Pawing the tangle, I detach an extension cord. Testing its length between clenched fists, I whisper, "This'll do."

I drag a crate, certain it's what he used, just below the gouged rafter. Twisting a loop in the center of the cord, I throw both ends over the beam, catching them as they drop. Then I wind the cord around the rafter to take up slack, finally hooking it around a nail jutting from the wood. Gripping it with both hands, I dangle for a ten count. It holds. Dad would be proud.

I step onto the crate. As I slip the loop over my head, I notice my cheeks are wet. Sweat, not tears. I can't believe I'm sweating in this refrigerated garret. Lifting my shirt, I blot my face dry. Then I just stand here, totally in control for the first time ever.

As I hover on the cusp of undone, random thoughts play a slideshow in my head. There's no common thread; some scenes are laugh-out-loud (I don't): Dad teaching Mom to skate; Gramp dressed as Peter Pan to Gran's Tink. I don't dwell on those featuring Lex, afraid they'll trick me into thinking I've got something to stick around for. Other images have the power to scramble my heart like an egg. But somehow I let them wash over me with as little impact as a public service announcement.

God's bound to be pissed, so I decide to pray. I do a whole rosary standing on the box. My back aches, my shoulders throb, but I won't move. Physical discomfort my temporary stand-in for emotion. Finally, legs going as numb as my heart, I realize it's time.

Finishing the rosary—". . . and all the evil spirits who prowl through the world seeking the ruin of souls. Amen."—I inhale. And I kick free of the crate.

There's a brief spark of clarity as the cord squeezes my throat—a moment of "Yes!" Then these peripheral flashes start. Ocean-sound fills my head, and I'm aware of my heart thudding, veins pulsing at my temples. My hands and feet tingle. I feel heavy. The attic seems to roll; it's washed in a deepening ruby tint.

Suddenly I see them: the life-size Nativity figures we made for Gran when I was ten. Dad cut them from Masonite; I painted them. They shimmer like moonlight in the corner, the room darkening around me. Gulping for air, I swear I smell Dad's wool sweater, his aftershave, feel his arm around me on Gran's front lawn as we admire the crèche. And then

I actually hear his voice: "This is what it's all about, Evan. This is what matters. Hope."

Of course.

Attempting this gymnastic move—legs swinging, fingers flailing for the beam—I have an undeniable sensation: Dad's hands under my arms, hoisting me. My ungainly lurch somehow loosens the cord. Coming undone, it relaxes its grip on my esophagus. As the plug swings past my head, I pull free and drop from the rafter, my ass slamming the crate corner. The pain is beautiful. Between coughs, I imagine the bruise seeping across my butt, an odd souvenir of my near miss.

It's over.

Once my breathing evens, I crawl toward the cabinet. Sliding the poster into its tube, I straighten the Christmas stuff, shut off the light.

Descending the ladder, I'm seriously blissed. I hope it's not brain damage from my brief oxygen deficit. Just what I need: a drop in IQ so close to SATs. But if I'd truly suffered cognitive impairment, I probably wouldn't realize it. I'll have to run that past Miss Delateski tomorrow. Right now, I feel simultaneously lighter and stronger, knowing all I do. I'm also shaking. But that's probably normal, considering what I just put myself through. This time, the wet cheeks aren't from sweat. And that feels great, too.

Staring into the bathroom mirror, I touch the raised pink welt already blooming at my throat. Good thing it's turtleneck season. Amazingly, I'm smiling by the time I hear her voice.

"Evan, are you here?"

It's Mom.

"Be right out!"

I'm eager to see her; I feel like I can finally put her mind at ease, reassure her I'm not going anywhere. That realization—I'm sticking around—is a major shift from an hour ago. I peek into the hall, and she's there, arms out. We hug for at least a minute, definitely a record.

Then she says, "I heard what happened at school. Are you okay?"

"Never better."

"Really?"

"Well, in all the ways that matter, yes. Listen, we need to talk. Got a minute?"

"For you, I've got all the time in the world."

"Thanks, Mom." I lead her into Gran's living room; we sit on the couch. "So, who told you what happened?"

"Well, school called to say there'd been some trouble. But then Denise filled me in."

"Mrs. Bottaro?"

She nods.

"What about Lex?"

My mother nibbles her lip, stifling a smile. "Her mom said Lex is 'indisposed.' Apparently there was talk of expelling her, but Father Brendan intervened."

"Expelling her? Why?"

"It seems she sent the Spiotti boy to the hospital for stitches."

"Sweet!"

"It is, isn't it?"

"So, there are some things I should tell you."

"I'm listening."

I tell the tale of these past weeks—with edits for content; she's my mom after all. The Father Fran stuff almost derails us. At one point, after I describe the worst of it, she goes down the hall to Dad's portrait. She just stands there for about five minutes, talking to the picture, repeating over and over, "You poor little boy. My God, you poor little boy."

Back on the couch, we hold each other. Even crying, she seems somehow at peace. It's like we both understand stuff now. Why Dad would get so distant. How come he'd never let me have a dog. The reason he hated spearmint. Though he was never as happy as we'd have liked, it's a relief to know it probably wasn't because of us. But awful knowing why.

Forty minutes in, she stops me with, "What would you say to pizza? I'm starving."

After she tips the delivery guy, I conclude the saga over a greasy, stuffed-crust with 'shrooms. Bad pizza's never tasted so good.

It's quarter past eight when we finally head home. I'm surprised when Mom pulls onto Jubilee Drive and stops the Outback in front of Lex's.

"Why are we here?"

"I think you owe Lex a thank you."

"Yeah, and an apology."

I swear, the butterflies in my stomach could probably manage the doorbell. Still, I knock. Lex opens the door and, before I can say a word, she embraces me. She smells like cupcakes and citrus toner—intoxicating.

I win the "No, *I'm* sorry" competition by a nose; then we both grin like idiots.

Lex's mom says, "And I'm heating the neighborhood, why exactly? Invite them in!"

The mothers chat over coffee in the kitchen while Lex and I head down to the family room. We plop on the futon. She smiles. Her hair's close to normal; still shorter, obviously, but sort of frizzy—just right.

"So, stitches, huh?"

"Eight. Turns out the skin around the eye area really *is* the most delicate."

I describe my attic episode. Pulling down my collar, Lex touches my throat. Her eyes stream as she makes me promise never to pull "such an asinine stunt" again or "I'll kill you myself."

"Deal."

Honking into a tissue, she smiles and says, "So, can I have my records back?"

"I don't know. What'll Tyler say?"

"All right, listen. I need to tell you something about Tyler." Looking embarrassed, she continues, "But you need to promise not to tell a soul."

"Scout's honor."

"That's impressive, but it'd have more impact if you'd ever really been a scout."

"Okay, okay, I promise."

She goes a deeper shade of pink and says, "Tyler's gay."

"What?"

"Well, not like definitely gay. I guess 'questioning his sexuality' is the correct terminology. I think he may have a wee crush on Kenny Nealson."

"I'm stunned." Good stunned, like winning Lotto. "What about you and him? You said—"

"I know what I said. And you deserved it! You were such a shit. But it's not true. We only ever kissed a couple times."

"Wow."

"It was sort of a decent arrangement for us both. It took the pressure off him, having people think he was serious about me."

"And you?"

"Well, I had a really cute boyfriend and no threat of physical contact." She looks a little wistful as she says, "He really was the perfect guy for a gal with intimacy issues."

"No, that's not true."

"It's not?"

I try to channel some of Dad's Old-fashioned Galloway Charm, as I say, "Nope. *I'm* the perfect guy for a gal with intimacy issues."

I lean in and kiss her, and though she doesn't exactly respond in Harlequin Romance fashion, she also doesn't upend the futon. Or send me for stitches.

She just says, "We'll see."

"That's good enough for me."

Just then Mom yells down, "Ev, we should go!"

She's got good timing for once. Lex kisses my cheek and I float up the cellar stairs toward home.

"Please pass the casserole."

We stare at Gran like she's a mirage, 'til she says, "I'd like a bit more."

This is new—she's rarely eaten Mom's cooking, forget seconds. Food's always been a crucial weapon in their domestic battle. And after last Easter, and the (mostly) unspoken blame they each harbored, it was a stretch to even picture them at the same table. I certainly didn't expect the hatchet to finally be buried in a bowl of slimy green beans and French-fried onions. But as Mom passes the Pyrex, Gran's hand lingers, patting my mother's wrist—an Easter miracle.

Gramp and Gran's dining room table's in storage, so eight of us crowd around the small kitchen table—Gran, Gramp, Reg, Ro, The Mothers,

Lex, and me. Gran's fighting major agita over the state of things. She can't help apologizing that the house is "in such shambles."

Gramp employs his special brand of reassurance: "Don't be a broken record, Maureen. Are you going to encore this same performance for another three weeks?"

Ordinarily, he'd be right—her apologies are usually just needy-housekeeper shtick—but it honestly is a mess in here. Crates and packing supplies are everywhere; they've begun the process of closing up shop, bubble-wrapping family history.

It must be difficult after forty-nine years, but I guess the attic's spell has finally trumped whatever good memories the house still holds. They're jumping ship. Aunt Ro seems thrilled with their decision. Aunt Reg is less enthusiastic; they're moving to her condo complex.

After eating, we migrate to the near-empty living room; just recliner, couch, and coffee table remain. Balancing cake plates on knees, we small-talk: dinner, the oddly warm spring. Harmless terrain. Then, somehow, Gramp veers to Spiotti—a.k.a. *that psychotic little pussy*, as in, "I wonder how that psychotic little pussy's spending *his* holiday."

Lex nearly shoots Coconut Lemon Sunshine Cake out her nostrils, and Aunt Ro says, "Daddy! Neither the topic nor the language is suitable for Easter Sunday!"

Aunt Reg smirks. "Oh, Rosemary, take a pill."

Gran just elbows him, shakes her head, says, "Nice, Fred. Very nice."

Mom and Mrs. Bottaro stay out of it and, though I don't exactly rush to Randy's defense, I'm pretty much over the whole thing. It doesn't hurt that Spiotti and Nealson no longer attend Sebastian's. They've been banished to the horror and desolation of the public school system.

Honestly, that horror and desolation probably isn't much worse than what we've got at Sebastian's—just different. I certainly didn't win fans on the track team, being "responsible for" the departure of our two best runners, but that's okay. Since my girlfriend spilled the school tormenter's blood, I feel pretty safe; it's rather like dating Jack the Giant Killer.

We manage to get the banter back on track. I start with Mrs. Bottaro's centerpiece, a spring lamb made of chrysanthemums, declaring it "totally lifelike." Lex rolls her eyes; she hates when I suck up to her mother.

Mom says she'll try something similar, "maybe orange mums, for Halloween. I'm thinking scarecrow."

We linger on holidays past: the Thanksgiving the tablecloth ignited; the Christmas Mom got lost at Donelan's Tree Farm; the July 4th I stepped on the hot briquettes. But last Easter no longer exists for us.

I'm impressed we tackle the holiday at all. One thing that helps is the date. It's April 20th, nearly a whole month after the first anniversary of losing Dad. Thank God, Easter floats. If it fell on March 31st every year, I think we'd have to convert.

We agreed to keep it simple this year, no big baskets or anything. I gave Mom a bouquet of tulips, tied with my brother's Easter bib. Of course, that made her cry, but she seemed genuinely happy to have it back. She got me "Perky Pierre," a chocolate-bunny-as-artist, wearing a foil beret. And, naturally, I got a little something for my two best girls.

Since we've reached the next level—Lex now refers to me as *mon significatif,* she suddenly hates the term boyfriend—I couldn't ignore our first holiday. I got her this cloisonné egg that plays Neil Diamond's "Song Sung Blue." Naturally, she was très appreciative.

There was also the matter of a certain missing birthstone. For some reason, after my rafter antics, I kept picturing Gran's ring. I guess it represented one of those little pits in the Galloway veneer, one I *could* fix. I decided to use the extra Angie cash, and Mom agreed. So when I went to bring in their mail, I pillaged Gran's jewelry box.

She's rinsing dessert plates when I tap her shoulder.

"What is it, honey?"

"I have something for you, Gran."

"Evan, we agreed no gifts. I'm getting too fat for chocolates, and your Gramp and I already have too much packing to do. The last thing we need is more stuff."

"Oh, well . . . then I guess I can return this."

"Not that I don't appreciate the gesture—" she spots the ring on my pinkie, "Oh Lord."

"I felt bad that Dad," my voice cracks, "let you down."

"Oh, honey."

"He was supposed . . . to fix it for you, and I don't like you not wearing it. Here, try it on."

I ease the ring onto her finger, only halfway, letting her finesse it past the swollen joint.

She holds it up and the new garnet glints, "It's beautiful, Jun—sorry, Evan."

"No, that's okay. Call me Junior. I don't mind."

"Happy Easter, Junior."

"Happy Easter, Gran."

Mom joins us in the kitchen, the three of us in a close triangle by the sink.

"So . . ."

None of us wants to bring him up, even though we've been thinking about him all day. Finally, I turn to Mom and say, "Remember how he used to love to hide the eggs?"

She and Gran laugh at the image of Dad in the yard with those fluffy rabbit ears and tail. Mom used to tease that he didn't need the disguise; he was all set for ears.

We do a quick group hug, and I sigh, thinking of all he'll miss. Then, for just a moment, I see the figures up in the attic, remember his voice, the sense of being lifted. And I think maybe he's not missing everything after all.

I turn to Gran. "You know the crèche figures in the—" I catch myself; we've learned not to use that word. "Upstairs? Since you guys won't really have a lawn, I thought Mom and I might take them."

Gran gets this did-I-leave-the-oven-on? look as she says, "The Nativity you and your father made?"

"Yeah."

"I'm sorry, honey. Did you forget? We got rid of it years ago. Remember? That nor'easter blew down the willow; cracked poor Mary and Joseph clear in half."

As my jaw drops, Lex comes in, touches my shoulder, and says, "You have a visitor."

It's Lupo, holding this humongous tray. It's a science fair project, a topographical map in frosted pastel: Italian cookies. I take the tray; it's like a bag of cement. Lugging it to the coffee table, I glance at Lex. True, she's never been a big cookie fan, but tears?

Turning back to thank Lupo, I see them: Angie's approaching the house, pushing what's left of Zio Joe in the metal chair. Head joggling, he grunts as she struggles with his wheels on the uneven walk. Lex slips her hand in mine and I try not to join her, crying over stupid cookies.

Then I rush past Lupo and down the front steps.

"Hey, Mondrian. Glad we finally found you. Me and Pop and Loopy Chenille been hauling this travelin' cookie show all over town." She's doing a decent impression of the same old Angie, even though she's not anymore, not quite. "We just came from your house."

"Hey. Long time no see."

"Yeah, sorry 'bout that. My plate's been mighty full." She runs her hand over Mister Alberti's buzz cut. "We're closing up."

"I know, I saw the For Rent sign. What'll you do?"

She shrugs. "Maybe I'll finally hit New York, go on some auditions."

"That's great."

"I was jokin'. Jocko here might need me to stick around."

Mister A makes this guttural noise; I realize he's laughing.

Pretending not to notice the scar bisecting his scalp, I bend, kiss his cheek. I don't expect the heat from his face, or the smoothness, like velvet. But mostly, I'm surprised when he lifts his left hand. The right one looks overlarge, a gag shop fake, stiff on his lap. Shaking, his fingers press my cheek, and he says, "Eev." It's good that Angie's behind his chair, because she loses it as he says, "Yyy gd-boy, Eevannn."

I catch it: deep inside his left eye, a spark of the real Zio. The right one is dull, dusty-bottle brown. Focusing on that tiny point of light, I say, "I love you, Zio Joe. *Buona Pasqua*."

He winks.

As Angie and Lupo heft him into the Civic, I spot Gramp peeking out the picture window. The vertical blinds snap closed, and as I walk toward the front door, I hear him say, ". . . rather you shoot me than let me live like—" he catches himself, with the help of Gran's elbow, as usual.

They're all expecting me to say something, but in that moment, every awful thing from the past thirteen months washes over me. And it's so weird, because I don't lose it. But it's not like in the attic, when I couldn't feel anything.

This time, the bad stuff seems important in a new way. Like part of the recipe: the bitter lemon that makes the coconut sweeter. I look from face to face, all of them surrounded by signs of change: boxes, bubble pack, the reverse shadows where portraits no longer hang. This house. My family. "All my dear ones" pops into my head; it's from a Virgin Mary prayer card that used to hang on Gran's fridge.

I struggle to take it in. To capture it. Considering my father's too-soon, I'm beginning to recognize it was also his meant-to-be.

Lex kisses me, says, "Why are you smiling?"

I can't answer. I'm not sure how to explain it's partly because I know I'll never understand, but also, because it seems I already do.

Acknowledgments

Writing seems solitary—isolated scribbling, interior musing, wee-hours key-tapping—but a finished book is a collaboration.

This novel began in my first master class at Wesleyan, Studies in Adolescent Lit, when Professor Anne Devereaux Jordan said, "Let's see where this story goes." Thanks also to classmate Betsy Feiner for sharing early chapters with her "friend in publishing," Joan Slattery, who offered inspiration and guidance.

To the Easy Writers, and to Monique Fitzgerald, Bonnie Goulet, Dierdre Moutinho, Andrea Petrario, and Joe Correll, friends, and insightful readers—appreciation for enthusiastic support. Thanks to countless friends—at NVCC and elsewhere—for believing in the book, sight unseen. Writer friends, Kim Stokely, Michelle Griffis, Julia Petitfrere, Courtney Sheinmel, and Nina Nelson, were voices of reason, inspiring me, keeping me going, occasionally talking me down. My dear friend, poet and teacher Edwina Trentham, was vital. Had she not asked to read more when there wasn't anymore, I might never have finished. Love and thanks!

Others were unwavering, especially Sister Angeline Dal Corso and Elaine Lavorgna—thanks for years of prayers and spiritual sustenance. For prayer—and technical support—thanks also to Terry Laslo.

My father said, "So get your masters," then helped make it possible—grazie, Ralph. To my sister, Cathy Mendyka; her husband, Paul; and my dear niece, Stacey, thanks for cheering me on.

Love, joy, and gratitude to my amazing wife, Janet, who never let me doubt—your faith makes it all happen. To Ben and Jilli, the best kids ever, for patience during hours devoted to your ink-and-paper sibling.

Thanks to CT Shoreline Arts Alliance for the 2011 Tassy Walden Award, an affirmation.

Gratitude to all at Gelfman Schneider Literary Agency, especially super-agent, Victoria Marini, a fierce, funny champion of my work. Your instincts greatly improved the book. You are amazing!

To the F+W Media/Merit Press team, I'm grateful to be in such good hands. Bravo to Skye Alexander's copyedit magic for making me seem delightfully consistent and clear. And to my editor, Jacquelyn Mitchard (still pinching myself!), thanks for faith in my writing and for sharing incredible insight and experience.

I can't forget my cousin, Mark. Although *The Namesake* is not an attempt to tell his story, Mark's "too-soon" definitely inspired my creation of Evan Galloway and his quest. I hope my work, in some small way, honors Mark's life and his family.

Finally, to survivors of sexual abuse, I honor you as well and stand with you as you journey toward healing and hope.